T0245993

The Hollywood Assistant

Also by May Cobb

The Hunting Wives

My Summer Darlings

A Likeable Woman

Other Books by May Cobb

Big Woods

The Hollywood Assistant

May Cobb

Berkley
New York

BERKLEY
An imprint of Penguin Random House LLC
penguinrandomhouse.com

Library of Congress Cataloging-in-Publication Data

Names: Cobb, May, 1973- author.
Title: The Hollywood assistant / May Cobb.
Description: New York: Berkley, 2024.
Identifiers: LCCN 2023051062 (print) | LCCN 2023051063 (ebook) |
ISBN 9780593546826 (hardcover) | ISBN 9780593546840 (e-book)
Subjects: LCGFT: Thrillers (Fiction) | Novels.
Classification: LCC PS3603.O225554 H65 2024 (print) | LCC PS3603.O225554 (ebook) |
DDC 813/.6—dc23/eng/20231106
LC record available at https://lccn.loc.gov/2023051062
LC ebook record available at https://lccn.loc.gov/2023051063

Printed in the United States of America
1st Printing

Book design by Alison Cnockaert

This one's for Amy, my very best friend, who brought me to Hollywood and also on too many fun adventures to count. How did I ever get so lucky?

Do people always fall in love with things they can’t have?

—Patricia Highsmith

The Hollywood Assistant

Prologue

SUNLIGHT GLINTS AGAINST the windows of the Sterlings' home, turning them opaque: a row of blank eyes staring back at me. The wind lashes at my car. An angry, raw summer day that stings like a fresh paper cut. The weather moody, unstable.

The sun slips behind the clouds. The windows are now two-way-mirror clear, the interior brightening into sharp focus. The cherry-red leather armchair in the parlor, a chenille throw dangling from the arm like a dog's tongue. The newspaper flung open and sprawled across the seat.

The stucco fireplace, the light-filled dining room. The upstairs bedrooms, all the windows bare and naked, curtains cinched back as usual, even at night while they sleep.

From my perch I peer into the living room. Glimpse a blur of dark hair. Marisol's, luscious and long, always lapping at her breasts. The back of her head, hair still swinging; Nate's hands flying up on either side of her in seeming exasperation.

They are arguing.

I can't hear them, of course, not from the front seat of my car, parked across the street, but I've witnessed their arguments so many times—the cracked accusation in his tone, the climbing in octaves of hers—that I autofill it, their voices throbbing from inside the walls.

Oh god, he's grabbing at her now, his hands wrapping around her neck. But she lunges forward, pushing him down.

The sun skids out from behind the clouds again, frosting the windows. The show is over.

1

THE TIP OF the X-Acto knife punctures the packing tape with a satisfying pop, the air inside the box hissing as if sighing, as if it knows it's the last one, the final cardboard square containing the remnants of my life in Austin.

I pry the sides open, remove the top layer of Bubble Wrap. My grandmother's set of Fiestaware dishes—glazed a candy-apple red—glistens in the afternoon sun, a stream of cloudy light that filters through the kitchen window. Even though the plates were clean before I packed them, I'm a bit of a neat freak, so I give them a quick rinse before stacking them on the shelf.

The kitchen is my favorite part of my new apartment. Which used to be a garage, converted years ago into a living space. All two hundred square feet to call my own, at least for the time being.

The kitchen window is an actual picture box, the molding carved from maple with a ledge that now holds my potted herbs in tiny clay cups. Thyme, rosemary, and basil. My life shrunk down in miniature.

But the view is spectacular, expansive.

Ropes of flaming bougainvillea with magenta petals twist down the crumbling outdoor steps that descend from the upper level—the main house—stopping right outside the back door, which leads out to a small patio.

The house is perched on the side of a jagged slope; beyond the patio, the hill is ribbed with terraced gardens, rows of bone-colored stone stained with mud-green splatters from the gurgling grotto above.

When I take my latte out there in the morning, the ticktock sound of the dripping water mixed with early morning birdsong makes me feel like I'm living in the French countryside, even with the faint buzz of helicopters constantly hovering over the canyons.

From the window, I can glimpse the starburst of bougainvillea, the sloping gardens, and a triangle of blue California sky. Beneath it, the gray road threads through the hills, a thin, meandering creek.

Because of the scant space inside the apartment, I didn't bring much with me out here, only what I could jam into the Nissan Leaf.

My closet. Kitchen stuff. My record collection (mostly made up of my grandmother's vintage jazz vinyl). My box of Moleskine journals, a cliché, I know. And my plants, or, at least, a fraction of them.

Lexie teased me a few months back just after the breakup. "I'm worried you're turning into the crazy plant lady," she said over FaceTime while I padded through my tiny apartment, the camera on my cell capturing the plants dangling from the ceiling, hugging the windowsills, lining the shelves. Her voice had that stretched sound to it, a thin timbre that it takes on when she's had a decent amount of wine.

On the other end of the line, I rolled my eyes, sighed.

Her words stung, but only because they were true. My heart was shattered, and I *had* tried mending it by filling my space with greens and more greens.

"Okay, I'm sorry I said that, but . . . you *could* take this chance to move out here finally, shake things up."

I wasn't ready just yet.

Not until several weeks later when she presented me with the new gig. Only then did I begin to warm to the idea.

And a few days after that, she called me, voice brimming with cheer, letting me know she'd found this apartment, fully furnished with a bed, dresser, and small dining table. That was the tipping point, the hinge upon which my decision hung to take the plunge and move to LA.

I saw it as a fresh start, a clean slate. On moving day, I dragged my larger furniture—including the bed Carter and I made love on, his breath ragged on my neck, my back arched in ecstasy—out to the curb and taped *Free* signs on everything, including most of my plants.

Now I flatten the final box, take it outside, wedge it into the bloated recycling bin.

I let out a pent-up sigh, releasing my tense shoulders.

That's enough housework for today. Locking the back door, I decide to go for a stroll. Though I've only been here less than a week, it's already my favorite part of living in the Hollywood Hills.

I head east, toward Griffith Park, zipping up my hoodie as a cool breeze rolls down the hill. Lexie has always groaned about "June Gloom"—the phenomenon that makes it sometimes chilly and overcast here in the summer—but I'll take it any day after the torch of Austin, the sun baking the back of my neck on walks, the temps already boiling into the low hundreds even in early June.

And I'll double take it after my scorched relationship, that last text from Carter, a dagger in my chest . . . don't ever contact me again, Cassidy.

2

THE TOPS OF my thighs singe as I push myself up a jagged hill. I'm in decent shape—thanks to my weekly yoga class in Austin and all the trails I used to hike—but half a mile into this walk I'm winded. It will take my body a sec to get used to these steep hills.

The road curves before it descends again, and as I round a knotted corner, I spy a hot guy (they are all hot in the Hollywood Hills) jogging toward me. Tall, sandy blond hair, hooded eyes, shirt wet with sweat, he's pushing a stroller (they're also all taken here), but I blush when he grins at me, jerks his chin skyward in greeting.

Is he being nice? Or does he find me attractive?

This is the pathetic state of my mind these days, my already slippery self-image deteriorating even further after Carter's abrupt departure.

I keep walking to push my ex from my thoughts, quickening my pace until the backs of my calves scream out, begging for a break.

Stopping in front of a wall of teeming jasmine, I suck in a deep breath. The pearl-white petals are so fragrant it makes me heady.

Another chilly breeze coasts over me, bathing me in the sugar-coated aroma.

A smile creeps across my face.

This was a good move.

I zip up my hoodie, start heading for the park again.

It's Sunday; I've been here since Tuesday, unpacking and getting acclimated before starting the new gig tomorrow.

On my first morning here, I spent the day sifting my things out of moving boxes, spritzing cleaner on the windows, placing my plants strategically in light both direct and indirect so they'll thrive out here.

Just down the hill is the grocery store with produce so fresh it glistens, so the next morning, I stocked up, packing the cart as if I were about to throw a lavish dinner party. I grabbed a rotisserie chicken—its skin perfectly roasted and dotted with black pepper—a fresh bunch of arugula, and a fistful of radishes for a salad. Jars of creamy Icelandic yogurt, exotic cheeses. A few bottles of pinot noir and even a bouquet of flowers.

In my well-worn feng shui guidebook, I read that fresh flowers, especially red ones, when placed in the relationship corner of one's home, can help attract a mate. So I let myself loiter in the towering flower display, selecting California's spectacular cherry-red ranunculus, crimson-velvet roses, and a few dark pink tulips.

On Lexie's suggestion, I spent yesterday morning at the Melrose Flea Market, strolling the aisles, passing couples, with their fingers laced through one another's, plucking wares from stalls—vintage china sets, retro chandeliers, handmade candles—no doubt to feather their nests even more lushly.

It made me sad to hear the coos from strollers, the scent of his-and-hers Starbucks, the easy, bubbling laughter that comes from stable relationships.

My stomach tightened when I thought about all the things I left behind. But then I asked myself, *What exactly was that?*

Shitty pay at a stressful nonprofit for the arts, which amounted to zero exposure with the actual creative side of things? Tortured hours spent at the Xerox, agonizing over punishing spreadsheets, getting worked up over nerve-wracking fundraising?

Three novels in a drawer, each one close to scoring a literary agent but no cigar?

My heart in flames over Carter?

No, this was the next right thing to do, as a good friend once put it, and that's what I have to keep reminding myself of.

Tears bit my eyes, but I tugged my sunglasses down, continued zigzagging through the aisles. I thrifted an antique set of juice jars, flicked through stacks of vinyl.

Near the exit, I spied a powder-blue café table with folding chairs, ideal for the patio. I nabbed it along with a few terra-cotta pots for an outdoor herb garden, Lexie and her plant teasing be damned.

After stashing everything in the car, I typed the Sterlings' address into my cell. I was already halfway there and wanted to locate it so I wouldn't be frazzled tomorrow during rush-hour traffic. I can't help it, I'm an antsy Virgo and crave control and order where I can get it.

Driving through the flatter part of Los Angeles, strip malls and palm trees throbbed past my window until the traffic slowed, creeping along until I reached the Santa Monica Pier, where it shuddered to a halt.

I didn't mind. A fist in my chest unclenched when I glimpsed the ocean, saw the giant Ferris wheel spinning above the frothy water. I let out a ragged sigh and lowered my window, letting the briny air fill the cabin.

Just before the pier, the highway curved into a tunnel, the 10 turning into the fabled Pacific Coast Highway, Highway 1. Traffic was at a standstill then, a sea of orange brake lights blinking like a Christmas tree in the darkness of the tunnel, before the tunnel opened, revealing a dazzling open view of the glimmering ocean.

I continued along the 1 as a row of sheer cliffs rose to my right. After several miles, I turned up a steep road that headed into the easternmost edge of Malibu, banked to the west by Topanga Canyon.

A blend of Cape Cod–style homes mixed with sprawling Spanish villas lined the wide, leafy streets.

I crept through a quaint little village that contained a tiny strip mall with an outdoor café, supermarket, and salon.

After several more turns, I snaked up a long road that finally delivered me to the Sterlings' enclave known as Monte Nido. At last, I located their street, a twisting road that encircled a hilltop, the ocean swelling into view once more.

The Sterlings' home was the last one on the curvy street, the lane dissolving into a cul-de-sac overlooking the Pacific. Their own freaking cul-de-sac.

Metal barricades shunted the end of the street with a small gap in the center that led out to an unpaved hiking trail.

Like so many of the homes in the Hollywood Hills, the Sterling place is Mediterranean styled. A pastel-yellow stucco mansion topped with the same rust-red tiled roof as those in my neighborhood.

I nosed my Nissan to the edge of the cul-de-sac, the ocean winking beneath me to my right.

Twin verdant lots flanked the two-story home, whose windows twinkled in the direct sunlight. An open, inviting house I could gaze right into if I weren't trying to be discreet. But because of its placement—the lone house on this wide perch of land atop a hill—it was otherwise completely private.

The sea breeze howled against my car as I idled, checking things out.

Next to the Dead End sign, a gray No Loitering sign glared at me, so I nudged the gearshift into reverse, slinking my way out of there. No streetlights in front of their house, I noted, just the hiking trail that hugged the cliff and the roaring ocean below.

3

I'M AT THE entrance to Griffith Park now. Strolling up the path, I pass a quartet of elderly gentlemen playing dominoes, the clapping sound of the bones striking against the metal table, their stubby cigars dwindling in the ashtray, shirts crisp with starch. Unlike the handsome jogger, they don't notice me, and I coast past them up the hill.

I still want to drive to the far side of the park to Griffith Observatory, see the famed location where that iconic scene in *Rebel Without a Cause* was filmed. James Dean jumpy, all crackling energy and chiseled cheekbones.

I still can't believe I live here, with the Hollywood sign tucked somewhere over my left shoulder. I'm a film buff—partly due to my proximity to Lexie, who studied film at the University of Texas while I majored in English—and partly due to my mother.

Lexie would drag me out on summer nights to the Paramount Theatre—a jewel box of a venue—in downtown Austin for their summer classics series. We'd dress in vintage gowns, share a bucket of greasy popcorn, and sip gin and tonics while watching films like *All About Eve*, *Gaslight*, and *Giant*. Afterward, she'd tell me about each one, things she'd learned—a detail about an actress, an anecdote about the script—her flawless face animated by the dollar-store candles we lit on our back patio, flame pulsing in the glass.

The real seed of my movie love, though, came from my mother, Angie, a film noir fanatic, who gobbled up Hitchcock and binged *Sunset Boulevard*, *The Third Man*, and the creepier ones (and my personal favorites), *The Bad Seed* and *The Night of the Hunter*.

Watching old classics, the black-and-whites flickering through our living room—darkened even during summer days—was one of the few things we did together before she split, abandoning my father and me when I was seven.

I'd sit on one end of our saggy sofa while she sprawled out on the other, the silk of her robe tickling my leg, her slender form in repose, clasping a cigarette, the ash growing dangerously long before she'd tip it toward the metal tray, her personal dare to the universe.

In the cramped living room of our tiny bungalow, I'd gaze hungrily at the screen and the ornate set designs that swept me away from my rocky home life in Dallas. Mom and Dad arguing late into the evening about money, Mom swiping the keys from the counter, leaving in her nightgown after dark to god knows where. Me underneath my Strawberry Shortcake comforter, stomach twisting into knots.

For the hours that the films rolled in front of us, though, Mom was mine, home safe on the couch, the nearness of her a balm, even if we didn't really speak. When I tried saying something, her palms would flitter up.

"Shhh, honey, I'm gonna miss the dialogue."

She hung on to these movies, too, like a life raft, hot rollers clamped around her chestnut locks, scarlet lipstick staining her mouth, dreaming, I imagine, that she was Stanwyck, Lake, Tierney, Bacall.

Not just ordinary Angie Foster living in a shoebox bungalow with cracking paint and a seven-year-old she never wanted in the first place.

MY THIGHS ARE burning again from the hike; I'm ascending a sharp stretch and when I peer over my shoulder, the grid of Los Angeles spreads out beneath me in the basin below. It's not dark yet, but patio lights are flicking on, a million tiny stars twinkling up at me.

Even though I love movies, I've never been dazzled by Hollywood itself, or celebrity.

"That's why you're so perfect for this job," Lexie said to me over the phone. "You won't be starstruck. I bet you don't even know who the Sterlings are because you practically live under a rock."

She was right, I didn't. Sure, I'd heard of Nate's films but had never seen them, and certainly didn't know him by name. Same with Marisol. Not that she's exactly a name. Not yet, anyway. I've done a fair amount of Googling since, though, and have caught up on Nate's movies so that I'm not completely in the dark.

I always fancied myself more serious, more academic than Hollywood. I didn't want to be an actress, like Lexie once did growing up; I didn't have the looks for it anyway.

I wanted to be Joan Wilder, Kathleen Turner's character in *Romancing the Stone*, face shining with tears as she sits alone at her typewriter in her Manhattan apartment, finally typing the words "The End" on her latest romance novel.

That was the last movie I remember watching with Mom before she vanished, slipping out one night to never return.

Chicago, drugs, stripping. My father speaking in clipped tones to my grandmother, Dad's mother (Mom's "people," as Dad referred to them, were never a factor in our family), late at night on the phone, my ears straining against the thin walls.

So, after college, I waited tables while writing in my off time, banging out smart, nerdy romances.

"You're a phenomenal storyteller, Cassidy," Lexie said during one of our long, lingering calls after I'd gotten another stinging rejection. "I'm just not sure you've found your medium yet. But I swear you'd slay out here. The way you write characters is freakishly brilliant—probably because you're always lost in your own thoughts, always overanalyzing the thoughts of others. You're a natural. And your dialogue—it's made for the screen."

She began her campaign for me to follow her out to LA shortly after she moved out here. And part of me wanted to. We'd been together nearly our whole lives, finding each other in middle school and staying best friends ever since.

But the times I'd fly out and visit her, tag along with her to industry events, it all felt overwhelming. Like a cult of personality that I could never belong to. Lexie was born with that dynamism—she's above it, actually, with not a fake bone in her body—but she has that command. Her sculpted swan neck, her lithe figure, her gorgeous face, pert nose, and high-wattage smile. Stick-straight platinum blond hair and crystal-blue eyes. Always shirking men off, never the other way around. Always lighting up the room and then dimming it with her exit. It's one of the reasons she's such a sought-after producer.

Her current beau, Harry, begged for her hand in marriage for years and Lexie would just shrug, tell him she's not ready. Only recently, during the pandemic, has she relented, finally saying yes. And now that she has it's like a switch has flipped. She's gone full-tilt boogie with the planning of the wedding, which is set for next spring.

And after batting away her pleas for me to join her here for seven years, *I* finally relented.

"Cassidy, listen to me, I have the *perfect* gig for you." Her voice was spiky with caffeine, sharp and insistent.

She then told me the details: I'd be a personal assistant to the Sterlings, working Monday through Friday for only six to seven hours a day, running errands, buying their groceries. And then there's the pay. Five grand a month.

"Why so much for basically doing nothing?"

"They all throw money at everyone out here. Main thing is, they just want someone they can trust. Someone who comes with a strong referral, who won't blab about their private lives."

"But you're not even gonna be there," I shrilled at her, already knowing there was no way in hell I was going to turn that kind of money down, but instantly growing anxious over the prospect of moving.

"But we can always text. And Harry will be here, if you need anything. Seriously, Cassidy, just take the money, the easy gig. And write in your spare time."

She was leaving for Prague for an extended shoot the following week. I agreed, hung up, my body buzzing with uncertainty.

But also, truth be told, with excitement. Lexie is probably right. Maybe I just haven't found my medium yet. I *am* always living in my head. Even in elementary school, I kept an exacting diary, the feral sound of the pen scratching against paper a release to me in the evenings as I captured each injustice of the day: a cute boy deciding to like someone other than me, a bad grade on a math paper, and always, always, Mom's and Dad's voices blazing in the next room, the flames of their bickering licking my bedroom wall.

The sun is beginning to droop in the sky, dissolve into the horizon. This is the furthest I've gone on this trail; I should turn back. I've just passed another sign warning about coyotes and what to do if you encounter one—no, thanks. I need to head home, get ready for tomorrow, grab a good night's sleep.

4

FOUR WEEKS LATER

THE POLICE ARE here, gathered just outside my apartment. Two officers to be precise. I'm hoping Mrs. Charlie hasn't noticed them.

I can hear the crackle of their handhelds, their sharp, back-and-forth banter. Holy shit; now they're knocking. Pounding on the old wooden door with such force it sounds like a gong ringing through my brain.

My heart is in my throat; my hands are shaking; I need to pee.

I wrench my robe around me tighter, creep toward the door with utter dread.

5

NOW

I WAKE AT six this morning, well before the alarm on my cell has the chance to bleat at me. It's still dark as I clatter around my tiny kitchen, brewing espresso for a latte.

My little machine—the kind that uses tin pods of coffee—was a big splurge. I bought it for myself at Christmastime, envisioning serving endless cups of perfectly made cappuccinos to Carter while we twined our legs together underneath the breakfast table.

Now it's just for me, coffee made for one. But I love it still.

While the machine growls and the sky outside begins to brighten from deep blue to peach, I froth a cup of oat milk, sweetened with a pinch of brown sugar.

Above me, the old wooden floorboards creak to life: Mrs. Charlie is stirring in her own kitchen. She's an early riser. Early to bed, too; she usually turns in by nine. That's why Lexie thought I'd make the most suitable tenant for her. She's somehow connected to Mrs. Charlie's granddaughter—a showrunner named Kate—who was looking for someone to replace the last occupant, who moved out this past spring.

Mrs. Charlie doesn't need the rent money—her late husband was a set designer who, according to Lexie, left her a sizable nest egg—but Kate wanted someone to listen out for her. Someone quiet, responsible, and not interested in having loud parties.

Or loud sex.

Someone like me. Sigh.

The rent is only twelve hundred a month, utilities included, which is unheard of in LA, not to mention in the Hills, so I leapt at it.

And anyway, I usually wind up doing what Lexie tells me to do. I might've been stubborn for years about moving, but look at me now; I've finally succumbed.

Lexie's the leader, I'm the follower. It's our roles, our dynamic. And it works, for the most part. She's far more savvy than I, and following her lead has normally only led me to good things.

And right now I'm feeling pretty grand as I empty the chocolate-brown shot of espresso into the bottom of a mug, gaze out my picturesque window, and watch as the morning bleeds pink light over the stone patio.

Carrying my latte and phone outside, I sit at the café table and tap on my cell, springing it to life. Scroll through NPR headlines without actually reading the stories themselves, as is my habit, then switch over to the BBC home page and do the same. Pathetically only clicking on something that's either catastrophic or has something to do with a celebrity or one of the royals.

This morning, all is seemingly quiet in the world.

I take a scalding sip, savoring the sensation of the espresso warming my veins.

Closing out the browser, I then tap on the Instagram app, something I know I shouldn't be doing, but I do it anyway, compulsively, every morning. I rarely post anymore; my feed is a ghost of its former self, but I open it so I can type in Carter's name, bring up his profile. Torture myself.

There's a fresh post from late last night. Carter at yet another bar flashing his incandescent smile in a string of selfies, rope lights winking behind him, young women of dizzying levels of attractiveness with their arms laced around his neck.

Fuck.

Any one of them could be his latest. The cherry-lipped blonde in the low-cut blouse, the wavy-haired brunette in a vintage tee that strains over her perky breasts. Or the goth girl with purple-stained eyelids and lips to match, all bedroom eyes and smoky voice, I'm sure of it.

"You're not my usual type," he said to me when we first sat across from each other at a hipster bar.

Heat flashed across my stomach, melting my core. I couldn't tell if this was meant as a compliment, but I took it as such while his dark eyes skittered over my face, dropping to my chest.

I'm not his usual type, but I'm special enough that I've made him stray from whatever his usual type is, I told myself as I sipped my sugary mojito, the rum clouding my peripheral vision.

Now, looking at these chicks—and thinking about all the chicks I've seen in his feed since we split up—I know that him saying I wasn't his usual type was not a good thing.

He's into magazine girls, Insta girls, the ones the cameras are hungry for. Not Cassidy Foster, brainy with mousy auburn hair. Camera shy and awkward.

I'm not saying I'm unattractive. I've had enough strangers hit on me that I've finally accepted I might be decent looking. But I'm no head turner.

I close out of Instagram, place my phone down on the table with a thud.

Carter is back there, and I am here, and I need to let him go. I literally shake my head, casting off the remaining thoughts of him.

In the silent pauses between the birds chirping, I can hear the whir of Mrs. Charlie's sewing machine. It's her hobby; she likes to sit in the little sewing nook, crafting creations with the windows tossed open.

I've been upstairs a few times since arriving. First time was on moving day. She'd laid out a platter of cookies for me when I popped upstairs to sign the lease, pick up the key.

Just off the master, Mr. Charlie had the original builders construct a miniature room, his wife's sewing room, complete with built-ins that house her candy-colored spools of thread. Her purring sewing machine rests beneath a set of hand-crank windows that open out over the tiered flower garden. Right now, yellow poppies are in bloom, their buttercup blossoms opening to the sun like cupped palms.

I take in another deep breath, try to center myself in gratitude like my yoga instructor back in Austin was always telling us to do. Over the years, I've tried gratitude journaling, but, as it turns out, I really just want to record the bad stuff that happens to me, the stuff that hurts. A great quality, I know.

But sitting here now, listening to the goldfinches chirp, I do truly feel grateful.

Flipping my phone over, I type out a text to Lexie.

Cassidy: First day today! Nervous but excited. And thanks SO much again for hooking me up with this place. It's perfect! xo

It's eight hours ahead in Prague and she's probably still on set, but three dots appear, inching across the text box like a caterpillar.

Lexie: Of course! So happy you like. And don't be so nervous. They're gonna love you! Xxx

6

I ARRIVE AT the Sterlings' fifteen minutes early. This morning, there are no other cars in the cul-de-sac, so I park as far from their house as possible, nudging right up to the metal barricades with the Dead End sign.

No June Gloom today. The sky is cloudless, the ocean shimmering outside my passenger window like a sequined blanket.

I'm literally in Paradise.

Still, my heart bangs against my chest—damn my nerves—and my hands are slick against the wheel. I shouldn't have made that second latte, which is all but gone, the remains cooling in the paper cup beside me.

Lexie's right, I shouldn't be so nervous. This is just grunt work, a job for which I'm profoundly overqualified. I think it's the unknown. That and my usual fear over whether people will like me. We didn't do an interview; I scored this simply on Lexie's good word—she's a friend of a friend of the Sterlings. I swear she knows everyone, so all the more reason I'd be filled with shame if they don't take to me.

Shut up, I whisper to myself in the soft hush of my Nissan. *Shut up, Cassidy, and just get your ass in there.*

The air is balmy, infused with the rosemary scent of eucalyptus trees that line the street. Tall, hulking things, their barks smooth and silvery. I'm dressed casually, in a hoodie and joggers, which felt like the right call an hour ago, but now that I'm in Malibu, strolling up to their sumptuous house, I'm second-guessing the choice. Of course I am. Too late.

The sidewalk is pitted with loquats; I step around the peach-colored blisters, trying to spare my new white sneakers from getting stained.

I've reached the edge of their expansive lot, and through the hedges, I glimpse a glittering aquamarine pool that I didn't notice before. I snap my eyes forward, careful not to appear as though I'm spying.

I reach the front walk that leads to the house. The arched front door is painted a pleasing mint-green shade that matches the trim. The velvety yellow stucco exterior is immaculate, unmarred by even a single dot of mold.

The row of large windows sparkles in the morning sunlight, but through them, I don't detect movement from inside the house. As I reach the front door, I pause, then press the glowing doorbell.

From inside, a burst of barking, chased by a female's voice—presumably Marisol's—ordering silence.

She opens the door, dressed in a lightweight robe over pj's—crisp white shorts with a matching cami—her olive-toned skin untouched by makeup but dewy and fresh nonetheless, a gleaming smile spreading across her lips. She looks even more beautiful in person than she does in her modeling spreads.

Two German shepherds churn at her ankles, both rumbling out low but subdued growls. Marisol bends down, caresses their salt-and-pepper coats.

"Boys, this is Cassidy, our new helper."

I inwardly cringe at the word *helper*, but shake it off because she's beautiful and beaming up at me.

Her flawless face is rimmed by a cascade of dark, glossy hair, appearing mussed from sleep but still so luscious it looks as though she could've been sitting in a stylist's chair for hours, going for a beachy look. Her legs are endless and toned, sculpted calf muscles flexing like a ballerina's as she's bent over.

"Cassidy, this is Oscar and Percy." She stands, appraises me with her friendly deep brown eyes, her lips crinkling into another smile. "They like it if you let them sniff the back of your hand. I promise they won't bite."

I'm not afraid of dogs, but still, I'm timid when I extend my hand, letting them smell. I once got bitten by a stray German shepherd in my Dallas neighborhood when I was little, and after, I had to have that god-awful rabies shot that stung like a bumblebee.

But Oscar and Percy nuzzle against my skin, staring up at me with kind, stately eyes.

"I love their names!" I chirp, my voice a high wire, my chest a bundle of nerves.

"Yeah? Thanks. I grew up a book nerd. My mom was a professor of literature back in Barcelona, where I'm from." Her accent is strong and intoxicating, shaping each word into an exquisite thing.

I don't tell her that I know this about her already—that I've done a bit of Googling about her and Nate. I have to walk that fine line of knowing enough to not ding their egos, but keeping my trap shut on the more personal stuff I *have* found out about, so I don't seem like a creep.

"Ah, that must've been so cool!" I say, in a most uncool, awkward way.

"Do you mean growing up in Barca or being raised by an English professor?" She tilts her head and there's a playfulness to her question that lets me know she's not really looking for an answer.

I offer one anyway. "Both! Huge book nerd here, too." To my shame, my hand springs up next to my shoulder like a toy soldier's. Why am I such a dork, always? I drop it, quickly recover by adding, "And I've always wanted to visit Spain."

She blinks at me, smiles, and bends back down to the dogs.

Oscar and Percy are now puddles by our feet.

"Relax here, boys, Cassidy and I have some catching up to do. Follow me. Let's go to the kitchen where we can sit and chat."

I trail her. Underfoot, terra-cotta tiles line the hallway floor, the clay a delicate blush-pink shade that gives the house a feminine feel.

As she walks, Marisol combs her hair with her long fingers, releasing a scent that smells like simmering sugar and tangerines.

"And ah, yes, Spain. I miss it. Haven't been back since before the pandemic," she says, over her shoulder.

We reach the kitchen, a sunlight-doused room that's lined with the same arched windows as the front of the house. Marisol gestures for me to take a seat on a barstool at the island.

"I'm sorry, you must miss your family so much," I say.

"I do. We are very close. I have a lot of sisters, and . . ." She hesitates, shakes her head as if she's warding off tears.

I stay quiet and wait for her to finish, not wanting to fill the silence.

She sucks in a sharp breath, shrugs. I get the feeling she wants to move on from this topic.

"Here, let me take that off of you." She's referring to my messenger bag, still strapped to me like a semiautomatic weapon.

I unpeel it from my chest, hand it over to her. She sets it on a low wooden bench, fixes me with a curious smile. "You can relax here, you know. Feel at home. Please."

The knot that was clenched in my chest begins to loosen, and I grin back. "Thank you."

She's still staring at me with that playful look as if she's trying to decode me. I decide that I instantly like her. Her direct way of being; her way of looking at me, as if she's amused; her casual air.

She floats around the island until she's standing next to the sink, facing me.

A trio of oranges the size of baseballs rests on the marble countertop. She places a hand on one, rolls it against the marble with her palm, almost like a soothing habit. "Just so you know, I didn't even want a personal assistant. I've never had one." An arrow of pride shoots through her voice. "I am much more, like, independent. I don't go in for all this Hollywood bullshit of needing a staff."

I swallow, unsure if I'm about to be dismissed.

She reads the confusion on my face, barks out a laugh. "Sorry, sometimes I am too direct. That's what Nate says." Her rich brown eyes dance with mirth. "Don't get me wrong, I'm happy to have you here, but this is all new for me. Having someone in my house, other than Elana, our housekeeper."

She twines a lock of chocolate hair around her finger. "Nate has a production office in Culver City, which he no longer goes into, not since the shutdown. They handle most of his day-to-day, so you won't be bothered with that stuff. I honestly wish he'd go back in. But I swear he loves staying home and would love for the two of us to stay here together forever, alone. But, I'm not cut out for that. It's stifling. I'm getting out more, ignoring stuff around the house, so he wanted to hire someone to help do the things I used to do. Like buy the dog food, run to the supermarket. Little stuff like that."

I suddenly feel overheated, like my hoodie has just shrunk against my skin, smothering me. Marisol's disclosed a whole lot rather quickly and I'm not sure how to react, how she *wants* me to react. I'm usually highly skilled at molding myself around other people's expectations and wishes, intuiting exactly what they want to hear, but I'm at a bit of a loss here, so I just nod dumbly.

Silence grows between us; I blurt out, "Well, I'm your gal!" with too much cheer in my voice.

She snorts out a laugh, most likely at my awkwardness. "Good, good. Thanks for getting me. I *like* people; I like to be social. Nate does, too, or he did. But he hasn't snapped back yet since lockdown. But I *have* to get out. Plus, I'm trying to build my career."

I nod. "I totally understand. These past few years have been insane." I don't tell her that I'm aware that she's a midlist actress at best, a former model turned actress five years ago. Decent foreign credits like a juicy role in a Pedro Almodóvar film, but nothing big in the States yet. I gnaw my bottom lip, wait it out.

Even though she's in pajamas, I still feel underdressed next to her. Like with most women, I scan her face, her body, for any imperfections. I'm not sure if this instinct to size one another up comes from social conditioning or is something more primal, something ingrained in our DNA, but my eyes graze over her poreless skin, her delicate curves in all the right places, and find zero flaws.

Marisol Torres is simply impeccable.

I'm hyperaware of my own appearance. Pale skin with freckles, frown lines already gripping my mouth at age twenty-nine. Bags under my eyes no matter how much sleep I get. Auburn hair wavy but not in any uniform kind of way that makes it flattering—more like perpetual bedhead versus beachy. I usually just run it through a flat iron, like I have today, which makes it more presentable but bland, like an outdated 1990s hairdo from *Friends*.

"So, like, I won't be working you to death is what I'm saying." Her velvet voice brings me back to the present. "I hope it will be an easy gig and that you can have lots of free time. There's no set schedule. Today, for example, I have to leave for a facial in a little while, so you really don't have to do anything; I just wanted to meet you, give you the keys. Which, hang on—" She slides open a drawer, plucks out a set of gold keys.

"Nate, he doesn't go in for electronic stuff, like keypads. Doesn't trust it, won't even let his scripts go over email until they're in production." She points her finger to her temple, makes little circles with it to signal that she thinks Nate is cuckoo.

"So we're old-school and have actual keys. Here." She slides them across the island to me. "He should be down in a sec to meet you. He has some things for you to sign. He's more into the paperwork stuff than me."

She closes the drawer with her hip, stretches her long arms above her, exposing a slash of toned abs. Yawns into her fist. "Sorry, I'm sluggish today. Late night," she adds, winking at me like we're in on some secret together.

"Understood." Stop it, Cassidy, stop saying stupid things.

"And so, like, each morning," she continues, which I'm grateful for, "maybe show up around nine-thirty-ish?"

She says this as if she's asking me.

I nod.

"I'll have a little list and you just work through it. Some days you'll be done in a few hours, others, it might take longer. See, I'm already terrible at being a boss of someone!" She places her palm to her cheek. "And sorry! I'm an even more terrible host. I haven't even offered you anything. Breakfast? I'm starved."

The second latte groans in my stomach. I ate a quick slice of buttered toast before heading over, but nothing more. I'm starving, but of course my first instinct is to decline, not make her fuss over me. "Thanks, but I'm good."

"So, you've already eaten?"

Shit. "Well, yes, a little breakfast—"

"Hmph!" she says, and literally pulls her shoulders back. "Well, I'm feeding you a *bigger* breakfast."

She slides a knife from the butcher block, halves one of the large oranges. Twists her back to me, placing the orange half in a manual juicer.

After two short glasses are filled, she slides one my way.

"And don't worry, this isn't all. I *eat*, unlike most people out here. This is just to start. Oranges from our trees!" She gestures through the air, thin wrists moving like a conductor's, motioning toward the backyard.

I swivel around, peer through the windows. A grove of orange trees, their bushy branches pregnant with fruit, borders the back edge of the oval-shaped pool I'd glimpsed from the street. Behind the trees, a tall stucco wall wrapped in climbing ivy cocoons the area in total privacy.

"It's my favorite spot. It's the most peaceful, where I can clear my thoughts."

"It's lovely." The surface of the pool shimmers in the sea breeze, like a dog's water bowl recently disturbed by drinking. A pair of slate-gray chaise longues sits at the lip of the pool. Next to them, a small table and chairs rest beneath a bright yellow-and-white-striped umbrella.

"You like to swim?"

I twist back around to answer, but Marisol is ducked into the refrigerator.

"Yes, I love the water."

"Bring your suit, you're welcome to it anytime," she says, speaking into their stainless-steel, French-door fridge.

She pulls out a sleeve of bagels, a package of bacon. She's tall and lithe, bustling around the kitchen like she's accustomed to cooking all the time, like it's her second skin.

"These bagels are addictive. They come from this little shop in Brentwood. You'll soon learn all the spots."

As they toast and the bacon sizzles, we sip our juice.

It's so sweet it tastes like candy, but without the acid burn of the store-bought carton stuff.

"This is delicious." I sip again and wipe pulp from my mouth with the sleeve of my hoodie.

"Thank you. It's one thing, well, one of the many things I love about living here. We have loquat trees, too."

"Yeah, I spotted those outside while I was—"

"I like making tarts with them," she says over me, as if she's not really talking *to* me. It's a trait I've noticed some rich people possess, a way of conversing where they are almost thinking out loud, not even really aware of their audience. "Especially if we're having a get-together."

I simply nod; don't want to trample on her thoughts.

She downs the rest of her juice, plunks her glass in the sink. Retrieves the bagels, their edges perfectly toasted, and flips the bacon with a pair of tongs.

Prying open the fridge again, she pulls out a glass tray that holds a square slab of butter and a jar of jam.

"Butter?" she asks. "Sorry, I ran out of cream cheese. I actually put it on the shopping list for you. Not that you *have* to go today. Tomorrow's better anyway because I'm cooking dinner and would love fresh fish."

"Butter's great, thanks!"

I take small, careful bites of the bagel, mindful not to smack in front of her. "And you're right, this is *so* good."

With the corner of a napkin, she wipes crumbs from the edges of her mouth. "You're welcome. And you're welcome to whatever's in the fridge anytime. I have to eat every few hours—I hate being hungry—so please, seriously, help yourself."

I nod and smile, continuing to chew through the bagel.

"So what brings you out here? You're from Texas, right?" She snaps a piece of bacon in two, nibbles. "I mean, you left behind cowboys and barbecue?" Again, that teasing smile that makes our interactions feel intimate, like friends, and not just strangers who've only just met.

I want to answer that I've moved across the country for this job, but stop myself, realizing how pathetic that might sound to her. She keeps staring at me, head tilted, waiting for me to answer. Because of her directness, I feel my heart slicing open, and thoughts of Carter spilling out. *No, Cassidy. Ugh!*

But it's too late. Marisol has already read my face, peered into my soul. "Ah, broken heart."

Tears flood my eyes, but I quickly blink, willing them away.

She drops the bacon down on her plate, reaches across the bar, grabs my hands. "Well, fuck him, whoever he is. You hear me? Men are dumbasses and he is not worth your time—"

The sound of footfalls creaking against the stairs makes Marisol pause.

"Oops," she says, her eyes sparking with mischief. "I hear Nate. We'll finish this chat later."

7

LIKE MARISOL'S, NATE'S skin is poreless, sun-kissed, and olive-toned. He's wearing a white button-down shirt—cuffed to reveal carved forearms—and an easy smile. He's tall, a couple inches taller than Marisol—they must be head-to-head when she's in heels—and his hair is thick, wavy. Sandy blond but on the darker side.

Black-rimmed glasses frame his eyes, which appear to be hazel with flecks of green.

Quite simply put, he's gorgeous.

Somewhere deep in my stomach, I register a ping of attraction, which I try to suppress. I neither want nor need to be attracted to him. Who wouldn't be, though? But he's safe from me; he's married. And as if on cue, Marisol rises, glides across the room to greet him.

"Good morning, darling!" She twines a lanky arm around his neck. They share a kiss, lingering enough to make my insides squirm, make me want to turn away.

Finally, they unlatch. Nate walks over to me, flashes me a dazzling smile, teeth as crisp white as his shirt.

"Hi, I'm Nate." That ping of desire in my belly swells; his tone is so pleasant, so sexy, and I'm a sucker for voices. "Very nice to meet you, Cassie."

He extends his hand and we shake. "You, too!" I say, with way too much enthusiasm.

"Tsk, her name is Cassidy," Marisol says, grinning and shaking her head like he's been a naughty boy.

Nate looks at me and lifts his eyebrows as if to say, *Why didn't* you *correct me?*

My skin burning, I swallow the lump that's expanding in the back of my throat. *Because rather than assert myself, I would just let you continue to call me by the wrong-ass name.*

"Well, nice to meet you, *Cassidy*," he says, cocking his head to one side, putting special emphasis on my name, which, coming out of his mouth, sounds like something almost sacred. When that easy grin spreads across his lips again, my face singes; I hope Marisol doesn't notice my swooning.

"Who wants coffee?" Nate asks, clasping his hands together, hitching his head toward a gleaming stainless-steel espresso maker.

"I'll have another shot of espresso, babe. Why not?" Marisol eyes me like she wants me to join in, almost daring me to say yes.

Instead of automatically declining, I follow her lead. "Sure! I'd love a latte!" I say, hoping I don't sound too forward.

"That's my drink, too," Nate says. "But we only have oat milk; hope that's okay."

"That's actually what *I* drink!" My voice springs out of me, girly and bright. I literally bite my tongue, will myself to act like some semblance of an adult.

As the machine groans and sputters out shots, Nate twists around. "You take her on the tour of the house yet?"

Marisol lifts the remainder of her bagel. "No, sir, not yet. I fed her breakfast like a good little hostess."

"Atta girl." Nate winks at her.

I'm enjoying their easy, playful banter.

"Those bagels are delicious. Marisol was telling me that y'all get them at some special place in Brentwood."

"Yep, it's not too far from my office in Culver. I used to bring them home on my way back, but I really don't go out that much anymore."

"I explained to Cassidy that you are a shut-in," Marisol says, her mouth curving into a wicked grin.

"Ouch. That's a bit harsh." Nate slides Marisol's espresso toward her, opens the carton of oat milk, and begins frothing it. "But not inaccurate. I do prefer to stay in these days, working quietly in my home office, which I'll show you in a sec."

Marisol sips her shot. "Mm-mm . . ."

As Nate works the machine, my eyes veer again to his forearms, hairless and taut. Like Marisol, he bustles around the kitchen like he's comfy here, like he'd be cast as the hot chef in a rom-com.

"Here we are," he says, placing a steaming mug in front of me. "And before I forget, I have some things for you to sign."

He walks over to the built-in, then returns with two packs of forms. "One of these is to set up your pay. If you don't mind, on your way home, you can drop it at our accountant's office in Century City. I don't like to send things electronically, don't trust it—"

"Yeah, I've also told her all about your weirdness," Marisol says, licking a foamy mustache from her top lip.

"Ha!" Nate guffaws. "Yes, I am particular about this stuff, but then again, I'm downright elderly compared to you two."

I smile, gnaw my bottom lip so I won't say something stupid. Nate is forty-five, I learned from Google; Marisol, thirty-three.

"So just fill it out, attach a voided check," Nate continues. "And this next form, it's a nondisclosure. Pretty standard stuff for Hollywood." His easy grin vanishes and his face takes on a serious edge.

He hands me a fancy ballpoint pen and the NDA; I scan but don't really read it. I don't want to hesitate, make it seem as if I don't trust them, so I scrawl my signature at the bottom of the page.

"I get it," I say. And I do. They have to protect themselves from some blabbing assistant, but I wonder if a former employee *has* done something underhanded, given Nate's sudden change in demeanor.

I push the document back toward him.

"Thanks, Cassidy. And thanks for being here. Don't know if Marisol's told you, but she's never had an assistant before."

I nod.

"But I have. Before we met. And, of course, I have my staff at the office, who you'll meet soon enough. They won't bite, don't worry. And you won't be doing much there other than picking up the odd package, that sort of thing."

"Sounds great," I say and sip my latte, which is nutty and perfectly sweetened as it hits the back of my tongue. "Thanks so much for this." I lift my mug as if to toast him before setting it back down. How awkward; I'm the worst. "It's divine!" I trill, clearly unable to stop myself.

"Glad you like it. Let's show her around, shall we? I've got a call in twenty—"

"You bet, boss," Marisol purrs.

"First, the backyard," Nate says, parting the French doors that lead to the pool.

Outside the air is still gusty, but less so behind their wall of tall, thick hedges.

"Not much you need to know about out here, but this is the pool, obviously."

"It's lovely. Marisol said I could swim anytime!" *Jesus, Cassidy.*

The breeze whips my baby-fine hair, causing it to lash into my mouth. It'll be a windblown mess by the time we get back inside.

"Oh, and the back gate there," he says, pointing to the far corner of the lot, "always stays locked. So there's no access to the house other than the front entry and the garage. Just so you know."

My eyes travel to the direction he's referring to. It's a tall wooden gate, arch shaped like their front door, that leads to the street.

Marisol rolls her eyes as if Nate's being ridiculous.

"What? I just wanted to give her the layout—"

"Next, he'll print you the original floor plans and—"

"My wife here," Nate says, snaking an arm around Marisol's neck, "thinks I go a little overboard with security."

"Ha! A little—"

"But . . . I've learned you can't be too careful. Not out here. Not in this business. That's why we like to keep a low profile." He looks at me meaningfully, as if referring to the nondisclosure I just signed. Again, I wonder if something happened with a past assistant.

Nate turns and files back inside, leading us down the hallway that connects to the front of the house. At the entrance, he sweeps his hand to the right. "The living room. Sometimes, I like to sit in here and read. It's quiet."

And looks out over the ocean, I think to myself.

The room is quaint, with a fireplace carved from the same chalky stucco as the walls. A red leather recliner is angled beneath a window, catching amber morning light. An idyllic reading place indeed. Across from it, a long sofa. No television in here. Just the far wall racked with book-lined built-ins. My kind of space.

Across the hall, he motions to the dining room. Like the rest of the house, it's simple and elegant, with an oval-shaped wooden table, scarred from use.

Next, he leads us down the hallway again, hooking left instead of right, which would lead us back to the kitchen.

Another sitting room. This one smaller than the living room, with a set of glass doors that opens up to an expansive lawn, the grass so green and manicured it looks as soft as a newborn's hair. A medium-sized TV is mounted above the fireplace in this room, artfully flanked by paintings on either side—portraits of their dogs, Oscar and Percy.

Next to the fireplace, an archway leads into another room.

"That," Nate says, jutting his chin toward the room, "is our guest quarters. Two bedrooms with a bath. Feel free to use this space as your own."

I'm not sure if this means I can't use the restroom I noticed off the kitchen earlier, adjacent to the laundry room, or if he's just being nice. I don't care, I decide. I'm grateful to have a little nook of my own here.

"The beds are great in there, too," Marisol says. "Like, if you ever want to nap. I'm a big believer in them myself."

We trail Nate up a long flight of wooden stairs, reach a light-filled landing that's lined with more arch-shaped windows on either side. To my right, I glimpse the pool, the street. To the left, the grassy lot with the ocean winking beyond the fence line.

"The master," Nate says, pausing in the doorway, but blocking it, making it clear that the tour won't be including their bedroom.

My eyes sweep around his form and take in a pair of massive windows. Through them, the silvery Pacific glistens and contracts. The room is long, rectangular, and easily larger than my whole garage apartment.

"More bedrooms over here." Nate waves a palm at the row of rooms opposing their master. "And finally, my office."

The office is clearly a new build, reached by a small set of descending steps. "Ta-da!" he says, sweeping his arm around the room.

It's more modern than the rest of the house but constructed to match with the same stucco walls and built-ins. High, rectangular windows line the walls, allowing the room to feel light and airy, while at the same time private, and a pair of French doors opens up onto a Juliet balcony overlooking the pool.

The room feels Mediterranean like the rest of the home but with a touch of Scandi-minimalism: a teal sideboard displays a vintage set of cameras next to a boxy sectional.

"Not too shabby, eh?" Nate asks, lifting an eyebrow at me.

"Not too shabby for a boy from the hood!" Marisol chimes, knocking her hip to his.

I know that Nate is from Connecticut, most likely from money, because Wikipedia identifies his father as an investment banker, and Nate a product of private academies that pipelined him to NYU film school.

"Straight outta Darien!" Nate jokes. "Darien is a posh suburb in Connecticut, if you've never heard of it. Most haven't. It's where I grew up. Marisol likes to tease me because it's so white-bread; I didn't get to grow up in an internationally famous city like her—"

"Oh! The poor boy was a whole hour away from the *most* international city of New York."

My eyes travel back and forth between them; I'm unsure of how to respond. I stand there grinning like a loon, hands tunneling deeper into my pockets.

"Cassidy here is from Texas, you know?" Marisol says.

"Yeah, Austin, right?" Nate asks, hazel eyes scanning my face.

For some reason, this makes me blush, both his soft, thoughtful eyes and the fact that he remembers this little detail about me even if he didn't get my first name right. I really am a sucker for any attention; my bar is so dangerously low.

"Yep. Dallas originally. So, straight outta Dallas!"

To my great relief, this elicits a bark of laughter from Nate and a grin from Marisol. She rolls her shoulders, slides her bare foot up her leg until it rests just below her knee on her exquisite calf: tree pose. With a figure like hers, she probably goes in and out of yoga poses all day long.

Gazing at the pair of them—her in skimpy pj's and Nate with his more buttoned-up look—I can imagine them in their bedroom, going at it. Hot and feral with the windows open, the warm sea breeze licking their bodies.

Do all people have these creepy, intrusive thoughts or is it just me? I shake the image away, paste a bland, neutral smile on my face. Exhale, letting out a pent-up breath I'd been holding in. *Focus, Cassidy, this is a great gig.* They are nice, they seem somewhat normal, and according to Marisol, there won't even be that much work to do.

From within his pocket, Nate's phone beeps, interrupting my endless inner monologue. "That's my call. Or my timer for my call. Listen, I gotta run—"

"Boi, bye," Marisol says, waving her hand over him with a flourish, as if casting a spell, before gently tugging me away.

8

I'M SOAKING IN the tub, an antique clawfoot, my second-favorite thing about this apartment after the charming kitchenette.

I'm relaxed, content, and dare I say, hopeful, for the first time in a long while. I really liked the Sterlings, and, more importantly, they liked me. I'm sure of it.

I inhale a deep breath, holding it for a few seconds before exhaling, letting my muscles go slack in the scalding, lavender-tinged water.

Soon after Nate took his call, I left. Instead of cruising up Highway 1 to the 10 to get to their accountant's office, I decided to veer down fabled Sunset Boulevard through the Westside to Century City. While rolling past the palm tree–studded sidewalk and storied mansions, a pang of sadness jabbed me: my mother. For the first time ever in my life, Angie Foster would've been proud of me, of where I've landed.

But I quickly shook that off, reminding myself—as I've had to do for years now—that Angie Foster didn't give two shits about me; she up and left, so there's no good reason to pine for *her*.

I arrived at the accountant's by eleven thirty, was home by noon. I can't believe my workday was so short. I'm hoping that Marisol was telling the truth when she suggested that more brief workdays like this are in my future.

I love that I'm not punching a clock, that I won't be imprisoned by going into an office anymore. I feel like I can breathe and still can't believe they're going to pay me five grand a month to basically run errands, flit in and out, hang around their luxurious house.

Next to me, on a little wooden stool, my phone chimes.

It's a text, from Lexie. Must be three in the morning there.

Lexie: Just checking in on ya, chica! How was the first day?

Cassidy: It went SO great! They really liked me, I think! You were right. Cannot thank you enough, am so excited!

Lexie: Yay! I knew you'd be aces!! Xx

Cassidy: Whyyy are you still up?

Lexie: Night shoot! And gotta run, but yay. So happy to hear and this is going to be a great move, I promise! Xxx

9

FOUR WEEKS LATER

DETECTIVES CRUZ AND Simmons are sitting on my futon, both perched on the edge, notepads open, pens hovering.

I can't sit; my nerves are so rattled my teeth are actually chattering. So I stir in my tiny kitchen, taking coffee orders.

"I'll take mine black. Double shot, please," Detective Cruz says.

Her hair is long and curly, thick with product, and her face is coated in full makeup as if she plans to hit a happy hour after her shift. I wish I could join her, drown out my sorrows.

"Same," Detective Simmons chimes, his voice booming but clipped. He's heavyset, balding.

So far, he's the bad cop to Detective Cruz's good one. But they've only been inside for a few minutes, so we'll see.

The room swirls around me, my hands clacking as I pull down the espresso cups. I'm playing the part of "guilty suspect" and even though I'm facing away from them, I can feel Detective Simmons's steel gaze needling my back.

I'm confident of two things: they're not here for a social call and they know I'm hiding something. I should've never let him rope me into all this. *What was I thinking? How did I think by agreeing to do something so crazy, things would end well? All love and light?* Obviously, I wasn't. And more than that, I should've never hit send on those texts.

That's why they're here, I'm positive of it. My spying, the photos, and then pressing send, flinging them out there, hoping it would bring us closer when all it's done is set something even more explosive in motion.

10

NOW

IT'S LATE. ELEVEN p.m. And dark. So dark the night is sooty black outside my window.

I should be long asleep by now. I'm much more of an early-to-bed, early-to-rise type of person—that's the Virgo in me—but my head is spinning.

Against my better judgment, I tip more wine in the glass, swirl it around. I'm not drunk; I rarely allow myself to get drunk. That's *also* the Virgo in me—I can't handle feeling like I'm out of control. But I am properly buzzed.

I was beginning to get tipsy at the Sterlings' tonight—Marisol kept refilling my wineglass—but before it got to the point where I'd be uncomfortable driving home, I snuck into the bathroom, emptied it down the sink, slapped water on my flushed cheeks.

But now I'm relishing the wine. The pinot noir warming the back of my throat, the numbing feeling spreading through my limbs, the simultaneous heightening and dulling of my thoughts. I only wish Lexie were here to hash out what just happened.

Nothing happened, Cassidy, I keep telling myself. It really didn't, but I'm still a bit jarred.

I consider texting Lexie, but she sounded busy the last time we messaged, so I resist, skid my cell away from me across the top of the comforter like a hockey puck. I don't want to bother her, run to her with every little thing, and plus, I want her to think things are still going well. And they are; I'm probably overthinking this like I do everything. Obsessing.

This morning, I arrived at the Sterlings' promptly at nine thirty. Marisol greeted me at the front door, dressed again in casual, but skimpy, pj's. A matching white cotton set with cherry print and a red cami peeking out underneath.

"Morning," she said, leaning in and kissing both my cheeks.

The gesture threw me off; I wound up jamming my nose into hers, giggles bubbling out of me like a small child.

"Ready for work?" she said, a smile drizzling across her face as if she knows this job isn't really work.

"Absolutely."

I trailed her into the kitchen.

A handwritten list awaited me on the countertop.

"I've got a pretty full day. A lesson with my accent coach, Andreas; a meeting with a producer; a massage; but I'll be back around four to make dinner. The grocery list is on the back," she said, motioning toward the paper.

I picked it up, turned it over.

Lemons

Dill

Asparagus

Arugula

Cherry tomatoes

Jarred olives, the good kind

Wild-caught halibut

Goat cheese

Fresh baguette (in bakery, they make them fresh every day)

Chocolate mousse (same)

Wine (any red that you like but spend at least $50 on the bottle)

Fifty dollars for wine? I'm so used to grabbing Two-Buck Chuck at Trader Joe's that spending that much stumped me for a sec, but I grinned and nodded.

"And if you see anything else that looks good, fresh, grab it. Like produce, I mean. I like to eat *real* food. None of this fad stuff, none of these powders or mixes. That's all junk. Humans need to eat things that come from the earth. That's why in Spain we live longer than here." Her cheeks blushing, she laughed at herself, waved her hand as if clearing smoke from the air. "But let's not get started on Marisol's lecture about skinny people in LA starving themselves on concoctions or the rest of America gorging themselves on fast food. How insufferable."

I like to think of myself as a pretty clean eater, but I know I'll be hitting the drive-through at In-N-Out on the regular. So I grinned, nodded again. "I hear ya."

I flipped the list over to read the front.

Dog food (My Pet Naturally–Santa Monica)

Joggers (Fred Segal)

Organize junk drawer

Groceries (I love Vintage Grocers)

"And here are the specifics on the dog food." She handed me a dry-food label and one peeled from a can. "Get two twenty-pound bags of the kibble and four cases of the canned. Someone can help you load into the car if you need. I know it's a lot, my boys eat like horses. Any other questions?"

"Joggers? Like, what size and color—"

"Oh, silly me. Size four, but hang on. I have a pair in gray, but I'd like a matching one in black." She slid out of the room.

I wondered about Nate, if he was upstairs in his office, and if I'd get to see him today. The driveway was empty when I arrived, but it was empty yesterday as well, so they must park in the garage.

Marisol returned with the joggers in hand. "Just take these with you. And you have the key, so just let yourself in and out. Nate's here, but he's lost in his own little world up there," she said, waving toward the ceiling.

So he *was* home. The thought of being alone in the house with him both thrilled and overwhelmed me. *Let's see how awkward Cassidy can be in front of Nate without Marisol as a sparkling buffer.*

"I've gotta take a shower, get running, but here, come look," she said, tugging open a drawer in the built-in desk. "Behold my junk drawer."

Inside, a tangle of keys, rubber bands, batteries, stamps, pens, etc., the usual, but it was as if someone had placed the contents in a giant Ziploc, shook it for several minutes, then dumped it back inside the drawer. My orderly Virgo brain felt assaulted, but I could immediately visualize order and how I'd execute this task.

"I don't even know where to begin—"

"I got this. Don't worry," I said.

Marisol leaned in again, pecked my cheek.

"Maybe I'm gonna like having an assistant after all." She winked at me, clicking her fingernails together as though she were about to open a Christmas present. "See you later, sweets!" She blew me an air kiss and floated out of the room.

I closed the junk drawer, scrawled on the bottom of my to-do list, *Target: plastic drawer organizer, binder clips, rubber bands.*

Other than the dishwasher, which hissed and sloshed next to me, the room was filled with quiet. Sunlight pulsed against the surface of the pool; I leaned against the counter gazing at their luxe backyard. The yellow-and-white-striped umbrella, tilted at the perfect angle, called to mind the beaches of the Italian Riviera.

Maybe I will take Marisol up on her offer, I thought, *and bring my swimsuit with me someday*. I love the water, it's one of the things I loved most about Austin. Languorous days on the shores of icy-cold Barton Springs, dipping in and out of the emerald-green swimming holes along the Greenbelt.

But a private pool perched high above the Pacific? This beats all. Eat your heart out, Carter. Oh, if he could see me now. I wished, and not for the first time, that he could still see my Instagram posts. I'd snap a teasing selfie by this pool. But he doesn't look at my account anymore; he blocked me. So I, in turn, blocked him.

Above me, louder footfalls snapped me back to attention. Nate. Probably heading down the hall to use the restroom.

I pulled out my phone, plugged in my various stops on the map app. Even with the Target run, I calculated I'd be finished well before four, before Marisol was due home.

I let myself out the front door, locking it with the key they had given me. It felt strange doing that, as if this were my home. Strange, but also, good. Just like the credit card nestled in my wallet that the accountant had given me to use for incidentals. Bearing Marisol's name, but still mine to use.

A lightness spread through me then as I walked down the sunny sidewalk to my car. It was the sensation of walking out of my old life and stepping into this new one, almost as if in a dream. I know it sounds cliché, but that's the feeling that overtook me.

My first stop was Fred Segal. Racks of buttery soft T-shirts greeted me at the entrance. I plucked one off, held it up to me. The fabric was whisper-soft against my skin, but when I fumbled with the price tag, squinting at the amount—$800—I inwardly shrieked, placed it back on the rack, headed over to the pants section.

The joggers were $325; I felt empowered as I whipped out Marisol's card, waved it over the tap screen without a thought about the cost.

Next stop, the Coffee Bean, where I treated myself (with my own money) to an iced latte. Santa Monica, in many ways, reminded me of Austin. All tank tops and leggings and beachy hair and laid-back vibes. Juice bars along the sidewalk next to salons, boutiques, taco joints. I almost felt like I fit in, save for the fact that my entire wardrobe comes from T.J.Maxx, not Fred Segal.

My final stop was Vintage Grocers, the grocery in Malibu. It was blissfully empty as I wheeled the cart through the produce section, plucking out a stunningly fresh artichoke. I then spotted a face that looked familiar. *Where did I know him from?* As I veered my cart closer to his, I realized it was Billy Crystal. Not some long-lost friend. I snapped my head in the other direction to hide my embarrassment over gawking at him.

By three o'clock, I was twisting the key in the Sterlings' lock. Oscar and Percy greeted me, tails wagging, noses nudging against my legs until I put the paper grocery sacks down in the hall to greet them.

Their coats are so shiny and soft; I kneeled on the cold tile, petting them as they licked my face.

"I bet you know I have your food in my car!" I chirped.

From down the hallway, the sound of Nate clearing his voice startled me.

"Those monstrous bags of dog food, I'll help you with those," Nate said, eyes smiling as he looked down at me, crouched on the floor, my V-neck tee probably exposing too much cleavage from his vantage point.

I shifted, brought myself to standing.

"That'd be great!"

"And here, I'll take those, too," he said stepping closer to me, his voice smooth like crushed velvet.

My pulse jangled in my neck. He lifted the grocery sacks, ferried them to the kitchen.

Walking with him to my car moments later, I felt embarrassed. A bland and basic Nissan when he probably drives a shiny Beamer.

I squeezed the fob and the hatchback lifted open.

"Dang, your car is spotless," Nate said, grinning, his eyes scanning the interior.

"I'm a bit of a neat freak, I'm afraid."

"We are, too. Well, at least I am."

He must have caught my surprised expression because he quickly added, "I mean, Marisol's no slob, I wasn't saying that, but I'm just wound a little tighter than she is, is all I meant."

He hauled the bags, slinging one over each shoulder.

"Well, here's to us both being tightly wound!" I replied, stupidly. *Shut it, Cassidy.*

Nate smiled as my face burned, trudging up ahead of me with the sacks weighing down his shoulders like saddlebags.

Inside, he set the food down in the mudroom just off the kitchen.

"I'm going to go finish up." He jutted his chin toward the ceiling.

"But thanks again for being here. It's going to be such a big help to Marisol, to me."

Obviously, he can't get away from my awkwardness fast enough, I thought.

"You're welcome! I mean, thank *you* for hiring me." *Oh god.*

He grinned again, then vanished from the room.

I SPENT THE next hour clearing my head by tearing apart the junk drawer, doing what I do best: organizing. On my iPhone, I selected a 1930s jazz playlist I'd created months ago to pipe through my headphones at work. Replicas, really, of my grandmother's record collection. Vintage compositions that comfort me.

When the hour was up, everything was in its place: stamps rolled neatly and cinched with a rubber band, pens packed side by side in their allotted slot, recipe cards stacked together with a binder clip.

I exhaled. The sight of my orderly handiwork filled me with glee.

From the front hall, Oscar and Percy burst into whinnying. Marisol. She was home.

She glided into the kitchen, looking resplendent in a yellow sundress. A strapless bustier hugged her perfect shape, the short hemline showing off her copper thighs, her sumptuous cleavage nearly bursting from the top, yet still somehow discreet.

On her cheeks, bronze blush made the soft angles of her face even more defined, and her lips were glossed in a petal-pink shade. An absolute knockout.

"How'd your day go?" I asked. "You look *gorgeous*, by the way."

"Thank you, love. It was fabulous," she purred. Her whole essence had a glow to it, as if she had just come off a titillating first date.

She picked up an orange from the countertop, began peeling it, popping juicy segments in her mouth. "Sorry, I'm starving. But what do we have here?"

She walked over to me, peered into the open junk drawer.

"Eeeee!" she squealed, pulling me into a hug. "Cassidy! It is beautiful! You are a genius! I could never!" Like yesterday, her skin smelled of citrus and sugar simmering on the stove.

I beamed back at her. "It's nothing, really."

"No, it's amazing. Ahh, will you do my closet next?"

"Of course! I'd love to! I geek out over this stuff."

"And where did you get that thingie in there?" she asked gesturing to the plastic organizer.

"Target."

"Never been there."

"Really?" I asked, baffled, with too much incredulity in my voice. "I mean, whatever, it's not that great—" I backpedaled.

"Yeah, I don't like the big-box stores."

You don't have *to like the big-box stores*, I thought. *You can afford to buy jogging pants at Fred Segal.*

"No, I hear ya," I said, even though I didn't.

I showed her the joggers next, then presented her with the artichoke.

"I don't know if you guys even like them, but it looked so good and fresh—"

"No, yes, exactly!" Her eyes danced over it. "It's gorgeous. And I love to steam them. Like I said, you're a genius!"

"And I picked this cab for the wine—" I slid it out of its paper sleeve.

"It's perfect!"

"Yay! So glad. And hope it all makes for a nice dinner for y'all."

I glanced at the clock on the microwave. Four thirty. "Is there anything else you need me to do today? I'm happy to—"

"Ah, no, you've done so much. Seriously. You're free to go."

I balled my keys in my fist, slung my messenger bag across my chest. "Okay! See ya in the morning then," I said.

"Wait! I have a better idea. Why don't you stay for dinner?" I was struck by the pleading note to her voice; it was hard to miss, almost a desperation. "We have more than enough."

I really wanted to get home, soak in the tub, watch *The Bachelor*, but how could I say no?

"Really? Are you sure—"

"Yes, of course, don't be silly. I'd love to get to know you better anyway, and vice versa."

Clasping the neck of the bottle, she wrested the cork out as fast as I'd ever witnessed anybody doing so.

"Here, let's have a little while I cook."

She splashed us each a small amount in a pair of large wineglasses. "But you sit, your workday is through."

"I don't need to sit, I could help prep—"

She put her hand up. "No way, you've done more than enough today and besides, I like cooking. It helps with my anxiety."

Anxiety? How could she possibly have anxiety? But it was an immature, fleeting thought. Of course you could have everything in the world and still be anxious, depressed. And be anxious and depressed *because* of it—the pressure. But unless they've scrounged the floorboard of their car for change in order to buy groceries, as I have, it's hard for me to drum up sympathy for someone in such a position of privilege. Still, I like Marisol and don't like to think of her suffering.

In her tight yellow dress with her long hair swinging over her delectable frame, she set about chopping the veggies, the knife striking rhythmically against the cutting board.

Soon, garlic sizzled in olive oil in a skillet and Marisol had a feathery pile of dill resting next to the fish. She sliced open a lemon, squeezing the halves over the halibut. "This is my secret," she said. "I like the fish to marinate in the citrus for at least half an hour before searing, then baking it."

As she was layering arugula and cherry tomatoes in a shallow wooden bowl for the salad, Nate entered the kitchen. He was dressed in another crisp white button-down, his hair still damp from the shower.

"Umm, you look . . . ravishing?" He sidled up to Marisol, snaked an arm around her waist.

"Thanks, babe." She pecked him on the cheek.

"Good day?"

"Very good. But we'll talk about it over dinner—"

"Yeah, I'm sure Cassidy doesn't want to hear our work stuff—"

"Oh, she will. She's staying for dinner!"

An almost imperceptible slouching of his shoulders, a flicker of disappointment across his face. A look at Marisol that seemed to say, *Why didn't you clear this with me first?* Then a quick recovery, a flash of his blinding smile. "Excellent, Cassidy! So happy you're staying. Marisol's such a great cook."

A pit formed in my stomach: *Yikes, he really doesn't want me here.* But maybe, I thought, it has nothing to do with me and everything to do with wanting to be alone with his drop-dead-gorgeous wife, especially when she looks so hot.

Marisol bumped him with her hip, popped a cherry tomato between his lips. "Now, out. Go walk the dogs or something. You know I don't like you circulating in here like a shark while I cook." She said it playfully, but I detected an undercurrent of angst, like she truly wanted him gone. I wondered why.

"Copy that," Nate said, winking at me before exiting the room.

"Whew. I love him, but sometimes that man gets on my nerves,"

Marisol said once the back door clicked shut. "Like, he says he loves my cooking, but if he stayed in here, he'd be micromanaging."

She didn't make eye contact with me as she was speaking; she spoke, instead, into the wooden bowl, tossing the salad with oversized tongs.

As she finished searing the fish, she hummed to herself, still radiating that crackling energy. And again, I wondered why she wanted space from Nate.

"Mm-mm . . . this is very good, Cassidy, nice and velvety," she said, clasping the wineglass.

"I agree! Cheers!" I tilted my glass to hers.

"To meeting you!" she said, toasting back.

"And you as well!"

I rolled the wine around in my mouth. It was insanely delicious, unlike any I'd ever tasted. Smoky, rich, but somehow still light as air.

WE GATHERED IN the cozy dining room. Nate and Marisol gave me the ocean view and sat opposite from me, their chairs pulled close together.

The wooden table was laden with platters of Marisol's perfectly cooked meal. The steamed artichoke, the salad dotted with goat cheese, the fish, its skin now golden and still sizzling. Nate dimmed the chandelier, lit a pair of slender beeswax candles, which flickered between us.

In addition to the wine, Marisol had laid out a pitcher of iced water topped with thin lime slices. I poured myself a glass to counter the effects of the alcohol.

"So, tell us," Nate said, dragging an artichoke leaf through the aioli sauce Marisol had whipped up.

"Well," Marisol said, nipping at her wine. "It went better than expected, let me just put it that way."

"Nah, we want details, don't we, Cassidy?" Nate asked, smiling at me.

My mouth went dry from being put on the spot like this, *and* from Nate smiling at me. "Sure. I'd love to hear more."

"Tell her your big news," Nate said.

"You know I don't like to jinx things before they're official, but, I'm one of three actresses up for the lead role in the new Guillermo del Toro film."

"Marisol! That's amazing! He's such a legend," I said.

"Thank you," she demurred, waving a hand in front of her. "But let's not get too excited just yet. I still have to book the part. But the meeting with David, the producer, went really well today."

Nate leaned over, tucked a lock of her curls behind her ear, whispered something.

She giggled.

Watching them being this intimate set off a feeling of unease in my gut. I felt like a third wheel.

Marisol speared a piece of fish with her fork, took a bite. "The thing I have to nail," she said between forkfuls, "is the accent. The film is set in Brazil, and as you may know, they speak Portuguese there, which I'm fluent in—I'm fluent in five languages, actually—but there are differences. In tone, in enunciation. That's why I'm working with Andreas, my accent coach."

"You've always worked with Andreas," Nate said, slinging his arm across the back of her chair. A gesture that felt protective, possibly even possessive. He scanned her face as if searching for a reaction. But she just grinned at him, a tiny smile that didn't reach her eyes.

"True." She lifted her wineglass to her lips, took a long sip.

Silence thickened between the three of us.

"He must be really great, then?" I offered, trying to knife through the awkwardness.

"Yes. And also, he's a friend. He's from Spain, too, so we are kindred. And I haven't seen him all that much since the shutdown. So we've been catching up. Having coffees, drinks. Like I was saying yesterday, Nate here is happy to stay at home with just the two of us. He's more introverted, but not me. I'm getting out now, even if he doesn't like it."

My gaze shifted to Nate. A wounded look rippled across his face. But then Marisol beamed at him, leaned in and placed her hand on his thigh. Under her gaze, he melted.

"She makes me sound like some freak, but yeah, I'll admit to being more of a homebody now." He looked at me, put his palms up in surrender.

It wasn't lost on me how Marisol had steered the conversation off of Andreas.

"I'm kind of a homebody, too," I said, but they had gone back to eating, my words dying across the table.

The fish melted in my mouth. Nate was right, Marisol *could* cook.

"So, Cassidy," Nate said, dotting the corner of his mouth with his napkin. "You're from Austin. Tell me more. What you did there, how you're liking it out here?" His voice was rich and silky and made my stomach clench.

"She's a writer, remember?" Marisol said, a flare of annoyance in her voice at having to remind him.

"Mm-mm. That's wonderful. What kind of things do you write?"

My pulse thrummed in my temples. I reached for my half-full wineglass. But before I could take a sip, Marisol refilled my glass to the brim.

"I write novels," I said, not wanting to go into any more detail. Not wanting them to know that I was still unpublished.

"Novels?" asked Marisol. "That's incredible! Like, what genre?"

Hands clammy, I cupped the wineglass like a goblet, took a long swig. I wasn't getting out of this line of questioning, apparently.

The sun had now set behind me, bringing our little trio lit by candles into sharper focus. Shadows pooled in the corners of the room; I could feel the edges of my sobriety softening with each sip.

"Well, I've written three so far, and they've all been romance," I ventured. "But not like the stuff in the supermarkets; I've tried to make them more literary, you know, paying attention to the sentences—"

But Nate and Marisol were already entangled again in each other, she with her hand still on Nate's thigh, he with his nose to her ear. Shame crept up my neck. Of course they didn't really want to hear about me, I'm a nobody. I pawed my glass again, took another glug. Slid my phone out of my pocket and checked the time: seven thirty. I was ready to go.

"I'm just going to the ladies' room," I said, rising from the table, glass in hand. "Be right back."

I veered down the darkened hall—lit only by sconces—to the guest quarters. Flipped on the light in the powder room and studied myself in the mirror. My lips were stained from the wine, making me look clownish, and my cheeks were blazing. After dumping nearly the rest of the glass down the sink, I splashed water on my face before heading back to Marisol and Nate.

AS I STEPPED into the dining room, Marisol was uncorking another bottle of wine. Sigh. I really just wanted to be back at home, swaddled in my pj's.

"Prosecco!" she announced, drawing the syllables out with a slur. "To go with dessert, which I almost forgot about!"

I swallowed the remainder of the red, scooted the empty glass toward her. The wine poured from the bottle cotton candy pink, fizzing brightly on my tongue.

"Let me get the mousse," she said, sashaying out of the room.

Over his own glass of prosecco, Nate peered at me, his face flushed like mine, his eyes probing and warm. "Like I said earlier today, thanks for being here. I'm really happy you are." This sent my stomach into cartwheels. I couldn't believe that he even remembered our earlier exchange. In the quivering candlelight, his eyes shimmered, flecks of green swimming in pools of hazel.

"I am, too," I replied, leveling my eyes on his, drawing my glass to my lips, taking another frothy sip.

We held each other's gazes until Marisol burst back in the room, a row of tiny dessert plates lining her slender arms.

"This is nice! Like a party! We used to have parties, remember, Nate?" She winked at him, speaking in the same teasing tone as earlier. But there was a dagger to her words. "We'd have these big, lavish parties. Tons of food. I'd cook all day in preparation. People congregating outside, around the pool, sometimes even taking a dip. Heady times. But—"

"But . . . the world went through a global pandemic and—" Nate said, his voice edgy, defensive.

Unease crept over me again. I started to feel like a pawn in some unspoken argument. Like an only child bearing sole witness to bickering parents.

"Babe, chill, I'm just relishing having someone else in the house!" She leaned over, nicked his neck with her lips, nudged her breasts against his shoulder.

Again, he dissolved under the sunlamp of her attention.

"This *is* nice," he said. "Like I was just saying to Cassidy, I'm happy she's here."

"To Cassidy!" Marisol said loudly, raising her glass in a toast.

We all clicked glasses, sipped.

"And to you guys, for having me here!" I added.

I barely moistened my mouth with this latest sip: I'm a stickler for not drinking and driving. But they both nearly drained their glasses, and the more they drank, they more they drew closer to each other, their attraction electric, palpable. Nate's eyes kept dropping to Marisol's chest, and she scooted so close to him I thought she might take to his lap next.

I inhaled the mousse, anxious to leave them to each other.

"This was so nice, but I really should be going." I stood up, retrieving my plate and glass from the table.

"No!" The word ejected out of Marisol's mouth, landing harshly in the air. "I don't want you to leave yet, we're just getting started." There was an urging in her eyes that tugged at me, but I really was tired of feeling like they needed to get a room.

She read my face, picked up on it. "I mean, of course you *may* leave; it's just been so long since we've done this. But I'm getting carried away." A jangled laugh barked out of her, discordant, sad sounding.

"I'm sorry, I'm just beat," I offered. "But this was *so* wonderful! And dinner was divine." I swiped the empty wine bottle, too, on my way to the kitchen, wanting to help clear the table.

Marisol was on her feet in seconds. "Oh, Cassidy, you are not allowed to clean! You are our guest. Please, leave it all on the counter." She trailed me into the kitchen.

"You sure? I don't mind—"

"I won't allow it! Plus, Elana, our housekeeper, comes tomorrow and she can tidy up anything I miss."

As if to emphasize her point, she clasped my forearms with her slender fingers, holding on to me like she didn't want to let me go.

But the vibe I got at the dining table was that they were ready to jump each other's bones, tear each other apart. She was probably just being nice, acting like she still wanted my company, buzzed and bubbly from all the wine.

"Hey, Cassidy." Nate's voice made us both turn in his direction. "Will you do me a huge favor?"

"Sure!"

"There's a package that needs to go to my office. First thing in the morning. Could you swing it by on your way over tomorrow? That'd be so helpful. It's important, or I wouldn't ask. It's for a table read tomorrow. Big actors will be there. I'll be Zooming from here, of course."

He crossed the room, picked up a white 8x11 envelope thick enough to hold a script.

"Got it!"

He handed it to me, the corners of his eyes crinkling into a smile.

Marisol slunk over to him, draped an arm around his neck. "Remember, this man is cuckoo," she said, corkscrewing her index finger around her temple again, the same gesture she did yesterday, "and won't send his precious documents electronically. So thanks for doing this. And for staying for dinner." She slurred her words, placing a flat palm on his abdomen.

His eyes grazed the taut breastline of her dress again.

I got the "they are ready to fuck" vibes again and said good night.

As I walked down the hall toward the front door, I heard Nate and Marisol burst into giggles in the kitchen.

"No, *you* behave," I heard her say to him, followed by another round of laughter.

Then their footsteps light and springy on the stairs.

When I reached the front door, my bladder screamed. Damn, I thought, I should've actually peed when I went into the bathroom earlier. Setting the package down on the slender entryway table, I crept back to the bathroom.

From upstairs, more chatter, more laughter.

OUTSIDE, THE NIGHT air frosted around me, sharpening my senses, snapping me out of any lingering tipsiness. The wind was sweeping through, wringing the tops of the eucalyptus trees. Below, lights glittered along the shoreline of the beach.

I was nearly to the 10 when I realized I'd left the damn package at their house. Nate's voice came roaring back in my ear: *It's important, or I wouldn't ask.*

Fuck. I'd programmed their cells into my phone, but didn't want to tip them off to my error, give them any reason to think I wasn't competent.

I turned around, headed back.

As I eased onto their street, I saw the upstairs master bathed in honeyed light. Good, they were still most likely up there. I practically tiptoed down the sidewalk, fearing they would somehow hear me. From my vantage point beneath their window, I couldn't make out much. Their room is so massive—the oversized king bed hugging the far wall—that all I could spy were a few pieces of artwork and the ceiling with the black ceiling fan doing lazy laps, swatting at the air.

My hands were sweaty and the keys nearly slipped from them as I aimed for the lock. The front door moaned when I opened it; I was terrified the dogs would give me away, but they stayed silent, most likely upstairs themselves, nestled in their doggie beds in the nook off of Nate and Marisol's room.

I stepped inside, bracing myself against hearing the sounds of them in the throes of it. Nate peeling off her dress, hoisting her up on top of him on their bed, taking her in front of the naked window.

But instead of the panting sounds of lovemaking, I heard shouts.

An argument. Feet pounding the ceiling as they churned right above me.

Muffled tones, then Marisol's voice, sharp as a knife, loud and clattering all the way down the stairs.

"You are *sucking* me dry, Nate! I can't live like this anymore—"

Then Nate's voice, rising in volume but still impossible to make out except for a single word: *Andreas.*

Then the smacking sound of a slap.

"Controlling *asshole*," Marisol hissed, her voice still shrill. Followed by the staccato sound of steps, most likely hers, ricocheting out of the room.

My heartbeat jangled in my neck. Snatching the package, I shut the door so quickly I nearly closed my arm in it.

NOW THE CONTOURS of my apartment are starting to blur. I sip the last shot of wine in the bottom of my glass, jam the cork in the mouth of the bottle. That's enough for tonight.

Switching my bedside lamp off, I slip under the covers.

Marisol and Nate's argument comes thundering back in my brain.

You are sucking me dry, Nate.

Andreas.

Controlling asshole.

That *slap.*

Should be super awkward when I show up in the morning. Of course, they don't have any idea I overheard their blistering battle. For all they know, the three of us had a nice dinner together. Save for a little bickering, the two of them outwardly appeared to be the model couple.

And for all I know, they fight like that every night, then make up for it first thing in the morning with primal, urgent sex.

Other than Carter, I haven't been in a real relationship, so how do I know how longtime couples behave? Who am I to judge? And also, it's none of my business. *Just run their errands, Cassidy, and collect your nice pay. Keep your eyes on your own paper.*

I fumble around on my nightstand for my earplugs, twist them in to deafen the sound of the helicopters. Screw my eyes shut, willing myself to sleep.

11

AS I APPROACH the Sterlings', my stomach wrings itself into knots. I hope they've smoothed everything over; I hope I can act cool, pretend I didn't hear their argument.

As promised, I stopped by Nate's office on the way over this morning to deliver the package. I was greeted by a petite woman with silver braids who introduced herself as Marta. In her yoga-toned arms, she clutched a pile of scripts for me to take to Nate, her face crinkling into a smile as she handed them over.

Staggering up to their house now, I still feel the pinch of a hangover. When I press the doorbell, Oscar and Percy explode into barks, their paws roughing up the other side of the door. They'll get used to me soon enough, I'm sure, but the sound is jolting, setting my nerves even more on edge.

To my surprise, Nate opens the door, shushing the dogs. His hair is tousled, and he's wearing a crisp white tee with joggers. "Morning!" he says, his eyes outlining my body.

With my hoodie, tank, and cargo pants, I look even more casual than he does. His gaze lingers over me, making my pulse quicken. I can't tell if he's silently judging my attire or if there's more to his stare. Probably the former. Ugh—why is my brain wired this way?

The dogs cease their barking, greet me by licking my hands.

"Shoo, boys, go," he says, ordering them away.

Their toenails click along the tile as they trot into the living room.

"Latte?" Nate asks, lifting an eyebrow.

I follow him into the kitchen.

"I'd love one, thank you so much."

"I'm on my second," he says, packing the stainless-steel filter with fine black grounds. "A bit of a late night." He winks at me, palms the filter into place.

"It was great, thanks again for having me—"

"Anytime. Like Marisol was saying, it was nice having a little dinner party, some company."

"It really was," I respond, wondering if she's upstairs, still sleeping.

"Oh, I have these for you." I dip my hand in my messenger bag, retrieve the packages from Marta.

Nate narrows his eyes, takes them from me. He tears one open, slides out a script. Emits a long sigh.

"I've really gotta stop agreeing to do this—" he mumbles more to himself than to me.

But I seize the opening to pry a little. "If you don't mind me asking, what is it?"

"Hmm?" he asks, eyes scanning the script. Shame knifes my chest; I've overstepped and seem nervy. Why did I think I had the right to ask?

He glances up at me, though, smiles. "Oh, it's a script one of my old college roommates wrote. And I know this is going to sound like such a dick thing to say, but I already know it's not going to be any good. He's one of those self-absorbed people that think their life story would make an interesting movie, so I'm sure it's something along those lines." He sighs again. "But I've agreed to read, give him notes, so—"

"Got it. Yeah, I bet you get hit up all the time."

The espresso machine growls, sputtering out the last drops.

"Yeah, it's endless and I can't ever seem to say no." He scratches the back of his neck and when he does, the bottom of his shirt creeps up, revealing his taut abs.

My eyes rest there a beat; he notices me staring. Heat flushes my face as I drop my eyes in shame.

"Hey, you said you were a journalist. Would you by chance be interested in reading this?"

His misstep stings and my mouth goes dry. *Journalist?* I don't even know how to respond.

"I'm a novelist, actually—"

"Oh, that's right. So sorry!" Crimson splotches bloom on his neck. He genuinely seems to have a bit of remorse. "The wine and all. I drank too much of it. Marisol, she loves to drink. I do, too, but I don't like to get soused."

"Yeah, me neither."

His eyes crease into a smile. "So? What do you say?" He holds up the script, tilts his head.

"I'll take a stab at it. I'm sort of a film buff, but be warned, I've never actually read a script before."

"I'm sure you'll do fine. It's a little different from novels, but I would say it's easier?" His sentence twists up at the end, forming a question. "And if you would, just write me up a page. Like a synopsis mainly, then, your thoughts."

"Coverage. I got it."

"Exactly! You already know the term and everything."

Lexie used to do coverage in her earliest days in LA. That's actually how she got her start out here, fresh out of film school, working at the very bottom in Francis Ford Coppola's office, reading scripts. She grumbled about it at the time, but was apparently very good at turning them around quickly, banging out a page or two about the screenplay, giving what turned out to be her savvy take on whether it had potential. She had an excellent eye and was quickly promoted to development.

"Yeah, my friend who lives out here, the one who got me this job, actually, used to do it—"

Nate's attention has wandered, though. He's combing through the rest of the pile that Marta sent, so I stop speaking, letting my words sink awkwardly in the air.

The muscles in his forearms flex as he flips through the stack of pages, toned and tanned, his hazel eyes focused, framed by his black glasses. With his bedhead, he has a dreamy schoolboy look.

My mind slips back to last night's fight, to the slap that landed on his cheek. At least I'm pretty sure it was Marisol who did the slapping. No trace of it on his immaculate skin, not that a single slap would leave a mark.

"Sorry, what were you saying?" He glances up at me, wrenching me out of my reverie.

"Oh, nothing," I stammer. "I just, well, I'm honored that you'd ask me to read." My insides clench. *Honored?* Someone please put a muzzle on me.

"You kidding me? You're saving me! This day is going to be insane as it is. I've got the read-through in twenty." Nate downs the rest of his latte. "And no rush, end of week is fine."

I smile, take a nip of coffee.

He gathers up the pile of papers from Marta, looks at me as if to say, *Why are you still here?*

"I guess I'll just wait for Marisol—"

A guffaw from Nate. "You might be waiting some time, then. Marisol's not here."

Did she leave last night after their fight?

"She left early this morning. Said she had a ton to do. So—"

I nod, lift the corners of my mouth into a smile, while trying to keep the rest of my expression neutral, as if I know nothing, as if nothing is wrong between them. And it very well may not be; their argument could long be in the rearview, but that's not the sense I'm getting from Nate.

"So, should I start reading now, then?" I ask.

"Well, she didn't leave you a list of what to do today. Sorry about that. She kind of took off. I mean, you're welcome to stay here and read, but since there's not much to do today, feel free to go, read from home."

Nate shifts his weight from one foot to the next. I get the sense he wants some privacy.

"If you're sure, yeah, I'll take off—"

"Positive."

The French door that leads to the patio bursts open. A middle-aged woman with stark black hair pulled severely into a ponytail enters the kitchen carrying a broom, a scowl stamped on her face. She eyes me and as she does, her mouth presses into a grim line.

"Damn loquats. Mr. Sterling, they are *all* over the patio. Such a sight. And the birds just make a mess of them. But don't worry, I sweep them all away." She has a strong accent, all angles, that I'm trying to place. Maybe eastern European? And her voice carries the weight of a martyr.

"Thank you so much. Um, Elana, this is Cassidy, our new assistant. Cassidy, this is Elana, our housekeeper. She's been with me for the past—" He cocks his head, aims a gleaming smile at Elana. "How many years has it been?"

"A decade, this past spring." She looks at me, shakes her head as if to say she can't believe she's been putting up with Nate for so long and deserves a medal for it, but in a loving, maternal way.

"Elana here is solid gold," Nate says, clamping a hand on her shoulder.

Her face brightens. "As long as you stay on my good side; that's what I tell him," she says, smiling at me, hiking up an eyebrow.

"Ladies, I'm going to leave you to it. Meeting in ten."

As he exits, Elana shakes her head again. "He is a good man. Very good."

I grin, nod. Eager to leave. But Elana continues.

"So, you like working for them so far?" she asks as she heads to the sink to rinse Nate's empty coffee mug.

"Yes. I mean, I just started Monday, but so far, they both seem really nice—"

A sharp *hmph* squeaks out of her. "Well, good." She yanks open the dishwasher, plunks Nate's mug on the top rack, slides it back into place with a thwack. Slams it shut. This woman should be a percussionist.

Her dark eyes, lined heavily in forest-green eyeliner, probe my face. "*He* is really nice. She is"—she casts her eyes around the kitchen and lowers her voice—"nice, too. But she's kind of, like, full of herself."

I must look baffled at her disclosure because she shrugs and adds, "Just my opinion. And sometimes, I feel a little bad for him. Mm-hmm."

My stomach sours as she speaks. As intrigued as I am to hear more, especially after what I was privy to last night, it makes me squeamish to be gossiping about Marisol, whom I really like so far.

"So where are you from?" I ask, trying to steer the conversation into a different direction.

"I live in East LA, takes me long time to get here." The martyrdom has crept back in her voice.

"But I mean, originally, are you from LA?"

"No, no. I'm Albanian. My husband brought us over here many years ago, then he dropped dead. Poof!" She flings her palms into the air. "He was a car salesman, bought us our house. Good life. But bad heart. Heart attack. So I started cleaning houses then, at fifty-three. I don't mind it; keeps me busy."

"I'm so sorry about your husband—"

"Don't be." She's moved on to the fridge, taking out leftovers and dumping them in the trash. "He had a good life. We had a good life. Where are you from, dear?"

"Texas."

"Oh, Texas! Oooh, I've always wanted to go! I love the show *Dallas*! Big money, big horses, eh?" She clicks her tongue.

"Kind of? But—"

"I bet you have a nice boyfriend?" She pounds her chest. "Big, strong man?"

A laugh barks out of me. "No, sadly, not me. No boyfriend. Not now."

"Well, a pretty girl like you, you won't be single for long. It's *exciting* here. So many young people." She winks at me, twines her stringy ponytail around her finger.

I lift the latte to my lips, swallow the second half of it. Walk it to the sink and begin to rinse but Elana is on me, wresting it from my hand. "I've got it," she says, as if she's overprotective of the kitchen. And of Nate, too, I think to myself.

"Well, I need to get going, but so lovely to meet you!"

"You as well! I'm here every Wednesday, so, see you soon."

AS I STEP out the front door, the wind whips off the ocean, blasting me again. The surface of the water is choppy today, steel gray with log-sized whitecaps forming. I'm happy I get to go home, still a tad hungover from last night's winefest, but I'm disappointed I didn't get to see Marisol. Read her face.

12

FOUR WEEKS LATER

IT'S NIGHTTIME. I should be asleep, but I can't still my nerves.

I'm nursing a cup of chamomile tea, trying to steady myself, but my hands are working overtime, my fingernail incessantly flicking the edge of Detective Cruz's business card.

I should call her, tell her what I saw. Spill everything. But the thought of that makes my throat close up, makes me panic. I mean, someone's dead.

And I had a hand in it.

13

NOW

BACK HOME, I click on my gas burner, melt butter in the cast iron. This day calls for my hangover favorite, a grilled cheese.

As the butter foams, I dredge the bread through it, then flip on the TV and watch yesterday's episode of *The Bachelor.* Trash TV is my catnip, my guilty pleasure. A counterpoint to my more serious side—neurotic novelist and overthinker of everything.

Once I've eaten, I draw a bath, making the water as hot as I can stand it. I grab the script from Nate out of my bag, sink into the tub, and begin reading.

Nate's right: the script is terrible. The plot centers on a self-made millionaire who works his way up Wall Street by stabbing his colleagues in the back. Stilted dialogue, scenes we've all seen a thousand times before.

I read the whole thing in one sitting, desperate to finish. After toweling off and slipping into my pj's, I flip open my laptop and create a fresh Word document.

Drowsy from the bath and the late night, I decide to go outside, let the cold, fresh air wake me up.

As Nate instructed, I start crafting a synopsis.

It's slow going at first; I agonize over my word choices. But once I'm into it, I find that I actually enjoy the challenge of hitting upon all the important beats of the story. Even though the script isn't good, it's still a fun exercise.

And it's the first time I've actually typed anything new into my laptop in ages that wasn't just for my old day job. After my last novel died six months ago, right before the holidays, I swore off writing anything new. I was crushed, devastated, my confidence assaulted.

The string of rejections from literary agents filled my inbox, crowded my head.

Compelling voice, but I just didn't fall in love with it enough to get behind it.

There is so much to like here, but ultimately, I didn't connect.

It's not for me, but I'm sure you'll find the champion you deserve, and when you do, I'll be cheering you on from the sidelines.

But then I met Carter, and I didn't need to write anymore. The romance I was searching for in the pages of my novels was suddenly in my life. For the first time. Sure, I'd dated before, had one-night stands. But Carter was the closest to the real thing I'd ever had.

Now that he's gone, though, now that I've returned to the keyboard, I realize I've been craving this. It feels good, it feels right. My brain is engaged, sparking for the first time in forever.

I wrap up my synopsis, leave Nate my thoughts at the bottom of the page. Press save, then print it out, since he prefers not to send stuff electronically.

I don't wanna bug Lexie, but I'm dying to share this latest development.

Cassidy: Hey! Hope all's well with the night shoots! Guess what? Nate asked me to do coverage! I mean, just for one script and it was awful but still! 😊

I have no idea if she's in the middle of filming or if she'll even respond, but just texting her makes me feel good, less alone.

A few seconds later, the three bubbles form at the bottom of my screen.

Lexie: Already?

My face burns. Why *wouldn't* he have already asked me?

But then three bubbles bounce into the frame again.

Lexie: Wow! Cassidy that's AMAZING!

God, I'm such a head case, always certain that people think so little of me, even my own best friend.

Cassidy: Ahh, thank you! Am excited!

The cell is warm in my hand. I feel uncertain about typing out the next text, but while I have Lexie's attention, I can't help myself.

Cassidy: And curious, have you heard anything about their marriage? Like if it's rocky or not?

There's a pause. Heat creeps up my neck. Lexie's going to think I'm being too nosy.

Lexie: Why do you ask?

I don't want to get into the whole story and tell her that I snuck back in their house, so I keep it brief, innocent.

Cassidy: I mean, no huge reason, just overheard them arguing the other night, so I dunno, was curious if they have like a reputation or something . . .

Lexie: Not that I've heard, but . . . most celebrities are kind of head cases, ya know?

I quickly reply: Absolutely!

Lexie: And put two of them together, and well . . . it's crazytown . . . but I do love me some juicy gossip lol! 👂 xxx

14

I'M KNOCKING ON the Sterlings' front door, but no one is answering. I rap louder, the sound of my knuckles against the wood ricocheting through the air like a woodpecker striking bark.

"Oh, Cassidy!" Marisol's voice comes threading through the hedges where the pool is. "I left the front unlocked. Come through the house and meet me out here!"

"Okay!" I holler back to her, though her form is shrouded by the bushes.

Making my way to the kitchen, I feel a ping of disappointment that Nate hasn't materialized downstairs yet. I'm eager to give him the coverage, even if I'm nervous about what he'll think. Digging in my bag, I leave it for him on the kitchen counter.

Through the French doors, I can see Marisol churning around the pool, cell phone clamped to her ear, graceful body wrapped in a red silk robe.

When I open the door, her back is to me, her form moving toward the deep end. She must've heard it clicking open because she turns, mutters something into the phone, ends the call.

"Morning!" she says, striding over to me. "Have a seat."

I drop into one of the two chairs that rest beneath the yellow and white umbrella, assuming Marisol will do the same. But she remains standing, walking in flip-flops in an agitated figure eight. As she prowls, she chews on a fingernail, her face crimped in a scowl. I can't tell if her expression is because of the morning sunlight, which glowers over us, bouncing off the surface of the water, or if she's anxious.

"Sorry, bad habit of mine." She flashes a brief smile that vanishes as soon as it appears. So, anxious it is.

Walking over to a wall of weathered stones, she slides her hand in a crack, tugs out a pack of cigarettes. Shakes one out of the battered package. "You don't mind, do you?"

"No, of course not."

She lights up, sucks in a sharp drag.

"Another nasty habit of mine." She winks at me, spews out a thin stream of smoke. "Nate hates me smoking, doesn't know I still do it."

My eyes flick to the balcony upstairs that leads to Nate's office.

Following my gaze, she says, "Don't worry. He's glued to a Zoom; his back is to us, so he can't see me. And fuck it if he does." She works the cigarette between her fingers. "Gah, sorry. It's just been a bit stressful around here these past few days." Her eyes are smudged with dark eyeliner; looks like she slept in her makeup.

I keep the muscles in my face stone-still, trying my best not to betray the fact that I heard their nasty fight. "I'm so sorry," I say, smiling warmly, nodding at her, hoping she'll open up to me, go into more detail.

"It's fine, really, I just have *a lot* going on." As she speaks to me, I notice that she avoids direct eye contact.

"Like today, for instance, I'm leaving soon and will be gone all day. I'm having lunch with Andreas, then meeting with a stunt trainer.

I know I don't have the part yet, but I want to be ready, show the producer that I'm the one. Figure out if I need to do a special workout, or extra strength training, that sort of thing."

As with the other day, it's as if she's talking to me but also talking out loud to herself. As if I'm just an extension of her psyche.

But like the other night when she begged me to stay for dinner, I also get the strong sense that she wants company, *needs* company. Perhaps my sympathetic presence acts as a balm for her.

She sucks in another stinging drag, blows the smoke out of the side of her mouth, so that it flows in the opposite direction of me.

Though I know a bit about her background, I decide to ask her about it, show interest. "When did you start? Acting, I mean?"

Her eyes are on me now, bright and warm. "Looking back, I think I was always acting. I was in ballet forever growing up, so I was used to being onstage. Loved it. Didn't love how it made my poor feet feel." She glances down at them, studies her feet as if she's still under the strain of practicing ballet, even though they are smooth, supple, toenails glossy, painted pastel pink without a chip on them.

"That's so cool!" I say. With Angie Foster at the helm, I never had the chance to do any extracurriculars. And after she took off, my poor dad was even more disinclined to take on anything other than seeing me to the school bus stop. When I got the call, freshman year of college, that he had dropped dead of a heart attack at the age of fifty, I wasn't even in shock; Angie had broken his heart years before.

"I was good," Marisol continues. "When I turned sixteen, a modeling scout from London approached my mother." Marisol walks back over to the stone wall, grinds the cigarette out on a bleached rock.

"Being a professor of literature, she didn't want me to sign. She wanted me to go to university first. I was a bit of a nerd and loved my studies, but I saw it as a ticket out of Barca. Not that it wasn't a great place to grow up, but I wanted to be somewhere more international, already wanted a more worldly life."

I shift in my seat, position myself under the umbrella, so that the glaring sun is blotted out.

Marisol continues her figure eight pattern, pacing in the space between me and the pool.

"So I begged my parents. They still refused. But I acted like such a brat and broke their will until we finally came to an agreement. I studied extra hard and tested out, finishing up high school a year early, at seventeen. *Then* I moved to London. And it was a whirlwind." A smile cracks across her face.

"I bet!"

"Like, I was a model for Gucci by eighteen, then Christian Dior, and on and on. Making more money than either of my parents ever had. Hanging out on yachts in the South of France, endless parties, five-star hotels, all of it. But I realized in my midtwenties that I was longing for something more. I *missed* my studies, missed reading, missed being challenged in that way." The wind blasts us; Marisol wraps her robe around her tighter, despite the blazing sun.

"That sounds like an incredible experience, though—"

"Yes, but, for me, it was ultimately empty. I mean, most people think models are stupid, but they're not. That's not what I'm saying. Try catwalking, for instance, while holding your neck and shoulders back like so." She demonstrates, and as she does, her robe slits open, revealing lilac lace panties and a matching push-up bra. "It's quite difficult and requires a lot of practice and focus, *and* you have to starve yourself. I hated that part of it. Watching every last thing I ate, it wasn't for me. It's one of the reasons I fell for Nate."

She raises her face, stares up at his balcony as if he's going to appear on it.

"He loves that about me. That yes, I have to work out and pay attention to my weight—it's my career—but I eat what I want. I guess the women he'd been with before weren't like that." She shakes her head; a small grin plays across her lips.

I don't want to pry, exactly, but I take this as an opportunity to find out more about their relationship. "How *did* y'all meet?"

I know from the internet they met at the Cannes Film Festival, but not much else.

"Ahh, it's a *story*." Again, her eyes brighten, a small laugh escapes. "So, we met at Cannes. I was twenty-eight, had been acting for already four years. I *loved* it, loved studying character, reading scripts, the research. And well, Nate, he is so brainy about all that stuff. I was just dazzled. Obviously, he's hot, too. That didn't hurt." Another laugh bubbles out of her.

I don't dare agree with her, even if I *do* indeed agree with her.

She sinks down into the seat next to me, and like before, her gaze is averted. I think of what Elana said about Marisol being full of herself. But Elana seems petty. Marisol just seems self-possessed to me, not necessarily full of herself. I mean, maybe a little self-absorbed, sure, but not narcissistic.

"But yeah, his film won the Palme d'Or that year and the buzz around him was *crazy*." She kicks her feet up on the table, crossing them at the ankles.

"And Nate, being Nate, all he wanted to do was hide. I thought it was so adorable. And more than that, I loved that he didn't care about the limelight. The celebrity, the ass-kissing of it all. So the night we met at a party, we hid in a corner and talked for hours before going back to his hotel."

The sun arrows down on her face; she swivels the umbrella, so that it covers us both. "Might be a good day to go for a dip?"

"Seriously."

"You really should bring your suit. Like, keep it in your bag or something. But Nate, ahh, I really did fall in love with his mind." She cocks her head, turning the conversation back to him. "*So* smart, and a book nerd like me. We fell in love literally overnight. Only problem was, he was still seeing someone."

Her eyes turn to me now, probing for my reaction.

I smile, nodding as if to say, *I get it, I would have totally bagged him, too.*

"Well, it wasn't anything serious, like more of a fling. But evidently *she* thought it was and didn't want it to end. And evidently, it got nasty. From the little he told me, I think she was obsessed, a bit of a nutjob. I think that's the reason he's so overprotective of us. And why he keeps everything a secret. Ever try looking at his social?"

I have. But I shake my head. "No."

From my few searches, I haven't found Nate on social media. I think back to my first day here, when he was showing us around and Marisol chided him for his hypersecurity. And at the time I thought it had to do with a former personal assistant, but sounds like it was a crazy ex.

"Well, he doesn't have *any*. Barely lets me have any. Like, I can't take any outside shots of the house, anything that shows location. And I get it. There are crazies out here. I've had a stalker or two myself. He would barely talk to me about his ex, he was so upset. And because of her, and that experience, he made me keep *us* a secret for the first six months."

"That must've been hard."

Like Marisol, I train my gaze on the pool, hoping that by not staring at her openly, she'll continue to spill it. The morning sun marbles the surface of the water and I'm getting so steamy in my hoodie and pants; a dip actually does sound nice.

"It was. I mean, I went behind his back and told my family. Good thing his Spanish wasn't so good then. He could never understand what I was saying on the phone." She lets her robe drift open and the sun glazes her torso with a beam of honeyed light.

"But keeping it from my friends in the industry was super tough. And having to sneak around with him. It was easier when he came to London to visit me, so much easier to be incognito there, but here, forget it. We basically holed up in this house, which, I'll admit, wasn't too shabby." She turns to me, winks at me again. "Why am I going into all of this?"

I feel even warmer in my clothes. *Because I'm prying and you haven't noticed?*

"Sorry if I'm boring you—"

"Oh my goodness, not at all. I asked."

She swats a hand in front of her face. "And I'm probably talking about the honeymoon days, so I can remember why I love him, and why I don't *actually* want to strangle him."

She snorts and I start laughing, too.

"Men, huh?"

"A hundred percent," I reply, even though I'd kill for a real relationship with one.

I wait for her to ask me more about Carter, since we never finished our chat about him the other day, but she dives back into talking about Nate. I wonder if she even remembers our little talk.

"So, that's one of the reasons I'm desperate to get this film. I'd get to be away from here for a hot minute. Have some space. We'd be filming in Brazil for like six months."

"Wouldn't Nate go with you?" My mouth goes dry as soon as the question exits my mouth; it's so none of my business.

"Ahh, maybe? For some of it? But he has his own thing going here, like he's very busy all the time, so I don't think he'd do more than visit. Which, don't get me wrong, I don't want to sound like such a horrible wife; I would miss him. It's just these past few years have been *suffocating.*"

I can't blame her. During the worst of the pandemic, I was all alone, which was its own kind of hell. But I think it would've been even worse to be bottled up with someone else, especially if you're more of a free spirit than your partner, which I'm quickly discovering is the case with Marisol.

"And he'll probably go into production soon on one of his films. Now that we're more back to normal, pandemic-wise. He has a couple of projects in the works, so one is bound to move forward."

"And you wouldn't want to be in one of his films?" I inwardly flinch at my question, which might sound like I'm inferring she can only get a role because of nepotism.

"No, no, no, no." The noes roll off her tongue rapid-fire. "I mean, sure, he's an incredible filmmaker, but we've always had an agreement: I won't star in any of his films because we would never want working together to come between us." She tilts her head at me as if to ask if I understand.

"I get that. Makes total sense."

Her hand travels to her mouth; she begins gnawing on a fingernail again.

She grows silent. It's as if a curtain has dropped between us. I glance over and see that her face is pensive, etched in worry again. Great. I had to go and open my mouth, ask her that invasive question, which has clearly thrust her into this anxious mood again.

Another gust shreds through the yard, causing the umbrella to flutter and its pole to squeak against the holder. Marisol continues staring at the pool, knees now wrapped against her chest.

I think back to their fight, to Nate saying the name *Andreas* before he got slapped. I wonder if this is the reason Marisol is tense today, because she's having lunch with him, and maybe Nate doesn't like it.

I wonder if that's who she was on the phone with. *It's none of your business, Cassidy*, I tell myself, but it's hard not to spin when she's all edgy like this.

"So, I don't have any real errands today," Marisol says, breaking my nosy train of thought. "And Nate's gonna be in meetings all day in his office. But I do have a project for you! I warned you!" She flashes me a quick smile.

"You did so well with my junk drawer, I'd really like you to tackle my closet, like I said. Now, be prepared, it's a war zone in there. Like, really. So it will probably take months. But maybe you can start on it today?"

This warms my organizing heart. "Yes, absolutely, I'd love to!"

"Great!" She clasps her hands together. "I need to shower and get ready to go, but come with me. I'll show you everything."

15

MARISOL'S CLOSET IS the size of my whole apartment. It even has a TV, its own A/C vent, and mini ceiling fan.

Even though it's beyond spacious, a wave of claustrophobia courses over me. Marisol is right: it's a war zone. The walls are sectioned into little cubbies that hold racks. Racks, in my mind, meant for organization by grouping: blouses, pants, tees.

But instead of things being in order, everything is muddled together. A bright red taffeta tutu hangs face forward, its hanger dangling precariously from the neck of a white T-shirt, as if Marisol intended this for an outfit, then got distracted.

Evening gowns that belong in their own segment are smashed in with designer jeans. Poofy satin shoulders are crushed and begging for their own rightful section. On the far wall is a white tallboy dresser, its drawers splayed out like decrepit stairs. A jumble of jewelry and perfume bottles vie for space on the surface of the dresser, pearl necklaces and baubles spilling from the top.

It honestly looks like a little girl was given free rein of her mom's closet and she went to town, raiding it, playing dress-up with half a dozen of her naughtiest friends.

"I told you it was a disaster!" Marisol practically shrieks as she reads the barely masked horror on my face. "Cassidy, help! I don't even know where to begin, so I just leave it like this."

An oval-shaped, full-length mirror on an iron stand catches Marisol's profile, her flowing hair, her silk robe, now cinched at the waist. And me standing next to her, a good three inches shorter, my hair limp and lifeless.

I survey the damage and already can tell that even though Marisol insisted this would take months, with a few trips to the Container Store and some alone time in here, I can have this closet whipped into shape in a week's time.

"It's not as bad as you think," I offer, sprinkling cheer into my voice. "Seriously. Let me at it!"

My eyes continue to rove. I'm shocked at how many items still have designer tags dangling from them. How many nice blouses and skirts and even dresses are tossed on the floor, brand-new. With an entire room to hang stuff, there's not an inch of space left on the rods.

"There is a lot of overflow, so—" I venture.

"I know, I know," she says, her voice taking on that squeakiness again. "It's one of the problems with being a model, and an actress. Designers are constantly sending me clothes and I have no idea what to do with them all! I was raised to never throw anything away, because it could be used as a hand-me-down for one of my sisters, but look at me now. I'm drowning!"

She leans down, starts picking through a pile of discarded clothes.

"Also, half of these aren't even the right size. I'm a two, sometimes a four. These here on the floor are sixes." She lifts up a white shirtdress, assesses it. "Like this. I've worn it a few times and I love it, but it really is too big."

She holds it to her svelte frame, studies herself in the mirror. Twists around to face me. "Hey, you're probably a size bigger than me, right?"

I don't flinch. "At least." I'm a six, sometimes an eight.

"Oh, this is *perfect*, then!" She anchors the dress to my chest, evaluating it. "Cassidy, I think this would look so great on you! And I was going to ask you to donate everything that's not my size, but you know what, why don't *you* have first dibs on whatever you think you might like?"

Butterflies tango in my chest. I've just been offered nearly half of this woman's glittering, glamorous, drop-dead-expensive wardrobe.

"Are you serious?" I ask, willing tears to not spring to my eyes.

"Of course, why not?" Marisol looks at me like I'm crazy.

But when you're used to raking through the racks at T.J.Maxx or Ross Dress for Less, an offer like this feels absolutely unreal.

"And shoes!" she says, kicking over a pair of knee-high leather boots encrusted with sequins. "What size?"

"Seven, seven and a half?"

"Okay, damn, I'm a six, but if you see any with the tags still on, like flip-flops, house shoes, Uggs, things where the size doesn't matter as much, you're welcome to those as well. If there's still a tag, I'm not interested . . . if they don't work for you, put 'em in the donate pile."

I have to force myself to close my big mouth, which is dangling open.

"Don't look so spooked." Marisol laughs, gently elbowing me. "You deserve it!" She leans in, pecks both my cheeks.

"Hey, what time is it?"

I dig my cell out of my pocket. "Ten thirty-five."

"Shit, shit, shit, I'm running late. Okay, dashing to shower, then heading out. See you later?" Her last sentence comes out as a question. I'm interpreting it to mean, *Please stay until I get back home.*

"Yeah! I'll just get started in here."

Marisol grabs a tee and a pair of jeans and swipes some diamond earrings off the dresser before she's gone in a flash.

16

IT'S FIVE P.M. and Marisol is still not home. But since she mentioned she'd see me later, I continue sifting through her stuff.

Early evening sunlight filters through the windows in their master, streaking the bed with slashes of light. From my position in the closet, I've eyed that bed with envy a few times today. The light and airy down comforter is as fluffy as soft serve. Their heavy wooden headboard ornately hand carved. The darting thoughts of what they must do to each other in there.

I'm nearly finished with Marisol's obscenely large pile of T-shirts. I decided to go all Marie Kondo with them, ditching the hangers and folding them into thirds, standing them upright, so that they nest neatly in the cubbies, resting orderly like a dozen eggs in a paper carton.

I've had a grin on my face all day doing this work. I'm pinching myself. This is by far the easiest money I've ever earned.

Not only have I tackled the tees today, I also started in on the clothes that still have tags, sorting them into three piles: keepers for Marisol, donations, and a mind-boggling-sized pile for me.

My bounty thus far includes the white T-shirt dress that Marisol gave me; three pair of Uggs (I've never owned a pair of real Uggs, just the knockoffs); a dozen dresses, mostly cocktail and sundresses; an entire rack of blouses; and a fat stack of skirts.

While I sifted through everything today, I occasionally snapped pics to share later with Lexie. She's going to be *so* jealous; she loves clothes far more than I do. She's always been the girlier one.

Even with the dent I've made today, my original assessment was correct: it's going to take me a full week of doing nothing other than this to get it fully under control.

I've been in here nearly all day, going downstairs only twice. Once to grab a bottle of sparkling water from the fridge, another time to eat my lunch, a sad little turkey-and-cheese sandwich I slapped together in haste this morning.

The first time I went down to the kitchen, I noticed my coverage was gone. Santa had taken the milk and cookies. Since then, I've had my ears pricked, listening for Nate, hoping he'll pop in and tell me what he thinks of my work.

So far, I've only heard him stirring in the hallway, probably going back and forth to his office, and haven't wanted to push myself on him. I'll find out soon enough.

From downstairs just now, I hear another sound. Voices. Raised voices to be exact.

I tiptoe out of the carpeted, nearly soundproofed closet for a better listen. The floors of their master are hardwood; as I creep toward the door, the boards pop and screech beneath my feet. Damn.

But by all accounts, they haven't detected me. The bickering continues.

I poke my head out of the door, ears straining.

Their voices fly up the wooden staircase; they must be in the kitchen.

"You're late. Again." Nate's voice is wounded, harsh.

"It's only five o'clock! And hello, traffic? This is LA, bro." Marisol's words are slippery, like she's had a little to drink. "Not that you would know because you never leave this house!"

I'm overcome with the peculiar feeling that maybe neither one of them realizes I'm still here. Maybe Marisol forgot that she told me she'd see me later. Maybe she didn't mean it literally, has forgotten all about me. Also, I always park my car far enough away from the house that I'm not even sure she'd clock it.

Yikes. I try to think of what to do, how to handle this. I feel like Goldilocks hiding in the baby bear's bed.

"And *you*, you can't get away from here often enough. It's like I don't even know who you are anymore." Nate's voice hisses like a steam press.

Silence.

I suck in a breath, wait for the sound of another slap.

Instead: "Go fuck yourself, Nate."

Followed by the sound of Marisol's shoes piercing the tiles downstairs.

Afraid she's going to mount the stairs and catch me, I cough, announce my presence.

More silence.

Then Nate, his voice now dimmed. "She's still here?"

The way he says it, I feel like an intruder, not their helper who's toiled away all day in Marisol's closet.

"Well, obviously. She's been helping me in my closet. I told you that earlier—"

"Shhh, okay, just keep it down."

I squirm back away from the door, retreating backwards to the closet, the sound of the squeaking floorboards betraying me.

The striking sound of Marisol's feet on the stairs jolts me firmly back inside the closet, where I turn my back to the door, feign organizing the jeweled mess on top of her dresser.

I even begin humming to myself in the hopes that she will think it was impossible for me to hear them, as silly as it feels.

"Cassidy, hey!" Marisol's frame fills the door.

She looks exquisite in her tight tee and jeans that cup her in all the right spots.

"Aaaaah!" she cries, clasping her hands together. "You are Wonder Woman!"

"Nah, it's nothing really."

Her face is made up, lips glossed with a deep scarlet, but her mascara has run down her cheek, leaving charcoal tracks. She clearly teared up while fighting with Nate.

"I can't believe I can see white!" She dashes over to the sectionals with empty rod space, shakes her head.

Standing close to her, I can smell the tang of alcohol, mixed with her usual candied citrusy scent. She turns to me, pulls me into a firm hug. Her hands stay clasped around my back, and then, to my surprise, a cry chokes out of her. She clings to me, her body wracking with sobs.

I don't know how to react, so I hug her back, smooth the back of her hair down.

She pulls away. Tears stream down her face, washing the rest of her mascara away. "I'm sorry." She sniffs. "It's just, I haven't had a friend—like, a real girlfriend—in such a long time that I feel kind of overwhelmed. Like this is something that my best friend from back home would help me with, ya know?"

I don't know whether or not to believe her. Is she truly crying about missing female companionship or just upset about the spat with Nate? Or a third possibility: she's embarrassed that I might have overheard them arguing.

She presses the neck of her tee to her face, blots it. "Sorry, I'm being silly. I'm just feeling a bit sentimental."

"I totally get it. You're probably homesick. And also, this is why I'm here! To help in any way," I offer. "Do you like it so far?" I ask, gesturing to the T-shirts.

"What in the world is all this even?" She plucks a perfectly folded shirt, hugs it to her chest like a toddler would a teddy bear. "You are a godsend, Cassidy! And you'll have to teach me this folding trick because I could never, ever."

I shake my head to deflect the praise. "I'm just kind of a freak about this stuff. So glad that some of my obsessive tidiness can be put to good use."

She wheels around, taking it all in.

"I'm just getting started. And I should be the one thanking *you*." I point to the heap of goodies on the floor that I'm claiming.

"Fabulous! I hope you love them!"

From outside the closet door, Nate clears his throat.

His feline frame is diffused in afternoon sunlight, making him look angelic, the tips of his hair painted gold.

"Well, well, well, what do we have here, ladies?" He cocks his head, beams at the pair of us.

"Cassidy here is just solving the world's problems, one closet at a time!" Marisol clasps her hands together again. "I banished Nate from this closet when I first moved in. His clothes hang in one of the guest room's closets."

"It's true, she did. But, you've seen my wardrobe." He plucks at his white tee. "This is astonishing, Cassidy!"

He is pouring on the charm; they both are, and it makes me feel slightly disoriented, like I'm complicit in sweeping their arguments under the rug. Not that it's any of my business, and it's not like they know I heard the first, nastier fight a few nights ago. But it's like they're forcing their cheer on me, so I will return it, let them know all is well. The whole situation couldn't be more awkward and I'm ready to move past it.

"Y'all are much too kind to me. Seriously, it's literally my job!" My cheeks ache from the large, fake smile that's stretched across my face.

I've always been able to read people and anticipate what they want, even before they're aware of it themselves.

If you call yourself an empath one more time, Lexie used to jab me, *I'm going to vomit.*

But it's true, I am. I'm keenly attuned to others' emotions, most likely due to how I grew up, tiptoeing around Angie Foster, scanning her moods, decoding her mental state, trying to become a buffer between her and Dad.

"Another thing that you're evidently astonishing at," Nate continues, forearm now resting against the doorjamb, "is coverage."

Oh my god, he read it! Glee spears my midsection.

"Really?" I can't help it; my voice twists an octave higher.

"I was just downstairs having a peek before Marisol came home." He glances at her, then shifts his gaze back to me. "And it's incredible. Seriously. Like, better than what the people on my staff produce. Marisol here is going to have to learn how to share you."

I feel as though someone has opened my chest, poured warm oil inside of it.

He steps into the closet with us, pulls Marisol into a side hug. She rests her head on his shoulder. All is seemingly forgiven.

"If you'd like, I have another stack of scripts coming to the house tomorrow and—"

"Are you kidding, I'd love to!"

"And no rush. End of next week is fine. And I'll pay you, of course, extra on top of your rate."

They turn to leave the closet and I stoop down, grab my pile of treasures. Now I'm grinning a real smile. Nate loved my work and he's going to pay me extra and I'm hauling all these clothes home!

IN THE KITCHEN, Oscar and Percy doze in the strip of sunlight, snoring, noses buried in their paws.

Marisol is half-hidden in the fridge, emerging with a chilled bottle of white. She shakes it at me. "Glass?"

"Ah, no, thanks! I'm actually meeting a friend for dinner," I lie. I have no friends here. Part of me would love to stay, but I've been here all day; I'm fried and really want to go home and watch trash TV.

"No worries. Nate's taking me out to eat tonight, if you can believe it." She winks at him; he rolls his eyes but in a loving way. "So I wanted to have a little nip before we go!" She shifts her hair from one side to the other.

After she fills her glass, she turns from us to take a sip, leaning her hip against the kitchen counter. In the sinking sunlight, her profile looks wistful, deflated.

I feel like I should circle the island, hug her goodbye, but I don't want to make too much of a show of things in front of Nate, don't want to out her earlier vulnerability.

"Seriously, thank *you*," I say breezily, wagging the overfilled bag of clothes at her. "Have a great dinner."

17

THE PAST FIVE days have been unbelievably great. Blissful, actually. I'm pinching myself.

It's Tuesday, early evening, and Marisol is upstairs showering.

Nate is in his office.

I convinced her to let me prep dinner tonight. She always cooks on Tuesdays, so I did the grocery run earlier, buying fresh shrimp, the makings for a homemade Caesar salad, red potatoes, a lemon curd with raspberries for dessert. And wine, of course.

As I dice the potatoes, I sip a glass—a pink sparkling rosé, which tastes like carbonated bubble gum on my tongue.

I'm not sure if Marisol'll ask me to stay for dinner, but tonight I'd actually be happy to: we three have been operating like a well-oiled machine for days now.

On Friday, the day after Nate told me he was pleased with my coverage and asked me to do more, I arrived to the house promptly at nine thirty. Marisol greeted me at the front door, wearing white cotton pj's, the bottoms of which were skimpy shorts; her hair was standing up: bedhead.

"Coffee? I'm just about to make some." She yawned into her fist.

In the kitchen, I watched as she prepared our espresso shots, topping mine with foamed oat milk, her eyes glassy and dreamy. She seemed lighter, less anxious. As if the previous day's argument had completely evaporated.

"Shall we go outside? I love listening to the birds in the morning."

"Sounds lovely."

Sunlight rippled off the pool and an easy breeze swept through the tops of the eucalyptus trees, just enough to release their piney scent.

"Hope dinner was great!" I said.

"Yes, *so* damn nice to get out. If you can believe it, this was our first meal out together since lockdown. I've been out in public a ton, of course, but Nate is still nervous, was nervous last night at first, even though we sat outdoors." Marisol shook her head, combed her fingers through her tousled hair.

"I get that."

"But once I got some wine in him . . ." She clicked her tongue; color rose to her cheeks.

Marisol peered around the yard as if to ensure that no one was listening to us, then dropped her voice a notch. "We actually had amazing sex last night," she said, twisting a lock of hair around her finger.

Now the heat rose to my cheeks; my tongue grew thick in my mouth. I had no idea how to respond. Just the day before, I was grinning like a loon in their closet with them after being an awkward bystander to their argument.

It was a little disorienting, the hot and the cold.

"Niiiice!" I said too loudly, going for cheery best friend but coming off all thumbs.

"Mm-mm," she murmured to herself, seemingly savoring the memory, her legs stretched out, coppery and long.

I kept quiet, waited for her to speak, to add to what she had just said. Even though it was a little destabilizing to hear, I'd be lying if I said I didn't want to hear more.

Overhead, the birds chirped as Marisol had promised; I tried to focus my gaze on a silvery piece of eucalyptus bark that was spinning lazily in the pool.

Marisol stayed quiet. When I glanced her way, a smile, lazy and satisfied, played on her lips.

So is he good in bed? What made the sex so amazing?

These questions tossed in my head, but I took a sip of my latte, the caffeine already making my synapses fire on double time.

Marisol lifted her own espresso cup to her lips, took the rest down in one long gulp. "I'm gonna be around all day. I've got some calls and stuff, people I need to catch up with. Emails, whatnot. So I thought you could work on the closet some more until the scripts arrive?"

"Absolutely!"

I spent the first few hours of the morning on the jeans, Marisol letting me know that I could keep any pair that were larger than a twenty-nine. I wound up with fourteen pair. Fourteen pair of designer jeans!

Over the weekend, I holed up in my apartment, only leaving for short bursts of walks, determined to get through the pile of five scripts that Marta had delivered to the house.

Nate wasn't expecting them until the end of the week, but since he's offered to pay me extra for them, I wanted to turn them around as quickly as possible, keep his excitement about me building.

I ordered in pizza, uncharacteristically ignoring my pile of laundry, which I'm typically so fastidious about doing.

Sunday evening as I was sipping on a glass of prosecco and double-checking my work for Nate, Lexie texted me, and I was finally able to gush about the latest turn of events.

Lexie: I'm on night shoots still and seeing double but how's everything? Any more trouble in paradise? Tea to spill? Sip, sip. 😉

Cassidy: Ha! Just one more spat so far, and then evidently . . . wonderful make-up sex? You're so right, they are kind of insane out here.

Lexie: Lol . . .

Cassidy: Oh, and Marisol let it slip that Nate had a crazy ex before they got together. You're officially caught up on all the gossip now.

Lexie: Really?

Cassidy: Well, her exact term was nutjob. Which is probably how Nate described her.

Lexie: Ick.

Cassidy: What do you mean?

Lexie: Makes me wary when a man refers to a female ex as crazy. It's always the woman, isn't it?

Cassidy: Yeah, totally.

Lexie: But . . . she prolly fucking was bc this town is full of loons lol.

Cassidy: Oh hey! Before I forget the most important thing . . . Look at my loot!

I sent her the trickle of pics I'd snapped of all the clothes and shoes I'd nabbed from Marisol. Followed by a pic of the five scripts splayed out like playing cards.

Lexie: Holy shit, she gave you all that? You know I get first dibs on whatever doesn't work for you the second I get back! Can't believe you get to raid Marisol Torres' freaking wardrobe.

A smile spread across my face, followed by a tug in my stomach. I missed Lexie, wanted her here with me to enjoy all this.

Lexie: And that's HUGE about the scripts. Gotta run but please keep me posted, please!

Cassidy: Will do and whennnn are you coming home? I miss you so much. Also I have no social life other than the Sterlings lol.

Lexie: Three months! It'll fly. And you can always go have drinks with Harry, he would love that!

Cassidy: OK! Will do! Love you!

Lexie: Love you more . . . xxx

It's not that I don't want to meet up with Harry, it's just that we're not close. Yes, he's my best friend's boyfriend, but I've only been around him a few times during my sporadic visits out here. I should text him, though, see if we can hook up. Maybe he has a hot friend.

YESTERDAY—MONDAY—I was tackling Marisol's dresser, sorting her sock and lingerie drawers, when Nate poked his head in the closet. His hair was damp from a shower and he smelled like honey.

Like last time, I had left my coverage for him downstairs on the kitchen counter.

"Hey, can we talk particulars?" He cocked his head to one side, smiled at me.

My face flamed. "Sure!"

"Well, I just glanced through your latest, and Cassidy," he started, his smile a sunbeam melting my core, "I don't know how to tell you this, but you're a natural. You have such a gift. I want you to take over reading most of my scripts. How does three hundred dollars a script sound?"

"Oh my gosh," I stammered, face flaming even brighter, "yes, sure, I'm in!"

"Deal!"

"Is it okay with Marisol?" I asked, gesturing around to her still cluttered closet.

"She's the priority, first and foremost. But yes, it's perfectly fine with her. And how often I'll need you will vary by how many scripts come in. So, it won't be the same every week, but probably an average of five to six a week. If you think you can handle it."

I didn't care if I had to spend all my weekends on his scripts. At $300 a pop, I'd be looking at picking up an extra $1,500 to $1,800 a week. I mean, it *would* cut into a lot of my free time and my potential writing time, but it could also mean really getting my foot in the door out here. Possibly into screenwriting. Let's face it, after three busted novels in and no bites, I *should* be trying to break into film and TV as Lexie has always insisted.

"I would *love* to. Seriously. Thank you."

He grinned at me even wider, kept his head tilted as if he were studying me, or possibly, marveling at me. "Great. I'm so thrilled." He finally turned and left.

IT'S NOW FIVE thirty. Dinner is all prepped and I'm still nursing the same glass of sparkling rosé. I've just finished rinsing the raspberries, have them laid out on a kitchen towel to dry.

Marisol's sandals click against the stairs.

She sweeps into the room, looking resplendent in another bustier summer dress, this one cherry red, her cleavage and immaculate shoulders oiled with serum. From her earlobes, gold hoops dangle, catching flickers of the oozing, setting sun.

"Ahh, thanks again for doing all this!"

She strides to the fridge, pulls out the bottle of rosé, fills a glass.

"Refill?" She tilts the bottle toward me.

I hesitate; I don't want to get soused, but one more glass won't kill me. "Sure!"

She gives me a heavy pour and we toast, the crystal glasses chinking together, making a bright bell sound.

The rosé fizzing on the back of my throat, I'm just about to comment on how delicious it is when we are both jarred by the sound of Marisol's cell ringing.

She sighs. "Now? I wonder who this could be?" Annoyance flashes across her face as she crosses the room to retrieve her phone from the charger.

She studies the caller ID, a small grin creeping across her lips. She swipes, answers. "Heeey," she says, warmly.

Her eyes dart to mine; she gives me a quick smile, holding up her index finger to signal she'll be back in a minute.

Stepping outside through the French doors, she tries to close them while cradling her cell, but they don't click shut, leaving a tiny gap of space in her wake.

From inside the kitchen, I can hear her laughter, loud and throaty.

"Are you insane?" she squawks into her phone.

I'm dying to know who's called her.

"I'm just about to cook dinner. It's not possible for me to get away . . ."

More laughter.

Her voice begins to die as she walks further into the yard.

I inch a little closer to the door, cock my ear.

"He would kill me, seriously. How can you expect me to get away this last-minute? At this hour? I *always* cook dinner on Tuesday nights, you know that—"

My insides are twisting. *Who is she talking to?*

As if she can detect me eavesdropping, she switches over to Spanish.

I inch back inside, afraid she's clocked me. But that's impossible; her back has been turned to me this entire time.

She keeps talking, and I take another swallow of wine, inch back toward the door so I can listen in again.

More conversing in Spanish; I only pick up the final word:

"Besos," she says, ending the call.

18

MARISOL STEPS BACK inside, face flushed, her body practically vibrating.

She crosses the room, drops her cell in her cavernous leather handbag.

"My god, it smells divine in here." Nate's voice booms across the kitchen as he enters it.

"Must be the garlic?" I suggest, shifting my gaze to the pan, where diced garlic slowly sautés, awaiting the shrimp.

Marisol clears her throat. "Honey, I'm so sorry, but I'll have to bail on dinner tonight."

"What?" Nate looks as though someone has punched him in the gut.

"You'll never believe this, but David, the producer, just called," she says, glancing at me as if I'm to verify her story, "and a group of them are meeting for dinner. Some Italian place called La Scala in Beverly Hills? Anyway, they want me to join them."

Nate folds his arms across his chest. "But . . . what about *our* dinner?"

Marisol goes over to him, wraps her arms around his neck. "I know, sweetie. It's totally last-minute and so inconsiderate of them, but, I couldn't exactly say *no*, could I? I mean, Guillermo's going, the DP will be there. Gael—"

Nate gently extricates himself from her embrace. Looks over to me.

My stomach squeezes with anxiety. I don't know what to think, but if I had to guess, it was Andreas who called, not David. The way that Marisol felt the need to step outside for privacy. Her throaty, lusty laugh. The way she switched over from English to Spanish. David Silver (I Googled the film after Marisol first told me about it and saw he was attached as producer) might very well speak Spanish, but . . .

I smile, nod once at Nate.

I have no idea why I just did that, but I somehow felt pressured to firm up Marisol's story. And seriously, for all I know, it *was* David that called, not Andreas.

"Cassidy here has prepped everything, you'll just need to finish up! And Cassidy, you want to stay, eat my portion?" Her Bambi-brown eyes are begging me to say yes.

And dinner solo with Nate doesn't sound like hell to me. Quite the opposite. "Of course, that is, if you want me to?" I level my eyes on Nate's.

He softens, his face rearranging itself from frustrated husband to doting boss. "Yes, I'd love that."

Marisol's eyes rove between us, seemingly calculating whether or not the coast is clear for her to leave. She gathers her bag from the floor. "I'll be home as soon as I can. Promise." She palms the side of Nate's face, kisses his cheek.

"You know how late these things can run," Nate grumbles. "So don't say that, but yeah, don't stay out all night, either." His body is stone-still as she tries to cover him with affection.

But because I am present, he has to return it *somewhat* or look like an ass, so he lifts one hand, runs it up and down her back.

"Besos," she says to him, planting a kiss on his cheek.

She floats over to me. "Besos." She kisses both of my cheeks, as if I were her daughter, like we're a family unit she's saying good night to.

She lowers her hand, clasps mine, giving it two squeezes. *Thank you for saving me, going with the flow* is how I interpret it.

I grin at her, pat her carved triceps. "Have a nice time!"

The room falls quiet; only the sound of the sizzling in the pan fills the air as she exits.

19

THREE WEEKS LATER

MY STOMACH IS sick with worry. Bile edges up the back of my throat and I'm aware that my nails are digging into my palms, causing pinpricks of pain, but I can't stop it.

The detectives want to talk to me again. And this time not just at my apartment.

I'm riding to the station in the backseat of their patrol car, jumping at every pop of traffic, every horn blast, nerves shredded beyond repair.

I can't believe I just arrived here a month ago, heart brimming with the promise of a fresh start, and now I'm about to be all but perp-walked into the police station, clearly their number one suspect.

A suspect in a murder.

My mind trails back to all the things I could've, should've done differently—to all the ways I got swept up—but it's too late.

This is bad. Really bad.

The walls are closing in on me.

20

ALONE IN THE kitchen with Nate, I suddenly feel overheated, like my clothes are too tight.

If I had known I'd be having dinner with just him, I would have at least made some kind of effort with my wardrobe today. Looking down and taking in my basic cami, shrouded mostly by my gray hoodie, I wince.

Nate's wearing one of his signature button-down white oxfords. His jeans form to his body in all the right ways.

"Well, shall we finish this up?" He grins at me.

We work side by side, me tearing the watery fistfuls of romaine into shreds, Nate whipping the homemade Caesar dressing together in a shallow bowl, his forearm flexing as he beats the side of it.

I sip the rosé, peer outside to the pool, and wonder, once again, who really called Marisol.

"That's so great that she's meeting with the producer," I say, instantly regretting bringing the topic back up.

An almost inaudible guffaw snorts out of Nate.

He continues whipping the dressing in a sharp, agitated motion.

"Yes, it's a good sign. There's so much schmoozing that goes on with these things, and Marisol's the best at it."

I detect a note of sarcasm in his tone, but when I glance at him, he flashes a smile.

"Gives me an excuse to cook dinner for once. I'm more of the breakfast chef. Pancakes, eggs Benedict."

"And lattes!" I offer.

"Yes, those, too. Speaking of beverages, this wine is great and all, but I could use something stiffer. Care for an old-fashioned? I make a mean one."

Jesus. I'm this side of tipsy after my glass and a half and I can't imagine driving after another drink.

"Sure!" I chirp. I'll figure it out. Sip slowly, maybe pour some down the drain like last time.

I watch with fascination as he drops sugar cubes into the bottoms of heavy-looking lowball glasses, drizzles them with bitters, and muddles the cubes with a wooden tool.

He brings the glasses over, places them on the counter right next to where my arm is resting. Reaching around me to open the freezer, he grazes my back, sending an electric current up my spine.

"Special ice," he says, winking at me.

He pops the rectangular cubes from a silicone tray, drops one in each of the glasses, uncorks the bourbon, and drizzles a healthy amount over them. The blocks of ice pop and hiss under the heat of the whiskey.

Reaching around me once again to open the fridge, he extracts a jar of black cherries.

"These are crucial," he quips.

"Want to take our drinks out by the pool before dinner? My mom was big on cocktail hour at our house and sometimes that ritual creeps back into my DNA."

"Ha! My mom, too. But cocktail hour was every hour at our house."

"Yikes."

I feel a prick of shame, blurting that out. Nate, from the sounds of it, was raised super Waspy; he probably can't even begin to relate to my sordid background.

I trail him outside, where he gestures for us to sit at the tiny metal table.

"Here's to our new partnership of you reading scripts!"

"I'll drink to that!" I tap my glass against his, with a little too much gusto. A splash of bourbon surfs the rim, drenching my hand.

I laugh, wipe my hand on my jeans to dry it. "I swear I'm not drunk."

"Well, you might be after this. Watch out." Nate grins.

In the dwindling sunlight, his hazel-green eyes shimmer, locking on to mine. My whole body flushes.

"I'd love to hear more about your novels."

Shit.

"Really? It's kind of pathetic, honestly. None of them have ever gotten published."

"That doesn't matter. Do you know how much rejection I faced starting out?"

I'm shocked to hear this. By all accounts, Nate was off to the races fresh out of film school.

"You did?" I sip my bourbon. It singes the back of my throat, but the sugar aftertaste makes it go down deceptively smooth.

"Of course! My first script didn't sell at all. And my first two films never got picked up for distribution. But, through all that, I learned my style, my brand. So, maybe the same thing will happen for you."

He leans over, nudges his elbow against my arm. I nearly drop my glass from this slightest contact.

"Well, thanks so much for the opportunity."

"Don't thank me, you're a natural, Cassidy, and clearly have a good eye for story."

I shake my head, demurring. Being out here by the pool—just the two of us, his full attention trained on me—sends a shiver pinballing through my system.

"I mean, thank you, is what I meant to say."

At this, Nate laughs, stretching his long legs out in front of him.

His glass is almost drained. Even though I've been taking small nips and mine is still nearly full, my vision swims.

He sucks the rest of his down, shakes the ice around in the glass. "Well, that hit the spot. Now I'm famished. Shall we?"

I don't want to break this spell, leave this spot, but I *do* need some food to sop up the alcohol. "Absolutely. I'm starving, too."

WE EAT IN silence, both of us dredging the petal-pink shrimp through the garlic-infused olive oil. And like the other night, Nate has lit a pair of slender stick candles, the flames winking between us.

Before I sat down, I shed my hoodie, adjusted my bra so that I have the slightest bit of cleavage exposed. As Nate refilled my glass of rosé, his eyes skimmed my neckline. So briefly, though, that I can't decide if I imagined it.

"This is so delicious."

"Mm-hmm," Nate says, his mouth full, dotting his lips with his linen napkin.

His cell beeps.

He checks it, shakes his head, glances up at me then back down at his phone. His palm grazes the back of his neck like he's trying to puzzle something out.

"Everything all right?"

He types something into the cell. Deletes it. Retypes. "Yeah, I'm just . . . trying to figure out what you women want," he says, almost under his breath.

"What?"

"Sorry, nothing." His eyes are glued to the screen on his phone, his brow pinched. "It's Marisol. Says they're just now at the bar getting drinks and haven't even been seated for dinner yet."

He grins up at me, but I heard what he said and feel the tension coming off him in invisible waves, like cologne.

He jabs his last piece of shrimp with his fork, jams it in his mouth.

I take another swallow of wine, followed by a chaser of ice water. The acute buzz I felt by the pool is numbing; I'd be okay to drive now.

Not wanting to be rude, I force myself to finish the last of the salad and shrimp. The air between us now is brittle, as if it could snap in two.

I stay silent, watching Nate finish the rest of his dinner, his jaw working in angry bites.

Once he's done, he lets out a long, ragged sigh. Over the flickering candles, his eyes smile wearily at me.

He slugs the rest of his wine. "Ahh. Care for a top-off?"

I hesitate. I should really get up and leave, but now that I know Marisol most likely won't be home for a while, I feel bad bailing on him.

"Sure, but just a little. I have to drive."

"Of course," he says, filling my glass to the rim, doing the same with his.

"So," he says, taking another long pull from his glass. He said the other day he didn't like to drink too heavily, but I guess he's revenge drinking after Marisol skated on dinner. "Tell me more about Austin. Only ever been once. For South by Southwest. My film premiered there, and we stayed downtown the whole time, so I didn't really get a feel—"

I take a sip; it tingles on my tongue like Pop Rocks. I tell myself that I'll alternate between wine and water now, take it slow. "Well, it's changed *so* much, I barely even recognize it anymore. That was one of the reasons I left. Too many rich white people everywhere I turned."

Nate cackles, his face reddening.

"Oh, sorry, I—"

"No, no, it's okay," he says, lasering me with his grin again, which has turned sloppy. "Guilty." He aims his wineglass across the table; we toast.

"So what were the other reasons?" He lifts an eyebrow at me and his eyes light on my chest. This time, I can tell for sure it's not my imagination.

My pulse jangles in my neck. "Well, my love life was on the rocks."

Nate's eyes are now serious, his face etched with concern. And intrigue.

"Care to talk about it?" His voice is honey, soothing, coaxing.

"Not really? But yeah, broken heart."

"What's his name?"

"Carter?"

Another cackle bubbles out of Nate. "With that name, I'm picturing some douchey tech bro, no?"

"Yeah," I say, laughing myself. "You nailed it, actually."

"Then, good riddance. His loss. Cheers!" Nate clinks his glass to mine.

As we sip, his eyes grip mine.

"So, back to your novels. I'm picking up that they're a no-fly zone, that you don't really want to talk about them. But I'm interested. What are they about?"

My stomach dips and curves as if on a roller coaster. I'm embarrassed to tell him, yet feel oddly intimate with him right now. "Exactly what we're talking about. My love life, or lack thereof. They're romance novels," I add, not knowing if he remembers me telling him that the other night. "So I was writing them to give myself a happy ending, I guess."

Oh god, happy ending? Please tell me I didn't just say that.

Nate tilts his head. "I get that. Writing is a compulsion for me, too. A way of making sense of the world." His voice is still smooth, but his words come out too fast, as if they're tripping on each other. He's soused. Or rapidly getting there.

"Yeah?" I ask, because I don't know how to form words right now. My stomach continues to have that free-falling feeling.

"Yes. If I don't write it out, I'll go crazy."

He traces the rim of his wineglass in slow circles, but his gaze never leaves mine.

"Have you ever thought about writing scripts?"

"I mean—"

"I'm not saying that since you haven't been published you should give up novels. But you really *are* so good at reading scripts, you might be good—no, *great*—at writing them, too. I could help you, if you wanted."

I draw in a thin breath. The candlelight wobbles between us, casting shadows across the strong lines of his face. With the wine I've been sipping, my buzz is renewed; I feel swoony.

"I'd love that." I keep my voice low, husky, trying to shed the schoolgirl gusto that I've only shown thus far.

His eyes skitter over my body again. This time, I don't look away. I hold his gaze, letting him know I see him looking at me.

My mouth lifts into a grin. "Thank you. That's seriously so kind."

He bats the air in front of him. "You're helping me. Us. It's the least I can do."

He empties the bottle of rosé into his glass, touches it to his lips. I watch his neck as he takes it all down in one mouthful, his jugular bulging as he swallows. I imagine pressing my lips there, trailing them down his chest.

Snap out of it, Cassidy, this is another woman's husband.

But I'm mesmerized and he catches my open stare.

He twists the stem of his empty glass around, bites his bottom lip. "I want to ask you something—"

His voice, again, is syrupy, tipsy.

"Okay—"

"Can you keep a secret?" His eyes are now laser beams, probing my face.

I don't know how to respond. Yes? No?

"Sure?" I finally say, as if it's a question.

"Great." Nate's chair scrapes the floor as he stands. "Follow me. I want to show you something."

21

I TRICKLE BEHIND Nate as he leads me down the hallway to the bottom of the staircase.

We're going upstairs? Alone?

My heartbeat hammers against my throat.

In his wake, I smell the expensive bourbon we drank and his clean, woodsy scent.

When we reach the landing, Nate pauses at their bedroom door. My breath hitches in my chest. *Is he . . . ?*

But before I can complete the thought, Oscar and Percy climb from their poofy dog beds and lumber over, smashing their noses against Nate's legs.

"Good boys, you guys are the *best* boys." He's crouched down, but twists his neck and grins up at me, as if in invitation.

"Hey there!" I say to Oscar and Percy, joining in on rubbing their coats.

Nate's hand knocks against mine. My breath hitches again.

After a lingering second, he rises and the pooches stagger back to their beds.

He heads down the hall toward his office. Instead of flicking on the lights, he goes to a far corner, switches on a sleek table lamp, which douses the room with soft light.

He motions for me to take a seat on the sectional next to the lamp.

From my perch, I can see through the pair of glass doors, down to the pool. I've never seen it at night before; it's magical. Strands of rope lights illuminate the loquat trees and jewel-green lawn.

"It's beautiful, isn't it?" Nate asks, stooped over, bangs cascading over his eyes. His hands rake through a filing cabinet.

"Absolutely. Like, pinch me."

"Ahh, here we go." He plucks a script from the cabinet.

Crossing the room, he plops down catty-corner to me. We're sitting so close that our knees are nearly touching.

His eyes scan the script as he flips its pages.

"Well, here's my little secret." He fixes his gaze on me. "This is nearly the latest version. The *latest* latest is on my laptop. But, I wanted to show you, instead of pushing a screen in your face."

He balances the script on his open palms as if he's a choirboy, offering the priest an open Bible to read during mass.

With shaky hands, I accept it.

The title sheet reads, `A KEPT WOMAN by Nate Sterling`.

Excitement zips through me. A secret script.

I glance up at him.

Eyebrows raised, he grins nervously at me. "Nobody knows about this, okay? And I want to keep it that way. I haven't shared this with one single soul. Until now." His whole body exhales, his formerly crisp white button-down now crimping with the release of his pent-up breath.

"What is this?" I ask. "I mean, I know it's a script, but why keep it a secret?"

A sigh whistles out of him. He leans back, crossing his legs at the ankle. His top foot starts wagging, mere inches away from my shin.

"So, Marisol and I have an agreement. Basically, that we won't work together, that she won't be in any of my films—"

"I know, she told me," I blurt out, wishing I could snatch the words back in my mouth. Afraid he'll think we've been dishing about their relationship.

Surprise flashes across his eyes.

"I mean, I kind of asked her why she hasn't been in any of your films—" I backpedal, hoping to cover my tracks.

"Ahh. Well, I'm sure she told you this, but we've never wanted business to come between our marriage. And it's worked out great so far. But, I really want her to have something in case she doesn't book this film. She'll be so crushed if she doesn't get it."

He's right. She will. I nod in agreement.

"And I'm not gonna lie, if this goes forward," he says, jabbing his index at the script, "we'll film in the South of France. I'd love to go back there with Marisol. It's where we first met."

His eyes take on a dreamy quality, but his face looks pained.

I smile, nod again.

"The thought of going away, after all this pandemic mess, and getting to be with her for a five-month shoot . . ." He shakes his head. "Let's just say I think it could be good for us."

My tongue is dry. I don't know exactly how to respond. "For sure."

"And, you could come with us?" He angles his head, steeples his fingers together.

The thought of parading around on a beach with Nate and Marisol is almost too much to bear. I smile, but literally bite my bottom lip to keep from acting too giddy. "That would be amazing . . . but again, why keep it a secret?"

"Ha! You're not gonna let this go, are you?"

A nervous laugh squeaks out of me.

"Because we've never worked together, and I'm not sure how she'll feel about any of it. I want to make sure the script is in the best possible shape before pitching it to her, let alone to the studios. It has to be the kind of project she won't be able to turn down. So, I've been working on it in secret. My own little pandemic project. Some people made sourdough." He angles his head even further, his eyes creasing into a smile. "I wrote a feminist, erotic thriller."

The word *erotic* being spoken by him leaves my mouth even drier. He must be drunk; I can't believe he just exposed all this to me.

But again, I'm grateful. I feel like he's really talking to me, versus how it can feel with Marisol, where sometimes I suspect I'm more of an extension of her psyche.

"An erotic thriller?" The question sputters out of my mouth.

Nate's foot stops wagging. He leans forward, placing his hands on his knees, face now a foot away from mine. "Yeah. Like an Adrian Lyne film, but for the female gaze."

He leans back again as if giving me space to soak it all in. His expression is thoughtful, his forefinger brushing his top lip. Just like earlier, I'm captivated watching him. Can't take my eyes off him.

"Whoa. Sold."

"Really?" he asks, his voice tender, vulnerable. "That doesn't sound clichéd?"

"No. Not to me. Not if it's done well."

He starts nodding, briskly. "That's precisely why I want *you* to read it. Not that I feel out of touch with women, but . . . I might feel out of touch with women?" A sheepish grin melts across his face.

"Ha!"

"So I'd love to have your amazing eyes on it, Cassidy. In secret."

He brings his index finger to his lips, making the shush signal.

Heat pricks my skin. I feel an invisible charge building between us. Crackling, sparking, electrifying.

I'm not sure how I feel about keeping this hush-hush from

Marisol, but if, in the end, it's all to help their marriage and cushion her from a possible fallout should she not get the role in the del Toro film, then I'm doing her a favor, I decide.

"I'll do it."

Nate stands, clasps his hands together. "Yes! Thank you!"

Taking his cue, I rise to my feet, take this as a sign to leave. Clutching the script to my chest, I head across the room. "I'll let you know what I think," I say, waving the pages at him.

"Ah, no, no, no. Script stays here."

Embarrassment floods my veins. "Really?"

"Yes. Top secret. I know it sounds crazy, but it stays in that drawer." He motions toward the filing cabinet. "Whenever you have time, just come in here and read. Marisol won't think anything of it since you're already reading for me. Just . . . keep in here *here*, okay?"

This sounds bonkers to me. He's being *so* secretive. And also, I can't imagine reading with him looking over my shoulder, but whatever.

"I understand." I smile, pass the script back to him. Turn to leave again.

Before I exit the room, I pause. Swivel back around to face him. "But my first note?"

A laugh barks out of him. "Already? You're really not going to go easy on me, are you?"

"It's about the title. I know I haven't read a single word of it yet, but that title is a bit . . . extra?" My voice comes out bold, a pitch too loud, as if some other being is speaking through me.

This elicits another laugh from Nate.

"So it better pay off, because right now, it sounds primed for cancel culture." Again, the words spill out of me effortlessly, as if I'm disembodied, watching myself speak. But at the same time, I feel keenly alive, buzzing not from the alcohol anymore but from Nate's trust in me, his desire to have my opinion.

He holds his palms up as if he's under arrest. "And again, that's *exactly* why I need you, Cassidy."

Holy shit! *He needs me.*

I slink out of the room before I have a chance to crush this idyllic moment.

22

IT'S ONLY NINE fifteen a.m., but it's already roasting. A heat wave swept through early this morning and is predicted to grip LA through the weekend.

I inch up to Nate and Marisol's, parking in my usual spot. My A/C is blasting, but my skin feels feverish. Not from the weather but from the titillating conversation with Nate last night, which comes flooding back to me now.

I feel lightheaded, the secret about the script building in my chest on the drive over.

I can't wait to read it, still can't believe Nate values my opinion so much. Trusts me. Wants me to give him feedback on work he's shown no one else.

I didn't tell Lexie, of course. I resisted the urge. Last night when I got home, I picked up my cell to text her, dropped it on top of my comforter, picked it up again. I finally placed it facedown on the nightstand, half hoping she'd reach out to me.

She didn't and I'm taking that as a sign to keep my lips sealed about this. Plus, as much as I want to share it with her, there's something delicious about having something strictly between Nate and me. Something that's just ours. For no one else.

Today I've made an effort to look more fashionable. I tried on Marisol's white shirtdress, the one she held up to me the other day, and it actually looks flattering on me, makes me look pulled together and not like some frumpy assistant who forgets her own needs.

I even took a little extra time in the bathroom this morning, applying light makeup, adding waves to my hair with the curling iron.

I flip my visor down, check myself out in the mirror. Smile at my reflection for a change. As I'm snapping the visor back into place, my cell chimes from within my messenger bag.

My hand dives in, retrieves it.

It's a text from Marisol.

Marisol: Hey!! Sorry for the short notice but we're running a bit behind this morning. Do you think you could give us like 30? Late night. 😘

She must think I'm still en route. Hmph.

There's no way I'm getting back into traffic. Since it's unusually balmy, I decide to take a stroll, stick to the path that rims the cliff overlooking the beach. I mean, shoot me now.

Cassidy: Absolutely!! See you soon!

The sun is a sultry kiss on my legs as I step out, the ocean below rippling in the mellow morning light.

I squeeze the key fob and step onto the sidewalk.

I reach the Dead End sign, am about to veer around the metal barricades cupping the lane when I hear Marisol's voice, distressed and angry, bursting through their hedges.

Ears pricked, I spin around, pad quickly in that direction. My strappy leather sandals tongue the pavement, not carrying me quickly enough like sneakers would. Damn my decision to dress up for once.

Then Nate's voice cuts through the air like a blade, sharp, searing. "Imagine being in my shoes! Being the one left hanging out to dry—"

He's nearly shouting at her as I slink toward the hedges, a wall of grass-green manzanita.

"It's not like I have a choice. I'm trying to build my career here," Marisol spits back at him, "and it feels like you're dragging me down by my ankles at every turn!"

No wonder she told me to get lost for half an hour.

It feels wrong standing here, eavesdropping. Yet I can't force my feet to budge.

"Did you even care how I felt last night?"

"It's not like I stayed out all night!" Marisol's tone is tense, tautly strung, the E string on a violin about to snap.

"You stumbled in at one in the morning."

As if sensing my presence, a flock of birds bursts from the top of the hedges, sailing over my head, toward the ocean.

Sweat pricks my armpits. I'm in danger of getting busted, so I retreat a few paces.

From within their walled-off yard, silence.

Shit.

I'm frozen in place, not wanting to budge another inch for fear they'll detect motion, hear me.

Then: the sound of water splashing.

"Hey!" Nate's protesting, but in an almost playful way.

Then, Marisol's squealing, followed by the sound of a body plopping in the water.

"You dick! I'm in my pj's!" A peal of Marisol's giggles cascades through the yard.

The sound of Nate jumping in the water. "Okay, so now we're both soaking in our pj's."

These people are truly mental.

The clapping sound of treading water, followed by the rhythmic sound of Nate and Marisol catching their breath.

I could walk away now, undetected. And I should. But, of course, I stay.

Silence again.

I suck in a breath, hold it.

"You make me crazy, you know that?" Nate's voice is low, husky.

No immediate response. Then a sound erupts from Marisol, rough and guttural.

I can't help it; instead of turning away, I push my face up against the hedges like some freak. I ease a branch to the side so I can peer through.

I gasp.

Marisol is naked from the waist up. Probably completely naked, but all I can see is her top half, turned away from me, glistening with water drops, hair slicked down her back.

Her arms are resting on the lip of the pool, breasts kissing the concrete, knees resting on the steps, underwater.

Behind her, Nate encircles her waist with his lean arms, buries his head on her shoulder. He's rocking back and forth, and as he does, those low, guttural sounds continue erupting from Marisol. She turns back to look at him, her face flushed with ecstasy.

Every nerve in my body is on fire with shame. I can't believe I've just caught them in the act.

As quietly as I can, I back away from the shrubs.

I'm unsteady on my feet, but as soon as I'm a few steps out, my cell dings.

Shit.

I pick up the pace and sprint away as fast as I can, hand on cell, silencing it.

23

ONCE I ROUND the corner I slack my pace, check my cell.

Lexie.

Lexie: How goes it?

Still heaving, I quickly reply: Great! Just got to work! Text ya later?

Lexie: Absolutely! No worries, just checking on you. Chaos here, lol! Talk soon. Xoxo

I continue walking. The mansions blur on my left, my head swarming with thoughts. The most pressing one being: it's clear that Nate and Marisol are the fight-and-fuck type. Also clear is that this isn't just some assistant job—it's a hot mess. Between their tremulous drama and Nate's secret script, I might just be in over my head.

Get ahold of yourself, Cassidy. Stop being such a drama queen. Stop making this about you.

I can't tell if that's good old Angie Foster's voice creeping back into my brain—if I so much as shed a few tears over a scraped knee, she labeled me a crybaby—or my own, good common sense. So *what* if I just caught my bosses fucking? At least Marisol gave me the heads-up, told me to stay away. I'm the stubborn one who hopped out of the car. Then . . . crept over to the bushes.

Eeeep.

I'm just as nuts as they are.

And I'm also now probably a good mile from their house and in danger of actually being late if I don't turn back soon.

I cross the street, head over to the opposite sidewalk, which overlooks the Pacific.

As the morning sun continues to blister the surface of the ocean, I rest my gaze there, feel my hamster-wheel thoughts beginning to dissipate.

I guess everyone out here *is* crazy, as Lexie warned me; I need to keep my eyes on the prizes: a juicy paycheck, access, breaking into Hollywood via Nate.

That's why I need you, Cassidy.

His velvety voice from last night skids across my mind again, making my pulse race.

I want to help him with his script; the thought of working with him thrills and exhilarates me. If Lexie knew Nate was letting me behind closed doors, wanting my input on the script he's keeping under wraps, she would slap me for even questioning things.

I check the time: nine forty-five. Marisol will be expecting me at ten.

I start heading back but keep my pace slack, wanting to give them every second until then to get it together. They'll need it.

24

MARISOL ANSWERS THE door, her lithe figure ensconced in a fluffy white robe, hair still wringing wet.

"Hey! Sorry about my appearance. We just took a dip in the pool." She twists her hair up into a jaw clip.

Uh-huh. Sure you did.

"It's blazing out, we couldn't resist." She smiles, but the grin is tired, saggy.

I trail her into the kitchen.

She wraps her fingers around her espresso cup, takes a long, lingering sip. "Mm-mm. I need this. Want one of your lattes?"

Though my pulse is still jittery, I nod. "I'd love one, thanks."

Marisol turns her back to me, digs out a rounded scoop of ground espresso from the paper bag. "Hey . . . thanks again for staying last night with Nate."

A lump lodges itself in my throat as I revisit being alone with him last night, being let in on his secret.

"Sure. It was nice!"

As the machine roars, she turns around, aiming a long sigh out of the corner of her mouth. "I'm happy to hear it. Because he was *so* pissed off at me."

She walks around to the bottom of the stairs, cocks her head upward. "Good, he's still in the shower."

"I'm so sorry," I reply, because I don't know what else to say.

She shakes her head as if she's just swallowed something distasteful. "Don't be. And fuck him. I mean, what was I *supposed* to do? Like, tell the producer, no, I can't come see you. My daddy will be too upset? Pshaw."

The machine belches out its final hiss. Marisol spins around to it.

While her back is turned to me, I wonder, once again, who really called her. Who she was with last night. Would dinner with the producer and film people really run until one in the morning? Possibly, if they closed the place down, went for drinks after. But she sure is acting defensive about the whole thing. Almost as if she needs to convince me, too.

Uneasiness swells in my gut: Marisol is being shifty, Nate's got a secret. And now *I* find myself in the middle, involved, keeping Nate's secret from his wife. What have I gotten myself into?

Snap out of it, Cassidy. Keep your eyes on your own paper. Stop wondering about their marriage and stay focused on the work.

"Here you are, my darling." Marisol slides my coffee over to me, another exhausted smile creaking across her face.

Even smelling of chlorine, hair stringy and wet in a bun, face devoid of makeup, she's flawless; this woman is dazzling.

"So, my head's not screwed on straight right now. I'll get it together for tomorrow because I actually do have some errands I need you to run for me. But for today, wanna just work on the closet some more? Do some reading for Nate?"

That last question makes the lump form again. I raise the mug to my lips, grin and nod at her as I take my first, scorching sip.

"I'm gonna be in and out all day, so honestly, just do whatever you like."

Butterflies swarm my stomach; I'm still uneasy, but I am giddy that I'll have time to peek at Nate's script.

"Sounds perfect!"

But Marisol's attention has already drifted elsewhere; her eyes are downcast as her fingers fly across the screen of her cell. The swooshing sound of texts being sent and answered swirls through the room.

"Sorry, what were you saying?"

"Nothing. Just that it sounds good, the plan—"

But her cell dings with another incoming text.

"Sorry. It's my stand-in, Jessica. She's going to drop by later today. We're just trying to figure out a time."

Marisol presses the side button on her phone with her thumb, locking the screen. She gently shoves it across the counter. "Ugh, my apologies. It's so rude when people do that. I hate cell phones. Hate all the accountability. The urgent need for people to find you." She exhales another sigh.

Above us, the floorboards wheeze.

"Uh-oh," she says, pointing toward the ceiling. "He's on the prowl. I'd better zip it."

I CHURN IN the closet for a good hour, but I'm not on my A game today.

I keep sorting through her handbags, nuzzling them into cubbies, then yanking them back out again because they still look jumbled, in disarray. But I can't focus long enough to figure out how to organize them. By color? By style?

My thoughts are twirling, my hands fidgety.

For all their perfectly prepared meals and shiny surroundings, there's something weird going on here with Nate and Marisol. Each of them seemingly guarding whole worlds from the other.

I finally scoop up all the clutch bags, sink to the floor, and force myself to try and concentrate on one menial task. I'll sort these by texture. Leather, silk, straw, satin.

As I'm making neat piles of them, finally homing in on the work, Nate appears at the door.

"Morning," he says, grinning down at me.

He smells clean and pure, fresh as a daisy. His crisp white tee inches above the waistline to his jeans. My eyes skitter across the tan, exposed flesh.

I see him in my mind's eye from a few hours ago, arms roped around Marisol, taking her from behind in the pool, the muscles between his shoulder blades flexing and unflexing.

"Morning," I reply, standing up, smoothing down Marisol's shirt-dress.

His smile widens. "I know that dress."

"Yeah, Marisol gave it to me—"

"Good thing she did. It suits you."

My stomach turns to hot jelly as Nate's eyes continue to prick over me. I haven't felt noticed like this since I first met Carter, and Nate is definitely noticing me. Both last night and right now. The sensation is almost excruciating. Exquisitely so.

"Thanks." A nervous giggle skitters out of me.

"So, Marisol just left. Wanna come have a look at the script?" He's still grinning at me, taking me in with his eyes.

"Sure. Let me just get these sorted—" I stammer, blushing under the weight of his attention.

"Don't worry about those. Just leave them. I'm not sure how long she'll be gone, how long we'll have."

I feel like I'm getting whisked away for a rendezvous. "Okay!" I dumbly say, and follow him down the hall.

Excitement trickles through my veins, but that same wave of uneasiness starts building again. What have I signed up for? I feel like I'm strapped into the seat of a roller coaster that's beginning to crest, right before its biggest drop.

25

NATE'S OFFICE IS the quietest room in the house; a womb immune from any outside noise. Perhaps because it's a new addition, unlike the rest of the home, which was built in the 1930s.

In the corner, an air purifier quietly hisses, but other than that, hushed silence.

He goes over to the filing cabinet, plucks out the script.

I cross the room, take it from him, then retreat to the sectional that we sat on last night.

Nate plops down in front of his computer, wiggles the mouse to awaken the monitor. "Don't mind me, I'm just gonna catch up on emails."

His back is to me, but in the blank quiet, I feel hyperconscious of my every move.

Settling back into the firm cushions, I tuck my feet underneath me, flip to the cover page.

A KEPT WOMAN

By Nate Sterling

I wince at that title but keep reading. Like his films, the writing is crisp, beautiful. The setting is Èze, a small seaside resort in the French Riviera.

In the first scene, he describes a beautiful, crumbling mansion that overlooks the Mediterranean. The lush grounds have a lagoon-style pool, expansive, the water turquoise.

I'm instantly transported.

From within the walls of the grand estate, we close in on Esme, our main character, who is at the large kitchen window, kneading dough. The scent of baking fills the room, her view of the ocean unobstructed.

She stands at the gleaming counter, working away, creating mock pastries that she hopes to one day sell at the local market.

Not that she needs the money—her husband, Theo, is a billionaire, but often away, and baking is her calling.

She only pauses when, through the window, she glimpses a tanned, muscular male scraping the surface of the pool with a skimmer. The pool boy, Gabriel. He shields his eyes, gazes back at Esme.

Nate clears his throat, snapping me out of the dreaminess of the script.

I shift on the sofa, try to reset my concentration, but am aware now of the sound of his fingers clacking on the keyboard.

A sigh escapes me, coming out louder than I intended.

Nate turns to me and grins. "Want me to get lost? I have a Zoom in an hour, but this space is yours 'til then."

"Yes, actually, if you don't mind?"

"Not at all."

As soon as I hear his footsteps bouncing down the stairs, I return to the pages.

The story centers on Esme and her controlling husband, Theo. She's in her late twenties; he's in his late forties. He's dashing, charming, unbelievably rich; they had a full-on, steamy courtship in which he, a widow, married Esme in a feverish affair, giving her everything she thought she dreamed of: a gorgeous, loving husband; an unbelievable home; her own giant kitchen to work in; and all the time in the world to bake.

The trouble is, Theo, a real estate tycoon, has a dark side. He's controlling, conniving. He cheats on Esme constantly, breaking her heart but gaslighting her into thinking she's imagining it all. She realizes that she's in a gilded cage of her own making and starts acting out.

In the opening scene, she drops her silk robe, exposing herself in the window, fully naked, to Gabriel. Slowly, erotically, she straddles a stool and begins caressing herself, touching herself in front of him. I'm impressed with Nate's attention to this, can't believe a woman didn't write it.

Thus begins a string of torrid affairs she engages in, all behind Theo's back. Or so she thinks. The more she acts out, the more controlling and menacing he becomes, to the point where she begins trying to control him, too, stalking his mistresses.

Devouring these pages, faster and faster, I become hot and bothered by all the steamy, explicit sex scenes. They're all carefully crafted and actually titillating—like porn for women—bold, unapologetic scenes that are driven by female desire and pleasure.

Damn, Nate has a good old feminist streak in him. And in Esme, he's written a complicated, fascinating female character who turns into a femme fatale, a role I believe Marisol would indeed have trouble turning down.

I still have thirty pages to go when Nate pokes his head in. "Time's up!"

He flashes me that goofy grin again, as if we are in on something covert, which, of course, we are.

As he did last night, he sinks down catty-corner from me, our knees nearly grazing.

His hazel-green eyes dart over my face. "Thoughts?" He clasps his hands together, rests them in his lap like a schoolboy.

"Well, yes. Lots of them. Do you have time now? Or—"

He chuckles. "Not really. Zoom's starting in ten. But just tell me, does it suck?"

"Ha! No. Quite the opposite. I was so pulled into Esme's story, her plight, and, if I'm honest, whew, the sex scenes are super hot."

My temples throb. I can't believe I just spit that out. *Who am I?*

His smile widens. "Well, I tried," he says, leaning back.

"But I definitely will have some notes for you. Like, how to give Esme more agency, for one. But I still have the third act to read, so—"

"See, that's why I'm *so* glad I asked you." His gaze lands on mine, holding it. "I know you can make it sharper, better."

"Are you sure I can't take it home with me tonight? Finish it—"

"Uh, no. Sorry. I trust you; it's not that. But I don't trust anyone else in this town and if for some bizarre reason it got into the wrong hands, I—"

"Aye, aye, Captain. I get it," I say, flashing him a teasing smile of my own.

"But seriously, thank you. I've been so nervous about this. Can't wait for you to finish and go over it with you at length."

Through the French doors, the pool below winks at us in the midday sun. I train my eyes there instead of facing Nate, who is still staring openly at me.

Go over it with you at length? This hot script?

Unable to form words, I nod, rise, and exit the room.

26

I PRACTICALLY FLOAT down the stairs, heart in my throat, whole body drenched with sweat.

I couldn't get away from Nate fast enough. I mean, I could've stayed with him all day in there, discussing the script, but I'm overheated. Need a breather.

Since Marisol invited me to raid their fridge, I yank it open, pull out a bottle of sparkling water. The cold fizz is exactly what my parched mouth is begging for.

I also slide out a wedge of smoked Gouda, slice off a piece to eat. I'm famished. I have a sad little tomato and spinach sandwich in my bag, but I need protein right now.

This has been *a day*. *Already*.

In the next room, the dining room, I hear the knocking sounds of Elana mopping the floor.

She must hear me in the kitchen because she suddenly appears, her hair tied back in another ropy ponytail, navy-glitter fingernails clasping the mop.

"I was wondering if you were here today!" she says suspiciously, as if somehow she knows I've been up in Nate's office reading his top-secret script.

"Yep! Just doing a little work upstairs," I offer, vaguely.

"I see. They are keeping you busy."

"So far!"

Her eyes narrow, rove over my shirtdress. "Somebody dressed up today!" She clicks her tongue, continues giving me the once-over, her mouth a tight line.

It's not a compliment; she's judging me.

"Yeah, well, Marisol gave me some things," I stammer, unsure of why I'm even disclosing this to her, explaining myself.

Elana twists around, bends down, and starts mopping the kitchen floor with such vigor I'm afraid the stick will snap. As she batters the baseboards, she starts humming; I take that as my cue to let the conversation die.

I finish the hunk of cheese and escape into the living room—the furthest spot away from Elana.

I can't stop thinking about Nate's torrid storytelling. And how he's chosen *me* to read it. Again, I consider texting Lexie. This is almost too much excitement to bear alone. But I know I can't. There's no way. I trust her completely, but even so, this is such a juicy secret I can't be one hundred percent certain that after a few drinks, she wouldn't blab it to someone on her film set. I cannot blow this.

No, this is between me and Nate, and that delicious fact sends pinpricks of heat all over me.

I'm halfway through my sandwich when I spy someone walking up the pathway that leads to the front door. A tall, thin brunette with oversized sunglasses who looks like she could be Marisol's twin.

Must be Jessica, Marisol's stand-in.

The doorbell chimes. Elana is running the vacuum so I hop up, answer the door.

"Hi! You must be Jessica! I'm Cassidy, the Sterlings' new assistant."

She cocks her head, studying me from behind her glamorous sunglasses with Dolce & Gabbana stenciled on the side.

"Yes, hi! So good to meet you." She shoves her glasses up on her head.

Her eyes are Bambi brown, the same shade as Marisol's. There are differences in their appearance, of course. Jessica's eyes are closer set, her frame is more slender, less shapely, and her lips aren't as full. Still, she's stunning and I can see why she's Marisol's stand-in.

"Let me guess," she says, pushing past me at the front door, "Marisol isn't here. She's running late."

Annoyance radiates off her body as she pounds down the hallway toward the kitchen.

"She's probably stuck in traffic but should be here soon," I say, covering for my boss, feeling oddly protective over her against this sassy double.

"Please. That woman is never on time." She plops her giant purse down on the kitchen counter, kicks off her sneakers. "Can't tell you how many times she'd be grossly late to set and I'd be standing there with a stupid grin on my face, trying to keep the director happy until she arrived."

I stare at her, blinking, but don't reply.

"Anyway—"

She starts to say more, but Nate appears in the entryway. "Hey, Jessica!"

"Howdy, Nate!" All of a sudden she's all smiles and her voice has taken on a syrupy tone.

"I take it y'all have met?" His eyes dart between us.

"Yes, just now," I say.

"Great." Nate whistles and Oscar and Percy come rushing down the hall, nails clattering against the tile floor. He grabs their leashes. "Cassidy, be back in thirty. Gonna give these guys a stroll."

Before the front door even closes all the way, Jessica starts yapping again. "I actually love coming to the house." She walks over to the fridge, pries the door open, stands there scanning the contents, leaving it open longer than is polite. I fight the urge to hop up off the barstool and go over, close it on her.

"It's so nice here," she says to the inside of the fridge.

She pulls out a cluster of green grapes, walks them over to the sink. As she's rinsing them, she cuts her eyes to me. "Nate, I mean, he's a total snack, right?" She snickers, stares at me for a reply.

I feel uncomfortable agreeing with her, even though I *do* agree with her—more than she'll ever know—but doing so would feel like a betrayal to Marisol.

I simply smile instead, a weak, half-hearted grin.

"Oh, whatever. Everyone thinks so. Marisol's a total head case, though." Jessica pops a grape between her lips. "But I still love her." Another snicker. "So how long have you worked for them?"

"Umm, I just started a couple weeks ago, actually."

"Like it so far?"

What I *don't* like is how pushy *she* is. "Yeah, absolutely. They're great."

"Don't get me wrong, and please for the love of god don't tell Marisol I said that about her—I would *never* hear the end of it—I really do love her. She's just . . . kind of a mess. But I guess most actresses are."

She pops another grape in her mouth, smacks it loudly.

Every nerve in my body revolts. I can't stand it when people smack their food. I wish Marisol would hurry up and get here.

"Let me correct that. Most *celebrities* are. I'm an actress, too."

And also a total head case, obviously.

"Just not a celebrity." Smack, smack. "Yet."

"So, what do you and Marisol have planned for today?"

"Well, when we're shooting, the studio pays me, obviously, but sometimes Marisol'll call me out of the blue, want me to come and run some lines with her. I mean, she has an acting coach, *and* a voice coach, and seriously a whole friggin' *staff*, but I guess she feels comfortable with me?"

I cannot imagine how. This chick is setting my teeth on edge.

"She's like a big sister to me. Guess that's why we bicker sometimes."

The back door that leads out to the garage swings open. "Hi, hi! Sorry I'm late!" Marisol rushes over to Jessica, a row of shopping bags dangling from her arm.

"Oh, yes, I was just complaining to Cassidy here about your tardiness—"

"Shut your mouth!" Marisol laughs. "Cassidy is *so* nice to me; you could take lessons."

"Ouch. Easy now." Jessica chomps on another grape.

"Cassidy. It's been a long day. Wanna take off now?"

I flick my eyes to the clock on the microwave. It's just two forty-five. "You sure? I could keep working on the closet?"

"See what I'm saying." Marisol winks at Jessica. "She's nice."

A sigh shakes out of Jessica, who rolls her eyes.

"And yes, you can totally go home. There'll be plenty of running around tomorrow."

I do feel strangely exhausted from this day.

"Okay, cool. Thanks!" I lean over, kiss Marisol on both cheeks as she's taught me to do. She returns the kisses in kind.

"So nice to meet you, Jessica." I plaster a fake smile on my face.

"You, too!"

"Besos, Cassidy!" Marisol's voice tickles the back of my neck as I head down the hall toward the front door.

27

THREE WEEKS LATER

MY HANDS QUAKE as I watch the red light glow on the recorder before us. Detectives Simmons and Cruz sit across the table from me, statue-still, expressions both rigid and hungry.

Why am I here without a lawyer? Oh, that's right, I can't afford one.

Blood pounds through my ears. I don't know how to convince them of the truth. Or, at least, what I think is the truth from what I saw.

Hysteria keeps building in me, gathering strength like a Texas thunderstorm, when Detective Cruz's voice cuts through my panic. "We need you"—there's an irritated edge to her voice—"to tell us the truth. You didn't just see him through the window, did you?"

But so far they've believed nothing that I've said, so why should anything I say now change that?

And my journals. They have my journals. Everything I wrote down that day in rage.

He can't just cast me off.

He can't just get rid of me. I'll make sure of that. I'll show him how wrong he is.

28

NOW

IT'S THURSDAY AFTERNOON. Four thirty. I'm in the Sterlings' kitchen, stashing the last of the bottles of wine away.

I'm bushed. Beat. Marisol wasn't lying. She had me running around all day. First to get her car—an inky black convertible Mercedes with sumptuous, gray leather seats—washed and waxed, then across town to Hollywood to pick up her herb order from her acupuncturist.

Then on to the posh liquor store to collect the cases of wine I'm now unloading, followed by a trip to the dry cleaner's, and a stop at the post office to mail presents to her twin nieces back home for their birthday. And finally, to the vet's, for flea medicine.

She's now upstairs getting ready for a party tonight in Malibu, at Guillermo's beach rental—or so she says.

Nate's still in his office.

As soon as she gives me the word, I'm out. I've got four scripts to read—not that Nate's tapping his feet, but I want to stay on top of it, keep the cash flowing in.

I hear Marisol's heels stabbing the stairs. Perfect.

She enters the room and, if it's humanly possible, looks even more resplendent than ever in a white halter dress, her hair glossy and ribboning down her shoulders. Her makeup is light, her pillowy lips glossed in a pale pink.

"Wow! You look amazing!"

"Ahh, you think so?" Her eyes rest on mine, swimming. She seems jumpy, fidgety.

"Yes! Absolutely stunning. Have the best time!"

"Hoping to! Getting nervous, honestly, that they're going to give this role to one of the others."

Penelope Cruz, Salma Hayek, Ana de Armas are all vying for it.

"Well, they'd be crazy to. They're all great, but you're a fresh face. And a killer actress. Don't you forget it."

Tears shimmer in her eyes, tumble down her cheeks.

"Oh, no, I didn't mean to make you cry!"

She flicks them away. "You're just . . . so nice to me. Thank you. This town can be . . . just awful."

Sympathy spears my chest.

I open my arms, wrap her in a hug. "I can only imagine."

Her slender frame shudders and I imagine more tears spilling.

After a moment, we pry apart.

"Is my makeup smudged?"

"Not at all. You look flawless."

The tears have actually accentuated her eyes, making them sparkle even more.

"Thank you, Cassidy."

"I feel like we are going to be thanking Cassidy for a long time." Nate's voice, teasing and warm, glides through the room.

I have no idea how long he's been standing there.

His tall frame rests against the archway. Behind him, the Pacific glistens through the windows.

I blush. "Ahh, stop it, you guys. Seriously. It's my job!"

Nate goes over to Marisol, twines her into a hug. "Hit it out of the park tonight, babe."

Wow, that's a different tack than he normally takes. Maybe the makeup sex in the pool healed all.

She responds with a kiss, light and brief. "See you later. And see you tomorrow, Cassidy."

She spills out the back door to the garage, her white dress squeezing her perfect form.

AS SOON AS I hear her Mercedes hum to life, I grab my messenger bag, strap it across my chest.

But Nate leans against the counter, beams at me. "Cocktail?"

Sigh. I really *do* want to get home to my little apartment, peel my clothes off, and slip into my pj's straight from a hot bath. And then binge trash TV. The latest *Bachelor* awaits.

But Nate is a foot away from me, tanned skin gleaming, eyes crinkled with mirth.

A flare sparks in my chest, bringing me back to life. I shed my bag, plop down on a barstool. "Sure. But help keep me honest and make sure I only have one?"

"Deal. What are you having?"

"What are you making?" I say, too much flirtatiousness in my voice.

"It's still warm out. Too warm for old-fashioneds. G and T?" He cocks his head, aims those swoony eyes my way.

"Sounds perfect."

First, he fixes us a fruit and cheese tray, using the last of the grapes that Jessica didn't gobble up, along with the smoked Gouda I'd snuck a bite from yesterday. He drizzles the little wooden tray with honey, scattering roasted pistachios across it.

Watching him work, delicately with the deftest of touches, his golden bangs spilling down his forehead, an earlier thought returns to me: hot chef in a rom-com.

My stomach twirls. I'm living in a Nancy Meyers film, except Nate is married and he and Marisol are my bosses. He is no Bachelor.

Next, he splits a lime into quarters, pulls out the jar of fancy cherries he used the other night in our drinks. From the freezer, he scoops out a few pieces of ice, rolls them in a hand towel.

"Ah, my favorite part." With a metal tool, he hammers the cloth-wrapped cubes. "I'm such a child."

My eyes trickle to his forearms, as usual. Watching them tense and untense as he beats the ice sends a delicious shiver over me.

He finishes off our cocktails, glides mine over to me.

"Cheers."

We toast and sip.

It fizzes bright and zesty on my tongue, the quinine in the tonic offering the perfect kick of bitterness.

"Well?" Nate's eyes dance over mine.

"It's *so* refreshing."

"I call it liquid air-conditioning."

"Ha! Yes, exactly."

I tip the glass to my lips, take another long swig.

Nate pushes the cheese tray forward, so that it's perfectly centered between us.

"Help yourself."

I select a slice of Gouda, drag it through a trail of honey.

"Thank you, this is nice. I didn't even realize I was hungry."

"Well, it's not all selfless. Now that I have you to myself—"

My heart lunges up my throat.

"—I know you haven't had time to read any more, but I'm *dying* to know your thoughts thus far on the script." He slices a grape into thirds, pops a piece in his mouth. Unlike Jessica, there's no smacking at all, and my crush grows even more.

"I really do want to finish it first before I weigh in, you know?"

Nate takes another sip, sets his drink down. Leaning forward, he rests his forearms on the counter, angling toward me as if he's about to tell me a secret. "I get that. I do, but yeah, still dying to know over here."

I'm already buzzy from the alcohol, and the way his eyes are probing mine isn't helping my lightheaded feeling.

"Well, I haven't stopped thinking about it." And I haven't. As I drove around town today, the vividly erotic scenes of Esme with her various lovers would spring into my mind. Also, her story, her rich character, her boldness.

"Really?" His voice is low, serious.

"Mm-hmm," I reply, not wanting to admit that his sex scenes have me obsessed with the script.

"What about it in particular, if I might ask?"

"I'll just say *this*." My voice comes out raspy, saucy. Like the other night in his office, it's as if some other sassy being is speaking for me on my behalf. "I'm dying to know how it ends. How you wrap it all up. Right now, it's so propulsive, so addictive, I think viewers are going to be knocked out."

"Really?" he repeats.

"Yes!"

"This is great to hear, but you're very adept at being cagey, ya know?" There's a playful note to his voice that makes me even more lightheaded.

"I swear I'm not trying to be."

"Well, you are." His gaze is direct.

I shift on the barstool, trying to still my body.

"I'm just invested in Esme. Her arc. And, like I said the other night, the sex scenes are super hot."

Behind him, the sun sinks into the Pacific, pouring orange light into the room.

I can't believe I blurted that out again. But it's true.

Nate gnaws his bottom lip. "Like I said before, I really tried."

I lift my half-empty glass to his; he clicks it against mine.

"Well, you knocked it out of the park."

"Ha! Thanks." Splotches of red stain his neck.

Again, he looks like some dreamy, preppy schoolboy.

His glass is drained. He tosses the shards of ice in the sink, reaches out for mine to do the same. "But . . . are the sex scenes . . . authentic?"

The barstool squeaks as I slowly rotate on it, back and forth. I can't stop squirming. "What do you mean? Authentic?"

"Well. I mean, from the female perspective. But before you answer," he says, waving my glass at me, "another one?"

I'm dying for another. "Remember when I said you should keep me honest?" I grin at him. "I'd love to, but I really shouldn't; I have to drive home and all that."

He blows out a puff of air that sends his bangs upward. "What if I put you in an Uber? Pay for it both ways?"

Now my neck is flushed.

"Okay."

"Okay!" A wide grin splits his face.

I grab the kitchen counter with both hands, force myself to stop twisting.

The sun is an orange-red cherry on the tip of a cigarette, almost completely now dissolved into the ocean.

I watch as Nate expertly mixes us fresh gin and tonics, his strong hands pinching the lime quarters.

He plunks a cherry in each of our glasses and they do the back float, spinning atop the surface.

God, I *am* the other side of tipsy.

"Let's go into the parlor. It's nice this time of night."

NATE GESTURES FOR me to take a seat on the red leather sofa while he sets everything down, cracks open the French doors.

Now that dusk has arrived, the air has cooled and it rushes in, soothing my clammy skin like air-conditioning.

"This *is* nice," I say, my voice wobbly.

Nate perches on the opposite side of the sofa.

"Cheers." He leans over, nudging his glass against mine.

Untethered from the prospect of driving, I take a greedy gulp.

"Ahh, delicious."

"Ain't it, though?" Nate replies. He's the other side of tipsy, too.

"You making fun of my Texas roots?"

OMG, I'm flirting.

"Ha! Not consciously. Sorry, but your accent—"

"I know. It's still there, latent from years away from Dallas, but it creeps out when I drink. Or *drank*, as they say back home."

"Do you miss it?"

Yes. No. No, I don't, I realize. I'm surrounded by literal paradise right now. But, fucker that he was, I do miss Carter. I miss being held at the end of the night. I miss our frantic lovemaking. My plans—which I thought were *our* plans—for the future. The way he held my hand under the café table.

"Or should I ask, do you miss him?"

Sorrow grips my chest. "Yes. No. Maybe?" Sorrow, but also warmth. I'm touched that he's asking.

"Sorry to bring it up. Love's a bitch, ain't it?" He cocks his head; his gaze is direct, causing me to forget all about Carter.

"Well said." I crash my glass against his, take in another mouthful of the limey drink.

I wonder what's brewing with him and Marisol. If the cordial, supportive words he spoke earlier as she was leaving were all a put-on, an act. And, I wonder if he's hoping I'll ask about it.

I bite. "So, what do *you* know about love being a bitch?"

I can't believe the question just fled my mouth; it's followed by a shaky pause. But it's a fair question. Nate doesn't know, after all, that I've been witness to two of their searing arguments.

"Hmph!" He guffaws, shakes the ice around in his glass. "Miss Cassidy, you sure are full of surprises."

"Like?"

"Like being this direct, for one."

"Well?" I shrug; heat creeps up my face. "But who's being the cagey one now? You're changing the subject."

My stomach twists. It feels like a bit of a betrayal to Marisol to continue this line of questioning. Maybe it's not some sassy other creature speaking through me, maybe it's the alcohol.

Nate's expression grows serious, his jaw muscles tense.

Great.

This is one of the reasons I don't drink; I hate losing control in social situations. But before I can continue inwardly berating myself, his voice claws its way to my ear through the thick silence.

"A lot, unfortunately."

As with Marisol's gripes to me about Nate, hearing this makes me feel uncomfortable. Like I'm being pitted between the two of them.

I'm the one, though, that invited this admission in.

But I'm sensing that Nate doesn't want to discuss it further, which is a relief.

An uncomfortable silence begins to swell.

"Sorry to hear that," I say, desperate to put a pin in it, give the conversation some closure.

Nate stretches out on the couch, kicking his legs up on the coffee table. He glances over at me with a tiny, playful smile. "Oh well, some days it's like *Romancing the Stone*, and others, it's straight-up *War of the Roses*."

Or, *Who's Afraid of Virginia Woolf*, I think but don't say, thank god.

"Hear, hear!" I reply, raising my glass to him for another toast. "Also, huge Zemeckis fan over here," I say, hoping to pivot this whole discussion.

"Really? I mean, I am, too, very much so. But you seem a bit young—"

"Not when you're raised by a television."

"Bah!"

"Yep. My mother, good old Angie Foster, god rest her soul, lived half in this world, half in the world of celluloid. Film noir was her alphabet, but also *Giant*, *Cat on a Hot Tin Roof*, *Breakfast at Tiffany's*."

Now the alcohol has me bragging about my movie knowledge . . . to an acclaimed film director.

"But *Back to the Future*, *Romancing the Stone*, we had those on VHS. *Romancing the Stone* is practically my origin story as a writer."

"See what I mean?" Nate asks.

"About what?"

"About you being full of surprises. No *wonder* you're so great at story. Look at your origin story, your mother's syllabus."

"Yup, Angie Foster, mother of the year—"

"Hey, it gave you character, smarts. Sometimes privilege isn't all it's cracked up to be," he says, casting his eyes around his fifteen-million-dollar home.

"Well, I'd love the chance to find that out for myself."

"Touché." This time, he taps his glass to mine, slings the dregs down his throat.

Springing up from the sofa, he clasps his hands together.

"Time for a refill. I'm gonna dash upstairs, powder my nose—"

I crinkle my own nose at him.

"No, not *that*. I don't do blow," he says. "I'm jittery enough on my own, thanks. My college days at NYU were definitely less Studio 54 and more *Inside the Actors Studio*. Nerd boy."

I chuckle.

"I'll be right back, don't you move."

I REMAIN MOORED on the couch, vision swimming.

I need more in my stomach, so I swipe a handful of crackers off the cheese tray, try to hang on to the last remnants of sobriety.

I stand, stretch my arms over my head. Step out the open doors, suck in a huge breath of fragrant night air.

Above me, the faintest band of the Milky Way pulses above the ocean.

Unbelievable. I didn't realize you could see the stars at all in Los Angeles. You can't from my perch in the Hills, but, of course, privilege affords a lot of things like ocean views, a peek into the starry skies.

I've read that the air is fresher, too, along the coast. That the ocean breeze filters the pollution, which hangs like gauze over the rest of the city.

Yeah, I'd really *love* to get the chance to find out for myself if privilege, like Nate says, isn't all it's cracked up to be. From my ringside seat into their marriage, it certainly does seem as if it has its pitfalls. Maybe you become numb to gratitude, to feeling it. Maybe you forget how lucky you are to find the one person who *gets* you, who sees you, in the way that Marisol described her courtship with Nate. Maybe you become blind to the paradise that's all around you, if that's all you see every day. If you stay holed up in this house, as Nate does, immune from traffic, cut off from seeing people plead for money on the streets, from driving past homes with bars bolted to the windows to keep burglars from stealing what few possessions are housed inside, then yes, you have no hell to compare your paradise to.

I kick off my sandals, letting the dewy, plush grass lick the hot soles of my feet. Spinning around in the yard, I take it all in. Making sure that *I'm* properly grateful. Beyond the lawn, the ocean shimmers underneath the full, pale moon.

"Hey!" Nate's voice calls to me from the small brick patio. "There you are."

"I could stay out here all night. This is seriously amazing. And makes me not miss Texas at all."

In his hand is a white FedEx envelope; I assume it's a script that's newly arrived. "Lap it up. I'm gonna duck back inside, mix our drinks."

Oscar and Percy trickle out of the house and join me on the lawn. "Hey, boys," I slur. "What a pretty yard y'all have."

They both curl up, their bodies shrimp shaped, around my feet.

I join them on the ground, the damp grass seeping through my joggers.

Squinting at the ribbon of Highway 1 below, I trace it north with my gaze, wonder what Marisol is doing at this exact moment. Is she having a good night with Guillermo, winning them all over? Or is she still antsy, a ball of nerves? I'm hoping the former is true. If, indeed, that's where she actually is.

Love's a bitch, ain't it?

Nate's voice floats back in my brain.

They are definitely tumultuous, dramatic. Fight and fuck.

Percy nudges his head onto my lap, snapping me out of my nosy train of thought. "Heeey." I stroke his fur and a satisfied yawn sighs out of him.

"Ahh, they really love you."

I twist around and see Nate back on the patio, two glasses of glistening gin and tonic in his hands.

"And I'm pretty crazy about them, too. Beautiful boys." I continue petting them, then slowly unlatch myself, getting to my feet.

They trail me inside, plopping down in the cocoons of their doggie beds in the corner.

"I seriously get why you prefer to stay home. I'd never want to leave this place, either."

Nate hands me my drink. "Marisol does *not* understand. So thank you."

I smile, and again, feel that by engaging in this back talk about Marisol, I'm in some small way betraying her.

But also, I *like* Nate. We obviously get along, have a connection, and I should feel zero guilt about that. At least I *think* that's how Lexie would advise me.

I wish I could snap a selfie of me and Nate right now, sharing cocktails, text it to her—or worse, post it to Insta—but Nate would be mortified, I'm sure. Especially since he's so secretive, protective. And I would feel like a jackass asking him for a selfie.

"Seeing double yet?" he jokes.

"Try triple."

"Oh, boy!" he laughs. "Feel free to finish off the cheese tray. I've had my share."

I top a cracker with a creamy wedge of Gouda, pop it in my mouth.

"This is my last drink, okay? I don't want to get sick in the Uber."

"Totally. I'm barely going to be able to function tomorrow as it is myself. So yes, Scout's honor."

My eyes are drawn to the crisp white neckline of his shirt collar. And his deeply tanned neck next to it. I can imagine what that smells like up close, what it tastes like.

As soon as he catches me staring, I look away.

"Hey, so, back to my original question. Which we've successfully veered off course from. The sex scenes in *A Kept Woman*. Are they authentic? From, like, your point of view?"

"Authentic? Meaning . . ."

"You know . . . do they . . . gosh, I don't know how to delicately ask this . . . but just making sure I got . . . the details right? That it was convincing? And . . . a turn-on?"

The way in which his face turns crimson as the words fly out of his mouth endears me to him even more.

A turn-on?

Blood surfs through my ears. Only the fizzing of the tonic water cuts through the whooshing sound of my galloping pulse. "Yes, I mean, as I said earlier, you hit those out of the park. You nailed them."

"Well, thank you. Not tonight or anything, but there's a few of those scenes that I'd like to go through with you, to make them as compelling and believable to a female point of view as possible. I would ask Marisol, of course, and I hope all this doesn't make you uncomfortable, but I can't, obviously, ask her."

He twists in his seat, tugs the neck of his shirt down.

"I mean, I'm setting out to do something groundbreaking here, and because I'm labeling it a feminist erotic thriller, it *damn* well better be, or the wolves will come after me."

I snort.

"And by wolves, I mean the critics, obviously."

I love how this praised director can be just as awkward as me. Fumbling with his words. "No, I get it. And you're right. We're adults and professional and I'll happily be your tuning fork. There are a few moments, a few beats I can already think of where we can really dig in, make it even *more* for the female gaze."

Again, I feel like someone wiser, and far more confident, is speaking through me. Maybe it's not the booze; maybe this is a part of me that's always been there, lurking, but hasn't found the right person to draw it out yet.

This feels good, right. My chest is bursting with the possibilities zinging through my brain: refining this script with Nate, him wooing Marisol with it, the film getting green-lit. The trio of us in the French Riviera, shooting it. Me shedding my work as a personal assistant and being promoted to Nate's right-hand woman in development. And the crowning jewel of my rapidly forming fantasy: penning my own script and Nate helping me get it sold, get it made.

"Whew," Nate says, shaking his head. "Like I said, you're full of surprises, Cassidy."

My mouth forms into a grin.

His arm is slung across the back of the couch, his broad hand mere inches from the nape of my neck. In his other hand, a freshly made drink. He takes a quick nip, shakes his head again.

He turns to look at me, dead-on.

"No offense, this has nothing to do with you, but when I hired an assistant, I wasn't expecting . . . *this*." He makes air quotes around the word *this* with his fingers.

My heart staggers in my chest. "What do you mean?" I ask, thinking of me reading for him, of our attraction. Our pull to each other. Or, rather, my attraction to him. I can't be certain that he feels it, too.

"This. This relationship. You being so adept at reading, at scripts. At being a sounding board. Don't get me wrong, I love my office staff, I do, but . . . this is *different*. I feel like I *know* you, and you know me. And I don't have to wear a mask around you like I do the others."

A pulse of chilled air from the lawn rakes through the room, causing me to shiver. I wrap my arms around my torso and simply grin again, nod. If I'm so good at story, then why can't I find my words right now?

"Which makes this next part all the more difficult to say."

Oh, fuck. Here we go. This is what I get for twirling around their backyard in gratitude, for allowing myself to daydream my way into a new, glittering future. What is he about to tell me? What shoe is about to drop? Nothing good ever lasts for Cassidy Foster. I should've learned this by now.

A pair of floor lamps flanks the sofa. The light from them is buttery and warm, but because it's pitch-dark outside now, shadows streak across Nate's cheeks. His eyes have dimmed, his handsome face is grave.

"Cassidy," he says, my name heavy on his tongue, "we have to talk."

29

MY STOMACH CLENCHES. Unclenches.

Nate's face has grown even more serious.

Jesus! What the hell is he about to say?

Is this honeymoon over already? All his buildup of praise and his hints of seduction, and then, bam, *we need to talk*; this reeks of a classic breakup. Have I done something to piss off Marisol? No, surely not. She was hugging me just hours ago, like she was hanging on for dear life.

Is he going to reprimand me for being too flirty with him? Have I made him uncomfortable? Misread the room? Holy shit—is he going to confide that he's attracted to me, too, but that we have to keep things straight between us, professional?

I feel like someone's ramming a hot poker in my gut and I want to yell at Nate to hurry up and tell me, get it over with already. The suspense is killing me.

"Well?" The question lunges out of me like acid reflux surging up my throat.

Nate shifts on the sofa, lifts his eyes to mine. "What I have to tell you, to admit to you, Cassidy, is this: the real reason I hired you is to watch my wife."

The air feels as though it's been sucked from the room, sucked from my lungs.

What in the actual fuck is he talking about?

Out of all the wild scenarios I'd spun in my head, *this* one would've never, ever occurred to me.

"Whaaat?" I spit out, as soon as I recover, making sure I've heard him correctly.

His face darkens even more.

"What are you saying?" I bleat. The room tilts, my vision blurs.

Is he just soused? Liquored up and blabbing nonsense?

He tosses back his head, spews out a long, ragged sigh. Rakes a tanned hand through his dreamy hair. "Look, I know I must sound crazy, but just hear me out."

Batshit crazy.

I nod, silently.

"When I set out to hire an assistant, I wanted someone who would, I don't know, keep tabs on Marisol."

I honestly can't say I blame him. I mean, I've had my own suspicions that she's running around on him. But still. Hardly my place.

"You hired me to spy on your wife." I say it as a statement, my voice flat, deflated. "So, all of this other stuff, how does that fit into—"

"That stuff is *real*, you have to believe me. Once again, no offense, but I didn't expect to take to you so much."

I'm both flattered and offended.

"I didn't expect, for instance, that you'd have such a natural savvy for scripts. I didn't expect," he adds, waving his hands into the air between us, "*any* of this. Our connection."

My tongue has swollen in my mouth; I don't know what to say, let alone what to think. I shake my head, stare down at my lap.

"I felt bad keeping this from you. And I *do* need someone to just—"

"Spy on Marisol?" The phrase flies out again, rapid-fire, through my lips.

"Yes, I—"

"But *why*?" I press. He doesn't know that I'm suspicious of her as well.

"Well, she's a free spirit. And I in no way ever want to stomp on that, but, for some time now, I've feared that she's been sleeping with someone else. Behind my back."

His eyes glisten, as though on the verge of tears. In one hand, he grips a cocktail napkin, which he's balling into a tight lump.

I can't argue with him. Marisol *does* seem to be up to something. But I don't want to get even deeper in the middle of things than I already am. And I *do* feel led on by Nate, unsure if he really thinks I'm some crackerjack or if he's been playing me this whole time.

"This might sound crazy," I say, a trace of sarcasm lacing my voice, "but have you tried *asking* her?"

"Yes, of course. And she just explodes on me." His voice is strained and even though I'm so pissed at him right now, and hurt, I feel a ping of pity.

I, for one, know what it's like to be deceived. It makes you want to scorch the earth.

"Well, what does she say?"

"That I'm being crazy, paranoid. That it's all in my head. That I don't want her to have a career—that's the latest thing she's throwing at me." He hangs his head, shakes it.

"This might be a ridiculous question, but has it ever occurred to you to install a tracking app on her phone?" I stop short of telling him how I know all about this.

He picks up his watered-down cocktail, gulps. "Yes. But (*a*) if she happened to find out, she would leave me forever, I just know it, and (*b*) I've been scared to learn what I might discover. And (*c*) how could I confront her if I did catch her being somewhere other than where she told me? 'Hey, babe, I've been tracking your location and guess what, you're lying to me?'" He shakes his head again.

Everything he's saying is true.

I feel shaky, like I haven't eaten for days. Black spots form around the corners of my vision. My mind is reeling. "Look, I have to admit I feel a little deceived here."

Not a little, a lot.

"I know, I know! I can't imagine what you must be thinking of me right now."

To my surprise, Nate reaches over the sofa, places his scorching hand atop my own. My head spins even faster. "But that's *precisely* why I've come clean. We already have such a great rapport, I don't want anything to endanger that, and it felt disingenuous not to be completely honest, not to show you all my cards. As psycho as I must look." He gives my hand a squeeze before releasing it.

"Look, I know what you're going through. Been through it myself—"

"You have?" he asks.

"Oh, yeah." But I stick my palm up, signaling that I don't want to go into it. "So I feel for you, I do, but what you're asking me is—"

"Insane?"

For the first time in a long stretch, his lips lift into a smile.

"Absolutely."

He's still grinning at me and I can't help it, I smile back.

"Why not just hire a private eye? I mean, it's not like I'm a professional—"

"No, that creeps me out. Some stranger following Marisol, chasing her. That feels invasive, also scary. I don't like it—"

I know that Nate is a control freak and overly concerned for their safety, so I actually believe his reasoning is true.

"I just don't think I can—" I mumble, while my brain is shouting, *What happens if you turn him down, Cassidy? What then?*

"Just once. That's all I'm asking here. I'm not talking about a three-month sting or around-the-clock surveillance. If she's doing exactly what she's supposed to be doing and is where she said she's going to be, then I'll drop the whole thing."

I paw toward my gin and tonic, drag it over to me. The ice has all melted and the condensation drips into my lap as I inhale a watery gulp.

"Just once," Nate repeats, his face pained, his exquisite features crimped with distress. "Please, Cassidy." My name in his mouth melts my resolve.

When I found out that Carter had gone on a date behind my back with a petite blonde who looked like a former high school cheerleader, my world shattered.

I know exactly what hell he's suffering through. And, if I'm being honest, I'm morbidly curious as to what Marisol is up to, if anything. How she could trash this dreamboat sitting next to me on the couch. Take him for granted. I know I never would. But for some people, life offers an endless parade of gifts, of opportunities. Some people are immune to loss.

I'm about to agree to it, but my earlier thought is grinding against me like a pebble in my shoe. "I love working with you, Nate. I really do. This is like the opportunity of a lifetime for me. But I have to ask, will this interfere with the work we're doing? Like, do you *really* want my feedback on *A Kept Woman* or were you just priming me for this?"

The bold, sassy voice that has been speaking through me intermittently is back.

"God, yes. Obviously, I desperately need your help with the script. I'm trying to salvage my marriage here. The pandemic has been hell on all of us. I'm hoping she's just blowing off steam, not truly betraying me." His voice is shaky. "I'm hoping, as I said, that if she doesn't get the part, this will be a cushion for her, because she will be crushed. And that working together, the very thing we feared—the work coming between us—may be the very thing that pulls us back together."

From his corner of the room, Oscar thumps his tail, rhythmically like a metronome, as if he agrees with his owner.

The cocktail glass, though nearly empty, feels heavy in my unsteady hands. I bring it to my lips, pitch the rest of it down my throat.

"Okay, okay. But just the one time. And if she's up to nothing, please let's never talk about this again."

"Deal," he says, rushing in, as if he's afraid I might change my mind. "And if she *is* up to no good? Then—"

"Then I guess you'll have a lot more to worry about than what I will or won't do."

30

"SO, WHAT WILL this look like exactly?" I ask. "Obviously, I've never done anything like this before."

"Whew." Nate pats his palms together as if he's dusting off flour, as if he's about to teach me how to bake a cake instead of giving me instructions on how to spy on his wife. "Well, actually this Monday would be the perfect day. She's supposed to be having lunch with her manager, Lisa. They always meet at the Beverly Hilton. But it's just . . . they met not too long ago and I'm kind of not buying that's where she's really going."

Me, too, I think, but keep my trap shut.

"So as soon as she leaves, you could follow her there."

The room contracts. I'm still digesting the fact that I've signed on for this.

"You could park a little ways down on the street, and just . . ."

"Watch?" I ask, my stomach becoming uneasy.

"Exactly. Make sure that's really her destination, see if you can tell who she's with. Lisa Schiffer is her manager's full name. Google her.

She's petite, dark haired. Also, I have a pair of binoculars for you to use."

The outside air billowing in has turned frigid; I rub my hands together, trying to warm them.

"Chilly?" Nate asks.

"A bit."

He goes over to snap the door closed and as he does, the white envelope he was holding earlier catches on his ankle. He bends down, swipes it up. Latches the doors together and returns to the sofa.

Thumping it against his thigh like a Frisbee, he looks at me, anxious.

Which makes me anxious. "What is it? A new script?"

He shakes his head, whistles out a sharp sigh. "No, I wish."

He pries the envelope open, slips out a single sheet of typing paper. Hands it to me.

In the middle of the sheet is a single typed line in boxy letters, much like a movie ransom note:

YOU NEED TO KEEP BETTER TABS ON YOUR WIFE

My blood runs cold; my limbs feel even icier. I pass it back to him, wrap my arms around my torso. "What the hell?"

"Yep. Creepy, right? Somebody left this here, at the front door, a few months before I hired you."

"And you have no idea who wrote it? Who's behind it?"

"No, none at all. I'm used to getting FedExes, and sometimes the office overnights me scripts. Sometimes they arrive by messenger. Sometimes Marta will reuse a FedEx envelope and stash a script in there and deliver it herself. So I thought nothing of it."

"Yikes."

"Yes, and I didn't even open it 'til the next day. I was kicking myself because I'd thought about having security cameras installed around the property, but honestly, I'm old-school and the idea of being monitored freaks me out. Plus, we have good old Oscar and Percy here as guard dogs."

The unease in my stomach returns. *What the hell?*

"I was already suspicious of Marisol before this. She had been staying out later than she promised, not answering my texts in a timely way. Just acting, I don't know—" His shoulders lift into a shrug. "Dodgy."

Arms now clasped around my knees, I realize I'm rocking back and forth.

"Jesus, Cassidy, you're shivering." Nate exits the room, returns with a white chenille throw, and drapes it around my shoulders. It feels like a warm hug.

"Thank you."

"Then when I got *this*, well, that's when my mind really started to race. I knew I needed to start searching for an assistant ASAP, someone I could trust."

"And you have *zero* idea who sent this, no suspicions at all?"

He scratches the nape of his neck. "None. Wish I did. I thought about taking it to the police, having it fingerprinted and all that, but, I thought they might want to speak to Marisol. It just felt wrong to get them involved. I didn't know *what* to do, honestly. I guess I wasn't ready for everything to blow up. Maybe I was engaging in some magical thinking. Like, one day she would just up and stop giving me reasons to suspect her."

"That's pretty frightening, though, that someone would trespass, leave this."

"Agreed. And it's clearly someone who'd been watching us, knowing that these kinds of things are left for me all the time."

At the sound of the garage door groaning, Nate and I both startle.

He stashes the paper back into the envelope, darts upstairs with it.

I hear the clap of Marisol's car door, the tweet of her key fob. The garage door wailing shut.

Nate's feet drum along the staircase.

The back door opens; Marisol spills through.

"You're home early," Nate says to her, warmly.

"I told you I wouldn't be very late tonight." There's a defensive ring to her tone.

Her hair is wild from the sea air; I imagine them all congregating on some fabulous deck right on the sand, the ocean lapping mere feet away.

"Feels good and toasty in here. I was *freezing* out there!"

"How'd it go?" Nate asks.

"Uhhh . . . it went *well*, I think? But I don't want to jinx it."

She clocks me out of the corner of her eye, sitting stock-still on the sofa. "Oh, hi, Cassidy!" Her eyes drift to my near-empty cocktail glass.

"Heeey!" My face flushes as my greeting two-steps out of me, sounding like I was raised on a farm in deep rural Texas.

"Hey, hey!" she says, shaking her hips as if she's dancing. "Nate! You got Cassidy drunk! I love it!" She goes over to the fridge, rattles out a bottle of prosecco.

I watch as she fills a glass; my belly twists. "Care for a nightcap?"

"Ah, no, thanks! I'm pretty soused, actually." My voice slurs as if I'm playing the role of "drunk person."

"Yeah, we had three gin and tonics already." Nate's beaming, as if he's trying either to impress her or to make her jealous.

Sipping the top off her wine before it sloshes over the side of her glass, Marisol doesn't seem the least bit suspicious that anything might have happened between me and Nate. Or maybe she doesn't care?

"I like tipsy Cassidy," she howls. "You're glowing. Alcohol suits you!"

I feel both guilty at what all transpired with Nate and me, our *plan*, and also a bit insulted that she seems so unbothered by the fact that I'm still here at eleven thirty at night, alone with her husband, boozing it up.

But maybe she's just super secure. Why wouldn't she be? And also, everyone has always underestimated me, including Lexie. I'm the wallflower, the perpetual third wheel, the friend you can leave alone with your boyfriend because you know she's not going to do anything wild like try and go down on him while you're passed out in the next room.

"I wish I could join you in a glass, but I really need to get going—"

"Yes, and we're putting her in an Uber," Nate says, leaving out the part that he offered, that he was begging me to stay for another drink.

Marisol sets down her glass. "An Uber? It's almost midnight! Nate, have you lost your mind? I don't trust those drivers. No, Cassidy, you're staying here, in the guest room."

"But I—" *Sigh. I have never wanted to be in my own domain as much as I do right this second.*

"I insist. No arguing. It's actually my favorite bed in the house."

Moments later, Marisol is turning down the sheets, fluffing the pillows. Fussing over the room as if anticipating a newborn arriving from the hospital. I'm struck by the thought that she has a maternal side, would make a great mom.

"Here you go!" she says brightly.

"Thank you." I smile, give her a quick hug.

To my utter gratitude, she closes the door as she exits, leaving me in my own cocoon, though I can hear the murmur of their voices in the kitchen.

My buzz is still clutching me, and as my head hits the one-thousand-thread pillowcase, the room starts to spin.

I clamp my eyes shut, clasp the side of the bed. Now, my mind begins to spin. I ask myself again: *What the hell have I gotten myself into?*

I WAIT UNTIL seven to text Marisol; I don't want to wake her. I myself woke at four thirty this morning in their guest bed, and unable to fall back asleep—nerves alight—I came on home.

Cassidy: Good morning! Woke super early so I split. But I'll be there at 9:30 as usual!

I need to tell Lexie. But I *can't* tell Lexie. Which makes this all the worse. I can't tell anybody.

My cell dings and I claw for it, assuming it's Marisol.

But it's a notification from my bank, alerting me of a direct deposit.

I sit up, open the app. My first paycheck has just pinged through. Happiness bleeds over me as I eye the amount: $4,000: 2.5K for the first two weeks with an extra $1,500 for the scripts I've read thus far.

Back in Austin, my annual salary was 65K. With that, I was barely scraping by. Now I'm on track to double that amount. Sure, I don't have benefits, but still. What I do have is a gateway to a possible dream career out here and I can't blow it.

Even though I feel ill over what Nate has asked of me, he knows he's got me. There's a million of me out here, and only one of him. I'm a dime a dozen. If I had said no, he would've replaced me, gotten someone else to say yes. I don't feel like he's cold and calculating, but he *is* desperate to find out if Marisol is screwing someone behind his back.

I stare at my balance again.

I need him more than he needs me; that is painfully clear.

Before I close out the app, a text from Marisol lands.

Marisol: No, no, no. You don't have to come in today. Stay home, read scripts if you want. Or not. Lol! Nate kept you up too late, and I appreciate you babysitting him 😊. We'll see you Monday! Besos! 😘

Thank god. I'm *so* glad to have this time away, to exhale, to hide. I feel a prick of guilt again, a gnawing sense of betrayal toward Marisol. First the secret script, and now *this*.

But as with last night, I also feel a flare of annoyance. She just thanked me for babysitting Nate, as if I'm not even remotely a threat.

31

SUNDAY MORNING, ELEVEN fifteen. The sun is scowling, ferocious against the cornflower-blue sky, continuing its torch of LA. I'm sweating, sitting in the shade waiting for Harry.

I couldn't bear to remain inside the four walls of my garage apartment one second longer.

Ever since I got home from the Sterlings' Friday morning, I haven't left.

I stayed holed up, tackling the pending scripts for Nate—seeing my bloated paycheck with my reading fees included gave me the motivation to push through the stack.

Plus, I needed to occupy my mind, keep it focused on something other than the giant task looming on Monday. And once I immersed myself in the scripts, I found, again, that I enjoyed it, that my brain hummed on a different frequency than normal.

I'm eager to get to *his* script. To roll up my sleeves and really start working together with him on it.

I ordered my meals in, feeling flush with the extra dough, trying out a new Thai place I now love.

By yesterday evening, though, I was beginning to climb the walls, craving company, so I did as Lexie suggested and texted Harry.

He offered to meet for brunch today, so here I am, fifteen minutes early, waiting outside the café, good Virgo that I am.

Multiple times throughout the weekend—but especially in the evenings when I'd had a glass of wine—I had to force myself to not call Lexie, Nate's secret burning on my tongue, waiting to be spilled.

But as with *A Kept Woman*, I just can't risk blabbing any of this to her. Not yet anyway. It's too juicy; I'm afraid she might not be able to contain it, especially with the false sense of removal she must be feeling in Prague.

I can't fuck this up.

I don't have a partner who pitches in for half my bills. Don't have a safety net. Hell, I barely have a retirement account. It's so pathetically small that I stopped looking at the statements because they sent me into spirals of panic. Instead of worrying about the future, I need to keep my present in check.

I need this break. It may be the only chance I'll ever have to truly follow my path, make a name for myself.

I'm hoping beyond hope, of course, that Nate's imagination—and my own—has simply gotten carried away. That Marisol is as faithful as they come, and that she'll be *exactly* where she's supposed to be come lunchtime on Monday so that we can forget this whole thing.

So I simply texted Lexie that Harry and I were meeting this morning.

Lexie: Omg yay! Hug that hunk for me and have the best time. You're making me homesick. xxx

Harry wheels up to the curb in a shiny Audi, sporty and sleek but also sensible. I instantly approve of how immaculately the car is kept, from the glistening coat of wax to the bare interior, devoid of any clutter.

I haven't seen him in years; I wave both my arms overhead like a madwoman, in case he doesn't recognize me.

When he walks over, we hug. My throat turns into a burning ball and to my embarrassment, I realize tears are forming. I hug him even harder. Not only because I haven't seen him in a long while, or because Lexie told me to, but because I feel like I've been lost in a foreign land for so long and I've finally stumbled across someone who speaks the same language.

"So good to see you, Cassidy! It's been what, four years?" Harry is medium height with thick, wavy hair that's beginning to gray, even though he's only in his late thirties. Sexy as hell. On men.

"Yeah, for Lexie's twenty-fifth!"

"I still feel hungover from that night."

"Ha, same."

A group of us had started out at dinner and then migrated to a tiki bar, where we lingered until closing.

"Shall we?" Harry opens the door, motions for me to step inside.

The café is nestled halfway up Beachwood Canyon in a small strip of shops.

"This place is about as low-key as they come in the Hills." Harry slides out two plastic menus from the hostess stand, handing one to me. "I love it."

We're seated in a sunny wooden booth overlooking the sidewalk.

"Thanks for meeting me. I've seriously only hung out with my bosses since I got here a few weeks ago, so I was kinda going batty."

"I hear ya. How's that going, by the way?"

The waitress sets down two ice waters on the table. "Anything else to drink while you're looking over the menu?"

"Oat milk latte for me, please."

"One for me as well," Harry says.

"It's . . . interesting?"

Harry hitches up an eyebrow. "Do tell."

"I mean, I don't know if Lexie filled you in, but the couple I work for can be a bit tempestuous. I'll just leave it at that."

"Nate Sterling and Marisol Torres, right?"

I peer around the crowded restaurant, wish that he would lower his voice. "Yes. Don't get me wrong, they are *great*."

"It's not just them, it's this whole town. But I've heard that he's actually pretty sane. I don't know about her, though. She's newer on the scene. And Lexie said you're already reading scripts for him?"

Our coffees arrive, steam rising from the mugs in thin wisps.

"Yes, I'm super grateful. Like, this could be a really great break for me." I stop myself there from saying more. Change tack. "How's the music biz these days?"

Harry is a sound engineer and in addition to having a world-class studio in their garage apartment, he's also consistently in demand from the big record labels—Universal, Sony. He's worked with everyone from Willie Nelson to Jay-Z to Lady Gaga.

"It was a bit of a roller coaster during the pandemic, obviously, but now I'm busier than ever. And damn lucky for it." He blows over his latte, takes a sip. "Right now, I'm working on a Björk album. Which is fascinating. Some of it involves me actually walking around my property, recording ambient sound."

"Love her! That's so cool!"

"Yeah, it's good. And hey, I'm really happy you're out here now. Seriously, call anytime to hang."

"What are we having, folks?" The waitress is back.

I haven't even glanced at the menu, but I don't want to keep Harry waiting, so I order pancakes with bacon and scrambled eggs; he orders eggs Benedict.

"I miss Lexie so much. It's excruciating finally being here and she's halfway around the world."

"Same. I mean, I miss her, too."

"Couldn't you visit her? I've always wanted to go to Prague myself."

"Yeah?" He shrugs. "I mean, I'd love to. But, like I said, I'm super busy and who would take care of the kiddos?"

Lexie and Harry have a trio of cats with cotton candy fur and ice-blue eyes.

"Hello, moi?" I saw into a pancake, jam a hefty piece into my mouth.

"Well, now that you're here . . ."

"I mean, I could do overnights, but actually, during the day I'm sometimes there until late in the evening."

"Honestly, I can't get away right now because of work. She'll be home in ninety days. I'll live. And then, we get to plan our wedding and I'm sure by the end of that we'll both wish the other were halfway around the world."

"Ha! But I can help with the planning!"

"How's everything else?" Harry has chocolate-brown eyes that exude warmth. I get the sense that he's asking about my love life. I'm certain Lexie told him all about how my and Carter's relationship detonated.

"Honestly? Lonely. Like I said, I've only been hanging out with the Sterlings, so if you happen to know a handsome, good-hearted bachelor—"

"Those are a rare species in La-La Land." Harry washes down a bite with ice water. "But I do have some buddies that I wouldn't be mortified to introduce you to. Tell you what, as soon as Lexie's back, we'll have you over for a happy hour on the deck?"

They live in the Hills, too, a few canyons over in Runyon Canyon.

"I'd love that!"

"But seriously, in the meantime, I'm around if you wanna grab a quick drink, bite to eat, whatever."

"Thank you. It's just so nice to talk to someone else besides them, ya know?"

"I can only imagine."

32

TRAFFIC IS A snarl this morning and even though it's only nine, the air is already parched, the heat unrelenting.

It's supposed to turn cold again tonight, and I can't wait. The heat wave is amplifying my mood—antsy, tense.

Everyone on the 10 seems jumpy, irritable. Horns blare, tires screech, and fuck-yous are pouring out of windows.

Los Angeles wasn't built for heat like this.

I heave a sigh of relief as I get sucked through the tunnel in Santa Monica and spit out onto the 1.

At least I'm out of rush hour. Up here, there *is* no rush hour, no one hustling to get to their nine-to-fives.

I crest the hill that climbs toward the Summit, the Sterlings' neighborhood, hands clenching the wheel.

I'm supposed to spy on Marisol today? What in the actual?

I take a long slug of coffee. Not that I need it; I feel like I've done three rails of coke, or what I imagine three rails would feel like.

Marisol's supple figure springs into view. She's out front, watering her herbs with the hose, face shaded by a wide-brimmed hat and her signature oversized sunglasses.

She's wearing a billowy peasant dress, stark white against her olive skin. Her feet are bare.

As she waves at me, my stomach grinds with guilt.

"Morning!" she trills.

My pulse thrums in my ear as I make my way up the sidewalk.

"Hot enough for you?" I ask.

"You know, I actually *love* the heat. Not so much back home. I mean, we had central A/C, but some of the older restaurants and bars did *not*. It'd be sweltering. But I love the feel of it. You really should bring your swimsuit, take a dip in the pool."

"I will! Just need to get a new one. Mine are all pretty ratty."

"Fred Segal has a cute collection—" She stops herself, probably realizing I cannot afford to shop there. "You know, next time you go for me, just grab one. Charge it to the card. My little gift to you."

So many gifts. So many possible strings.

My stomach grinds even harder.

"Really? That's so generous!"

"Pshaw. What's the point of having all this"—she tosses her free hand in the air—"if you can't share it with friends?"

The rosemary plants are shriveled, the soil around them crumbly. As she waters them, it's as if I can see them drinking in the nourishment, standing up straighter.

"Nate told me you have *a lot* to read today, so don't worry about my stuff. Just make yourself at home in there. I'm going out in a little while to lunch and a few other places." She aims the hose toward a row of silvery sage bushes, twisting her body away from me.

"Okay, if you're sure! But if you need anything, just holler."

Oscar and Percy greet me in the entryway, tails swishing, faces prodding my hands.

"Hey, Cassidy!" Nate calls from the top of the stairs. "Can I see you a sec?"

"Be right there!" I set my coffee down, unslinging my messenger bag from my chest, my stomach tightening.

Plodding up the stairs, I feel as though I can barely catch my breath.

"Howdy!" Nate greets me, smile pasted on his face. In a lower voice he asks, "Marisol still outside?"

I already hate this, this sneaking around behind her back.

"Yes, she's still watering."

"Great, listen. As I said, she's heading, allegedly, to lunch with her manager at eleven. Just hang out downstairs, read, but the second she leaves, you go, too, okay?"

"Got it." I sigh, louder than I intend to.

"Just this once, 'kay?" He grins at me again. "And don't text me what you see—I'd never want her to come across that. Just relay it all when you get home. And here, this is for you." He hands me a small white envelope.

I open it. It's stuffed with starched hundred-dollar bills.

Nate brings his index finger to his lips, mouths, "Shhh."

I don't know whether to accept this or give it back. It feels like literal hush money. But Angie Foster's face springs into my mind. She might have been short on parenting, but one mantra she drilled into me was this: *Never, ever turn down money.* ("We're too poor for that kind of foolishness, Cassidy.")

She'd mainly been referring to the odd times Gran would hand me a ten-spot to run to the corner store, or when Lexie's dad would offer to buy me pizza. I always felt guilty accepting gifts, which probably had something to do with my low self-worth.

I fold the envelope in half, stuff it in the front pocket of my jeans.

"And Marta dropped this off first thing this morning. Not that you don't have a pile already waiting for you—"

"I don't! I actually finished them all over the weekend."

Nate guffaws. "You don't have to work on the weekends—"

"Well, Marisol *did* give me Friday off, so I wanted to jump in. It's nothing—"

The front door whines open; we both freeze and fall into silence, like we've been caught doing something naughty.

I raise the volume of my voice a notch. "Great, I'll just start with this one. And aim to have the coverage to you end of day."

"Perfect!" Nate's eyes widen in approval at my cover story.

33

BY THE TIME I reach the foot of the stairs, Marisol is in the kitchen, mixing up the dogs' food.

I slip into the parlor and curl up on the couch, begin reading.

Or pretend to.

It's ten. She must be heading out soon to make lunch by eleven.

I hear her bare feet climbing the stairs, strain to listen to her and Nate's muffled voices. But I can't make anything out.

I slide the envelope of bills out of my pocket, open it. Start counting and continue counting. Holy shit. There are fifty one-hundred-dollar bills. Five thousand dollars. Just for doing this once.

After a few moments, the ticktock sound of her heels stabs the stairs.

"Bye, Cassidy," she calls out, glancing at me from the kitchen.

I shove the money back in the envelope. "See you later!" *See you in five.*

My heart is in my throat as I wait to hear the garage door squawk open.

I leap up, dash to the front door.

Their driveway from the garage spills onto the street, far enough away from where I park that it would be nearly impossible for Marisol to detect me, but still, I creep into the front yard, then stealthily make my way to my car.

Hands slick on the wheel, I press the accelerator until Marisol's car comes into my view. I really don't know what I'm doing, but I reckon I have her obliviousness on my side: I'm not even entirely sure she could pick my car out of a lineup.

Still, when we hit the light on the 1 that takes us to Sunset Boulevard, I put on my sunglasses, tug down my visor to hide my face.

At least the heat wave is causing her to keep the top on her convertible, which makes me feel less exposed.

Marisol is a fast driver, I'm learning, and as we curve around the bends on Sunset, she darts in and out of the right lane, passing cars that are moving too slowly for her.

The time is 10:45; my GPS on my cell is indicating that our arrival time is 11:08.

We coast through Brentwood, and as we cross over the 405, I glimpse the Getty Museum over my left shoulder. Next we enter the storybook part of Sunset with the mansions, the palm trees, before cruising through the campus of UCLA.

I don't know that I've taken a normal breath since I left the Sterlings'.

Calm down, Cassidy, breathe in, breathe out.

So far, Marisol is heading *exactly* where she's supposed to be.

Over the weekend I did as Nate suggested and Googled Lisa Schiffer, her manager. Not that she's going to be out in front of the hotel waiting for Marisol. But maybe, just maybe, I'll park and walk in, try and get a look at them dining from a distance.

We turn off Sunset onto Beverly Glen, winding our way down to Wilshire Boulevard.

The fabled hotel comes into view: seven stories high, Mediterranean chalk-white exterior with the Beverly Hilton insignia in lipstick-red lettering.

I slow my car, wait for Marisol to turn into the valet turnstile, but instead of pulling into the hotel, she continues on Wilshire until we hit Santa Monica Boulevard.

My GPS—which I have programmed with an endearing male, Irish accent—is befuddled, the directions on the screen spinning as he attempts to reroute me.

Adrenaline zings through me.

Where are you headed, Marisol? I want to shout at her, warn her that I'm watching and to please reroute herself.

She continues down Santa Monica.

Damn, damn, damn.

It's 11:10 and she's definitely not going to lunch at the Beverly Hilton.

Maybe they changed their lunch spot? This area is full of posh places; perhaps Nate didn't know the latest plan. Oooh, maybe they're heading to the Ivy, that star-studded spot nearby.

But that hope is punctured as we sail past Beverly Boulevard, which would have taken us there.

I'm staying one car length behind Marisol, and drivers keep swerving in to fill that spot. Which is fine; it's a slow crawl on Santa Monica anyway.

I want to turn around, head back to the Sterlings', lie to Nate. Tell him that yes, she's having lunch with Lisa at the hotel, so can we just drop all this.

I hate it.

But, as much as I hate it, I think of his pained expression the other night, his exasperation, and I remember the sick feeling I experienced when I learned of Carter's betrayal.

As much as I'm tempted to lie to get out of all of this, I'm invested. *I* want to know what Marisol's up to, if she's a cheater or not.

I follow her through West Hollywood, and then scramble to change lanes as we approach Bronson and she weaves into the left turn lane.

What the hell?

Bronson is the road *I* take to get to my apartment.

For a few panicked moments, I worry that she's onto me somehow, that she knows I'm following her, is going to lead me home, have it out with me, fire me.

She turns onto Franklin, the next road I would take to go home, and my breath seizes up in my chest.

But my body relaxes, the wind hissing out of me like a balloon, as we continue down Franklin, past my turn.

Again, I'm wondering if perhaps Lisa picked a new spot. Maybe the scene at the hotel wasn't all that today? Maybe they want to go somewhere quieter?

The Griffith Observatory fuzzes past my window, and we continue down Franklin into Los Feliz.

Marisol then turns up a winding street, which corkscrews through the hills, sending my stomach turning.

We follow the switchbacks until, below in the distance, I see the metallic pond of Silver Lake.

We're away from restaurants and anything commercial, twisting further into a cramped residential area.

Marisol slows, finally, and parks in front of a red stucco home. It's modest, with a garage on the bottom level and two stories stacked on top.

I halt a good ten car lengths away, parking on the opposite side of the street under the cover of a stringy willow tree.

As Marisol exits her car, she looks both ways before sashaying up the sidewalk. The sunlight douses her—earth's very own spotlight on a leading lady. She's dressed in a nude-colored cami with toothpick-thin spaghetti straps, bronzed legs on generous display in high-waisted pink shorts.

She flicks a glance in my direction, but her face is swallowed by her sunglasses and hat.

She clutches her bag as she hurries up the walk to the front door of a house that is most definitely not the Beverly Hilton.

34

A MAN DRIFTS out of the house to meet her.

Tall, strong jawed, dark haired. Handsome from a distance. Could be Spanish, could be Andreas.

He leans in, grazes her cheekbone with the back of his hand, a tender gesture. She takes his fingers, brings them down by her side so that they're touching her thigh.

Shifts her weight, cocks her hip, a flirtatious signal. Their hands are still latched; she tosses her head back in laughter, their laced fingers swinging like lovers'. She tugs him toward her, kisses both his cheeks like she does with me, then releases his hand, disappears inside with him.

Hmph.

I can't tell if they are just very close or if there's something more.

I suck in a few steadying breaths to try to quiet my spiraling mind.

I still have a choice: I can start the car, head back to the Sterlings', and lie to Nate, sparing his feelings.

He didn't ask for photographs or any evidence; only my word.

Maybe he shouldn't be so trusting. But people have always trusted me, and for good reason. I'm good old solid Cassidy Foster.

I imagine him upstairs in his office, pacing the length of the room, wondering what's lying in wait for him; the suspense must be eating him alive.

I'm *so* relieved he instructed me not to text him. That would make me so much more jumpy, the back-and-forth, the barrage of questions.

I'm jolted out of my thoughts by the scraping sound of a pair of skateboarders zooming down the hill.

I check the time: 11:18. I haven't even been here five minutes and already it feels like hours.

Gauzy curtains line the front-facing windows on the bottom floor, obscuring what's inside, so that it's like trying to see through sheets of cotton candy. I lift the binoculars to my eyes. They feel like dumbbells in my grip, cumbersome as I hoist them up to peer through. I feel silly doing so, like some PI from central casting. Through the filmy gauze of the curtains, it's hard to make out much, but I can tell that the room appears to be vacant.

The upstairs window, however, is bare.

Through the lenses, the room—or at least the top half, what I can glimpse from my angle—comes into crisp view. It looks like a bedroom. I spy the top of a headboard, a macramé wall piece hanging above, holding a leafy plant. Other than that, it's minimalist, save for a wooden floor lamp.

But the lamp is off and the room is devoid of Marisol and the mystery man, as far as I can see.

I study the house. It's a bit shopworn; its blood-red paint is shedding and clots of mold splash the chimney.

The petite front yard is lush, though, a pool of sea-green turf blanketing the ground. Twin palm trees jut from the earth, their pineapple trunks standing guard on either side of the walkway.

I aim the binoculars to the bottom floor again, twisting the lenses to bring the room into sharper focus. Something passes in front of the window—a figure—but it's gone as soon as I've glimpsed it.

Sigh. This is so stupid.

I drop the binoculars in the passenger seat, pull out my phone.

Against my better judgment, I tap on Instagram, bringing it to life.

I haven't posted anything since moving out here; I've been in hiding, only hopping on to lurk.

There's a new post from Lexie. She's on a rooftop in Prague, ancient buildings knotted together behind her, a short blond woman tucked under her arm. In the selfie, they've got glasses of champagne raised.

The caption reads: `Night shoots are wraaapppped!!!`

She hasn't been posting a ton—probably because she's so busy—but each time she does, I'm simultaneously happy for her and filled with pangs of missing her.

What would she think of me if she could see me now?

I shudder at the thought.

I scroll through my feed, checking on friends from back home, and before I know it, I'm typing Carter's name into the search engine to pull up his profile.

But before I'm finished typing, I sense movement out of the corner of my eye, gasp when I notice the upstairs lamp has been flicked on.

Closing out, my cell thuds in my lap as my hands scramble for the binoculars.

Through the undressed window, Andreas and Marisol come into view. Okay, maybe it's not him, but that's what I'm going with for the moment.

My shaky grip causes the image to bounce, so I place the binoculars down, peer into the window with my own eyes.

Marisol steps to the glass, hair glossy, covering her shoulders like a sheet.

Andreas has slipped from sight, but Marisol stands there rooted, gazing out the window. With just my naked eyes, I can't make out her expression.

I lift the binoculars again.

She's staring straight ahead, hands planted on a slim table.

She twists her head back, as if looking over her shoulder.

And then Andreas comes into view again, standing right behind her, his hand caressing her hair, pulling it over to one side. His lips are now dancing along her bare shoulder.

From the collarbone up, she is naked, her shoulders bare.

With her perfectly manicured hand, she reaches behind her, grabs the side of his face. He continues grazing at her neck. Marisol's head falls forward ever so slightly, her hair now covering most of her face.

Her lips are parted, eyes closed, and I can't be sure, but I think she's rocking back and forth, hair swaying forward with each jerk.

No, I'm pretty certain that's what's happening.

I feel swoony, but I fumble for my phone, tap on the camera icon, hold it out in front of me, snapping a few photos.

Nate didn't tell me to do that; I'm doing it anyway, to study the images later.

The last pic I take is a blur because Marisol is moving away from the window with Andreas right behind her.

If they are in the bed together now, I can't see it from this downward angle. The show is over, and I'm not entirely sure what I just witnessed.

I wish I could stand on the roof of my car, get a clean view into the bedroom. To be absolutely certain. But what I saw was pretty damning.

I twist in my seat, trying to get comfortable. Exhale.

Zooming in on the trio of pics I snapped, I'm frustrated. There's no clear shot of Andreas, just his fuzzy form in the background.

Doubt creeps in like tendrils rooting in my brain. Was my mind playing tricks on me? *Were* they making out? Fucking, as it most definitely appeared?

It sure looked to me like she was getting it on with Andreas, unless, of course, they were reenacting a scene from the film.

Would they do that? He's not her acting coach; he's her *accent* coach. But maybe those lines are blurred?

It was *so* quick, what I saw; I can't really be sure.

He was definitely kissing her neck. But was that all? And what the hell am I going to tell Nate?

Before I can chase that train of thought any further, Marisol spills from the house, gushes toward her car.

Her brake lights illuminate—two red globes blinking in warning that she's about to take off.

I release the parking brake and slide it into drive, creep behind her.

I really *don't* want to keep doing this—trailing her—the adrenal letdown has exhausted me already. But I'm sure Nate will want to know where she's going to next.

In my bag is the envelope stuffed with five thousand dollars. One more stop, I tell myself, then I'm off to their house.

35

MARISOL THREADS DOWN the 101 to the 110 to the 10, heading west.

She speeds along and, like earlier, causes me to drive faster than I'm normally comfortable with, but I never lose sight of her inky bumper.

As she exits into Santa Monica, I'm forced to jam on the brakes right behind her as she stutters to a stop at a red light.

Again, I snap down my visor to shield my face, silly as it makes me feel.

After a few turns, she glides into a valet station in front of Blow, a high-end salon.

Whew. Perfect.

My work for the day is done.

At least this unpleasant portion of it. Now that she's in a seemingly benign location, I'm heading back.

As I twist through the canyon that leads to the Sterlings', I think about what I should tell Nate, how to phrase it, how to possibly shield his feelings. But no matter how I word it, there's no hiding the fact that Marisol lied to him about where she was going.

I'm moving up the walkway in the front when Nate opens the door, causing me to jump.

His eyes are wild and his hair looks messier than it did earlier, as if he's been clawing at it, twisting up the ends.

"Well?" He seems as if he's almost out of breath.

"Let's go sit somewhere and talk, okay?"

"That bad?" His voice is brittle, a bone china mug waiting to shatter.

"No. I mean, yes, but also, no." I'm flustered; I have no idea what to say to this man.

"Here." He gestures to the leather sofa in the parlor where we drank the other night. The fact that he can only manage to utter one word guts me.

I sink down and Nate perches on the far end, hands steepled over his nose like he's warding off a headache.

"Just tell me. Rip off the Band-Aid. Where *was* she?" he seethes.

"Well. It was strange. At first, I *thought* we were headed to the hotel. I mean, she drove there and everything. But once she hit Wilshire, she hopped on Santa Monica Boulevard and drove away from the Hilton."

"God *damn* it, I *knew* it." Nate's fists clench, pound the wooden coffee table.

I flinch.

"Sorry, I—"

"Don't be, I understand. But just listen, okay?"

"Okay, go on." He stares out the French doors, training his gaze to the sea.

"So, she drives to this house in Los Feliz, a little two-story red stucco—"

"Andreas's place. Unbelievable." He leans back, kicks his feet up on the coffee table, clutches at his hair.

I don't rush in with words of sympathy; instead, I give him the dignity of space, of someone *not* telling him how he should feel.

"I know his studio—which is basically his house—is in Los Feliz. I don't hound Marisol about that sort of stuff. But I've had an inkling about him. The way she talks about him sometimes, that sort of thing."

I nod.

"And it's so strange; they've been friends for a few years now. I just thought it was great that she knew someone else from Spain, so that she didn't feel so isolated here. But—" Nate's hands are trembling. He clasps them together to make them stop. "After I got that note, I began to pay closer attention to her comings and goings, naturally. And I realized how much time they actually spend together. And evidently it's *more* than I've even known about."

As he's speaking, he's staring straight ahead, as if in a trance, using the same disembodied voice one uses after they've experienced trauma.

I stay quiet, unsure of what to say.

After a few thick moments, he turns to me. "Tell me exactly what you saw. I *need* to know." He thumps his chest on the word *need*.

Sucking in a deep breath, I exhale, tuck my hair behind my ears, and begin telling him what I witnessed.

Marisol parking, getting out. Their affectionate exchange. Slipping inside the house together.

I have to force myself to say the next part out loud. "And this next part, well, I'm not really sure of what I saw. Even with the binoculars. But they went upstairs—"

Nate sighs, a ragged sound whistling out of him. "Go on—"

"And I saw Marisol at the window. At first, it looked like she might be topless, but—"

The house is stock-still, quiet. I can hear Nate gulp.

"Don't spare me, Cassidy."

"But *you* saw what she was wearing today. A nude cami, so that's why I can't be sure."

"What else?" His voice is soft, measured.

My stomach tightens.

"I saw Andreas come up behind her."

Now *I* gulp.

"And?"

I think of the photos on my phone but decide not to show them to Nate. They *aren't* conclusive, would probably just drive him insane. Plus, he didn't ask me to photograph Marisol, and doing so felt like trespassing, so I'll just keep them to myself.

"It looked, to me anyway, like he was kissing her neck?"

"Oh god." Nate's face is ashen, the color gone.

I don't have the heart to tell him it seemed like Andreas was taking Marisol from behind.

"I know. I'm sorry."

Instead of drumming his knees, Nate's fingers are now on his mouth, thrumming his lips, gnawing on this latest intel.

"How long did this last?"

"Just a few minutes, or a few seconds. It was seriously all a blur, and part of me hesitated to tell you because I'm *not* sure what I saw. Like, what if they were working out a scene?"

"Ha!" An angry laugh scrapes out of his throat. "Sounds like they were working out something, all right."

The scab that formed over the wound Carter made is now getting picked open again. In a very empathic way—Lexie's judgment of my use of that word be damned—I *feel* Nate's pain, viscerally.

The sting of it, the betrayal, the hollowness of *what now*.

Carter leading the tiny blonde out of the bar, his arm draped around her. The pair of them giggling into the warm Austin night. The kiss at her car, long and lingering. And then him following her in his own car.

The bastard.

As ambiguous as some of the details in my mind might be, Marisol and Andreas *looked* like they were together. I know he kissed her neck, I know I saw him sweep her hair to the side, I'm nearly certain I saw her rocking back and forth.

It makes me furious at her, and ill on Nate's behalf.

"I need some time to process this. Sorry, I don't even know what to say, what to think—"

I stand. "I'm so sorry, Nate. And even sorrier that I can't tell you anything for sure, so—"

"Yeah, but it doesn't sound *good.* Whoever sent me that note has most likely seen them together."

He hasn't made eye contact with me since we've been upstairs, but he looks at me now, his gaze direct, open.

"Thank you, Cassidy. For everything."

"Of course." I strap my bag across my chest.

I nod, turn to leave.

"One last thing."

I pause, ears ringing with dread over what I know he's about to say. "Since this time was kind of inconclusive, could you just maybe follow her one last time? Please? She's allegedly running around all day tomorrow—to the spa, to meet with her wardrobe consultant—"

Even though my throat constricts at the thought of trailing her again, Nate is right. Neither of us is closer to having the answer to the million-dollar question: *Is Marisol really cheating?*

And here is this man, laid vulnerable in front of me. I feel another flare of anger toward Marisol.

"Just one more time. If you don't see anything damning tomorrow, then I really will drop this. Figure out some other way to handle this. You have my word. Swear to god."

"Okay," I say, "okay."

I want to ask him, *But what if I do see something?*

36

THE HEAT WAVE broke in the middle of the night.

Driving over to the Sterlings' this morning, I don't even have the A/C on. My windows are lowered and crisp morning air filters through, helping to wake me up.

I park, lingering along the sidewalk, letting shards of oceanic wind continue to blast me.

Marisol pulls the door open.

She looks demure, hair pressed down by sleep, luxe figure hidden in a gray hoodie.

"We're just in the kitchen talking, come in."

I wonder what about.

"Morning," Nate says to me, not looking up. He's hunched over on a barstool, steaming mug in front of him; he's immersed in reading something. Looks like a script.

A heaviness hangs over the air, as if the particles themselves are having a standoff.

Marisol moves away from Nate, circling the other end of the

kitchen counter. "I'm leaving soon to get a facial, then shopping with my wardrobe assistant, so I've made a list of things for you today. Simple things, but, whew, here we go, it's kind of a lot. Work in the closet, pick Nate's shirts up at the cleaner's, stop at the pharmacy to grab Nate's sleeping pills, pop into Fred Segal. I'm going away this weekend on a little beach trip, up to Zuma, with the film people. Staying Friday and Saturday night. And, believe it or not, I have nothing to wear." She snickers. "Would you mind running over there today and grabbing a bunch of stuff? A swimsuit, shorts? Beachy stuff, you know? All my things are so last season. Oooh, and you could get yourself a swimsuit like I said the other day. Sound good?"

"Oh my gosh, yes, thank you!" I beam at her but try and tamp down the enthusiasm in my voice so as not to betray Nate, so as not to act like I'm on Team Marisol all of a sudden.

Her eyes scan the list. "And last but not least, dash into the grocery store to shop for dinner tonight—"

Nate clears his throat, sets his mug down with a thump. "*You* can run by the cleaner's. On your way back. Also, the pharmacy, too, is on your way home."

Marisol opens her mouth, closes it.

"*I* need Cassidy today." His tone is serrated; my face flushes from being thrust in the middle of whatever is going on between them. "I'm seriously considering this one script and I need her to read it today, tell me what she thinks." He winks at me, making me flush even more. Not because the gesture feels intimate, but because Marisol's mouth drops open again as she looks between the two of us. I feel like a pawn.

"Fine, it's just, I'll be gone for a *while* today." Her voice is raw, sounding on the verge of tears, and as I study her face in the pale morning light, I notice that her eyelids are puffy.

She exhales, cuts her eyes at Nate. "Remember about Thursday?"

she asks. He's glued again to his script, only gives a clipped nod in response.

"Cassidy, we're having this big table read on Thursday. For the leading role. So, it's a huge deal." Her eyes stay on Nate; he continues boring his own eyes into the pages of whatever he's quite clearly pretending to read, mouth gnawing on a pen.

She sighs, looks at me, and rolls her eyes at him as if to say, *Whatever.* "They've just cast Gael as the male lead, so he'll be there reading with each of us. They want to see who he has the best chemistry with." A devious grin plays across her lips as she says it, and she glances back at Nate, who remains still as a statue.

"I *love* him. I wish I could go with you."

"If I get the part, you'll be on the set all the time, of course. The whole shebang!"

I feel Nate's gaze on me like a dart, but when I look his way, he's dropped it. Ugh, I feel like I'm betraying Nate again by being excited for Marisol, but I *am* excited for her, no matter what she's doing in her marriage.

"Fabulous!"

"Yeah, so today, I'll be out. But honey, I'll be home in time to cook—" Her eyes reach for his, but he continues to avoid contact. Though crimson streaks are beginning to paint his neck.

"I'll start now on the closet!" I say, desperate to escape this marital quicksand that's sucking me down. "I'm almost done anyway, am itching to finish."

"Perfect. I'm taking the boys for a long jog this morning, so work in there now before I need to be in there to get ready." Marisol blows me an air kiss.

As my feet thud against the stairs, I can hear their voices, low and sharpened. Unless I stop, though, I can't make out their words, so I continue my ascent.

The closet is a mess. It's my fault I haven't finished the organizing job, but Jesus, it's as if Marisol tried on everything in her wardrobe and kept looking for something better.

Starting with the floor, I sift the discarded clothes into two piles: those that look as though they've been worn and need to be washed, and . . . everything else.

Next, I move to the top of the dresser. All her jewelry is in a twisted mess; I start at the left corner and work my way across, carefully untangling the delicate strands. I shouldn't be so judgmental: no one gives a shit what I look like, but for Marisol, her appearance *is* her work, or such a huge part of it. I can't even imagine getting ready to present myself to the world every day like this.

The TV screen flickers, but it's muted, tuned to CNN, and as I work I watch the news updates flicker across the bottom. When the time reads 10:53, Marisol pokes her head in.

"Yay! Looking great! Gonna shower now, get dressed, so if you wanna go read whatever script is ten miles up Nate's ass, now would be a good time." As she's done before, she corkscrews her index finger around her temple to indicate Nate is crazy.

As soon as I hear Marisol twist on the faucet, I find Nate in his office.

"Do you really have an urgent script for me?"

He's sitting at his desk and rolls in his chair toward the filing cabinet. "Yeah, mine." He grins up at me. "You have the remaining third to read, so I thought you could look at it while she's getting ready, before you, you know—"

"Okay, but not sure I can finish before then."

"Of course, but I *am* anxious for your thoughts."

I plop down on the sofa; he brings the script over to me.

"I'll be downstairs in the kitchen. I'll let you know when it's go time."

I nod. Ugh. I dread following Marisol again.

How in the world does he expect me to focus on this right now?

I finger the pages, scanning the lines until I find where I left off.

Esme has just learned that one of her lovers, a local sculptor named Damian, has been murdered. She walks home from the village, cheeks soaked with tears, and on the ground in front of her along the leaf-strewn path, she comes upon a photograph that has been shredded, pieces of it laid out on the trail like the breadcrumbs in "Hansel and Gretel."

A chill shudders over her as she pieces the photo back together. It's a shot of her with Damian, both of them half-dressed by the sea in a sensual embrace.

Fearing for her life, she decides to turn around and walk back to the village instead of going home to Theo.

Despite the more pressing thoughts crowding my brain, I find myself—as before—wholly engrossed in Nate's storytelling. I fly through the final pages, am sketching my thoughts in the journal I keep stashed in my messenger bag when he startles me by appearing in the doorway, no footfalls in the hallway announcing his presence.

"Jesus."

"Spook easy?"

"Obviously."

"Ahh, you finished?" His eyes are bright, dancing over me, his script in my lap.

"Yes, and it's *staggering*." I *don't* ask him if he's aware that, with the infidelity, his script, in some ways, mirrors his own life right now.

"Whew. Thank you. So happy to hear this, and want to hear your thoughts on the end, but—" He jerks his head toward the staircase, lowers his voice to a whisper. "She's about to leave. For her facial." He puts rabbit ears around the word *facial*.

I stuff my journal in my bag, weave around him.

"Can you come back here, right after?"

"Sure."

His eyebrows crease into a frown. "Well, whatever you see—if you see anything at all—it helps me, Cassidy. Please remember that. I'm trying to save my marriage here; I want to give her the benefit of the doubt, but it's tough. She's acting like I'm being controlling. Like this morning, right before you got here, we had this huge fight because I tried to pry a little about yesterday." He shakes his head. "I just need more intel."

My heart thuds against my rib cage as I climb down the stairs, catch the sound of the back door closing.

37

MY FINGERS GRIP the steering wheel as I tail Marisol up Highway 1, her Mercedes cutting up the slender highway, a black water moccasin skimming the surface of a river.

We enter the darkened tunnel that takes us to Santa Monica.

When we emerge, Marisol exits by the boardwalk instead of going left into Santa Monica proper.

I have no idea where her spa is, so I cling to her bumper, hoping, again, that she's too oblivious to notice me in her rearview.

We cruise down Main Street, the ocean brewing slow waves on our right. She jerks a hard left into a car park.

I decelerate, select a spot ten cars away from hers.

She hops out, donning a giant, navy floppy hat that nearly shields her whole face. Her signature oversized sunglasses swallow the rest of her face; it looks as if she wants to be incognito.

She's dressed in a simple white summer dress, copper skin popping against the bleach-bone fabric.

I scan the area for a salon but can't see one, so I'm forced to step out of the car, follow her on foot.

She heads up the sidewalk that borders the beach. The boardwalk is packed today; if she weren't wearing that floppy hat, I'd have a hard time tracking her.

Sweat pricks my armpits. I feel anxious trailing her on foot, like she can make me anytime if she just turns around.

I've got my shades on, but other than that, I didn't think to wear a hat, only my hoodie, which I hastily yank over my head.

The sea air tastes clean; the sand is the color of pale gold; I chide myself for not coming down here before now. I should be living, exploring, not having my life totally consumed by the Sterlings, but here I am, stalking Marisol, weaving around Rollerbladers and skateboarders.

My heart bangs in my throat when she stops, twists around.

I duck behind a tall man, slowly slide to the edge of the crowd, away from her and toward the beach.

She glances in the direction of a row of shops and restaurants, then shuffles across the crosswalk.

I quickly follow, afraid she'll evaporate into a building and I'll lose her.

I watch as she enters a place called the Water Grill.

Great, what am I supposed to do now?

I tug the hoodie down lower on my forehead, nudge my sunglasses up my nose, and head through the crosswalk.

I can't see her.

I have no choice but to enter the restaurant.

As soon as I clasp the front door, though, I spy motion in the corner of my eye, clock Marisol's floppy hat.

A waiter is seating her at an outdoor table that is semiprivate, shrouded from the street by waxy tropical plants.

Which is actually perfect, because she won't be able to see me if I stand right here, behind a giant bird-of-paradise.

God, I feel like such a creeper.

But this is no spa and she's clearly not here for a facial.

Poor Nate.

I hear shoes clacking along the sidewalk and nearly jump when Andreas brushes past me. He's dressed sharply in a button-down with designer jeans, his thick dark hair and strong jawline making him look like a movie star as well. Before he enters the restaurant, he stubs out a cigarette with the toe of his fancy leather shoes.

Marisol stands from the table, brushes his cheeks with her signature kisses.

I'm about fifteen feet away, can see them perfectly this time. There's only one other outdoor table occupied, and the couple seated there are at the very far end.

Marisol and Andreas have nearly complete privacy.

Except for me, that is, lurking in the foliage.

Instead of sitting across the table from her, Andreas takes the seat next to her. It's a four-top and they're both facing the ocean. Which makes sense; who wouldn't want that view? But it also tells me that they are definitely more than friends.

I lean against the wall, pull out my cell, thumb through my apps. Try to look like any regular twenty-something hanging out on the boardwalk. I even jam in my earbuds for appearance's sake, but obviously keep them on mute.

Over the clapping ocean breeze, the din from the street and foot traffic, it's difficult to hear their conversation, save for Marisol's burst of laughter.

The waiter sets down a pair of flutes filled with something pink and bubbly. Sparkling rosé, her favorite.

They toast and after they sip, Marisol leans into Andreas. He winds his arm around her shoulder, and just like yesterday, lifts her hair out of the way. Under the table, I watch as she places a hand on his thigh. Flings her sandals off, runs a toe along his shin.

Small, shareable plates arrive.

They eat, drink, and laugh. Marisol pops a ring of calamari into Andreas's mouth. From my perch, I can see that his muscles are ropy, strong. His lips are sensuous. Rose petals.

For a second, I don't blame her one bit. Andreas is yummy.

But then I think of Nate, home alone, upstairs in his office, doting on her every whim, trying to please her, trying to create a whole-ass film for her to star in, and my stomach sours.

I tap on the camera app, snap a pic of them together at the table. Marisol's head on his shoulder, Andreas's arm linked around her.

They very much look the couple.

As soon as the plates are cleared, the waiter refills their glasses.

Dessert is next. A tiny ramekin of crème brûlée. Andreas spoon-feeds Marisol delicate bites. He pays the waiter, then shoves the plate away, grabs her cheeks, and pulls her into a long, lingering kiss.

The other couple is gone and the waiter is out of sight.

Her hand snakes further up his thigh.

They pull apart, sip more rosé.

Then Marisol leans in, kissing Andreas. When they unlatch again, he cups the back of her neck with one hand, brushes her lips with his thumb. Kisses her again, a slow, smoldering one this time. His hand stays on her neck, fondling her hair. The other one travels under the table.

I snap another pic, ease back around the plant, feeling like a total perv.

My breath is jagged and my hands quake holding the phone.

I peer around the tropical again.

They are locked in another kiss. Andreas's fingers slowly crawl up Marisol's leg, tracing her hemline. He pauses for a quick, teasing moment, then his hand disappears inside her dress. She tips her head back, lets out what looks like a moan, while shifting in her metal chair; it looks like she's sitting right on top of his hand.

I aim the phone, take another pic. And another one. And another one.

Like yesterday, Andreas is now devouring Marisol's neck, his lips traveling along until he's nibbling on her ear as his hand continues to work, faster and faster, inside her dress, causing her to stir back and forth.

It's only because of my angle that I can see what they're really doing; a passerby might only notice them kissing.

Snap, snap, snap. I must have taken a dozen pictures by now.

I've seen enough, far more than enough, and don't want to get busted when they pour out of the restaurant.

I cross the street, sink my feet into the velvety sand, and wait until they emerge.

While I loiter, I swipe through the photos. They aren't grainy like yesterday's; they're crisp, sharp, in focus. Marisol's lips are parted, her head tilted back as Andreas's mouth pecks her neckline. Her legs are parted, too, as his hand roves beneath her hemline.

A cyclone of emotions roils through me. A prick of shame, for having watched them all but have sex, for spying on them, invading their privacy. An undercurrent of anger on Nate's behalf. And a red-hot top note of jealousy mixed with fury. Marisol has a perfectly good husband at home yet he's not enough for her. I get the feeling that nothing is. That's how cheaters are. After Carter played me, I read a piece in *Cosmo* about how serial cheaters are more likely to continue cheating. That they can't get enough; they can't be satisfied. They seek the chase, the thrill, and will usually continue the pattern of infidelity indefinitely.

It actually helped me begin to move on. The realization that Carter was a loser and a lost cause. Not that I'm totally over him, but the rational side of my brain can convince the impulsive side that I should be.

Marisol surfaces from the restaurant first, head swiveling left to right, as if clearing the street, making sure she doesn't spy anyone she recognizes.

She's heading across the crosswalk toward me, so I slip behind the pop-up stand of a portrait artist.

She saunters down the boardwalk, hips catwalking, the confident, victorious strut of a woman who has just triumphed in her life.

Andreas strides from the restaurant next, aviator sunglasses shielding his eyes, hand cupped around a cigarette, his lips inhaling post-coitally.

38

I DRIVE THE few blocks to Fred Segal in a daze, tumble inside the store.

Thankfully, I'm greeted by a tall young woman with impeccable platinum fringe and jewel-green eyes. "Help you find anything today?"

She exudes the same, utterly carefree Southern California vibe that everyone but me seems to possess. On her long, bony fingers, silver rings are stacked and her shapely arms are sleeved with intricate tattoos.

"Yeah, actually, I could use some help. My boss wanted me to grab some things for her for a beach trip this weekend. She's tall, but size two. A couple of swimsuits, cover-ups, shorts, whatever you think? Also, I need a swimsuit?" I say that last part as a question, though I don't know why.

She cups a hand, motioning me to follow her. "We've got a *great* summer line in the back. Just came in. Super cute stuff." She turns back, catches my eye and possibly my mood, which, at the moment, is the opposite of utterly carefree. She winks. "Don't worry, I gotcha."

In the jet stream of her pleasant, floral, spicy perfume, I trail her.

She delicately lifts items off the rack, hanging them on an empty one while muttering to herself—"*This* is darling; this is *so* hot."

I'm so relieved she's taking the wheel here.

"And you said you needed a suit, too?"

I nod.

"Size?"

"Six."

She takes a step back, lasers her jade eyes over me, from head to toe.

"You know what, I've got the *perfect* piece. Just trust me."

She heads over to the window, plucks a red bikini off a rack. There's barely enough fabric for it to stay on the hanger.

Reading the doubt on my face, she thrusts it at me. "Seriously, try it on. I know, I know, it looks skimpy, but I think it'll be super hot on you. And I'm rarely wrong."

Face reddening to match the barely-there two-piece, I vanish inside the dressing room. The top of the swimsuit *is* skimpy but halter-style; it actually looks flattering on me. It's the bottoms I'm nervous about. They're the latest fad, the "thongkini," which I swore I'd never get caught dead wearing. They basically show your whole ass, so I can't believe I'm even entertaining trying them on.

Fuck it.

I slide into them, twist in front of the mirror, checking out the suit from all angles. I can't believe it, but I feel sassy, bold in this.

I step from between the curtains and she squeals when she sees me, clasping her hands together. "Well, what do you think? Because you *look* absolutely amazing!"

"I feel . . . naked but also good, like, really good. I'm shocked!"

"This is my favorite part of the job, selecting things for someone that they would've never picked out for themselves. See how the high cut on your hip makes your legs look longer? And the top is exquisite on you. The coloring looks *so* good with your strawberry blond hair. Seriously, you have a great bod and need to show it off. Like fuck it, we only live once, right?" She leans in with her palm raised, slaps me a high five.

When the tag tickles my underarm, I check out the price. Four hundred and thirty-five dollars. Holy shit! I can't, no way. But then, Marisol said to get it and she knows the cost of things here, so screw it.

"I'm taking it!"

"Excellent! And the rest of these?"

"Yeah, all of it. She can bring back what she doesn't like, or, have me bring it back." I roll my eyes.

"I hear ya, girl."

AS SOON AS I'm back in my car, heading up Highway 1 to the Sterlings', my momentary giddy feeling evaporates.

Now I have to face Nate.

When I get to the front door, I knock.

And wait a few moments.

No one answers.

I'm positive Marisol's not back yet, but Nate should definitely be here.

I pound harder, and from within, Oscar and Percy erupt.

I press the doorbell and then it hits me: Nate could be on a Zoom. So I select their key from my key ring, twist it in the lock.

As predicted, Nate waves from the top of the stairs, points to his headset, indicating he's on a call.

Good. I have a little more time.

Smothering the pooches with kisses and hugs, I call them into the kitchen, fish a few bacon treats from a bag.

"Hey!" Nate calls from upstairs.

Adrenaline fizzes through me. I clutch Marisol's bags from Fred Segal, head up the stairs.

"Those all for Marisol?" Nate grabs them from me, sets them carelessly in the hall.

"Yeah, but she'll probably return some. I just grabbed a bunch—"

"I don't care about that; I don't even know why I asked." He tilts his head at me, runs his hand through his hair. "Shall we?" He hitches his head toward his office door.

"Sure."

We take our usual positions on the sectional. Weak afternoon light leaks through the room. Through the west-facing windows, the Pacific quivers below, metallic and silvery like spilled mercury.

"I can already tell this isn't going to be good."

My throat swells with emotion. "I—" I stammer.

Nate leans back, crosses his arms around his chest, like he's protecting himself.

"She didn't go get the facial. At least not yet, anyway."

He nods his head, a quick, jerky set of nods, a manic, jagged energy radiating off him. "I figured. Go ahead."

"Well, she went to this beachfront restaurant in Venice, down on the boardwalk."

"And she met *him* there, am I right?"

I suck in a shaky breath, force my head to move up and down.

I can't bring myself to tell him what I saw, to put it in descriptive language—I don't know, shoot the messenger and all that—so I dig my phone out, tap on the photos app. Select the first of my series, hand it over to Nate.

He reaches for it, but his eyes drill on mine, as if to ask, *Do I really want to see what you're about to show me?*

I raise my palms upward, shrugging. *Definitely not.*

He takes the phone from me, puffs his cheeks, and sighs upward, like he's blowing out a smoke ring. He's dressed in his signature white button-down and a pair of slim-fitting, charcoal-gray cargos. On the edge of his collar, I can see his jugular begin to pulsate, a raised river of stress.

He looks down at my cell in his hands, taps on the screen to wake it back up.

My eyes are glued to his. His face is turning the shade of cherry wine and from behind his glasses, his hazel eyes register anguish, but also, confusion. Not likely because the pics aren't clear as cleaned glass, but rather because he can't believe what he's seeing: that he has definite confirmation that this is really happening.

He swipes through the sequence of torrid pics, his mouth hanging open as he does. When he gets to the end, his jawbone tightens and he flings my phone back to me.

"I can't . . . I can't fucking believe this. Hearing about it is one thing, but seeing it . . ." The rest of his words die in his mouth.

I shrink inside. *Why* did I show him the pics? I guess because I know what it's like to see it with your own eyes. It lands differently; there is no more guessing, no more letting the person off the hook.

But I feel lightheaded, like I'm on the edge of a precipice, about to leap.

I just crossed a line. Marisol might be the one who is cheating, but I feel like I'm the catalyst in all this. I feel shaky inside, stupid for showing him the pictures.

And for the first time, I'm questioning my own motives. Am I really trying to help him or do I want to break them up? Does some part of me want to watch them explode? I feel icky, filled with shame, self-disgust.

I open my mouth and my voice creaks out small, tinny. "I'm so sorry, I shouldn't have showed you. Probably shouldn't have even snapped the pics—"

"No, no, no. That's not what I'm saying at all. I'm actually"—he scratches under his chin—"relieved that I finally know. Like, for sure know that they aren't just friends. It was the not knowing and feeling like I was being paranoid, controlling, and her fucking gaslighting me that was driving me over the edge." His voice wavers; his eyes have the polished look of threatening tears. "Oh god, who am I kidding?" He tears off his glasses, drops his head in his hands.

My stomach lurches as I watch him break down.

"I'm trying to put on a good face for you, but I'm destroyed," he says, his eyes still obscured by his hands.

"Nate, I'm so sorry. I truly am."

His torso quakes.

When he looks up at me, his face is slick with tears. "I feel numb. Hollowed out. I just need a little space—"

I spring to my feet. "Of course!"

"No, no, you stay. I'll be right back."

39

ALONE IN NATE'S office, nothing to keep me occupied, I squirm on the sectional, try to settle, but I can't. I'm jumpy. My insides are antsy, my body crying out for a long, punishing walk, but I have no choice but to wait for him to return.

I hear water running in the sink in the bathroom, then, splashing. Nate sighing. Clearing his throat.

I just tore his heart out and stamped on it. No, Marisol did, but I'm the reason he knows about it.

"Cassidy." He stands in the doorframe, his face splotchy from crying. The three syllables of my name tumble out of his lips in a sonorous, rhythmic way. "I don't want you feeling bad about this," he says, as if reading my thoughts. "This is *her* fault. I would say I want to be alone right now, but that's actually the last thing I need. I need a drink. I need to take my mind off this 'til I can confront her."

His long form leans in the doorway, his eyes twin orbs of resin, fawny and kind.

"I'm not going anywhere." I lock my gaze on to his. "I know exactly how you feel. Well, not exactly, I wasn't married to the guy, but still, it stings."

He nods; his eyes crinkle into a small smile but still have that haunted look to them.

"How are you going to confront her, though?"

"I don't know. But don't worry, I'll leave you out of it. I promise."

"Okay. And the pictures?"

"It'll be like I never saw them, okay? The last thing I want to do is get you even more tangled up in my crazy marriage than you already are. Let's change the subject. I will seriously lose my mind if I don't distract myself somehow. What do you say? Join me in the kitchen for an afternoon cocktail?"

"I'd love to."

"Can we talk scripts?"

"Deal."

IN THE KITCHEN, he begins making us old-fashioneds. "Cold front and all," he says. "Can you handle it?"

"I can handle one. It's three in the afternoon. No judgment, but—"

"Lightweight." Nate winks at me, then drops a block of ice into each of our highballs.

In the entryway, I hear the front door whine open. Followed by a thwacking sound.

Nate rolls his eyes. "I forgot Elana's here today. That's the sound of her beating the rugs in the front yard. I'm really grateful she never had children," he jokes.

As he stirs our drinks, Elana announces her presence even more dramatically this time, by slamming the front door, barking out a few sharp coughs. Her feet thud in the hallway toward us.

"Whew!" she says. "So much dirt!" With the back of her hand, she wipes her eyes, which are watering.

"Sorry, Elana," Nate says. She's the kind of person who makes you feel like you need to unnecessarily apologize.

She shakes her head, scuttles out of the room. Sneezes. Batters the baseboards with what sounds like a mop.

Nate places my drink on a coaster, slides it over my way. "I would say cheers, but that doesn't feel right. How about, fuck it?"

"I'll drink to that," I say, clicking my glass against his. "Fuck it all!"

Elana drums even louder against the walls.

Nate sighs, rolls his eyes at me. "Elana!" his voice thunders.

She thuds back down the hall. "Yes?" she answers, a look of irritation streaked across her face.

"You can actually go for the day."

"What? I just got here. I have the whole house to clean."

He walks over to her, smiling, places his hands on her shoulders. "I know, I just need to talk to Cassidy here."

She cuts her gaze over to me, looks at the drink in my hand, skewers me with her eyes, as if I'm the one asking her to get lost.

"Leave it, seriously. It can wait until next week. Cassidy and I are working on a script today, and kind of need to talk in private."

Heat licks my face as he says this.

"Suit yourself!" She grips the Swiffer in her hand even tighter. "Place is a pigsty, though. At least let me finish getting up all the dog fur." She shakes the Swiffer back and forth.

"Sorry, but not today. I can live with it. Thank you, darling." Out of his pocket, he slides his wallet, opens it. Tweezes out a hundred-dollar bill. "You'll still get your check, as always, and this is for your trouble today, okay?"

She shoots me another soured look but accepts the cash. Without speaking to Nate, she tears off the furry Swiffer sheet, discards it in the trash. Stashes the stick in the laundry room. Storms down the front hallway, wrenches open the door. Lets out an exasperated huff, slams the door shut.

"I can't even with her." Nate's face breaks into a grin. He chuckles into his highball, slings it back. "She's so . . . extra, that one."

"Seriously. I feel like I'm in deep shit and all I did was sit here."

"Shall we?" he asks, cocking his head up toward the second floor.

Warmth seeps over me again. I clasp my drink, follow him up the stairs.

I take my usual spot on the sofa while he combs his file cabinet for the script.

When he plops down, I notice he's sitting closer to me, his knees brushing against mine.

"So, the ending? Let's hear it."

"Like I said before, it's staggering. I don't think the ending needs any work at all, actually. The way that Esme transforms into a femme fatale just before the third act is . . . chef's kiss." I actually blow an air kiss at him.

"You liked that, huh?" His face brightens with pride.

"Yes! And the actual ending? How, after stalking Theo's mistresses, she actually befriends Beatrice? Has Beatrice lure him into that cave so that Esme can kill him herself? Five stars, no notes."

Nate takes a long, lingering sip of bourbon, keeping his eyes aimed on mine while he does.

This feels good; feels like it did the other night when we were talking story before Marisol came home, interrupting us.

"I worked my ass off on that. Like I said earlier, this was my pandemic project and I sort of walled off my mind and created this reality. Some of it had to do with wanderlust, with wanting to travel and not being able to—"

"Yeah, the scenes of the village, of the sea, are luminous—"

"And part of it, I realized while I was writing it, was taking Marisol and me back to the place we met. To the South of France. Maybe even then, I knew I was losing her." His voice shakes.

"Well, it's masterful," I rush in and say, trying to keep his mind off his wife.

"I'm *so* happy to hear that. Usually by now in the process, Marta would have read it and my whole staff would be swapping notes, even Marisol. But you're the only one I've shared it with. This is such a massive relief."

"Are you kidding? I'm thrilled you've shared it with me." The bourbon incinerates my stomach, which, I realize, is completely empty. Nate is sitting so close I can smell the whiskey on his breath as he talks.

"I want your notes—"

"I haven't even had time to type them up!"

"I know, I know, but just off the cuff—"

"Okay, my notes are bigger picture. Like I said earlier, giving Esme even more agency."

"For instance?" His bangs spill down his forehead as he leans in closer.

"I want her to be dissatisfied in her marriage even sooner. And stepping out on Theo much quicker. Earlier. So that it's not just all in reaction to him, but could have more to do with her own desires, you know?"

Nate bites his bottom lip, nods. "Wow, Cassidy, I don't know what to say. And I don't know how in the world I found you. So lucky."

My solar plexus splinters with fever. It's as if there's static electricity building between us; if he were to reach out and touch me, I'm positive we'd shock each other. His eyes probe mine, serious and level, but there's the smallest tug at the corner of his lip, a playful smile. He's probably just buzzed. Probably revenge flirting against Marisol.

"Welp, you found me because my best friend is well-connected out here, so it's her we should be thanking."

Nate's eyes stay serious. "I will send her flowers sometime. For real."

"Ha," I chuckle.

"Don't be so modest. You must know how talented you are, how special."

"Pshaw," I say, totally self-conscious but loving every second of it. I wave away the compliment, pick up my whiskey glass, take another scorching sip.

"And I was thinking, the sex scenes, again, are super hot, but we could have even more of them. Nothing gratuitous, but a few more of Esme. Because they're *that* good. I don't know how you tapped into the female gaze so well, but damn—"

Now Nate chuckles, shakes his head.

"Sorry, once I start talking, especially if I'm drinking, I don't shut up—"

"That's just it. I could listen to your voice all day."

The bourbon roils in my stomach, fire snaking up my chest.

"Oh, yeah?" I say with a kittenish purr. The booze has emboldened me. That and the fact that this impeccable man is being cheated on. I want to stay in here with him all day, comfort him, talk film. And more. Our connection is real, strong, palpable.

"Your thoughts, but also your voice. It's . . ." He rolls his drink around in his glass. "Sexy. Your accent."

I feel a tug toward him; he brushes his knee against mine again. I'm certain it's no accident. But then he stands, the last few moments between us a shooting star I'm not even certain I've actually seen.

"Well, I'm getting us another round. Then you can switch to water, eat, sober up. No arguments." The small smile has now spread into a crackling grin.

My vision blurs as he leaves the room. He is openly flirting with me—I know he is—just called my voice sexy. Our chemistry is so strong that in a parallel dimension we would've already started making out. My palms are slick against the sweating glass.

What is happening here and what is about to happen?

I feel a shift, tectonic plates drifting beneath my feet, and I know that whatever is coming next, I'm going with it.

From downstairs, I hear the crash of ice in the glasses, and on top of that, Nate whistling. Nate whistling like one does in a romantic comedy when they're drunk on love.

His feet are heavy on the stairs, most likely leaden with the liquor. When he enters the room, I swear another button on his shirt has been undone, exposing a tanned triangle of his luscious flesh. His bangs are still tumbling down and his cheeks are flushed, rosy and whiskey kissed.

My heart jitters in my chest, an engine revving, the rpm jumping just before the gear is shifted.

Instead of sitting catty-corner from me this time, Nate lands right next to me. After he hands me my drink, he slings his lean arm behind the sofa. The whole side of me that is next to him lights up.

I can smell him, clean, woodsy, his breath alcohol soaked but with a hint of mint. "So, I thought we could go through this one scene together, like, tear it apart."

I can't make my mouth form words and he's not looking for an answer anyway; he's leaning forward to grab the script.

He sets his drink down on the ottoman in front of him, flips through the pages. His face brightens. "Ah, found it!"

He passes the pages to me.

My eyes scan the words and I nearly gasp. It's one of the more scorching sex scenes in the whole script. Esme is lying out by the pool when Gabriel, the pool boy, comes over to the house.

She's lying on her stomach, hands dropped by her sides, topless. She appears to be dozing, but as Gabriel skims the pool, edging closer to her, she shifts, spreads her legs a bit. She's wearing a string bikini, the summer sun baking her from above.

She doesn't care that she's nearly fully exposed. Theo is at work. Or at least she thinks he is.

Gabriel approaches her chaise longue, greets her with a hello.

She parts her legs even more.

He sinks down beside her, begins massaging her shoulders, working his way to her lower back.

My mouth is so dry I pause my reading, take a sip of the old-fashioned. As I do, a strand of hair falls over my face. Nate brushes it back, his fingers sizzling against my cheek. I nearly choke on my drink. *Why is he having me read this scene?*

I don't acknowledge his gesture; I keep reading.

Gabriel is now raking his fingers up Esme's inner thighs until he's touching her on the outside of her bikini, over and over, making her moan. And more.

They never trade a single kiss in this scene, but somehow that makes it even hotter.

And then he leaves, not looking for anything in return, which stirs something in Esme, causes her to become all the more attracted to him.

"So?" Nate asks.

"Umm, I—" Desire mangles my voice. I can't even speak properly. I clear my throat, try again. "I think this is the hottest sex scene I have ever read."

"You're joking."

"No. It's exquisite. There are no strings attached, no expectation from the man, no pleasing of the man that has to be done—"

Even though my hair is still tucked behind my ear, Nate brushes his hand against my cheek again as if there is.

"So, no, there's no need to tear this one apart."

I've been staring at the script, averting my gaze from him, the words dancing on the page, but now I turn to him, risk a glance.

In the silky afternoon light, his eyes are resin colored, flecked with green slivers. He leans over and kisses me. His lips are firm, but yielding at the same time. Delectable, his kiss volcanic. I'm trembling, but I kiss him back.

He breaks away, flits his eyes to the floor.

"I'm sorry, I got carried away—"

He takes my hand, but it's more of a paternal gesture, a checking to see if I'm all right. He's still staring at the floor, head hung in what looks like shame.

But I'm already blazing inside, so I take his hand, bring it to my mouth, run his index finger over my lip. It's rough, rougher than I would've imagined, and it makes me want him even more. I begin to nibble on it; Nate groans.

What am I doing? What are we doing?

But I shush the voice in my head. This feels right, even if we're doing the same wrong thing that I've been judging Marisol for. I keep nibbling, then take the tip of his finger in my mouth.

"Cassidy." He slurs my name.

His hands are now moving on their own, clasping the sides of my face. His lips are on mine again, his tongue teasing and frantic at the same time. The room spins around me as he tugs me closer, so close that our chests are touching.

The sound of the back door opening, then slamming, jolts us both.

Marisol's voice wafts up the stairs. "Nate? Cassidy?" She sounds leery, as if she's somehow onto us.

We untangle, smooth down our clothes as the ticktock sound of her feet pummels the stairs. Nate moves to the other section of the sofa, catty-corner from me. Before I know it, she's at the door.

Her eyes lick from Nate's to mine. And for the first time, I detect a whiff of jealousy. "Hey, you two!" Her face has that blushing and glassy look from just having had a facial.

To my surprise, I don't feel a ping of remorse. Only a smidge of fear that she can pick up on the current moving between me and Nate.

"Hey!" I say, pasting on a smile.

Nate tenses, says nothing.

"Hey, honey!" Marisol tries again.

Silence.

The air is molasses that can't be stirred.

"Your stuff from Fred Segal is in the hallway!" I trill. "We were just going over that script, but I can show you—"

She doesn't even look at me; she keeps staring at Nate. "I'll look at the clothes later, but thanks." Her voice is small, sad.

"Well, I better be going," I say. She doesn't try to stop me.

"See y'all tomorrow!" I add awkwardly before scooping up my cell with the damning pics, blasting myself from the room.

I'm not even to the bottom step when I hear the tinder of their bickering, their voices puncturing the walls. I can make out some full sentences, while others are just blasts of words. I linger at the end of the stairway, ears pricked.

"You smell like cigarettes"—Nate's voice. "What the fuck, and also—"

"Nate, what are you saying? Come out and say it."

"Where *were* you?"

Voices muffled, footsteps traveling down the hall.

I snap to, head toward the front door. I step outside, but before I creak it shut, I hear Marisol shouting, ". . . trying to sabotage my big day!"

40

THE MORNING IS crisp, overcast. I'm wearing a hoodie that Marisol gave me and yet another pair of her designer jeans.

But a fresh heat wave is on the way, predicted to descend later this evening.

Marisol opens the front door without a greeting. Her eyes are blank, her mouth a thin line.

Shit. I bet she and Nate had it out.

I wonder what he said, how he confronted her. Of course he'd leave me out of it, but the frostiness coming off her right now makes me unsure.

"Hi!" I say, too brightly. "Look!" I tug at the hoodie, stick my leg out to show her the jeans.

She just lifts her eyebrows at me as if she doesn't understand.

"These are some of the clothes you gave me!"

"Ah!" she offers, but nothing else.

Her flip-flops slap the tile floors as she pads into the kitchen.

She grabs an espresso cup, sips from it. Doesn't offer to make me a latte.

"So," she says, studying a slip of paper that's in her other hand, "since you didn't make it to the grocery store yesterday . . ." A pregnant pause. "I thought you could go first thing today. I'm out of everything."

When she levels her eyes at mine, I detect fury swimming in them.

"No problem! I'm sorry I—" I stammer, my tongue a thick wad in my mouth.

She swats the air in front of her with the slip of paper. "No worries, but here's the list." It makes a scratching sound as she scoots it across the counter to me.

She's pissed. Her body movements are tense, jagged, and the edginess coming off her is almost too much to bear. I guess that's what she was talking about when she told me about her anxiety. But this is more like anger. And once again I feel like a pawn in their spousal chess game; I'm getting the shit end of the stick and can do no right.

"I'll go now, if that's okay?" I ask, trying to smooth things over.

"Perfect." She nods, but it's a formal gesture, her eyes never reaching mine. "I'll be leaving at noon for a massage. To help relax me for the table read tomorrow."

"Oh, that *is* tomorrow, how exciting! Are you—"

"I'm fine," she spits, her tone a scalpel, sharp, cold. "See you when you get back."

Sighing under my breath, I turn and head back down the front hall.

AT THE GROCERY store I race around, careening my cart through the aisles as fast as I can. I feel as if I need to make things up to Marisol, show her some extra effort. Even though it's not on the list, I swipe a bottle of that prosecco she loved the first time I had dinner with them, charging it to my own card.

Lugging the sacks of groceries into the kitchen, I find her sitting on a barstool, her eyes newly puffy. I wonder if they had another fight while I was gone.

"I got you this. On me!" I brandish the bottle of wine, slipping it from its paper bag with a flourish.

"Thanks, Cassidy." This time, a small smile glimmers across her face.

I inwardly exhale.

But as I unpack the groceries, placing the produce in the crisper, Marisol sits there wordlessly, studying her phone, the silence only punctuated by the occasional sniff.

"What else can I help with today?" I clasp my hands together, fix her with a grin.

"Oh, nothing." That cold scalpel is back in her voice. "Why don't you go upstairs and see if you can help Nate some more?" Another small smile rakes across her mouth, but her eyes remain like blanks, and there's a sour note to her voice when she says Nate's name.

Heat pricks my neck, but not because I feel bad; now I'm just pissed and sick of being punished for doing my job.

But you're not just doing your job, Cassidy, are you?

As if Marisol can sense my frustration, she stands, shakes her head, and rolls her shoulders like she's warming up before exercise. "Sorry, I'm just . . . there's just a lot going on right now. And tomorrow is important."

I reward her apology with a smile. "Of course! I totally get it. And hey, did any of those pieces from Fred Segal work?"

Her iciness melts a little further. "I'm sorry. I haven't even had a chance to look."

"Gotcha. And hey, thanks for the new swimsuit! I totally scored!"

"Of course. It's nothing."

"I'll just head upstairs, then? See if Nate—" I leave the rest of the sentence unformed.

She nods.

Even though her mood has seemingly brightened, she doesn't circle the kitchen counter, peck my cheeks with kisses as she normally would. But beggars can't be choosers; I'll take this as a win.

She's already intensely fixated on her cell again as I plod toward the staircase.

41

I'M SITTING OUTSIDE on my thin metal chair when I feel it, the first licks of what's sure to be the heat wave returning. The air, which was just cool and moist moments ago, is now dry, parched. A dragon's breath.

I'm sipping a frigid glass of chardonnay, my skin blistering from remembering Nate's mouth on mine, his finger between my lips. The way he moaned my name. A shiver courses over me as I think about it. And just like in high school and, later, college, I feel the compulsion to share this with Lexie, to validate that it actually happened. That I didn't just imagine it.

But, of course, I can't. Not right now. I have to keep this deliciousness to myself, see where it leads.

I feel oddly numb to Marisol. To how she might feel if she found out. I absolutely don't want to lose my job, but I guess I feel that since she's cheating—and that Nate and I have an obvious attraction—the math seems fair? I'm sure I'm supposed to feel more remorse for kissing another woman's husband, but I can't dredge that feeling up. I'm certain this makes me a terrible person.

Nate's lips were electric against mine and the biggest emotion I'm feeling right now—aside from my intoxicating attraction to him—is curiosity: Will this happen again?

Obviously he wasted no time confronting her. But I wonder what happened next.

I clasp my wineglass, give it a spin, inhale the buttery-sharp scent. After downing the remains of it, I head inside. I know I won't be able to sleep without help tonight, so I dissolve a melatonin under my tongue, plunge into bed.

I WAKE EARLY, sweat soaked. Between the ridiculous heat and a series of scorching dreams about Nate, I'm wrung out. But also, exhilarated. Ready to get to their house and test the mood.

It's Marisol's big day, her read-through, which should mean I get some alone time with Nate. God, I hope so.

Because of the temperature—they've predicted not only a heat wave but also the more serious heat dome—I've dressed in a pair of Marisol's cut-offs and one of her cute white tanks. I also slipped my new swimsuit in my bag before heading out.

When I arrive at their front door, I rap on it as usual. But just like the other day, nobody answers.

Sigh.

I try the knob before fishing out my keys. It's unlocked.

"Hi!" I announce loudly, hoping not to startle anyone.

But no one answers back.

My nerves are on overdrive from the anticipation of seeing Nate; hell, also seeing Marisol. My legs feel shaky as they ferry me down the front hall.

I hear laughter trickling in from the parlor.

Stepping around the corner, I see that the French doors are parted, and spy Nate and Marisol outside. Her back is to me, and she's wearing even shorter shorts than me. Hot-pink running shorts, her perfectly shaped ass cheeks peeking out of the bottom. Her glossy hair shimmies down her back as she giggles up at Nate, who leans against the fence, a lazy grin oozing across his face.

She places a hand on his arm, laughs even louder.

My chest burns with jealousy at the sight of them.

Did they fight and fuck as usual?

Did Nate just forget about the pics I showed him on my phone? About us?

Before I can even think about it, I find myself marching out there toward them.

Nate clocks me first, lifts his chin in greeting. "Morning, Cassidy!"

Marisol spins around.

But it's not Marisol at all.

It's Jessica. Her stand-in.

Now a sharper jealousy flares within me.

Is he like this with everyone? Aggressively flirty? Is what happened with us de rigueur for him?

Off Nate's greeting, Jessica twirls around, gives me the once-over with her Bambi-brown eyes that I can't help noticing are closer set than Marisol's, making her much less attractive than her boss.

"Heeey," she says. "Amazing that you're still here." She laughs into her hand.

A chuckle erupts out of Nate. "Easy."

She twists her torso back around, flinging her hair over her shoulder, preening in front of Nate. Again, she touches his arm. "Come on, you know I love her, too, but she's . . . a hot mess."

I rock my weight from one foot to the other. With her back turned to me and her position—standing in front of me and Nate—I feel walled off from him, unsure of what to say, what to do with myself.

After one more awkward moment of listening to their private banter, I swivel around, head back inside.

42

MARISOL CLATTERS DOWN the stairs, nearly bumping into me as I head into the kitchen.

"Hi!" She leans in, kisses me on both cheeks.

She's dressed in a green silk romper, legs flowing flawlessly from the hemline, gold hoops dangling from her ears. Her face is in full makeup, hair blown out and shiny. It's disorienting how beautiful she is.

And what a good mood she's in.

They must have fought and fucked.

Dammit.

But I'm also relieved she's being nice to me.

"You look adorable!" she says, scanning my outfit.

"Well, these are yours." I pluck at the tank, then the shorts.

"Just perfect! Oh, and I love *all* the clothes you picked from Fred Segal! I'm keeping everything!"

She hustles to the kitchen, the back of the silk shorts rippling across her impeccable ass.

"I can't take credit, I didn't pick them out—"

She's bustling around, cranking up the espresso machine, glances up at me as if she's listening, but her distracted eyes tell another story. "Hmm? Don't be shy about it, you're a genius, Cassidy!"

"Thank you." I don't have the energy to correct her.

I watch as she bangs the filter against the rim of the trash can—emptying grounds the color of wet coal. She hums as she flits around and I'm stabbed again by the thought that she and Nate made up, that all is forgiven, swept under the rug.

Studying her now as she bends to fill the dog bowls—her satiny hair spilling down, her immaculate figure—I can't believe I thought I ever stood a chance with him. I'm such a fool. Always have been.

"Will you help me pack tomorrow? For my trip?" Marisol asks, snapping me out of my self-pity.

"Of course! And oh my god, thanks again for the swimsuit from Fred Segal!"

Her cell chimes and she tugs it toward her.

"They have the best stuff." Her eyes are trained on her phone, fingers tapping against the screen.

Again, she's talking at me but not really to me.

Whatever.

My ears grate at the sound of Jessica's annoying laughter gushing into the room. She stares at Marisol on her cell, rolls her eyes.

Nate walks in next, wearing his headset. He catches my eye, points to his ear, signaling he's on a call.

I study his face, try and decode it, but he turns away before I can, exits the room.

Jessica has plopped herself down on a barstool and to my dismay, she's grazing on an orange. Smacking on the slices like she did with the grapes.

This bitch.

"I'm going with Marisol today to the table read. Super excited." She picks the white membrane from a slice, pops it into her mouth. "And she's letting me drive her fancy-ass car."

"More like making you." Marisol bumps her with her hip.

"Well, I do hate the way you drive, so—"

"Cassidy, what are you up to today?" Marisol asks.

I'm afraid that she's going to invite me along with them. Last week, I would've leapt at the chance to go, but now, I want to be alone with Nate, figure out what's going on. If anything is going on.

"I was going to ask you. Do you need me to do anything? Because if not, Nate has a fresh stack of scripts for me to read—"

A huff tumbles out of Jessica's mouth, like she can't believe I'm reading scripts for him.

"No, no. I can't even think about anything else today other than the table read. So yeah, make yourself at home, catch up on reading. Hell, go for a swim—"

"I did actually bring my suit, since it's so hot out."

"Yay! Yes, take a dip later. Nate told me he's going to be up there in meetings all day. So enjoy the pool. I might join you later. I can never get Nate to swim with me anymore."

Except for the other day, I think, bitterly.

Jessica's eyes are glued to mine. She pops another orange slice between her lips.

I stare back at her like, *What the fuck do you want?*

I don't like her, don't like that she was flirting with Nate.

He's a total snack, I remember her telling me when we first met.

But there's something else pulsing behind my eyes, bothering me. It's the fact that Nate was flirting back with her, and that same sourness seeps into my stomach. Does he behave this way with everyone?

"Enough, piglet. Let's roll," Marisol says to Jessica.

"Yes, ma'am!" She slides off the barstool, picks her skimpy shorts out of her crack.

Marisol dots my cheeks with kisses. "See you later!"

"Good luck! Not that you need it. You got this!" I raise my balled fist, plant it against hers.

"Thank you, sweetness!"

Another eye roll from Jessica. "Peace out, Cassidy," she says, her tone haughty.

THE KITCHEN FALLS quiet after they leave.

I don't know what to do with myself. I actually don't have any scripts on me; I'm all caught up.

Above me, I hear Nate's footfalls, his hushed voice. He must still be on that call.

Butterflies tango in my stomach at the thought of us upstairs together the day before yesterday. But then, he and Marisol seemed sunny this morning.

I don't know what to think.

I go to the bathroom in the guest room, check myself out in the mirror.

In the reflection, I actually don't look half-bad. It's amazing how much better expensive clothes conform to the body. Marisol's tank, which was probably two hundred dollars, curves around my breasts, then slims at the waist in a flattering cut.

I wonder if men do this. Surely they must, but do they constantly look at themselves through the filter of the world's eyes? A calculus that females, I know for certain, use to figure out how something might look to a potential lover, how another woman might perceive an outfit, how something will pop on Instagram.

The sound of Nate clearing his throat rips me to attention.

"Busy?" he asks, a teasing smirk on his face. He's still wearing the stupid headset.

"Just freshening up."

His eyes rake over me; his mouth hangs open. "You look great to me, no freshening up needed."

Every nerve in my body tingles. He's standing in the doorway and I'm wondering if he's going to come over to me.

He doesn't budge, so neither do I.

"Thanks," I mutter.

"So, I have a ton of meetings today. Otherwise, we could've picked up where we left off—"

My heartbeat stutters.

"—with the script." He looks at me carefully. It's as if he's testing the waters with me, not wanting to be the first one to acknowledge what happened between us.

And I get it; he *does* have to be careful. He's the one in the position of power. He's the one with everything to lose.

But I don't have it in me to close the gap between us, make the first overture.

"Gotcha."

"But I do have a new script. The office actually emailed this one—I'm printing it for you, should be finished in a sec. It's time sensitive, has to be read by end of day. It's from Nicole Kidman's company. I won't have time to read it, so, counting on your good judgment."

"Jesus. Okay. No pressure or anything," I joke.

"You got this."

The way he's staring at me makes my stomach drop, as if I'm riding in a too-fast elevator. Still, I stay rooted in my spot, safe and immune from being rejected.

"I'll bring it down in a sec." He winks at me.

As he pounds up the stairs, I hear his printer belching, then his ringtone pealing, signaling an incoming call.

"Yes, I hear that," Nate says, his voice still reaching my ears, "but it's more important to me to like who I'm working with than to get some hotheaded star. So, it's a pass from me on her."

He springs down the stairs, still mired in his call, passes me the script. Before he turns to head back up, he winks again.

My heart beats double time again and I sway into the kitchen, drunk off his attention and the promise of what it might mean.

But I can't. I have to wait this out. I don't want to show my hand too early. Hell, I don't even know what my hand is, other than being hopelessly, heedlessly attracted to Nate. A married man.

Nice going, Cassidy.

Settling into the parlor, I begin to read the urgent script, a television pilot with an ensemble cast set at a crumbling manor in New England.

It's good, edgy, atmospheric, but even though the writing is strong, I have the damnedest time staying focused. I literally have to force my eyes to stay focused on the page. But finally, I finish. Then mount the stairs.

Nate is parked in front of the computer monitor on Zoom; a sea of faces stare back at me. I creep away from the door, head back downstairs.

Fuck it, I'm going for a dip.

In the guest bath, I step into my racy bikini, grab a towel from the cabinet.

As I'm walking from the guest room to the kitchen, the blast of the A/C hits me, punctuating how much skin I actually have exposed. I feel naked waltzing through their house. Oh well.

Outside, the high noon sun is piercing, scalding, but it feels good against my chilled skin. I'm used to the Texas summer sun, how punishing it is.

I unroll the towel on a chaise longue, twist the umbrella so that it partially shades my face. My skin is fair, and I burn easy, but I'm craving a little bit of a tan.

Lying on my back, I close my eyes and breathe. Try to relax.

But every time I try to clear my head, Nate springs to mind. His kiss, the way I feel with him. More delirious thoughts spin: what would've happened between the two of us if Marisol hadn't come home just then? I let myself wander down that delicious path, pulse fluttering as Nate and I take it further and further in my mind.

From where I'm lying, I can see his office window, the set of French doors that opens onto the Juliet balcony. Squinting my eyes, I gaze up there, willing him to look down.

But I know his back is to me, his eyes trained on his computer screen.

The pool water gurgles in the filter and the hushed sound of cicadas buzzing in the heat makes the air itself seem like it's vibrating.

MY HAND DROPS to my side, jolting me awake.

Shit!

I can't believe I fell asleep, but I slept so poorly last night that I'm also not surprised. The time on my cell reads one o'clock. I've been knocked out for nearly half an hour.

My skin is sizzling, so I sit up, take a long drink off my sparkling water, flip over on my stomach.

Instantly, I feel exposed again, can feel the sun grilling my almost totally bare ass, and I almost decide to flip back over.

But Marisol is not due home until probably three and Nate is locked away in his room, so I stay facedown, the warm rays melting my muscles, making me feel dreamy, blissful.

This is why the rich have pools and no jobs: so they can do this every day.

I hear a car grumble past, but the hedges are so thick, it's nearly impossible to see the yard from the road unless you're parked right at the edge of the curb, or standing on the sidewalk, peering through the bushes like I did when I saw Nate and Marisol fucking.

The thought comes unbidden.

Did he get all hot and bothered with me and then see it through with Marisol, after their bickering? I cringe at the thought, but that *is* their pattern. Fight and fuck.

A creaking noise from above startles me.

I push myself up on my elbows, twist my head in the direction of the sound.

The French doors to Nate's office are flung open, and he's standing on the postage stamp–sized balcony, staring down at me, mouth curved into a flirtatious grin.

"Well. I step outside to take a break, get some fresh air, and . . . well."

Even from this distance, I can tell that his eyes are tracing my backside, my ass, my legs.

"Yep, just taking a break. Marisol said I could swim—"

I see him gulp. "And have you? Swum?"

"Not yet." I cock my head, daring him to come down here.

"I'm blowing off my next Zoom, then."

He disappears inside his office.

In what feels like seconds, he emerges from the kitchen in a pair of burnt-orange swimming trunks and nothing else.

His chest is as scrumptious as I had imagined, his skin burnished, his abs toned. A small trail of hair leads down to his waistline, and my eyes follow it.

Now I gulp.

I should flip over, shield my bare ass from him, but he's staring at me openly and fuck it, fuck it all.

Marisol really ought to treat him better.

He drops onto the chaise next to me, sitting on the edge. I slowly churn over, come up to sitting, adjusting the skimpy top so that it covers, at least partially, my breasts, which his gaze flits over.

"Wow. Umm, this suit. It suits you." His voice cracks at his lame pun.

"Thanks. A gift from Marisol. Well, *I* picked it out while shopping for her, but she said to."

"I'd say you have good taste."

As his eyes drink me in, I feel like someone has just doused me in gasoline and is about to light the match.

I don't tell him that I would've never picked out something this bold; I own it, letting him believe that this is who I am. Like the person who—after a few drinks—speaks openly and brazenly about scripts and screenwriting.

The urge to lean over, grab him by the back of the neck, and kiss him is fierce, but I tamp it down.

This is precarious. I know he's being cautious and has to be, but I'm being cautious, too. I've just had my heart torn out by Carter and I can't take another blow.

But he did come out here to swim with me. Another shiver sizzles over me as I think about what might happen next. And it's not lost on me that he had me read that torrid swimming pool scene.

"Shall we?" Nate stands, aims a shoulder at the pool.

"Definitely."

We wade down the steps into the water.

"Jesus!" I shriek.

I'm used to the tepid pool water of Texas; this feels like an ice bath against my skin.

We're hip-deep, but Nate dives in, swims the length of the pool, breaking the surface on the other side.

"Show-off!" I say to him.

"It's chilly, but you're also kind of being a wimp?" He mock-splashes me.

My top half is scorching from the sun, but my bottom half is frozen.

"Get in all the way or you'll never get used to it."

"Okay, okay."

I dive under the water, swimming toward him, heart barreling in my throat. The water burns it's so cold, but it's also refreshing.

When I come up, we're just a foot away from each other.

"Whoa! It's cold, but it does feel so damn good," I say, treading.

Nate's arms are spread out on either side, muscles sculpted while hugging the edge of the pool, and somehow, he looks even more delectable with wet hair.

He gently kicks his legs as I tread in small circles in front of him.

We are near the deep end. Figuratively and literally.

"Let's move to the shallow end; looks like you're out of breath."

He slinks against the wall until we can both stand. My breasts are just above the surface of the pool and Nate's eyes skim them again.

"So?" he asks.

I have no idea how to respond to this open-ended question.

"Well, I finished the script."

"Already?" Surprise coats his voice.

"Yeah, I read super fast, if you haven't picked up on that yet." Now I'm the one winking at him.

"Ha! Yes, of course I have. And?"

"It's terrific. Like, should you sign on to direct? You have to read it first, but it's this big, juicy ensemble cast, lots of tension, lots of drama, and the setting is moody, evocative. Like your films."

He's smiling at me in admiration. "You're a dream."

His words slice through me, cutting me open, making my pulse echo throughout my whole body. Again, I want to close the space between us, wrap myself around him, and never let go.

"You're not so bad yourself."

He cocks his head, studies me, really looking into my eyes as if he's seeing *me*.

"Cassidy." His voice is low, husky. "What are we doing?"

It's not so much a question as it is an invitation. His eyes are still locked on to mine, and now they're smoldering.

I don't think I've ever been this turned on in my entire life. I can't help it; I feel my toes spring me forward toward him.

Our chests are now inches apart.

"I can't answer that," I say.

"Why not?"

"Because I have no idea." My voice comes out raw, throaty.

I lean in, close my eyes.

His lips find mine. So does his tongue.

His hands move underwater, gliding up my sides, pausing just before he reaches my breasts.

He pulls away. "What are we doing?" he asks again.

Above us, the sun thunders down, torching us.

"You tell me." I lean in, kiss him again.

Longing pinches between my legs, so much so that I can barely stand it.

Nate unlatches from me but keeps his hands on my cheeks. "Wanna know what I sometimes do out here?" His voice scratches in my ear.

The sun has now slipped behind a jagged cloud, making it feel dusky.

Marisol said Nate won't swim with her anymore, so I wonder for a sec about that. Does he swim alone, instead, when she's not around? Is this part of the separate lives that they lead? But he's now choosing to swim with me?

"Of course."

"I love to lie on my back, stare up at the treetops, sometimes close my eyes and just float. Here, try it."

He says it like I've never floated on my back before, which is hilarious to me, but maybe pools aren't as popular in Connecticut as they are back home?

I do as he says, taking in oxygen to help buoy me. His hands skitter across my back, supporting me. "I'll hold you."

He's at my side. I feel my bikini bottom riding up, and as I put my hands over my head, my top inches up, too, so that the bottoms of my breasts are peeking out. I don't try to adjust it.

"Oh, Cassidy, you are so beautiful." His breath is rapid, quick, as if he's treading water instead of just standing here still, holding me.

Even though my eyes are closed to block out the sun, I can feel his raking over me from the way his voice is aimed.

"Really?" I ask, genuinely surprised. Because compared to his wife, I am *not* beautiful.

"Yes. Your skin, for starters, is just gorgeous. Peaches and cream. And your hair. And, of course, your body. I hope you know that. You're not some LA beauty but a real beauty. Stunning, unfiltered."

I want to say, *Well, so is your wife*, but I don't.

Instead, I ask, "What happened the other day, after I left?"

A serrated sigh; I feel his hands shift beneath me. "The usual. I tried to question her, she gaslighted me. I'm so over it."

Did you fight and fuck? I want to ask. But clamp my mouth shut.

After a second, I ask, "Y'all seemed fine this morning. You seemed chipper, actually."

I want to spear him with a question about Jessica, but decide not to ruin this golden moment.

"An act. All of it. It's her big day and no matter what she accuses me of, and what she's doing to us, I would never spoil that for her."

One of his hands grazes up my side. His fingers are now on my shoulder, teasing the top of my strap. I'm absolute putty in his hands.

With his other broad hand, he starts to spin me slowly, until I'm facing him. Both his hands now rove to my hips, pulling me into him. I'm still on my back—he's going to have to do everything from this point on—but I wrap my legs around his waist, feel him against me, stiff.

"Cassidy." My name comes out as a moan.

Ever so slightly, he starts to move against me, and everything inside me catches fire. I open my eyes and the sun, still buried behind the cloud, pulses. The treetops seem to pulse, too; the sawing of the cicadas swells.

Everything is alive.

I'm about to sit up, move the rest of my body closer to his, when I hear the back door snap open.

His hands drop and my feet thud to the bottom of the pool.

I snap my torso up, come fully upright.

Standing in the doorway, hands on her hips, is Marisol.

Her eyes are a lancet, moving between me and Nate.

My face scorches with shame.

But really, other than him holding me while I was floating, what could she have seen from that distance? All the action was happening underwater, thank goodness, hopefully a blurry mess from her vantage point.

"Nate? What are you doing?" Her voice is a lancet, too, cutting, sharp.

I feel a twinge of guilt, but more than guilt, just pure shame at being caught.

"I was just helping Cassidy learn to float. Believe it or not, she's kind of a beginner."

Marisol snorts. "Sure. Cassidy," she says, her words cold and weighted, "you can leave now."

Fuck.

I scramble up the steps and as I do, Marisol takes in my scanty swimsuit.

"Thanks for this." I tug at the side of my suit. "I really love it."

But she greets my effort with silence and I can feel her eyes skewering me as I walk.

Wrapping myself in a towel, I do the walk of shame in front of them, slithering inside the house.

"Well, how'd it go?" Nate asks Marisol, casual, playful, as if she didn't just walk in on something.

I purposefully left the door cracked, so I could hear them.

"You've got to be fucking kidding me," Marisol says, her words coming out of her like machine-gun fire.

"What? What's the big deal?"

"What were you doing with her, exactly?"

A pregnant pause.

I hold my breath.

"Nothing. I told you, showing her how to float—"

"Tsk."

"I know, I know it might've looked bad, but we were both taking a break. We just happened to take one at the same time."

"Well, you better watch it with your little lapdog. She may not be as innocent as she seems, or acts."

"She's done nothing wrong."

Pride washes over me; Nate's taking up for me, even if what he's saying is a lie.

"Whatever—"

"Yeah, you're one to talk—"

I feel their voices creeping closer, so I rush to the guest room, peel off my wet swimsuit. Fully towel off, then toss on my clothes as fast as I can. Grab my bag and escape out the front door.

43

MY CAR CRAWLS to a stop in the Sterlings' cul-de-sac.

Ugh. I don't want to be here, don't want to face Marisol. But at least she's leaving town at lunchtime to head to her beach bash.

I can't believe Nate and I got interrupted again yesterday by her. More than disgraced right now, I'm pissed that what we were getting up to was cut short, as awful as that sounds.

I know it's irrational of me to fantasize any further than making out with him—I could just be a rebound; he could just be blowing off steam—but I can't help it. My thoughts snake to a future of working with him, being with him, rationality be damned.

But when Marisol opens the door, my fantasy is immediately dashed.

She's positively glowing, dressed in a pair of shorts and a flowing, slightly revealing top from my Fred Segal run.

I'm no match for her, and I'm ludicrous for even entertaining anything beyond a fling with Nate.

As dashed as I am, though, I'm equally relieved. I don't want some huge confrontation with her. I honestly didn't know if she was going to answer the door with a knife in her hand, dagger me for fucking around with her husband. I would have.

He must have smoothed everything over; I shudder inside to think what that might look like.

"Hiiii!" she chimes.

"Good morning," I say in a measured tone, unsure of how to behave.

"Listen, first off," she says, leading me by the hand to the front living room, then lowering her voice, "about yesterday, I was just pissed. Don't take it personally, okay?"

"So, you're not mad? I know it looked weird, but we were—" My tongue tumbles in my mouth.

"God, no," she says, as if it's the most ridiculous thought in the world.

Wow. Even after what she witnessed—which I know was ambiguous; thank god we were no longer kissing—she's still not jealous of me.

She grabs me into a hug, then takes me by the shoulders, levels her eyes with mine. "Cassidy, I trust you implicitly, okay?"

"Okay, good!" I say, beaming at her, feeling a pinch of guilt for two-timing her.

"But . . . the deal is, if I don't make a fuss, Nate gets insecure, ya know? So, like, I'm an actress? And sometimes I act. I learned this a long time ago and you will learn it soon enough: men's egos are as fragile as glass, so you have to sometimes put on a little show. Make a fuss."

I want to feel nothing but pure relief, but instead I feel deflated, dismissed: I'm no threat to Marisol Torres and she's letting me know it, in the nicest possible way. Or the most passive-aggressive. I can't tell. But she genuinely seems unfazed.

"I guess I have a lot to learn, but whew, you sure fooled me," I shoot back, hoping to dagger her just a little, even though I know I'm walking a dangerous line here.

"I can pour it on thick when I need to. It's how you handle them, how you stay in control." She winks at me, tilts her head, gives me a small smile like she feels pity for me for not grasping the world—and men—like she does. "Just remember: male ego, fragile as glass." Another wink and she's off down the hallway.

Her winks, and her words, not only make me feel small, they chill me, let me know just how very manipulative she can be.

Her hips sway slightly, all but prancing in her delicate sandals into the kitchen. She smells of her signature sugary scent and her sumptuous breasts peek from the top of her silky, low-cut blouse.

Today I dressed demurely—my own cargos and a T-shirt, to not draw any attention to myself. Being in the kitchen with her, I feel positively dowdy, plain.

"So, you'll help me pack? I wanna get an early start. Friday traffic on the 1 and all. And after that, you're free to go. Nate's going to be crammed with meetings all day." An almost imperceptible smirk tugs across her face.

Is she fucking with me? Marking her territory?

"Okay, sure."

"But first, I'm gonna walk these pooches since I'm going to be away all weekend. Back in twenty. You can just hang here if you want."

I smile.

After I hear the front door close I move up the stairs, quickly.

Nate's in his office, but not on the phone or a Zoom; he's sitting peacefully on the sectional, reading a script.

"Cassidy," he says, removing his glasses. His voice is warm.

"Hey, so, real quick, Marisol's out with the dogs. Is . . . everything cool?"

He puffs up his cheeks, lets out a sigh. "Define cool?" He grins at me.

"I mean from yesterday, from us—"

"Yeah, I *guess*? I'm not sure what she actually thinks, but probably because she knows she's actively fucking some guy behind my back—or damn near close to it—she could only question me so far without getting into dangerous territory herself."

"I better go back down; she'll be back in a sec. Also, she wants me to leave after I've helped her pack. Which, if you ask me, is kind of strange if she's cool with everything. But she's acting to me like it is so—" I pause, not wanting to tell him the rest of what she and I talked about, obviously.

"Who knows."

"So, I guess I'll see you again on Monday?"

"I was actually thinking . . ." he starts, then nibbles on the end of a pen.

I can't breathe. I'm sure this is it; he's gonna tell me not to come back, that I'm fired. That this is all too sticky.

"That I should take you to dinner Saturday night."

My stomach drops ten floors.

"Just you and me. Give us a chance to really go through the script, and—" He keeps gnawing on the pen, doesn't finish his sentence, but rather, raises his shoulders in a shrug as if to say, *We'll see.*

Sunlight spatters through the windows; my vision blurs.

Nate has just asked me out.

While Marisol is going to be out of town.

"I'd love that," I finally say. "Very much."

"Me, too." His eyes linger on mine. "Come over at seven? We'll go somewhere quiet, chill."

What he means to say is, we'll go somewhere where he hopefully won't be recognized.

"Sounds fabulous," I blurt out, before he changes his mind.

I turn to leave.

"Oh, and Cassidy, feel free to wear something nice. I'm not just taking you to Fatburger. I mean, you don't have to dress up, that's not what I'm saying, but—"

"I gotcha," I say, letting him off the hook.

His schoolboy shyness and rambling are so endearing; I would cross the room, leap in his lap if Marisol weren't about to walk through the front door.

44

IT'S SATURDAY. TEN a.m. I've been up since six, unable to sleep, my whole body buzzing, thrumming with excitement over my date tonight with Nate.

A date! With Nate!

A real date. Not stolen moments in his office or a tryst in the pool while Mommy's gone.

No. He asked me out.

I still can't believe it.

Now that the stores are open, I'm going shopping for something for tonight. Obviously, it doesn't feel right to wear one of Marisol's hand-me-downs.

I head to Anthropologie. The prices make my teeth grit, but I can usually count on a worthy splurge, so I scour the color-laden store, grabbing as many items off the rack as I can carry.

Once I'm in a fitting room, I narrow my options.

A hot-pink summer dress, or a white romper, with a cut-out stomach.

I try both on, checking myself out from every angle.

Ugh, I can't decide.

I whip out my phone, snap a pic of me in each outfit, text them to Lexie, praying she's near her cell.

Cassidy: Halp! Haaalp meee. Which one looks best?

To my glee, I see her typing back right away.

Lexie: Love 'em both. What's this for?

Fuck. I hesitate. Then say fuck it.

Cassidy: Actually . . . well . . . I didn't want to tell you just yet but Nate is taking me out to dinner tonight.

Lexie: ???

Lexie: !!!

Lexie: Lol . . .

Cassidy: I know, I KNOW.

Lexie: Just the two of you? Where's the wifey?

Cassidy: Out of town . . .

Lexie: what?!?!

Cassidy: I know . . . omg . . .

A lull. I wonder what's going through Lexie's head right now.

Then, a few seconds later, her text pings through.

Lexie: Okaaay . . . just . . . I don't know. Be careful. You know how you can be.

Ouch. I feel like I'm a little girl who just tripped and busted her lip on hard pavement after being warned that I was running too fast. Lexie's text stings.

I know exactly what she's referring to. My proclivity to get too attached, to become a bit too obsessive. There was Jimmy in college, who I crushed on so hard that after a one-night stand, I was convinced we would start dating. He never called again. But I couldn't let it go. My heart was shattered, and Lexie was there to pick up the pieces.

And there was also Carlos, in high school. I nursed a crush on him all throughout freshman year, and one Friday night after a football game when we were all partying around a bonfire in the woods, I thought we were finally going to get it on.

It was the first time he ever took notice of me, talked to me, flirted. Brought me foamy beers from the keg. Next thing I knew, Lexie appeared, staking claim to all that attention. I kept looking at her, trying to signal that this was finally *my* moment, dammit, but she acted oblivious. Tossing her head back, coyly touching his biceps. Essentially cockblocking me when she could've had anyone. Later telling me she went to second base with him that night.

She claimed, afterward, that she hadn't known the depth of my crush, and it's possible she didn't. I kept a lot hidden, under the surface, and boys, to Lexie, were like candy. She didn't take them all that seriously. But I stayed mad at her for months after that. Not that I showed it; Lexie was really my only true friend, so what was I gonna do, punish her forever?

But the grudge remained. It *still* irritates me, after all these years, as childish as it sounds. That just goes to show how big a hole my heart has in it.

So, I don't blame her for being overly protective, but still, I'm steamed.

I toss my cell on the stool in the dressing room, ignore her for a few seconds.

But shit, she's gotta help me with the outfit.

Cassidy: I'm fine! He asked me out! Gotta run, but which outfit?

Lexie: Hot pink. Looks super dope on you. Seriously, you look HOT in it. But grab the white one, too. For another time.

Cassidy: Kk, thx!! Xxxoooo

Be careful. You know how you can be.

Grrr. That makes me ball my fists. But then I have to remind myself, Lexie's in the dark here. She has no frame of reference. She doesn't know about the secret script, the kisses, our connection. She doesn't have a clue, so I shouldn't let myself get all worked up when she's honestly just looking out for me.

At the checkout, my cell chimes. I air-tap my card over the machine, check out.

Missed call from Lexie.

Exiting the store, I ring her back, phone pasted to my ear.

"Sorry, was just checking out, but hiiiii!"

She must be in a bar somewhere because I hear earsplitting synth music, loud voices in a foreign language, most likely Czech.

"Heeey! Oh my god, I had to call you. Girl, what?"

"I know, I know. I can barely hear you—"

"Stepping onto the roof now, hang on—"

The music becomes mute as Lexie's voice crackles over the phone. "So, I'm listening . . . whaaat?"

I'm weaving through the parking lot, trying to locate my car. "I have *so* much to tell you," I tease.

"Spill it!"

But I'm not going to. I can't. But I do decide to tell her about the secret script. And about his suspicions about Marisol.

"Wait, *what*?" Lexie's voice is etched with alcohol. I wish I were there with her in person, doing shots.

"Yeah, he's just, like, super suspicious. She's acting dodgy, sneaky, not coming home on time. That sort of thing."

"Hmm. That sounds super toxic!"

"Yes, it's batshit! Come home and help me, please," I say, then laugh nervously.

"And what's this secret script, whaaaat, Cassidy, holy shit!"

"I know. I *know*!" I squeeze my key fob, open the door, slide inside my car. Now that I'm in this enclosed space, I feel like I can divulge a little more. "It's this sexy, femme fatale script and he basically wrote it for Marisol to play the lead in. It's such a long, convoluted story, but he's having me read all the scripts that come through now, and I'm the only one who's read it. Lexie, you have to *promise* me that you won't say a word about this to anyone—"

She scoffs. "Oh, please. Of course not! I would never! And I'm running ninety to nothing here and am drunk right now, so I prolly won't even remember, but *holy shit*!" She squeals. "And dinner tonight?"

"Yup."

A pause. A little static. I think I've lost her. But then she comes back.

"Cass, is there something going on between y'all?"

I bite my lip. I *so* want to tell her about everything, but I can't. It's all in the ether right now, the early stages. "No, there's not," I lie.

"Cassidy—" She says my name as if it's a question.

"No, I swear."

"'Kay—"

"But . . . if there were?"

"Is there?"

"No, but I *do* like him. I feel like we have a connection."

Another stretch of silence.

"Look. I get it, he's dishy. So talented. So connected. All that," she slurs. "But just . . . protect yourself. Protect your heart. Protect this *job*."

My face burns; my mouth goes dry.

Everything she's just said is true, and yet I'm going to do the exact opposite of her advice.

"I will! I swear," I say, when I recover my voice. "It's just dinner. Not to worry."

"Okay, love you, woman."

"Love you, too."

I'm suddenly overcome and don't want to let her off the line.

"When are you coming home again?"

"In ninety short days. Soon as this circus is wrapped!"

"'Kay. Love!"

"Mwah." She air-kisses over the phone.

45

I DRIVE OVER to Nate's in a narcotic blur, so worked up by the thought of seeing him I can barely focus on the road.

I blew out my hair, finishing it off by putting beachy waves in it with my curling iron. Brushed on a light coat of makeup—remembering Nate's throaty words that I was a natural beauty—and spritzed on a little perfume.

He's my first date since Carter, and I can barely sit still in the car. I keep shifting, fiddling with the A/C, the radio.

The sun hangs over the ocean, apricot and bright, and I park—not in my usual spot but right out in front of their house.

I suck in one steadying breath before opening the door, stepping out.

The heat is a balm to me, warm velvet caressing my skin as I make my way up the front walk.

Like in the pool the other afternoon, cicadas buzz all around me, fizzing in the air. It must be mating season, I think, grinning to myself at the thought of that.

Before I'm even to the door, Nate opens it, greets me with a smile.

Somehow he seems even taller tonight, dressed in a sleek black suit that looks like a Tom Ford.

We study each other, grinning.

"Wow. Just wow," he says, eyes skittering over me. "You're breathtaking."

He leads me to the parlor, where, from the stereo speakers, jazz music plays. Duke Ellington. The breathy, golden sound of an alto sax fills the air.

"Johnny Hodges," I say.

"Very impressive," Nate replies.

"Music is my first love, stories my second. Movies, third. And my gran had a great jazz collection."

"I got into it through film scores. Ellington in particular."

"*Anatomy of a Murder*," we both say at the same time, then laugh.

He takes my hand, pulls me over to the red leather sofa.

"I didn't know if you wanted a drink here first, or not?"

"Do you?" I ask.

"Not particularly. I'll have one at dinner, of course, but I don't want to be fuzzy tonight." His eyes shimmer as he stares at me. "We have a script to discuss, remember?"

I smile. "I don't want to be fuzzy, either. I want to remember and feel everything," I say, my voice coming out chalky, lusty.

"Your hair is gorgeous tonight." He lifts a sheet, his eyes dropping from my head to my legs. "And the rest of you as well."

My pulse throbs in my neck. I lean in, place my mouth on his. Our lips dance in time together, but it's his hands I'm aware of: desperate, seeking. Cradling my face, traveling downward.

I sigh as he cups my breasts, lips trickling to the plunging neckline of my dress.

I'm going with whatever happens. And whatever comes of it, so be it.

He keeps a hand on my breast, fingers outlining it through the fabric. His other hand is inside the skirt of my dress, warm and papery, inching up the side of my thigh.

I reach down, touch his pant leg, move my hand to the front of it.

"Cassidy." His voice crackles in my ear.

Through his suit, his skin is molten. I begin to rub, slowly at first, then a bit faster. My fingers fiddle with his button until I get it undone, zipping his pants down.

His hands haven't stopped working over me; a light glaze of sweat coats my skin.

I'm slipping my hand down the top of his boxers when we both jump at the sound of the back door banging open.

What the fuck?

Nate retracts his hands, zips up his pants.

Adjusting the top of my dress, smoothing the bottom of it down, I spring to my feet, moving as far away from him as possible.

"Honey?" Marisol's voice, bright and buttery, cuts over the soft-playing jazz. "You in here?"

Her heels click against the tile, ticking closer like a time bomb, until she's under the stucco archway, gaping at both of us.

"Well, aren't y'all all dressed up?"

I expect her to be pissed, but instead she's beaming at both of us. "What kind of party am I missing?"

I wait for Nate to answer.

"Hey, babe!" he says, straightening his jacket. "Back early?" he asks as if there's no care in the world.

She crosses the room, twines her arm around his. "I missed my honey." She nuzzles her nose against his neck, grins at me.

Even though I'm dressed in my finest, I'm still no match for her. And she knows it, in her white cotton eyelet dress that kisses her ungodly curves.

"Well, how'd it go?" Nate asks, smiling down at her. "Everything okay?"

I shift my weight from foot to foot; I feel awkward, the third wheel again, like I should go.

"Far better than okay." I can hear the tipsiness in her voice. "But more on that in a sec. What are *you guys* up to?"

"I just wanted to take Cassidy out, for all her hard work. She's new in town and all. I really wanted to go with the three of us to celebrate everything that's happening, but you're so busy, so—"

Marisol punctures me with her eyes. For a fleeting moment, they turn to steel, cold and unforgiving, but when Nate glances at her, they change back to sparkling, caramel brown.

"Yes, of course, and sorry to burst in like this. I would've called, but I wanted to surprise you." She draws him in closer, runs her knee against his leg. "With the good news."

"Well, do tell!" Nate says.

"Yes!" I chime in.

"I got the part! Eeeee!" she squeals.

Nate pauses for a second; I see his face fall before he recovers, smearing on a wide grin. "You did? Already?"

"Yes! Guillermo told me this afternoon over wine out on the deck! Can you believe I beat the others out? I mean, Penelope, Ana—"

Nate wraps his arms around her waist, pulls her into a hug. "Congrats, babe! This is the best news ever!"

"Yes, huge congrats! I'm so freaking happy for you!" I say, from my lonely corner of the room.

"Well, I thought we could go celebrate?" Marisol looks up at Nate, studies his face. She's clearly asking, without asking, if I can be cut out of the picture.

She turns her gaze to mine and when she does, Nate looks over to me, gives a quick roll of his eyes. "Yes, of course!" he answers.

"I hate to interrupt your plans, though—"

Even though she clearly does not.

"No, absolutely, y'all should go out!" I rush in and say. "No big deal for me. The three of us can have dinner another time and celebrate! Sound good?"

"Yeah," Marisol answers me, though her attention is twisted back to Nate, her fingers spiraling his hair at the nape of his neck.

I couldn't feel more uncomfortable. Or more disappointed. The only thing that's keeping me from falling to the floor is the quick eye roll from Nate, a message that he, too, was annoyed by her disruption of our evening. That he doesn't really give a shit about her good news.

Marisol continues her PDA, so I clear my throat. "See y'all Monday?"

Marisol finally unlatches herself from Nate, comes over to me, pecks my cheekbones. "Yes, besos, Cassidy! See you soon!"

"Congrats again! I'm thrilled for you!"

She squeezes both my hands, shoots me a genuine smile. "You're a gem, you know that?" Her eyes look watery, as if on the verge of tears.

I shake my head, smiling, dismissing the compliment.

"Have the best night!" I scurry out of the room.

46

MY CELL PHONE wakes me, gyrating next to me on my nightstand.

It's a stream of texts from Lexie. The first one was sent an hour ago, followed by two just now.

Lexie: So, how did it go last night?

Lexie: Well?

Lexie: ??? You best check in!

Cassidy: Hey, sorry. Just waking up! Short answer: it didn't.

Lexie: What do you mean?

Cassidy: Wifey came home.

Lexie. Damn . . . that's a bummer!

Cassidy: Total bummer.

Then I remember I'm not supposed to have real feelings for Nate, at least not in Lexie's mind.

Cassidy: Whatever!

Lexie: Yeah, maybe it's for the best, tho?

An arrow to my heart. I know she's just looking out for me, but I don't want to hear that right now.

Cassidy: Prolly.

Lexie: Welp, gotta run. Make Harry take you to happy hour somewhere so you can wear that fabulous dress! Xxx

Cassidy: Will do! Xoxoxo

My whole body sags as I exhale. Fucking Marisol. *Of course* she had to come home early and fuck up my date with Nate. I could scream.

Right before she busted in, I'd already gone to third base with him in my mind, my head in his lap, him grinning down at me. Her coming home was like being ripped out of the best dream ever; I wish I could go back to sleep, dream it all over again. Grrr.

But something hits me. She got the part. Which means she'll be leaving, maybe sooner rather than later, for Brazil. Probably with her sidekick and accent coach, Andreas, by her side.

I remember her telling me that Nate would come visit, but that he also would stay behind a lot because he's so busy. Which means . . .

The thought is almost too delicious to keep rolling around in my head. But it's enough to launch me from bed to my little kitchenette.

I never ate last night, just came home, chased a melatonin with wine. My stomach is empty, rumbling. I crack two eggs in a bowl, beat them to death before dumping them into my gran's cast-iron skillet.

They come out fluffy, perfect. I run my toe along my bare leg, shaved to the skin for Nate's sake.

I'll get my chance with him yet.

47

MONDAY MORNING TRAFFIC is a knot and the air outside is so dry and hot it feels like a sauna.

I park, amble up the sidewalk.

After a few knocks, Nate answers the door.

His hair is still damp from the shower, his T-shirt smells fresh, and his designer jeans hang just right on his hips. I nearly swoon when I see him.

"Good morning," I practically sing.

"Hey, Cassidy," he says. He's leaning in the doorjamb, but doesn't move to let me in.

"Listen," he says, stepping outside, pulling the door nearly all the way shut behind him. His brows are creased into a look of consternation, causing my knees to wobble. "Marisol's still in the shower."

Still? As in, she was in there with you and you got out? And why are you telling me this, I want to shout.

My eyes wobble up to meet his. "Okay. Want me to just read—"

"Not now. Why don't you take the day off? I'm sorry one of us didn't call you before you came all the way over here, but . . ."

I bristle.

I want to reach out, take his hand. Pick up where we left off Saturday night. But there's an invisible fence between us. Not chain-link but a thick, stucco wall that I can't penetrate.

"What? Why?" The words come out as if they've been strained through a colander.

Nate whistles out a sigh, looks around as if to make sure no one can hear him. "Look, I know this will be difficult to hear, and believe me, it's difficult to say, to explain—and I wish we could talk in private—but, Marisol and I are gonna try to work things out."

"But she's fucking some other guy!" I practically shriek.

This instigates Nate to close the door completely.

"I don't know that. She swears she's not sleeping with him—"

"But what about *us*?" I don't like the whine in my voice, but I can't help it.

"Cassidy, please. I like you. A lot. More than I should, actually. But I can't right now. I have to see this through—"

"But you can't just cast me off—"

He takes me by the wrists, his fingers pulsing against my skin. "I'm not, okay? I just need . . . time. So, I'll still pay you and everything—"

"I don't care about the money—"

"Yeah, but it's only fair. So just, I don't know, take a free week off? Give me some time. Please." He drops my hand, pleads with his eyes instead. "I'll see you next Monday, okay?"

I'm gutted. I feel like someone has taken a knife, hollowed me out. I have no play here, no power. But I do have something else to say. "Just be careful, Nate. She's playing you. I know you don't want to believe it, but I care for you and I know what I saw with my own two eyes."

He leans in, pecks me on the forehead. Even though the contact makes my skin sizzle, the gesture is paternal, condescending. "Thank you for understanding. See ya next week."

I turn, let my shaky feet carry me down the walkway.

As I reach the sidewalk, Nate calls out to me. "Cassidy," he says. For a second, I feel like he's going to tell me he's made a mistake, that of course he wants to leave Marisol.

What he actually says cuts me to the quick, makes me wither like the torched plants along the freeway.

"And enough with the spying. Okay?"

I blink at him, then keep walking, wishing that a sheet of wind would pick me up, carry me out to sea.

MY HANDS CLATTER for my keys; I'm quaking so badly I nearly drop them.

I feel Nate still watching me from the front door, but will myself not to turn around, not to give him any more of me in this moment.

Cramming the key into the ignition, I twist it, fiddle with the buttons until the A/C is blasting.

I get out of Dodge.

Slowly at first, drifting down the hill, then punching the accelerator once I hit Highway 1.

As usual, there's no traffic down here; the people who live in these glass houses don't work. Instead, the traffic flows from the east, the Elanas and the Cassidys of the world shuffling to make their nut.

Enough with the spying. Okay?

What the fuck did he mean by that? It's almost as if he were insinuating that it was something *I* was doing on my own accord, when *he's* the one who asked me—no, begged me—to follow Marisol. His words torch through my brain, but I try and breathe; I'm probably overreacting. He likely just meant that I should cool it, since they are trying to work it out.

But I still don't like how he phrased it. As if it were my idea to begin with, when he had to plead with me. Pay me extra.

I mean, I'll admit that by the end, he didn't even need to ask me, and perhaps me snapping those pics spooked him, made him think we might get caught, but fuck him for saying that.

And for dumping me like this.

Asking me out to dinner, telling me to dress nice, snaking his hands all over my body, then shutting me out like I'm dispensable. Kicking me to the curb when I became inconvenient.

The rational part of me knows that they are still married, that Marisol is still his wife, but he was all but giving me signs that they were heading for the rocks. That the pic of Andreas fingering Marisol was enough evidence for him. But now he's saying he doesn't know for sure if she's sleeping with him.

Seriously? Give me a break.

I'M SO UPSET that when I step inside my place, I go over to my shoebox of journals, slide out the most recent one.

Flopping on my bed, I pour my thoughts out. The pen moves so tersely over the paper that it nearly tears it.

He can't just cast me off, I repeat on the page.

He can't just get rid of me. I'll make sure of that. I'll show him how wrong he is.

Take the week off. With pay. Fuck you.

After scribbling down a whole page, I clasp it shut, chew on the tip of the pen.

A thought flickers inside my overwrought brain, then several thoughts, brightening like an old-fashioned light bulb glinting when first turned on.

First, I know that what I have with Nate is real. Aside from the burning attraction, I'm certain our connection is real. Our bond over storytelling, our ability to be real with each other, unmasked. Naked. Our true selves. *Real.*

And the attraction. I feel his lips on me again, scorching, urgent. His hands inside my dress, hungry, coarse.

My name spilling out of his mouth, dreamily, as I undid his pants.

What I *know* with certainty was going to happen next if Marisol hadn't barged into the room, her presence splitting us apart.

I'm not gonna let what just happened with Nate on their doorstep ruin all of that.

He might have blinders on right now to Marisol, but I do not.

He's wrong about her. Dead wrong.

The next thought brightens in my mind so brilliantly that it almost blinds me.

And it's this: I still have the binoculars and I'm gonna keep watching her.

If he's saying he doesn't know for sure that Marisol is screwing around on him, I'll just have to prove it to him.

48

YESTERDAY, I LAY low. After Nate dismissed me, I never left the apartment again; I was too zapped, wrung out.

But not today. It's ten a.m. and I'm already buzzing, itching to go, binoculars ready, stashed in my bag.

I practically fly over to the Westside, zipping in and out of traffic like a hummingbird.

Marisol normally leaves the house midmorning; I want to catch her when she does.

I park in my usual spot, this time facing the other way, so that my bumper kisses the Dead End sign and I have a clear shot of the house.

I feel ridiculous, a bit scared I'll get caught, but honestly, I don't know if Marisol would even recognize my car and Nate is always tucked away upstairs, out of sight, in his office. His windows aren't street facing.

I lift the binoculars, swing them toward their bare windows.

They immediately pick up on Marisol.

She's dressed in a robe, flimsy pj's underneath, moving through the front room to the dining room like a dancer.

She plops down at the dining room table, espresso cup in one hand and what looks like a script in the other.

I scan the other windows, but no sign of Nate.

She sips, flips the pages, sliding her hands through her silken hair, her face studious, immersed in whatever she's reading. Which is most likely Guillermo's script.

Her whole life, her whole trajectory, just changed over the weekend.

With this role, she'll go from supermodel turned side-role actress into star.

Somewhere deep in my chest, I register happiness for her, genuine delight that she's getting this break she more than deserves.

But also watching her now, wrapped loosely in that robe, perched at the table that another woman polishes each week, doting husband upstairs who will literally do anything for her—write a leading role in his film, turn a blind eye to her cavorting—and not a care in the world about anyone other than truly herself, I also feel my blood start to curdle.

The way she burst in on us Saturday night, knowing I was all dolled up and not even considering my feelings, that just maybe I would've wanted to join them. She's despicable. This woman has always walked on clouds, high above the rain.

I'm not saying she hasn't worked hard, but by some formula of grace and genetics and luck, she entered this world too gorgeous for any bad thing to befall her.

I'm not jealous of her, not in the slightest. I don't want her house, her career, or even her looks. But I am into her husband, the one she so casually toys with.

She slings back her espresso and when she does, her robe gapes open, exposing more of her lilac satin pajamas.

Soon she folds the script shut, retreats into the kitchen.

I realize I've been holding my breath watching her, so I thud the binoculars in my lap, inhale slowly.

And wait.

While I sit, I fumble with my phone, rereading my and Lexie's latest text exchange, the one where she said she thought it was for the best, prolly, that we didn't go to dinner.

It still singes me.

The judgment.

The cavalier way in which she wants me to move on past my feelings. In her defense, I played my feelings down. I had to. Which is why I haven't told her about what happened yesterday with Nate.

Thinking about divulging that makes me feel ashamed, like she would say—or at least think to herself—*I told you so.*

I'm trickling through our entire text history when, out of the corner of my eye, I detect movement.

It's the garage door, creaking open.

Marisol's black Mercedes nosing out.

I slink behind the wheel like a PI in a TV show and wait a beat before starting my car, sliding in behind her.

We wind our way up the hill into the village.

Marisol tosses on her left blinker, pulls into the grocery store parking lot.

Of course.

It's Tuesday, the one night a week she routinely cooks dinner. And I'm not there to do her shopping for her.

Disappointment oozes over me. This isn't the salacious chase I'd hoped for.

I park as far away from the front door as possible and watch as she floats inside.

Half an hour later she emerges, paper bags banging against her hips.

I follow her home but circle the block a few times before settling back into my spot.

Once the garage door closes, I lift the binoculars again.

This time, Nate is in the kitchen, lifting the grocery sacks from her arms, leaning down, brushing her cheek with a kiss.

My heart lurches.

But I can't take my eyes off them.

Marisol lowers a bundle of asparagus into the sink, begins rinsing it.

As she does, Nate comes up behind her, folds his arms around her waist, kisses her neck.

Watching them makes my stomach sour.

She leaves the water on—because, well, rich people don't have to think about ordinary things like water bills—twists around and pulls him in to her.

They kiss. Long, slowly.

Nate lifts her up onto the kitchen counter.

She's wearing a wrap dress; he undoes the tie, exposing a red lace bra that he tears at with his teeth.

My cheeks are damp; I hadn't even noticed I was crying.

My vision blurs, the heat from my tears fogging up the binoculars, so I set them down, allow myself a good cry.

Motherfuckers.

After a few seconds, I wipe off the lenses, peer through.

Her bra must be front-opening because it's ajar and Nate's feasting on her perfect breasts.

Her head is tossed back, toned legs clenching his waist.

Anger spears me.

This was us in the pool. Well, we were *almost* there, just a few days ago while Marisol was getting good and felt up by Andreas a few days before.

I feel tiny. Small. Inconsequential.

I can't look anymore, can't bear to see them going at it.

As if they're all back to normal.

In anger, I throw the binoculars down on the passenger-side floorboard, tear away from the curb.

As I speed down the freeway toward my apartment, I think, *Marisol, you're a damn fine actor indeed.*

49

MRS. CHARLIE WALKS the length of her kitchen upstairs, back and forth. She must be baking.

Normally, the sound is comforting, but this morning, it sets my teeth on edge. The creak of the floorboards, the shuttling around: these are normal sounds and my life is anything but normal now, so they feel discordant, taunting.

After witnessing Nate banging Marisol in their kitchen, I was useless the rest of the day.

The only thing that kept sparking through me, the only flicker of hope—and this is pathetic—is that Nate was the one who initiated things with Marisol. Just like that day at the pool when I saw them having sex.

Marisol is just going along with it, I'm sure, biding her time until she gets whisked off by the film crew to an entirely different country, far away from Nate.

Unless she's truly in love, or in lust, with two people at the same time.

She could be, but I'm positive she's not. There were too many hints dropped about how she's going stir-crazy at the house, how Nate is trying to hold her back, and then I *saw* the way she was with Andreas. Brimming with desire. Couldn't keep her hands off him. Allowing him to pleasure her, even in public.

No, there's a chasm in their marriage—that's why Nate was driven to my arms—and I'm going to pry it open even further.

It's ten a.m. Marisol should be getting ready to leave, if she's going anywhere today, and I'm certain she is; she never sticks around that house for too long.

I want to catch her doing something she's not supposed to be doing, so I can bring it to Nate.

I still can't believe I have to wait until Monday to go back to work. Feels like an endless stretch of days with nothing to do. So, fuck it, I'm gonna fill them.

THIS TIME WHEN I round the corner to the Sterlings', my breath catches in my throat.

Marisol is out front watering.

I skid to a stop, put the car in reverse, slowly back down the street.

Shit.

My heart rate panics through my veins and I keep inching backwards until I'm out of sight.

What the hell am I doing? Have I completely lost it?

If they do catch me, what *will* my excuse be?

I'm about to blow this whole gig.

Maybe I should bide my time, be patient. Be chill.

Keep my head down, do the work, coast until Marisol is out of the picture and then entertain thoughts again of me and Nate together.

That's what a sensible person would do. And I'm usually sensible. The orderly, dependable Virgo.

Except when I'm not. Except when things get messy.

Like Carter dumping me for someone else. Giving me the heave-ho, jarringly, suddenly, with no real explanation.

And why should Marisol get away with cheating on Nate? Why should she get to waltz away, unscathed? If I don't catch her now, I may miss my chance to.

I lower my window, letting the tangy sea air swirl through the car.

After fifteen minutes of deep breathing, quieting my nerves, I restart the car, creep back toward the house.

No one is outside.

Perfect.

I park in my spot, kill the engine.

Squeezing the lenses together, I bring the home into focus.

Marisol is scrambling around the kitchen, stuffing things in her bag, lifting her keys from the countertop. Her body is squeezed into a lemon-yellow dress that barely covers her ass. It's strapless and the neckline clings to her breasts, which threaten to crest over.

Bingo.

She's going to meet Andreas. I'm positive of it.

MY SUSPICIONS ARE confirmed when she routes to the 1, hitches onto Sunset Boulevard just as she did the other day. We notch our way through stoplights until we hit Santa Monica Boulevard.

Her Mercedes glints in the heavy sun; my eyes never leave it as she corkscrews her way through the hills, ending again on Andreas's street.

Before she steps from her car, she primps in the mirror, swiping on fresh lipstick, pushing her breasts up, teasing her hair with her fingers.

I park further away this time.

I have a different plan.

Through the binoculars, Andreas swings the front door open, steps out, folds her into his arms.

She stares up at him as if he's her savior. Her stance is supplicant, imploring.

His index finger drizzles down her neck, runs along the top of her breast.

Again, I can see why she can't resist him.

Once they vanish inside, I step from my car.

This is risky, but I can't get a clear shot from sitting inside, so I have no choice.

I prowl down the sidewalk, pulling my ball cap down, jamming in my earbuds. Over my sundress, I'm wearing a jean jacket, collar up.

I'm just another walker out, getting their steps in.

Except this walker pauses behind the chubby trunk of a palm tree, one house down.

I left the binoculars behind. If I need to zoom in, I'll use my cell.

I pretend I'm getting a text, palm my phone out in front of me as if I'm checking it. But behind my glasses, my eyes are glued to the upstairs window.

Nothing.

But when I lower them, a grin lurks across my face.

The gauzy curtains that were pulled over the monstrous first-story window the other day are parted. Just enough to where I can make out a sofa resting in the middle of the room.

As if on cue, Marisol tugs Andreas through the space by his shirt collar.

They are wasting no time today.

Before I know it, he's shirtless, chest ripped with muscles, washboard stomach sinking into his low-waisted jeans.

I aim my phone toward them, zooming in through the camera app.

Marisol wrenches him to the sofa, her hands on his hips.

He sits.

She's now on her knees in front of him, fingers dancing along his waistline, wresting him out of his jeans, sliding them down just so. They hug his thighs.

His hand rubs the back of her head as it dips up and down.

Click.

I snap my first photo.

After a moment, Andreas clasps the side of her face, bringing her up to him.

He slathers his long body across the length of the sofa, the top of his jeans still splayed out, and jerks Marisol on top of him.

The willow tree in his yard bends to the hot wind, its stringy mane getting a blowout.

I can't believe they're going at it like this in front of the window, but then, I have to remind myself that the curtain is parted just so, the sofa retreated far back enough into the room that unless someone is actively spying on them, parked right out front and zooming in like a freak with her cell phone, then what they are doing inside would largely go unnoticed.

His lot isn't very wide, but it's deep, the front a good fifty feet from the sidewalk. The strings of the willow tree provide a screen of privacy.

Marisol's dress rides up her hips.

She's sitting on Andreas, her back arched as his hands work the top of her dress, inching it down. Her breasts spring out and soon the dress is just a pool of yellow fabric around her waist, the rest of her exposed.

I take a series of pics, my finger pressing down the camera button as it makes the scissor sound of a camera at a model shoot.

Marisol is *definitely* not acting here.

Andreas tugs a rope of her glossy hair, causing her spine to arch even further as she rides him, her face grimaced in pleasure.

Click, click, click.

I feel vindicated, self-righteous. I was right. Nate was wrong. And now I'm getting proof. All the evidence I'll need, or one would think.

I feel off-kilter watching them.

This is different from my first time here. Different from the restaurant, even.

This is real, carnal. Private.

And I'm violating that.

But I can't stop.

I feel violated, too.

Snap, snap, snap.

Andreas clenches her bare ass as she moves back and forth over him. They're frantic for each other, desperate, their movements gaining speed now.

No acting going on here at all.

I take one last shot, stagger away before they finish, before someone spots me.

My sneakers thump the pavement as I climb the sharp hill, lungs panting.

Once inside my Nissan, I don't wait for Marisol to leave; I don't need to.

I only do one thing, which I hope I won't come to regret. But that I have to do before I chicken out.

Hands unsteady, I swipe through the photos.

It's as if I've directed and shot a porno all by myself.

They are perfect. Clear. Vivid. Bold. *Graphic.*

Leaving nothing to the imagination.

God bless the iPhone 13 Pro with its three camera lenses.

Breath craggy, I select Nate's name. Stare at his 310 number.

Hesitate.

Then press send.

50

I'M DRIVING TOWARD my place, lacing through the hills.

Trees squeeze past me as I thread around the canyon, twisting along the front side of Griffith Park.

I don't want to go back to my apartment just yet and sit and stew, so I pull into Griffith, park in the shade of a scraggy oak.

My phone sits in the seat next to me, riding shotgun, a very quiet passenger.

Dammit.

But what do I expect? Nate to receive these lurid photos and text me right back, all thumbs-up?

No.

In all likelihood, he's clutching his stomach, swaying with anguish in his upstairs office.

Which brings me no joy. Honestly.

I don't want to hurt him, don't wish harm on anyone, but I couldn't help but rip the Band-Aid off, expose his marriage for the deeply troubled gaping wound it is.

I feel jostled, a martini being convulsed in its shaker by an exuberant bartender.

Will he hate me for sending those? Hell, for taking them in the first place, especially because he told me to stop watching her?

And is that the underlying reason he called me off in the first place? Because he knows she is getting up to no good and he can't bear to face it?

Prying myself from my seat, I clamber out of the car.

I have to hike through this, even in the crazy heat.

I pass the quartet of elderly domino players, inhale the scotch-scented aroma of their smoldering cigars, continue up the hill.

My legs begin to burn, that gratifying sensation gripping my muscles that comes from a good workout. I've missed this, I realize, just a simple hike. I haven't been taking care of myself. I've allowed myself to get swept up, swept away into the Sterlings' marriage, and again, I'd be ashamed to tell Lexie everything that's been going on.

Especially the little paparazzi episode I just went through back at Andreas's house.

Is that even legal? Snapping photographs of people while they're in their homes, completely unaware that they're being watched?

I'm certainly not dumb enough to Google it. But damn, it's one thing to have them on my phone, it's altogether another to have sent them to Nate.

A gust of hot wind rattles the treetops ahead of me, making me shiver. I'm all alone on this trail, the only sucker hiking in this swelter. I think about the bobcats, the coyotes with their splotchy coats, and turn around to head back.

Plus, I left my cell in my car, and obviously I can't stand to be away from it for even twenty minutes.

I nod to the old guys, thwacking their dominoes on the metal table. They nod back.

Slipping into my car, I grip my phone, study it.

Nothing.

Except now under the stream of photos I texted Nate, the notification has changed from *Delivered* to *Read*.

51

HUH. SO HE'S read the text, seen my pics. And still hasn't responded.

But it's only been less than an hour since I pressed send; I need to chill.

I coast down the hill toward the fancy supermarket.

My cupboards are practically bare, no fresh produce, no beverages other than coffee. I might as well chew up a little more time before going home.

I'm parched, so I head to the juice bar in the back of the store, order a carrot-and-orange juice. While it's being made, I tuck a few rounds of Brie in my cart, a few boxes of crackers.

The juice hits the spot; I devour it as I roam the aisles, grabbing a few bottles of white and prosecco, some sparkling water. Grapes, strawberries, salad stuff.

I check my phone, yet again. Nothing from Nate.

I continue shopping. The prepared food aisle is in the back of the store, just past the produce; I head there, swiping a tub of bougie pimento cheese, hummus, olives, and a garlic rotisserie chicken.

I'm checking over the expiration date on the chicken when I hear it. Throaty and familiar laughter at the register with the checkout clerk.

The voice belongs to a tall, slender blonde.

But it couldn't be her, could it?

Lexie is halfway around the world in Prague.

A stocky man enters the checkout lane behind her, obscuring my view. Surely I'm just imagining it.

I'm too far away for me to call out without sounding like a freak, so I weave through the rows of produce toward her.

All I catch is a glimpse of the back of her head as she exits the store. But it looks just like her.

I abandon my cart, nearly tripping a small child who rounds the corner as I try to catch up to the person I think is Lexie.

Staggering out into the parking lot, I scan for the blonde, but don't see her.

Lexie drives a white Toyota Land Cruiser; there isn't one in the lot.

Hmm.

Maybe I'm actually going crazy. Maybe I just miss her so much I'm conjuring her?

But that was her laugh; I swear to god it was. And the owner of the laugh had the hair and the figure to match.

Back inside the store, while waiting in the checkout line, I text her.

Cassidy: Okay so this is going to sound crazy but are you back in town? If not I just saw your doppelganger at Gelson's, lol.

My cell feels like a weight in my hands as I grip it, awaiting her reply. When she doesn't text me back after a few moments, I dart over to my text with Nate.

Just to be sure I haven't missed anything.

Of course I haven't.

Sigh.

It's nearly three o'clock, almost midnight in Prague. Which, I'm fairly certain, is where she actually is. She's going to think I'm so crazy.

But am I? That laugh, Lexie's scratchy, jazz lounge singer laugh, scrapes across my eardrum.

I follow the road that curls up to my apartment, but before I get to my final turn, I make a left instead, decide to drive by her place.

I'm really just using up more time, I tell myself. Even though that's not true.

When I enter the canyon where their house is, I pull onto their coiled street and spy Lexie's Land Cruiser in the drive, hatchback popped open. Inside, rows and rows of paper sacks.

What the fuck?

I peel away, flying back down the hill.

When I hit a red light, I squeeze the side of my cell, command Siri to call Lexie.

On the second ring, she picks up.

"Hey, chica!" she says. Breezy, raspy.

"Hey! Did you see my text?"

"No, hang on—"

My cheeks burn as I wait.

In the background, I hear her whisper something.

"Oh my god, I was going to call you in a few! Swear to god!"

My throat grows thick.

"Hang on, lemme go outside." Her voice is lower, conspiratorial.

I hear the scraping sound of her back sliding glass door opening. She and Harry have an enormous deck that juts out over the canyon. It's both glorious and dizzying at the same time.

"You're freaking back? I'm sorry, but . . . when did you get home?" My voice comes out whiny, clotted with threatening tears. I feel hurt that she hasn't let me know yet, that I had to find out by spotting and chasing her in the goddamn grocery store.

"Late last night. Look, I know you're prolly mad, but don't be, it was *super* last-minute. Chris got Covid and you know he's one of our principals, so we're shut down for the week. I wasn't going to come, but I wanted to see Harry, work on some wedding planning, and was *dying* to see you! So, I hopped on a plane yesterday, literally got a ticket just before boarding."

Chris Evans is the star of the film she's producing.

"Okay, but you could've texted me—"

"I know, I know, but I wanted to surprise you! Harry was actually going to call you today to see if you'd come over tomorrow night and I was going to waltz into the room," she says, her voice sagging. She sounds tired. Jet-lagged. "But now . . ."

I want to be mad at her—I want my pent-up anxiety to be unleashed on something, someone—but I can't. She's my best friend in the whole world and now I get to see her.

"Can you just come over, like tonight? I'm dying to see you, woman!" I plead.

"I don't know, I just got here and Harry'll kill me—"

A fire poker singes my chest. I know I'm being an irrational little bitch right now, but I'm sick of all this coupling off and being the third wheel.

"Please? There's so much—" The unspoken words dangle in my mouth. Am I really going to tell her what's been going on? "So much I have to tell you. Like, in person. And right fucking now." I laugh, trying to splinter my own seriousness.

A gravelly sigh from Lexie. "Girl, I'm so beat. But yeah. Dying to see you, too, obvy, and hear *everything*. Lemme rally. Go give Harry a hand job or something, so he'll let me come over."

52

I'M SPEARING AN olive with a toothpick for the charcuterie board I'm making when she knocks on the door, her knuckles pounding rapid-fire.

"Heeey!" She practically tackles me with a hug.

"OMG, heeey! Thanks for coming over!" I grip her as tight as I can and she clutches me back.

We're practically dancing in place. Tears burn my eyes and when we pull apart, she's crying, too.

We haven't seen each other since before the pandemic when she flew to Austin for a girls' weekend.

I can't believe she's actually here in the flesh. Even though her face looks tired, she's resplendent in her simple black romper, cottony and crinkled but in a cool way. Gold bangles dangle from her thin arms and her champagne blond hair has beachy waves dropping beneath her shoulders, her customary length.

Looking me over, she shakes her head, her arctic-blue eyes still shedding tears. "Damn, I'm crying. I didn't even cry when I saw

Harry." She chuckles, wiping the tears away with the back of her hand. "I just can't believe you *actually*, *finally* live here."

"Thanks to you!" I beam, spreading my arms out like Vanna White, indicating that I love my digs. "This place is *so* fabulous!"

"You like?"

"Yes! It's perfect!"

"I liked it, too, but glad you do as well, you picky Virgo."

I clamber for another hug, squeezing my arms around her neck. "I've missed you so much." My voice catches in my throat. It's been way too long since I've seen my friend. "But this is just a big ol' tease."

"I know, I know, but it's better than nothing and I'll be back for good in just a few months. Promise."

"Until your next shoot."

"I'm not taking an out-of-town job again. Not for a long time, anyway. I've got some TV prospects lined up; they mostly all shoot here. Harry would *kill* me if I took off again."

"How *are* you guys?"

Lexie rolls her neck, a longtime habit of hers. "We're fine. Better than fine, actually. Absence making the heart grow fonder and all that. Only stressor is trying to plan a wedding from afar. He's actually taking me to Laguna Beach Friday morning to scout sights. So I am *ready* to be home. With him. With you."

"Ah, Lex, he's *so* great. And I'm so happy for you guys. Hey, let me know if I can help at all with the planning? You know I'm detailsy."

"Believe me, I will! And you know me. I'm a Gemini, not a Virgo. I kind of exist in the ether, like some specter. Better at big-picture stuff. So yeah, this is definitely way more your bag." She cracks a grin, her perfect teeth gleaming.

She toes the door back open, grabs some bags in from the patio. "I packed an overnighter in case we get too crazy?"

My heart melts at the thought of that. I didn't realize how lonely I actually am. It took someone who is like family being here, right next to me, to make me grasp it.

"And, I brought *presents*!" She lowers a paper sack into my arm.

"What's this?"

"Stuff from Prague!" she practically squeals. "Told ya I was gonna surprise you!"

I pull out something glass and weighty. Tear the tissue paper off. It's a bottle of absinthe. "What in the world? This looks delicious. Thank you!"

"Oh, it is!"

I unwrap the rest: adorable, hand-painted ceramics from the Czech Republic. A set of Bohemian crystal highballs.

"Lexie! It's like Christmas! Thank you! I love it all."

"Let's get into the absinthe!"

"But I have wine—"

"Obvy. But let's just have a shot." She peels off the paper sticker from the lid, uncorks it. "This is the good stuff, the real stuff."

She snatches two of the highballs, rinses them in the sink. Pours the emerald-green liquid in the bottom of the glass.

"Got any sugar?"

I open up a cabinet, pass her the sugar jar. After whisking some in with a spoon, she passes me my drink. "Naz Dravi! Cheers in Czech."

"Naz Dravi!"

"Sip it slowly," Lexie warns.

The liquor is both cool and molten on my tongue. Herbal. Almost medicinal. Not bad.

"Let's go outside for a sec," she says.

I lift the char board, carry it out with my drink. At the small bistro table, we sip and snack as the sky above us purples.

"So, you said a lot has happened?"

Gah. I wish I hadn't opened my damned big mouth. Last time I checked my phone, there was still no reply from Nate.

"You could say that."

"Cassidy, tell me." She nudges. She's always been able to get everything out of me; I don't know why I'm pretending like it's even possible to keep this all from her, especially now that she's sitting right next to me and not an ocean away.

"It's fine, really." I jam an olive in my mouth, roll it around.

"Okay, someone needs more alcohol. Clearly."

I try to wave her off, but she grips the bottle, slops more in my glass. "This stuff is good for you. I was drinking it like milk over there."

"But you don't even drink milk over here!" I joke, kicking her leg with my foot.

"Okay, you know what I mean. *Drink*."

"One more and then we're hitting the prosecco."

"Deal."

The liquor slides down my throat, slippery, fiery. The woods around us begin to go fuzzy.

"Hey, before we get into all that, you need to raid Marisol's shit!"

"Oh, yes. Holy shit, I forgot!"

We burst inside, head for my tiny closet, which is spilling over with her treasures.

"This is insane!" Lexie wrestles a beaded dress off its hanger, steps out of her romper. She slips it on, looking like a movie star herself. "Well?"

"Yours! It looks *much* better on you!"

"Eeeee! This is fun!"

She raids the shoes next, trying them on, kicking them off, separating her finds into her own little pile.

"Your glass is empty. Get the wine."

I fill two stems with the bubbly. After the absinthe, it tastes like cotton candy on my tongue and I down half my glass.

She gets to my new red swimsuit. "Well, look at this!"

The memory of Nate and me together in the pool floods back. "Yeah, no, that's actually mine—"

"It *is*?" she asks, surprise lancing her voice.

"Yup!"

"Like, who are you even? I *love* it, but it's *so* not you. I'm so fucking proud of you! See, LA looks good on you. Sorry to say, but, told ya so."

She's talking, but my mind is still picturing Nate, feeling his lips on mine, feeling him tug me into him. My groin pulses with the memory.

When I look up, Lexie's halfway into one of Marisol's one-pieces. "What do you think?" she says, yanking up the straps.

"It's yours!"

"I love this game!"

I sink down on the side of my bed.

"Cassidy, what—" Her eyes rake over my face, flecked with concern. "Okay, I'll stop and focus." She steps out of the swimsuit, shimmies back into her romper. "Tell me."

And I do. I tell her everything. Starting at the beginning, with Nate slipping me his secret script. Then on to our exchanges about it and how good that all felt. How natural. Our connection. Then on to the spying.

My face sears when I tell her that part. I feel so dirty, so ashamed for spying on another woman. But Lexie listens in her usual nonjudgmental way, assessing, nodding in all the appropriate spots. Pausing me only to ask pertinent questions.

The only one that jabbed me was actually about the script.

"So, was it any good?"

"It's utterly brilliant, explosive. Sexy as hell."

"And he wanted your feedback? No offense, but—"

"I'm telling you we have a connection. It goes beyond our attraction," I reply, my voice growing loud.

"Okay, okay, I didn't mean anything by it, but damn, that was a fast pivot on his part from *hey, will you buy our groceries* to *hey, here's my top-secret script that's also super erotic, let's read it in my office together.*"

"Fair enough." I chuckle, feeling a twinge of self-satisfaction at how quickly things did indeed move between us.

I describe our last foray, how we were inches from sleeping together when Marisol came home.

"Brutal. That is *brutal*, sister."

"I know, I know. Fucking hell."

"And, like, I can't even get mad at you for falling for him because I get it. He's a total hottie."

I finish by telling her how he gave me the week off. Told me to quit spying on Marisol. "As if it were my fucking idea in the first place! The nerve."

"Seriously." Lexie empties the rest of the wineglass down her throat, locks her eyes on to mine. "But have you? Stopped spying?"

Heat licks my neck. I'm tempted to lie. This last stunt I pulled might be the thing I'm most ashamed of. I stick my nose in my glass, take a long pull.

"Oh my god, you haven't." It tumbles out of her mouth like a statement, not a question.

There's no point in lying.

"Well, I just wanted to see. And maybe gather some evidence for him so he'll know she's a two-timing ho!"

"Cassidy!"

"I know!"

"And?"

"Caught her. Red-handed." I slide her my cell.

Her mouth hangs open as she swipes through my photos. She literally gasps, covering her lips with her hands. But she's also laughing. She's drunk. "I'm sorry, but this is all too batshit crazy!" she howls.

"Give me that back!" I say, lunging for the phone. But she's too fast for me in my tipsy state and maintains control of it.

"No! These are super hot. I mean, look at them. No offense; I'm on Team Cassidy, not Team Marisol. But OMG you fucking pervert!"

"It wasn't like that!"

"I know, I'm kidding. Don't be stupid. But dayum, woman. You've kind of gone a bit outer limits, dontcha think?" She cocks her head, clicks her tongue.

Ouch. That stings. But, she's not wrong. And at least she's laughing about it. Which makes me feel a tiny bit better. Less like a wretch. As with all things in life, Lexie makes everything seem less grave.

She's looking at me with something like shock but also pride in her eyes. "I mean, who have you become? A rabbit boiler? A homewrecker?"

And I haven't even told her the worst of it.

I sock her in the arm. "Shut up!"

"We'll find you a nice boy out here, one who's not married." She howls again, clutches her stomach. I take the opportunity to snatch my cell back. "You know I love you, right?"

"Yes. Thank god. But shut the fuck up. I have one last thing to tell you."

"Oh, shit!" she squeals, rubbing her hands together.

"I texted Nate the photos—"

"Did not!"

"Did, too!"

"And?"

"Well, that was earlier today. And I haven't heard back."

"Shit, shit, shit—"

My paranoia about doing something illegal flares back up. "Do you think I'll, like, get in trouble—"

"God, no. Believe me, if I were her husband, I wouldn't want these being seen by another soul." She swirls the wine in her glass, takes a nip. Her brilliant blue eyes twinkle.

"And obviously, you can't repeat any of this to anyone! Not even Harry, okay?"

"Pfft. I'm so fucking sure! You know you don't even have to tell me that," she says, sounding slightly hurt.

"Sorry, you just know so many people out here that probably know them—"

"I really don't. Just Ramona, my producer friend who told me they were looking for someone. And I'd never fucking tell her. C'mon, Cassidy—"

"Okay, okay, sorry. I'm being ridic!" I exhale, blowing the weight of the world off my shoulders.

"That is the *last* thing you should be worrying about. So, whad'ya think he'll do?" she asks. "Maybe he'll leave her? I mean, this is out-and-out proof. Who could stay with someone after this?" She tsks. "Total baller move on your part to send them. Well played."

She clasps the throat of an unopened chardonnay—we've depleted the prosecco—and wrenches out the cork.

She's moving around the apartment now, circling. Another old habit of hers. When things get too serious, she busies her body. Reaching into the closet, she pulls out another pile of Marisol's stuff.

"What about your job?" she asks, fastening a kelly-green bikini top over her romper. She's soused. "Like it?"

"Yeah, it looks *awesome* over your clothes," I joke. She looks like a little girl playing dress-up; my heart surges with affection for her. I have missed my friend so much.

"This job," she continues without looking at me, fiddling with the straps of the bikini instead, "could turn into so much more. I can tell you really like him, but you're playing with fire."

Ouch.

"You might want to let that part of things go? Keep it professional, so you can milk him for the screenwriting stuff? Sounds like things were really catching on there, ya know? This town is so tough. Competition for everything everywhere. It'd be hard to get this kind of opportunity again."

She stares at me now, reads my face, which has turned to stone.

"Shit. You really *are* in deep with him." Concern pinches her perfect face. "Fuck the wine, I'm getting the absinthe again."

She crosses the room, tipsy, traipsing over to the kitchen counter where the bottle rests.

"I'm already trashed!" I plead.

"Drink. Now *I* gotta get something off my chest."

53

I TAKE A sip of the absinthe, swish it around in my mouth. It kinda tastes, and looks, like mouthwash, so why not? Man, I really am tipsy.

And not prepared for whatever Lexie is about to unload on me. Her features are still creased with concern, even as she's wearing Marisol's bikini top over her romper.

"What is it?" I ask.

Lexie clears her throat. "Fuck it, I just wanna be totally honest with you. Because that's what we do."

"Okaaay."

She sucks in a quick breath. "So, Chris *did* get Covid and we are shut down for at least a week, but I wouldn't have flown all this way just to see you and Harry for a few days, ya know? Even with the wedding stuff coming up. It's a trek."

She undoes the bikini, tosses it in the pile.

"I came back because I was worried about you."

There it is.

As soon as the words leave her mouth, I feel a precipice forming between us, dark, dusky, treacherous. A gorge in our friendship.

"What do you mean?" My voice is small, a miniature version of me echoing from the void.

"Look, as I said in my text, I wanted you to be careful. Because . . ." She waves her hands in front of her. "We both know how you can be."

My stomach roils.

"But you didn't even know everything. Like, I only told you we were going to dinner, so—"

"Cassidy. Come on. I *know* you. And I love you. I'm saying this as your best friend: I was worried. I could already tell you were becoming obsessed with him—"

"But how?" My mind reels back to Jimmy in college, my one-night stand, and even further back to Carlos, in high school, my crush whom Lexie cockblocked me with. "That was how I *used* to be, but that's been literal years. I don't need your *concern*, thank you very much. What's going on with me and Nate is different, it's real. Like what I had with Carter. Well, before we broke up."

Lexie looks up at me, her eyes wary, almost sheepish. Like she's calculating my current mental state. I wish I could slap her right now.

"Listen, I talked to Carter."

Mic drop.

My face stings, my whole body stings with shame and confusion. "What? You did what? When? And how? Why would you—"

"Because I was *worried* about you and couldn't get to Austin, so I DMed him on Insta, and Cassidy—"

Tears fill my eyes. I'm so angry, so hurt that blood pounds through my head, clouding Lexie's voice. It sounds like she's underwater.

"You weren't with him for six months. You were only with him for two weeks."

54

THE OLD SAYING, the air has been sucked out of the room, is a tired one, but it's true.

With her proclamation, Lexie just vacuumed all the air out of the room, out of my lungs. Tears surf down my cheeks. I'm sobbing, gulping and gasping. And ashamed. *So* ashamed. My dirty little secret is finally out.

I feel grimy, naked. I only wanted Lexie to think that I was capable of being in a long-term relationship. I wanted everyone to think that, that I was worthy of such a normal thing, instead of being perpetually single, unwanted. Unnoticed.

So yeah, I embellished a few details; I'll be the first to admit it. But she's wrong. Carter and I were together for three weeks. Twenty-two days to be exact. We met late in January, after the new year, and he ended it, fittingly, just before Valentine's.

I didn't have the heart or will to tell Lexie that I'd been unceremoniously dumped. So, I pretended. Snapped pics of a vase of roses that were allegedly from Carter. A few weeks later, I took a selfie at the coast, posting it on Instagram, captioning it, `Here with my one and only.`

Pathetically, I meant myself, but I wanted the world to think I was still with him. But by the time April rolled around, I was done pretending. I was ready to admit to Lexie, and really, to myself, that we were over. That the whole thing had been a sham.

She knew he'd cheated on me, that I'd caught him red-handed. But she didn't know the rest.

Did she?

Through clenched teeth now, I ask her, "And what did y'all talk about? I'm fucking furious you went behind my back!"

She scoffs, a full-body scoff. "Lady, you lied to me about him for months! I'm the one who should be pissed!"

"Well, what all did the asshole say?"

She plants her lips on the rim of her glass, downs the whole thing. Wipes her mouth with the back of her hand like a sailor in an old film. "That you freaking stalked him after! Stalked *them*! That he had to threaten you with a restraining order. And only then did you stop."

Tears brim in my eyes again; my throat tightens as if someone is gripping it. When I speak, I sound like I've been sucking on helium. "Okay, okay! I went a little crazy, I'll admit it. But Lexie, I know I was with him for a short amount of time—it was three weeks, for the record—but it was the best three weeks of my life! He told me he loved me! I mean, he was drunk and boning me and I should've known better, but—and I'm sorry I didn't tell you, I just felt like such a loser."

She places her hands on my shoulders. "But you're not. That's crazy talk. And I will *never* judge you. I get it. Men are *assholes*, most of them anyway. Like ninety-nine point nine percent of them, and you've always gotten the short end of the stick when you don't deserve it."

I wipe my eyes, nodding. Flail my hands out to her for a hug.

She embraces me as fresh tears spring and my body wracks with sobs.

"And I love you for being so passionate, so fucking romantic, but you *can* go overboard sometimes—"

I nod. "I know, I know." I sniffle into her collarbone.

"I mean, remember Jimmy? And parking outside his apartment and blaring 'Nothing Compares 2 U' over and over until he freaked out?"

"Yes." I'm humiliated by the memory, but the way she recounts it also makes me laugh, deliriously so. Laughter and sobbing blending together so that I feel lightheaded, on top of being slobbering drunk.

"So, I'm being serious, maybe just let Nate go? Like, not the job, obviously, but the other stuff? You deserve more than some gropey guy who's mad at his wife—"

Those last words assault me. "But that's not all that's going on here. We *do* have something."

Her eyes grow wide, as if she thinks I've lost it. She nods. And the smugness, again, infuriates me. I know I've been over-the-top in the past—too naïve, too out of touch with what's actually going on with guys, too desperate, too needy, too willing to believe in my own fairy tale—but it's the script that the patriarchy writes, the one in which they want us to believe we are merely half of, instead of whole, if we don't have a partner that drives us to these edges. And it's not my fault that there's a shortage of good men. Of Harrys in the world. Easy for Lexie to sit here and judge, even if she's pretending that's the opposite of what she's doing.

"Look, you're into him. So, be into him. Just, be more low-key, okay? Maybe see what happens months from now. You don't have to *actively* explode their marriage, ya know? If it's over with them, it'll be over and you won't have to do any more meddling. Also—and I know this is going to sound super douchey—but, if you can't cool it for yourself, could you maybe cool it for me? For my good word? I am the one that got you the job, after all, so . . ."

Every pore on my skin is filled with humiliation. She *does* sound douchey, worrying about her reputation, but she's also right. And I know it. Relationships and partnerships and word of mouth in Hollywood especially are trellised on trust, and I'm about to blow all that for her, if I haven't already.

"I'm sorry. I didn't even think of that—"

"I know, and don't beat yourself up. You know I couldn't actually give two shits for the most part, but—"

"No, you're right. And I want to be honest. I'll *try*. No promises, but—"

"Like, just cool it. Is all I'm asking. Just for now. Show up Monday like nothing's happened. Seriously."

"Got it," I finally say. But she and I both know I'm going to do damn well what I please. "I'll do my best, Lexie," I say, sniffling like a wounded child. "Promise."

55

I JERK AWAKE.

Marisol's pile of clothes is littered on the floor, the char board rests on the dining table, half-mauled. The other side of my bed is empty.

My hand gropes for my cell; I can't find it on my nightstand.

Steering myself out of bed, I swerve across the room, locate it on the kitchen counter next to the half-empty bottle of absinthe.

My god.

It's not a small bottle, either.

The room lurches.

I brighten my phone. No notifications. Nothing from Nate, still, dammit. And nothing from Lexie.

But next to the espresso machine, she's left a note.

> *Couldn't sleep. Jet lag. Heading to crawl in my own bed. Call me when you're up. Xx*

Looking at her familiar handwriting, I sigh, feeling a sliver of guilt and trepidation that I've potentially put her in a tricky spot by fucking things up with Nate and Marisol.

She's right. I'm wreaking havoc over here and I need to chill. Calm the hell down.

But that's the last thing I feel like doing. I stare at my cell, willing a reply from Nate to appear. When it doesn't, I go over to my desk, grab a sheet of paper. Pen poised above it, I think of what to say. But a better thought takes over, and I flick on my laptop, quickly type a few lines, hit print.

Before I leave, I down a whole glass of cold water. I feel as though I've been backed over by a bus. But it was worth it. As ashamed as I feel for spilling everything to Lexie, it was necessary. How long was I supposed to keep all that shit to myself? And I'm actually relieved she knows the truth about Carter, that I don't have to harbor that sneaky, cringe-inducing lie anymore.

I climb in my car, roll down the hill to In-N-Out. I need something nasty and sloppy; a 4x4 is calling my name.

On the way, I try Lexie. It goes to voicemail. It's ten and she's probably finally sleeping. I leave a quick message.

The line at In-N-Out is blissfully short, and before I know it, I'm in animal-style heaven, devouring my whole order while driving.

Instead of turning east, to head back home, I go west, as if an invisible string is pulling me.

Fuck it.

I can't help myself.

I want to go over and investigate, see if there's been any fallout from my text. Those pictures.

I CURVE AROUND to my usual spot, park. Wipe my hands clean before picking up the binoculars.

The lights are on downstairs in all the rooms, as usual, but I don't pick up on any movement.

Nate, of course, is probably upstairs in his office, and it's doubtful Marisol's still asleep. She must be gone, I surmise.

Maybe she's at Andreas's.

I'm about to pull away when movement jerks my attention back to the Sterlings'. I see a form moving through the house so I sweep the binoculars in that direction.

It's Nate, settling onto the sofa in the front living room.

His clothes look crumpled; his hair is mussed.

I twist the lenses, focusing them so I can see his face. His expression is angry, anxious.

In his hand is his cell, and his features darken even more as he swipes the screen.

He's studying the photos I sent, no doubt. Torturing himself. Or maybe he's searching for a divorce attorney.

Either way, he appears to be alone, and I have to stifle the urge to call him, tell him I'm right outside and that I'm sorry his wife is a cheater. My fingers grip my door handle. Screw calling him, I should get out of the car, knock on the door. Apologize for sending them, ask how he's doing.

But Lexie is right. I have to play it cool.

So as soon as I see him exit the room, I climb from the car, slink up the sidewalk. In a FedEx envelope that once held a script, I tuck the note inside, leave it at the front door. As if sensing me, Oscar and Percy burst into barking. I hear Nate's heavy feet pounding down the stairs. And as fast as my own feet will carry me, I race back to my car, pulling away in time to see Nate open the door, glance down, and retrieve the note.

Good.

I crank my car back up, ease away, when my cell rings.

My heart jumps in my throat thinking it's Nate, that he saw me pull off.

But it's Lexie.

Shit.

"Morning, chica," she says, voice scratchy. She must be able to hear me driving because she asks, "Where are you?"

"In-N-Out on Sunset," I lie. "Well, just left or I'd offer to—"

"Oh my god, don't bother. The thought of food makes me wanna retch right now."

"Tell me about it, Ms. Absinthe."

"Oh, come on, you know you liked it." I hear a smile in her voice.

"I did last night. But Jesus."

"I hear ya. I'm just tossing and turning but saw you called, wanted to check in. You okay?"

Sure. All good—no biggie. I'm just heading over to Marisol's lover's house to spy on them again.

"Yes. Thank you, Lexie. You're the best."

"Okay, cool. Can I call you later? I'm so not in my right mind—"

"Me either."

"Harry was saying you should come over tomorrow night. We've gotta go wedding locale scouting in Laguna in the morning, but after we could have a few friends over for—drinks on the deck? Since I'm leaving Sunday morning and all?"

A trickle of happiness oozes over me. "Yes, I'd love it. That actually sounds perfect. But," I venture, "I know I'm being greedy, but could we get mani/pedis today? A quick girls' day? Please."

A pause.

"Ah, Harry's gonna kill me, but sure. Gimme an hour; let me revive myself with caffeine. I'll pick you up."

"You're the best!"

Perfect. Lexie may not like what all this girls' day will entail, but it'll give Nate time to digest what I've just dropped at his front door. Surely that will prompt him to wake up, to get back to me.

I tell myself I'm going to exit the 10 and head home, but I let it blur past, driving on until I reach the exit for Andreas's house.

I turn down his street. Marisol's car is nowhere in sight. Hmph. She does have other places she meets him, obviously, so they could be together at another restaurant, or, they might not be together at all. Nate might have totally lost it, confronted her. Has he shown her the pics I took? I wonder.

I shudder at the thought, and again, worry about the consequences. Will she press charges against me? I probably would.

But surely he wouldn't do that. If he did, he'd need to explain the history behind the photos, the history behind the spying itself. And that would implicate him.

Maybe he just got in her face, and then they fought and fucked again.

My head spinning with wild scenarios, I'm grateful Lexie and Harry are having me over tomorrow night. That I have something to look forward to instead of this nonstop, all-consuming obsessing over the Sterlings.

56

"YOU SHOULD TOTALLY go with power pink!" Lexie's nails click along the brightly colored bottles of polish. "I'm picking demon death black, of course."

Minutes later, our feet are soaking in tubs of scalding water, our back muscles being kneaded by the soft leather massage chairs. Lexie flicks through a crinkled *Us Weekly* as I grip my phone, waiting for a text from Nate that will probably never arrive.

"You know what? Can we just do the pedis, skip the manis? I want you to take me somewhere right after and I know Harry's waiting."

Lexie lifts an eyebrow. "Okaaay. I guess."

Half an hour later we are driving to the Sterlings'.

"Only reason I'm going along with this batshit plan is that I'm morbidly curious to see their digs." Lexie lowers her window. "Explain to me again what exactly you expect to get out of this mission?"

I'm not really sure. Another glimpse of Nate?

"It's *killing* me waiting 'til Monday. I dunno, I just, like, wanna see if there's anything telling." I didn't mention, obviously, my trip here this morning.

We climb the spindly road that threads through the canyons of Malibu, leading to their house. As we round the corner, my stomach drops ten floors.

Nate is walking down the sidewalk, Oscar and Percy tugging him forward on their leashes.

His hair is damp, his eyes shielded by a pair of Ray-Bans.

"Should I slow down or speed up?" Lexie asks, her voice uncharacteristically tense, which, in turn, puts me even more on edge.

"Just stop. We're far enough away, plus, he doesn't know your car."

Nate's striding toward us, but we're parked on the other side of the street, and I've pulled my own shades on, am slinking down in the passenger seat.

I'm scanning his body language, looking for clues; if I'm guessing right, his strong jaw is tensed, head hanging low. I'd say he's still in distress.

From my photos. From my note. From god knows what, if any, confrontation he had with Marisol.

"Hubba-hubba," Lexie purrs. "Dayum, I can see why he's got his hooks in you. He's even more dashing in person."

Instead of making me feel better, her words make me feel even worse. A familiar unease crawls over me, the feeling that if we *were* to hop out of the car and approach Nate, he'd have eyes for Lexie, as all men have when we've been together.

"Let's get out of here," I reply. "Before he clocks me."

57

IT'S FRIDAY MORNING. I'm parked outside the Sterlings'.

A moth to a flame.

The heat wave is over. In its place, the weather lashes. Sunny one minute, dark and broody the next, as if it can't make up its mind.

Like me.

I swore to myself I wouldn't come back here until Monday, but something about seeing Nate's haunted form yesterday, twice, twisted me all up.

I guess because part of me feels guilty. I'm the one who snapped those nasty pictures, sent them to him. I'm the culprit here.

But another part—the louder part of me—knows that what I did was right. He needed the Band-Aid ripped off completely; wasn't getting there on his own.

With just my naked eyes, I glance up at their house.

First, I get a clear view inside, and then the sun sneaks out from behind an angry cloud, placing a glare on the windows.

This is stupid. Foolish. I need to hang it up, come back on Monday.

I lower my window, letting the wrathful sea breeze pelt my face, and when I do, I hear the creak of their garage door opening.

My pulse threads through my temples.

Marisol backs out of the drive; I see her face shielded by her oversized sunglasses.

I tail her to the 1 until she veers on Sunset Boulevard, her well-weathered path to Los Feliz, to Andreas's house.

A feeling of smugness trickles over me; as crazy as I'm behaving, she *is* the one at fault here for her disintegrating marriage.

We wind around Sunset, then drop down Beverly Glen.

When we hit Santa Monica Boulevard, though, she turns right, instead of heading left.

What the hell?

Her blinker pulses and she's pulling into the valet turnstile at the Beverly Hilton. Shit, shit, shit. I pump the brakes, nearly getting rear-ended as I do.

I watch her car door open, but traffic is nudging behind me, so I'm forced to keep going.

After I circle the block, I park across the street in a metered spot.

I don't even know why I'm staying; this is her usual lunch spot with her manager. But I pathetically have nothing better to do until I go to Lexie and Harry's tonight.

I lean my seat back. Check my phone for the zillionth time to see if there's a text waiting for me from Nate. As if.

Open my browser, navigate to NPR. Scan the headlines. Nothing interesting. But not much can hold my interest these days. I wish Monday would hurry up and get here. I try and visualize strolling up to their front door, being greeted by Nate.

Me acting all nonchalant. Him letting me know that Marisol is out. Inviting me in for a latte. Then thanking me for being the Band-Aid ripper-offer.

I glance up at the Beverly Hilton, wonder if I should go in. Just to see who she's with. But that's probably a stupid idea. I decide to sit here for another hour, then leave. Maybe kill some time at the mall, go for a hike.

My brain is working overtime, cycling through what I should and shouldn't do with my day, when I see Marisol bursting through the sliding glass doors of the hotel.

What the fuck?

She's only been in there for fifteen minutes. Tops.

Her long hair flows behind her; her enormous sunglasses devour her face.

But even from this distance, and even with her expression mostly covered by her glasses, she looks stressed. In a hurry. Charged up.

She feeds her yellow ticket to the valet, chews her nails as she waits for them to retrieve her car.

Once she's in, she speeds off, jerking onto Santa Monica Boulevard, gunning down the road.

Shit.

I punch the accelerator, thread into traffic, trying to catch her.

Shit. Shit. Shit.

She's gone.

But I keep heading west.

Finally, I see the top of her convertible.

She's driving so fast, crazier than I've ever seen her drive before, darting in and out of lanes, blowing through yellow lights.

I'm out of breath as if I'm running and not driving, but I manage to stick close behind her.

I slow my pace once she turns down their street, watch as she wheels into the drive. She doesn't even bother with the garage, she just flies out, racing through the back door.

The hell?

Nestling into my standard spot, I slide down in my seat, watch as she pounds through the kitchen, then disappears.

A few minutes later, she's standing with her back to me in the front living room.

Nate is with her.

He's facing the window.

His hands fly up to his sides, exasperated; her head shakes back and forth, her long hair ribboning down her back like a stream.

They're shouting at each other; I'm positive of it.

Did he call her at lunch, interrupt it?

What happened that made her race home, get into it with him?

It's a blur, but I'm pretty sure I just saw her raise her hand, strike his face.

I remember that slap I heard a few weeks ago.

Palms glazed in sweat, I lift the binoculars, try to get a better look.

But the sun is not cooperating. Every time I focus, it skids behind a cloud, darkening everything. I drop them; they're pissing me off.

Her head is shaking back and forth still, as if she's telling him off. And then, oh god, he's lunging at her, his arms gripping her sides as if trying to get her to calm down.

Her arms fly up, flinging him off, but now he's grabbing at her throat.

My own throat goes dry; I don't know what to do.

She dives forward, pushing him down. The sun pops back out at just that moment, turning the window almost mirror-opaque.

Everything seems to be spinning and also still, all at once.

It's impossible to see inside now.

I wait, my own breath suspended.

When the sun finally slips behind another cloud, I glimpse into the room.

Marisol is stooped over, as if looking at the floor. But I can't see any further than that; the window cuts her off at the knees.

She scurries from the room.

There's no sign of Nate.

Is she running toward him, or away from him?

I can't just sit here and wait to find out. She's liable to erupt from the house—either by the front door or back—at any second. He is, too.

I can't be caught watching them.

I stab my key in the ignition, turn it. Hands wobbly, I pull the gear down into drive and coast away.

58

I DON'T KNOW what to do with myself. Where to go.

I feel like I should call Lexie, tell her what I just saw. Out of all their fights, this one was the most serious and disturbing. Sure, I've heard them yelling before, even heard that slap, but I've never witnessed, or overheard, them getting physical like this.

What have I set into motion?

It's only one o'clock.

Six hours to kill before I'm due over at Lexie and Harry's.

She's gonna read this shit all over my face. But maybe she'll be distracted by the other guests.

No; I'm not going to call her, not going to tell her what I just saw. She'll be so upset with me for continuing my stalkery behavior and I already feel grimy enough as it is.

I head home, tell myself I'll stay in the rest of the day until the party, binge-watch all the trashy TV I've been missing out on.

I WAKE TO the sound of car doors clapping shut, handheld radios crackling.

I must've fallen asleep because it's late afternoon; I can tell by the angle of light through my curtains.

The noise outside makes every hair on my arms stand up. I've watched enough murder TV to know what that sound is: the police.

Somewhere deep in my gut, a sense of foreboding starts to build.

I creep to the window, peel back the curtain an inch.

It's two officers, a male and a female.

I don't know how I know, but I just know they're here because of Nate and Marisol.

Their fight earlier was bad. Explosive. I probably should have intervened. Or, at the very least, stayed there. It's like leaving the scene of an automobile accident.

And it's all because of me and what I started.

Shit. Shit. Shit.

Nate confronted her, showed her the pics. They went at it.

Now Marisol has gone to the police, let them know my psycho ass is the one who photographed her.

And here they are to arrest me.

Their radios continue to crackle; I'm hoping Mrs. Charlie hasn't heard them. They're getting closer. I can hear them talking right outside my door.

Even as I'm expecting it, their knock makes me jump.

I wrench my robe tighter around me, drag myself to the door.

My hands are literally shaking as I clasp the knob.

Jesus fucking Christ, Cassidy, get it together.

I flick my eyes to the microwave. It's five forty-five. I need to be at Lexie's soon. If I'm not in jail.

The knocking starts again, so I open the door.

"Evening." The male detective tips his head to me, gives me a bleak smile.

I'm speechless.

"I'm Detective Simmons, this is Detective Cruz. Mind if we come in?"

I can't remember if I'm supposed to allow them to come inside or if I need to insist on an attorney or what, so I step back, nod yes.

"Please, have a seat."

I motion to the futon.

They each pull out their notepads.

Which is never a good sign.

"Cassidy Foster, is that right?" Detective Simmons asks. He's short and balding.

Detective Cruz is attractive with glossy curls spilling down the side of her face. She's smiling at me, exuding warmth where he is cooler.

"How can I help you?" I ask, feeling like I'm playing the role of key witness in a TV show. "First, can I offer you coffee? Espresso?" Bingo. I know for sure I'm supposed to do that.

"I'll take mine black, double shot please," Detective Simmons replies.

"Same," says Detective Cruz.

My hands clatter as I work the machine, wrench two cups down off the shelf.

"We have a few questions for you. Mind if we start?"

"No," I say, keeping my back to them, hoping they don't notice my hands convulsing.

"You work for Nate Sterling and Marisol Torres, is that correct?"

Blood surges through my neck. I practically drop their espressos. "Yes," I say, crossing the room, handing them their coffees. "I'm their personal assistant. Why—" But I stop. I'm not supposed to ask that. "I've been with them for about a month now."

Detective Simmons nods. Clicks the tip of his pen. Scratches something down on his notepad.

"So, you were there today?" he asks. Casual. Not looking up from his notepad.

My throat swells. I don't know how to answer this question.

Detective Cruz looks up at me, her kind eyes smiling, but imploring.

"Uh, no, actually, I wasn't. They gave me this week off." My face burns.

Fuck. I've just lied to the police.

He looks up from his notepad now, fixes his gaze on mine. "You just started working there a month ago and they've already given you a week off?" He scoffs. "Must be nice?"

I grin, nod. Keep my lips sealed shut.

Detective Cruz sips at her espresso, sets it down on the saucer with a clink. "So, Cassidy, we just have to ask," she says in the calm, almost apologetic voice of a gynecologist who's about to perform a Pap smear, "have you noticed anything unusual about the Sterlings lately? Anything going on between them?"

She tilts her head, waits for an answer.

My mind whirls. They *must* know about the photographs; I wish they would just come out and tell me that's why they're really here, instead of leading me into this web so I can entrap myself.

"Uh . . . well, I've only been with them a short time, so I honestly don't know what their normal is, you know?"

My fingers drum the dining table. I lower them, balling them in order to make myself stop. I'm actually quite pleased with my answer. It's not a lie, really, except possibly by omission.

"No, I get that," Detective Cruz says.

Detective Simmons fixes me with a flat stare.

Good cop, bad cop.

"So, when's the last time you saw them?" he asks, clearing his throat.

Fuck.

Well, today while I was peeping through their windows. Oh, and I saw Marisol mounting her lover just a few days ago, having sex.

"Last Saturday."

It's not exactly a lie. Is watching the same thing as seeing? As being with someone? No, it is not.

Alarm floods my bloodstream, causing my ears to ring, though. If they *do* have the photos of Marisol and know that I'm the one who took them, I'm all but digging my own grave here. Further and further into the earth.

"Would you say that you have enjoyed your work with them?" Detective Cruz's soft voice travels across the room, lands in my eardrums.

I tilt my head, paste a thoughtful smile on my face as if I'm giving this question serious consideration.

"Yeah, for the most part."

The way she says *enjoyed*, as if it's in the past, all over with, wrenches something in my chest. Does she know I'm about to get canned because I took pornographic photos of my boss?

"I mean, yeah. Like, they are very generous and the work has been pretty easy so far. I feel like it's a compatible fit. For the most part."

What I want to say—no, shout—is, *Why don't you fucking come out and tell me why you are here?*

"And for the other part?" Detective Simmons asks, a smart-ass smirk playing on his lips.

I pause.

Think, Cassidy.

"I mean, they are people of very high means. Lots of money. Lots of power. So, it's not like we're best friends or anything, you know?"

Damn, that was lame.

"But they've honestly been lovely to work for; *are* lovely to work for."

"And what kind of work do you do for them, exactly? You're their assistant, so, I imagine it's a lot of grunt work?" Detective Simmons is trying to get a rise out of me.

"I don't consider it grunt work. I enjoy it. I'm a writer and it's so much better than being jammed in a cubicle all day. But yes, it can be basic things, like doing their grocery shopping, buying their dog food, trips to the cleaner's—"

Detective Cruz nods at me, but for some reason, her deep brown eyes hold pity, as if I've just told her something sad.

"And Nate, Mr. Sterling," I correct myself, trying to sound not so intimate with him, "has just started letting me read scripts for him."

At this, Detective Simmons's pen starts moving across his notepad again.

That might've been a dumb thing to say.

"Sounds to me like you're getting on with them quite well, then. Especially him?" he asks.

This elicits a nearly imperceptible gasp from Detective Cruz.

My skin reddens even more. "Yes, but I would say with *both* of them. She's very happy with my work, too. I reorganized her whole closet," I say, and a pleading edge creeps into my voice, "and look"—I gesture to the pile of clothes strewn across the floor—"she *gave* me all these as hand-me-downs."

"Wow!" Detective Cruz replies. "Now that's *my* kinda job!"

"Exactly. Like I said, they're very generous people."

"But Cassidy, if there's anything, even if it seems small to you, insignificant, that you've picked up on, that might be off about them. Any arguing, anything, you can tell us," she says.

"Why?" I blurt out, because I can't stand it anymore. "Has something happened?"

It's lightning quick, so fast that I almost miss it, but Cruz and Simmons exchange a glance, conferring on something.

Detective Simmons gets to his feet. “Don’t worry about that now. We’ll be in touch if we need to ask you any further questions.”

Detective Cruz rises, too, places a hand on my shoulder. “Thanks for talking to us today, Cassidy. Here’s my card. In case something comes to you later.”

As the door is closing behind them, I feel like I’m falling through the floor into an infinite, nightmarish pit.

Part of me is relieved. If they were here about the pictures, then surely they would’ve said so eventually, after I didn’t offer that up.

But if they’re not here for the photos, why *are* they here, questioning me like cops do during a crime investigation?

I see Marisol in my mind’s eye again, lunging toward Nate, grasping at his throat.

Then standing over something, looking downward. Rushing from the house.

Holy shit.

The nightmarish pit expands and I’m free-falling into it.

59

MY CELL CHIRPS, causing me to jump, hoping it's finally Nate.

It's Lexie.

Lexie: See you soon? Xxx

Damn. I'm due there in an hour.

Me: Yes! Running a little late tho. Prolly 7:30! Xo

Lexie: 👍

My feet stayed glued to the floor. I can't move; I'm immobilized, like in a dream where you're trying to run from danger but can't lift your legs.

I need to think. Calm down. Breathe.

I can't believe I lied to the cops. Twice. First about not being over there today, second about the last time I saw them being last Saturday.

This is not good.

The only thing I can do now is hope that my mind is spiraling out of control. Maybe they got a domestic dispute call from Marisol or something. Maybe they don't know about the photos that I took. Maybe Nate wasn't actually sprawled out on the floor with Marisol standing over him. Maybe my mind was, and is, playing tricks on me.

Inhale. Exhale. *Think*.

Cell still in my hand, I scroll through my texts until I reach Marisol's name, then open our last text thread.

I tap out a casual message.

Cassidy: Just checking in! See you guys Monday! Lemme know if you need me to pick up anything on my way. Scripts from Nate's office, stuff from cleaner's! Xo

This might be the stupidest thing that I've done yet, but why not act like nothing at all is wrong? Why do I always assume the worst?

If something *has* happened, or is amiss, why not pretend on text, as a sort of written record, that everything on my end, at least, is perfectly fine?

I stand in my sweat-soaked robe, staring at the cell, willing Marisol to text me back. Or, at least, for an indication that she's read it. But no matter how many times I blink at the screen, my text just lolls there, unread, un-responded to, ignored.

60

I'M HEADING OVER to Lexie and Harry's numb, careening around the canyons.

I managed to make a little effort with my hair, toss on one of Marisol's cute wrap dresses. A floral print. Which feels like the opposite of what I should be wearing.

A trickle of cars spills from Lexie's drive.

I need a drink and I need one fast to get through this social event.

I park and am ambling up when Lexie sails down the drive, hair up in a messy but chic bun, exquisite figure hugged by a little black dress, face pink from the sun.

She's walking barefoot, which is so Lexie, it makes me smile.

"Yay, you made it!"

She threads her arm through mine, guides me up the steep hill.

"Come on, there's a hottie I want you to meet." On her breath, I smell gin. She loves her martinis.

"God, really? I mean, I'm not sure if I'm ready—"

But she digs her nails into my arms, cracks open the front door. Steers me into the living room.

It's an expansive, midcentury space with a bank of glass serving as the back wall overlooking the deck, and beyond it, the canyon.

Harry is at the stereo, nestling a record onto the turntable, and a few clumps of people are gathered throughout the room, clutching cocktails.

"The looker in black," Lexie hisses in my ear.

My eyes land on a tall guy in the corner, hanging out alone. Black jeans, tight black T-shirt, dark hair. Gorgeous, but not too gorgeous. My stomach spins a little as I stare at him.

"Hey, everyone!" Lexie yells above the music.

Harry twists the volume down.

"I want you to meet my best friend in the whole world, Cassidy Foster! She just moved here from Texas, so y'all give her a warm welcome!"

My throat burns as a sea of eyes feasts on me.

"Hey!" I squeak out.

Some lift their glasses to me; others nod, smiling; but thankfully, no one bum-rushes me.

"Let's go." Lexie tugs at my arm.

"Can I at least have a drink first, Mommy?"

"Oh, shit! Sorry. Yesss, follow moi."

Harry gives me a quick hug on our way to the kitchen. "Thanks for coming."

"Thanks for having me!"

"Well? Whatcha having?"

"I'll have one of your famous martinis. I can crash here, right?"

"Absofuckinglutely!"

Lexie tugs open the freezer, pulls out a fancy bottle of gin and also vermouth.

"You're all sun-kissed and gorgeous!" I say. "How was the beach?"

She swirls the vermouth in the bottom of a martini glass before dumping it; it frosts along the sides. "Glorious! Harry rented us a convertible. But it was too brief. And also . . . stressful? Like I knew planning a wedding would be! We narrowed the venue down to three spots, though."

She screws open a jar of green olives, drains a shot of the juice in the cocktail shaker before plucking out two olives.

It's delicious. Icy. Salty. Peppery. Dinner in a glass.

"My god, this is *so* good."

In the dwindling sunlight, her eyes shimmer. "I can't believe we're here together, toasting." She raises her drink to me, clacks it against mine.

"To us!" she proclaims.

"Hear, hear!"

"And to Felix, the hottie in the next room."

"Shhh, not so loud!"

As the liquor rolls through my bloodstream, I begin to relax. To soften.

Louis Prima pipes through the speaker in the living room; Lexie grabs my arm again, leads me back in there.

Felix is still alone in the corner, holding what looks like a glass of bourbon.

On the wall above the fireplace, their flat-screen hangs.

The sound is off, but the Dodgers game is on.

I dig my feet into the rug. "Not just yet. Lemme get a little more liquored."

"Fine!" Lexie pauses next to me, eyes dancing with mirth.

Louis Prima gives way to Rosemary Clooney singing "Mambo Italiano," and I actually feel my hips twitch to the infectious tune. It might be the gin, but there's a loosening in my chest from being in this room with these people, doing something very normal. I'm with my sister and feel invincible by her side, the visit from the detectives earlier a receding memory.

The room brims with possibility, that shaky, buzzy feeling at the start of a very good party. There's Felix now, leaning against the wall, stealing a glance at me as Lexie and I bump hips.

She lifts my drink from me, sets it on the sideboard, then twirls me around the room. She's always literally the life of the party. A magnet. All eyes are trained on us.

I'm getting lost in the song when Harry turns the stereo down.

"What the?" Lexie says.

But then she follows his gaze and her expression twists into curiosity.

A hush falls over the room as Harry completely silences the record, stabs the remote, raising the volume.

On the TV, where a shot of the Dodgers crowd just was, is the local news. A red ticker runs across the bottom of the television, streaming words that my eyes can read but that I can't compute.

Acclaimed Hollywood director Nate Sterling
found dead in his Malibu home this afternoon.
Police are investigating . . .

61

HOT TEARS CLOUD my eyes; I'm dizzy, like I might faint. I feel Lexie's hand on my shoulder, but other than that, I'm not of this world. It's as if I've left my body and I'm floating above the room, a kite on a string.

It can't be. But somehow, it is. The ticker at the bottom of the screen continues to stream and now my brain registers the sight of the Sterlings' house, the yellow stucco exterior, the walled fence of green shrubs, but now a reporter is standing out front, feet planted on the sidewalk.

I hear the words she is speaking but can only decipher some of them. The rest sounds like the teacher in the Charlie Brown cartoons I watched when I was little: "*Waa, waa-waa.*"

The reporter punctuates the part that I can't stop hearing: "Investigators are treating this as a possible homicide."

Harry lowers the volume; the room fills with hushed voices that are climbing louder.

"Did anybody know him?" someone asks.

"She *works* for them," Harry proclaims, causing every neck to twist in my direction.

He doesn't say it in an accusatory way at all, but somehow, it still lands in my ears like that.

Bile surges up the back of my throat. I feel like I'm going to be ill.

"Oh my god, so sorry," people seem to mutter around me.

Lexie's pressure on my shoulder becomes deeper as she squeezes it, steers me outside onto their vast deck.

As if they just heard the news, too, the towering grove of eucalyptus trees brays in the wind that gusts from the canyon.

Tears strangling my throat, I stagger to the railing, let them pour out.

Nate is gone. Nate is dead.

Lexie wraps her arms around me, hugging me from behind.

"Cassidy—"

I can't stop crying.

Finally, she swivels me around. Her face is etched with distress, as if I'm a hand grenade whose pin has just been pulled.

How can he be dead?

He was just here, roaming through his house yesterday.

The memory of Marisol lunging at him, then swaying over something on the floor, comes flooding back.

As does the detectives' visit to my apartment.

Why didn't I knock on the door when I saw them fighting? Why didn't I stop this very thing that I helped put in motion? I know the answer, of course: I couldn't have thrown myself even more into the middle of things than I already had, and I certainly couldn't have predicted his death, his possible murder, but . . . if I had inserted myself, he might still be here.

Lexie knows some of the behind-the-scenes stuff, but not the latest. Her eyes are scanning my face. Eyes that know me the best.

"I'm so, so sorry, Cass. You really fell for him, and I didn't want to feed this the other night, but it sounded like y'all really clicked. This is so awful I just don't even know—"

"I can't fucking believe this." Fresh tears spring to my eyes. "If I hadn't sent him those pics—"

"Wait, what? You think *that* had something to do with this? It was probably a burglary gone bad . . . you're not saying that you think Marisol—" Her voice trails off as her eyes continue to laser my face.

I look up at her, sheepishly. Guiltily.

"Whoa, whoa. What are you *not* telling me?"

"Nothing." I swallow. "Just that I—" My eyes drop, tracing the thick cedar planks of their deck.

Her hand is back on my shoulder, squeezing it, as if imploring me to keep talking.

"I saw something."

Silence pulses between us.

"Cassidy." She says my name as if asking me a question. "Tell me you did not go back over there. That you didn't keep spying—"

"I did, okaaay?" I answer, my voice wild with emotion. "Just twice. Once yesterday. And then again today."

"And?" Lexie asks calmly, carefully. Coaxing.

"Didn't see anything yesterday really. But today—" I shake my head at the memory of it all.

Marisol at the valet. Marisol bursting from the hotel in a heated state. Driving home like a maniac. Having it out with Nate. Big-time. Then standing over him—now I *know* it was him on the floor.

Lexie's hands are on my wrists, kneading them. "Tell me."

I go through it all with her, piece by piece. When I finish, she tilts her head to the sky, shakes her long blond hair, as if asking the universe, *Is this all the crazy you got for us?*

"Oh my fucking god, Cassidy. It sounds like you witnessed a murder."

I don't really want to think this of Marisol, but I also don't know what else to think. Except . . . "Yeah, or like self-defense. I mean, he was going at her, too. She could have just gotten a little carried away—"

"A little?" Lexie's voice hisses out of her.

"I don't *know*!"

"Well, don't you think you should go to the police?"

"I probably should've called them when I saw all that, but . . . I just thought it was another one of their nasty fights. I didn't think Nate was *dead*. Not until—" I pause. I don't want to tell her this next part.

"Out with it." Her blue eyes are frosty, serious.

"Not until the detectives came over this afternoon." It rushes out of me before I can stop it.

"Hold up. *What?*" Lexie's eyes are now steel blades. "Actually, hang on. I'm getting our drinks."

Shit. I shouldn't have told her. But how could I possibly keep all this to myself?

While she's inside, I slip out my cell.

Look at my text to Marisol, about going over on Monday.

No reply.

But now, the notification has changed from *Delivered* to *Read*.

Should I text her? Let her know how very sorry I am that Nate is dead?

My thumbs are on the keypad when I hear the sliding glass door open. Lexie approaches with the watery remains of our martinis.

We sink down on the bench that rims the rail and sip, my throat welcoming the punishing burn of alcohol.

Lexie stares straight ahead—not at me—as she asks this next, biting question. "Cassidy, I just have to know—" She rolls her shoulders. "Is there something you're not telling me?"

A knife to the chest.

"What do you mean?"

All around us, the sickle-shaped leaves of the eucalyptus clatter in the wind.

"You just told me you were at the Sterlings' earlier today. And now—"

"Oh my fucking god," I erupt. "You don't think—"

She gives her head a hard, jagged shake. "Of *course* not. It's just," she says, then sighs. "If you by chance went inside the house, like during, before, or after, or hell, I don't know, if there's something you're not telling me. Because honestly, you haven't been telling me *a lot*, so—"

"No, I didn't go inside. I haven't been back in their house since last Saturday. Swear to god. I only wanted to see what they were up to, you know? After I sent those pics."

"Okay, okay, I'm just trying to help. Run damage control—"

"Damage control?" My voice contorts, rises up a few volumes in pitch.

"Cassidy! The cops were at your apartment today, hello?"

"But I haven't done anything wrong—"

But that's not true. That's not true at all. I've instigated nearly all of this. Spying on Marisol, snapping pics of her, sending them to Nate. *Not* intervening when it seemed they were in distress. Fleeing the scene. I can practically hear the bars of the jail cell clanking shut.

"I know you didn't. But your hands aren't clean here, either."

Panic squeezes my chest. I down the rest of my drink.

"What should I do?"

"Just stay cool. And maybe get a lawyer—" She snorts, laughing.

"It's not funny!"

"I know, I know, it's *so* not funny that it actually is."

This is classic Lexie behavior. Laughing at the most inappropriate of times.

"I need to go home. Seriously. Need to think about what I'm going to do."

"You should stay here—"

"I really don't want to. The party and all. I need to get into my own bed—"

"And tomorrow, you should call those detectives again. Tell them exactly what you saw—"

The panic squeezes me harder; I clamber to my feet, try to inhale a few deep breaths. "I don't want them to know I was *spying* on them, though—I don't know what to do."

Lexie stands up, grips me into a hug. "You're going to be *fine*. But you probably should tell them what you saw, dontcha think?" She pulls back from me, blue eyes swimming over me.

62

I'M WRENCHED FROM sacred sleep by the sound of pounding at the door.

Nate is still in my head as I lurch from the bed. I was suspended in a thin state of dreaming all night, seeing his face, feeling the brush of his lips against mine, his voice like aged bourbon in my ear.

In one dream, he looked up at me through the window. I was sitting in my car while he and Marisol wrestled in the living room. His face was sad, pleading. Begging me to help.

The pounding continues.

I plod across the room, clasp the doorknob.

Detectives Cruz and Simmons stand on my stoop, their figures framed in frothy morning light.

Last night, when I got home from Lexie's, I sat at my dining table, nursing a mug of chamomile tea, flicking the edge of Detective Cruz's card.

I wanted to call her, tell her everything, but I was still torn about outing myself, admitting I had all but been stalking the Sterlings.

Now I wish I had.

"Morning," I offer.

Detective Cruz gives me a sad smile; Detective Simmons nods, a quick, jerky gesture.

"Come in, please." I step aside, letting them pass. "I was actually going to call you last night," I stammer.

"That would've been the smart thing to do," Detective Simmons growls.

"Coffee? Same as last time?"

A look passes between them. "No, thanks. We're here to talk." Detective Cruz keeps up her solemn smile, though she's basically just given me code for: *Cut the shit, this isn't a social call.*

They perch again on the edge of the futon, pens poised above their notepads, ravens on an electrical wire.

"Why don't you start by telling us what you left out last time?" Detective Simmons says, eyes narrowed at me. "I'm sure you've seen the news. Your boss," he says, clearing his throat, "uh, former boss, is dead."

Against my will, tears cloud my eyes.

Detective Cruz is on her feet, reaching for the box of Kleenex. She plucks a few out, squats down in front of me. I retrieve them from her hand, sop my eyes. To my surprise, she hugs me. "I'm so sorry. I know you guys were close."

This at once comforts and alarms me. I know I mentioned to them about Nate letting me read his scripts and I remember how Detective Simmons had reacted, insinuating that Nate and I were close.

After a moment, she returns to the futon.

"So, Cassidy. As my partner here just said, we know there's more for you to tell us. Things you left out yesterday."

Man, she gets an A-plus in diplomacy. She doesn't say that I out-and-out lied to them, even though I did.

I sigh upward, blasting my forehead with air.

"Why don't we start from the beginning? When is the last time you saw the Sterlings?" she asks.

I have no choice but to start spilling.

"On Friday. Yesterday." It already feels like a month ago. "I was . . . in their neighborhood and stopped by. And—" My voice wavers.

"Go on. We need to know everything. It will enormously help us with our investigation." She pastes on a warm smile.

"Well, soon after I got there, Marisol left in her car."

"And?" she asks, her eyes expectant.

"And, well, I followed her."

A look passes between them.

Great.

"Is this something you did regularly? Hang out in your car outside their house? Follow her?" Simmons barks. "Never mind, we'll come back to that in a minute. Go on."

A metal taste floods my mouth.

"She drove to the Beverly Hilton. Left her car with the valet. Nate told me she regularly lunches with her manager. So I figured that's what she was doing. But then—and this was really strange to me—she bolted from the Hilton like twenty minutes later."

Another look passes between them. This time, Detective Simmons squints at me as if he's trying to decode me.

"And so, I followed her back home—"

"As one does," he mutters under his breath before Cruz slaps his knee.

"And she raced home, driving pretty wildly. She seemed upset. And when she got home, that's when I saw them." My hands start to quake in my lap, recounting the memory of it.

"Saw them . . ." Cruz looks at me, nods.

"I saw them arguing, in the living room."

Yet another glance between the detectives.

A pit of guilt roils in my stomach; I'm all but hanging Marisol here. But I don't know what else to do; I can't keep on lying to the police. Lexie is right about that. And if she did truly kill him in self-defense, then she won't go to jail. At least that's what happens in the movies. I feel myself swaying back and forth, rocked with emotion. I haven't even *thought* about what Marisol must be going through. She was cheating on Nate, yes, but she still most likely loved him. At least I think she did? Unless . . .

"And you were just sitting in your car the entire time?" Detective Simmons cuts into my stream of consciousness, his voice jarring.

"Umm, yes."

He clicks his pen, scratches a long note on his pad.

"Yes. Like I told you guys, they had given me the week off. I was due to go back Monday, and I guess, I don't know, I felt like going over there." The words jumble in my mouth. I have the teetering sensation that I'm walking down a steep hill in stilettos, ready to take a tumble at any second. "Okay, okay. Listen. The truth is, they had been having problems. Bickering. Fighting."

Simmons lifts his eyebrows at me in mock surprise, an apparent silent chide for me withholding this information yesterday. "About what, would you say?"

I swallow. I have no idea if they know about the photographs on Nate's phone yet. Surely they must. But I'm still going to keep that little detail close to the vest for now. "Mainly about Marisol being gone a lot. She's been on a long audition for a big role, and she's been scattered here and there. And, well, Nate, he didn't like it."

Simmons clicks his pen. Over and over. The sound sets my teeth on edge.

As if sensing the surge in my anxiety, Detective Cruz takes over. "Cassidy, you can tell us everything you know, okay? Did you ever see Nate get physical with his wife?"

Other than catching them screwing in the pool?

I almost chuckle at that absurd, intrusive thought.

Then I think of the slap, though I'm still pretty certain it was Marisol who was doing the slapping.

"No, no, I didn't."

Click, click, click.

I want to snatch the pen from him, stab him in the leg with it.

"Okay, let's get back to yesterday. You saw them fighting." Cruz says this as a statement. "What did that look like exactly?"

I tell her everything. About the sun darting in and out from behind the clouds, partially obscuring my view. About Nate lunging for Marisol, Marisol lunging back at Nate. Then, when the windows became clear again, Marisol looking down at the floor, as if at something. Or someone. Then rushing from the room.

"And what time was this, would you say?" she asks.

"Around one o'clock."

They silently confer again, study each other.

Shit. Shit. Shit.

"I'm gonna be real honest with you here, Ms. Foster," Simmons says. Hearing my surname in his mouth makes the back of my neck tense. "What you're telling us doesn't add up. At all."

Fear coats me like a weighted blanket. Here comes the part about the photographs. He's about to let loose on me, tell me that I was lying about my reason for being over there.

"I don't understand—"

"Then let me be real fucking clear with you. *You* were at the house at the time of Mr. Sterling's death." He stabs his notepad with the tip of his pen, like that proves whatever point he's about to make. "But Marisol Torres was not."

63

THE ROOM TILTS; the detectives' faces blur.

What the hell is he saying? Of *course* Marisol was there. I saw her with my own eyes. She's lying. Maybe she *didn't* kill him in self-defense and she's covering her ass about whatever did happen.

Because when they find out she's a cheater—if they haven't already—that's Motive 101 to off a spouse.

"I'm sorry, what? I don't understand." My voice cracks. "Marisol was *there*. I saw her, followed her home—"

Detective Cruz gives a sympathetic nod. "You're right about one thing. She was at the Beverly Hilton. Only," she starts, her eyes oozing with the sympathy one reserves for a troubled child, "she never left."

"But that's impossible!" My voice climbs an octave. "I saw her leave! Followed her home. Saw her in the house with Nate. Arguing. She's *lying*."

"No, you're the only one who is lying here." Simmons jabs a chubby index finger at me. "She stayed at the Hilton until nearly two thirty and there are witnesses."

My heartbeat is a coked-up woodpecker thrumming against my temples.

This can't be. Are the so-called witnesses lying for her or am I losing it? "Could she maybe have said she was going to the bathroom, slipped out for a bit, then came back?"

"Absolutely not. She never left the table, in fact." Simmons crosses his arms on his chest, fixes me with a sour smile. He's enjoying this, the bastard.

Cruz taps my knee. "Cassidy, you've been through a lot. Are you *sure* that's what you think you saw?"

Am I sure? Am I sure of anything at this moment?

I falter, reel back in my mind to yesterday.

Hell yes, I'm sure. I saw her leave, trailed her home, saw her struggle with Nate.

"Yes." I grit my teeth. "Marisol is lying."

"And why do you think she would lie?" Simmons asks.

"Because she was cheating on her husband!" I practically shout.

"So when we asked you yesterday if anything was off about them, you didn't think to mention that?" Simmons cocks his head to one side.

"I—I didn't—" I'm stammering again.

"Didn't what? Want to implicate yourself in Mr. Sterling's murder?"

"I—"

"Look. We have his cell. And we saw the photos you texted him. Which is illegal, by the way—taking pictures of someone in their private residence without their knowledge—"

"But I—"

"Let me finish. We already know about the affair Ms. Torres was having. So if you think that's some trump card you were holding, it isn't. She came clean about the whole thing. We've already talked to her lover—who was at the doctor at the time of the murder, before you start in on accusing him, too—and sadly, having an affair doesn't equal murder. Like you might've thought." He finishes, leans back, triumphant.

"What are you saying? You think I—"

"What *we* think," he says, glancing at Cruz, "is that you were in love with Nate. *Obsessed*—that's the word Marisol used to describe your feelings for her husband—and something happened. Maybe he didn't want a relationship with you. And, well, you've obviously been watching Marisol. You took those photographs, you sent them to her husband, trying to blow up their marriage. Why else? And then he winds up dead and you're telling the police you watched his wife possibly kill him? When she wasn't even there? But you were?"

The blood drains from my head; I feel like I might faint. This is so much worse than I could have ever imagined.

But I know I saw Marisol. None of this makes any sense. Someone is lying. Big-time.

"I—" I struggle to form words. "I wasn't *obsessed* with Nate, ahem, Mr. Sterling. And I wasn't just arbitrarily spying on Marisol. Mr. Sterling ordered me to do so. Paid me extra for it."

There. It's all out on the table now for all to see and judge me for.

The detectives eye each other again.

"Cassidy. Let me see if I'm understanding. You're saying Mr. Sterling is the one who had you watch Marisol?" Cruz asks me without a trace of smugness in her voice, like she's genuinely curious.

"That's correct."

"And when did this start?"

I tell them everything. His suspicions about Andreas, the times I spied on her. I even hand them my cell to flip through the photos I snapped. Simmons's eyes nearly pop out of his head as he views the pictures.

"And you said he paid you for this?" Cruz asks.

I gulp. This makes me look so bad. "Yes. It's complicated. Like, I didn't *want* to do it, but I felt sorry for him and—"

"And he was apparently promising you a career jump of sorts?" Cruz nods as if she wants me to agree with her.

"Exactly. I mean, not exactly. One wasn't contingent on the other, but he had indeed just begun to let me read scripts for him, so, yes, I was in an awkward position."

"I'll say so," Simmons chortles.

"And he paid you. Would this be on your paycheck? Can we verify?" Cruz asks.

My stomach sinks. "I get paid by direct deposit. And no. He paid me in cash. I didn't even want to take it, but he gave me an envelope with five thousand dollars in cash—"

"Do you still have that? We could run fingerprints—"

"No. I tossed the envelope and deposited the cash. I can show you the cash deposit, though."

She's scratching in her notepad, seemingly unimpressed by this.

"And these photos you sent to Mr. Sterling. Is that the only text exchange you guys had?" she probes. "Any emails? Did he not want these other photos?"

"No, no. He was super private about everything. So I showed him the pics when we were together. Those last ones I sent—I sent them a few days back, when I had the week off. I wanted him to know the truth. That he wasn't crazy about Marisol. That she really was cheating."

"So, there is literally no record that Mr. Sterling actually asked you to perform private investigative services for him," Simmons coldly states.

Dammit.

Hysteria clasps my throat.

"I'm not lying!" I screech. "And she *was* cheating on him! He told me it was the real reason he hired me: to watch her."

A guffaw coughs out of Simmons.

"I'm afraid the photos I sent were the reason for their fight."

Cruz gnaws on her bottom lip. "But we've told you, Marisol was not at the house. There *was* no fight."

I want to scream. I want to fling open the door, run from this place. Hop in my car, drive back to Texas. I don't understand what the hell is going on.

I *saw* her. I saw *them*. At the time of the murder.

My mind clicks and clacks around like spokes on a wheel, whirring. Thinking. *Think*, Cassidy, *think*.

I blink my eyes shut, force myself to—once again—replay the events of yesterday.

Then my mind does a jump cut, leaps back to that morning when I arrived at the Sterlings' for work. Let myself in. Heard the trickling of laughter from outside. Saw Nate and Marisol on the lawn, giggling.

Except it *wasn't* Marisol.

It was Jessica.

"Cassidy, are you all right?" Cruz places a tentative hand on my knee again, breaking my train of thought.

"Yes. I'm more than all right. In fact, I think I've just come up with our suspect."

Simmons sighs. "This oughta be good."

"Okay, hear me out. I don't know her last name or where she lives or anything, but Marisol works with a stand-in. A body double. Looks *just* like her. Her name is Jessica. I met her a few times. She was always flirting with Nate. Like, big-time. Told me she thought he was, and this is a quote, a 'total snack.'" I lean back, cross my own arms over my chest. "Maybe, just maybe, somehow she was following *me*, watching the Sterlings herself, and led me on a wild-goose chase to their house. And killed Nate. But made it look like it was Marisol."

I know I'm reaching, but also this theory is starting to take hold, become my predominant reality. "She really could be her doppelganger. So you should definitely look into her. And, also, I never liked her. There was something about her—" I shiver.

Detective Cruz gives me another encouraging nod. "We'll follow up on this, too. Thank you, Cassidy." She rolls her pen around in her hand. "Have you told us everything?"

I suck in a breath.

No, I haven't told you that Nate kissed me. More than once. That we were on the verge of having hot sex. That he was having me read a secret script of his. That I was pretty much in love with him. And I think he had real feelings for me, too.

But I can't tell them that. Why should I have to? It will only make me look worse and there's no way they can find out that we made out, almost made love. He's dead.

"Yep. That's it."

She looks over to Simmons, who shrugs, slaps his notepad shut. Stands up so harshly that the metal feet of the futon scrape against the pine floorboards.

"We're leaving now, but I think you know we're not done here," Simmons says. "Don't leave town. Stick close to home, keep your cell on you. We'll definitely be in touch."

64

I'M SHAKING; RATTLED. I need to call Lexie.

She answers on the fourth ring, something that annoys me, given my current situation.

"Heeey," she answers. Breezy. Casual. A bit cold.

"Hi," I say, my voice tremoring. "What are you up to?"

"Just hanging with Harry. Remember? I'm leaving in the morning?"

I feel like I can't breathe. I forgot all about Lexie heading back to Prague. She simply can't leave me.

"But I think I'm gonna push my flight 'til Monday. Harry wants me to stay since we haven't had all that much time together, so—" Her voice dwindles. She doesn't come out and say it, but it feels like she just insinuated that my drama has interrupted their alone time.

"Got it." Hurt swells inside me.

"Hang on." The swishing sound of the sliding glass door opening fills the line. "Stepping out onto the deck, so we can talk in private. You talk to the police again yet?"

"They actually just left. It's why I'm calling. Lexie, I'm freaking the eff out. They think *I* had something to do with Nate's murder."

A silent pause blooms between us, one she doesn't attempt to fill. An icky feeling creeps over me: does Lexie also think I murdered Nate? Is that why she's icing me out?

"I *know* I saw Marisol arguing with him; I followed her home from the hotel. But . . . but they are saying—" Tears strangle my throat. I feel like I'm trying to convince my own goddamn best friend of my innocence.

"What are they saying, Cassidy?" she asks, concern sharpening her voice.

"That she never left the hotel!"

"What?"

"I know! Look, can I come over? I'm flipping out!"

Lexie sighs. "Chica, I wish. But Harry's cooking for us right now and I promised him a quiet, romantic evening, just the two of us. *And* we're crash-planning the wedding."

I can't believe how incredibly childish she sounds, and Harry sounds, right now. And selfish. My boss, my love interest, just got axed and I'm on the hook for it, but they're more concerned about having date night than they are about me, who is falling to absolute pieces. Sometimes, I really detest coupledom.

I can't help it; a rattly sob erupts.

"Hey, hey there." Lexie's voice is warmer now. "You're going to be fine. I promise. Listen, I'll push my flight 'til Monday for sure. Come over tomorrow, okay?"

"Okay," I blubber out, still feeling stung.

"Gotta run. Harry's waving me in. Hang in there, chica. See you tomorrow."

65

I HAVEN'T SLEPT other than fits and starts.

I'm at my kitchen window, staring out. A blanket of fog hugs the basin below. I give my latte a quick, jagged stir before dumping it from my ceramic mug into a to-go cup. Snatching my keys off the counter, I march outside before changing my mind.

I've never seen the fog before in LA; it's mystical, a stratus cloud suspended over the usually smoggy streets.

It feels strange driving over to the Sterlings', knowing that Nate isn't home. Will never be home. The house now belongs to Marisol.

Marisol, who didn't murder Nate. Who was nowhere near the scene of the crime.

But who still might have been behind it all.

Last night as I tossed and turned, a new theory took root in my mind. One I haven't been able to shake: what if Marisol and Jessica are in cahoots?

Marisol had been feeling constrained by Nate, hemmed in, and now that she landed the dream role she'd been vying for, she didn't need him anymore. Didn't need his connections to give her a leg up in Hollywood.

What she does need is his money. His house.

And him out of the way so that she can fully take up with Andreas.

I'm not certain how Jessica fits into the picture, only that I never liked the bitch and that this could've been the stand-in role of a lifetime. If Jessica *had* been spying on me, watching me, keeping tabs, then she knew I was watching *them*, and staged the whole thing to lure me back to their house and witness the murder.

The impossible murder because Marisol is alibied to the hilt.

And Jessica is a phantom.

Except for the fact that I've fingered her to the police.

Even with their banter, she and Marisol seem like fast friends—Jessica driving Marisol around in her convertible Mercedes, staying on the payroll even when there's not an active film shooting.

Jessica probably wasn't even flirting with Nate, but playing him. Going along with things. Biding her time.

If this is all true, I bet Marisol is going to take really good care of her, and Jessica, a starving wannabe actress, will be set.

As I turn on the Sterlings' street, my heart flutters.

There's Marisol, about a hundred feet from the house, walking Oscar and Percy. Damn. I'm not prepared to see her right this second.

But even though I'm a ball of nerves, this might even be better; I couldn't count on her answering the door for me.

I cruise up beside her. As oblivious as ever, she *still* doesn't seem to recognize my car. This, too, works in my favor.

I lower the window. "Hey! Marisol!"

She twists her head in my direction and the expression on her face is unmistakable: unadulterated fear. She wrenches the dogs' leashes and starts racing toward the house.

I call after her again, this time more urgently. "Marisol, wait!"

She keeps trucking, so I hop out of the car, bound down the sidewalk toward her. I've got to say something so she won't be this spooked by my presence.

"I'm so sorry about Nate!" I yell to her backside. "And I'm so sorry I sent those photos. I didn't mean—"

This stops her. She jerks around. Oscar and Percy lunge toward me, tails wagging, and it's excruciating to me that I can't pet them.

"You knew *exactly* what you were doing," she hisses.

"I'm sorry! I shouldn't have ever agreed to go along with it, to let Nate talk me into spying on you! I got carried away—"

Her face twists into confusion. "What are you talking about?"

She sounds genuinely confused. But it occurs to me that I only *just* told the cops this and if Nate never brought me and the spying up when he confronted her, then she truly doesn't know what I'm talking about.

"You really don't know? Nate hired me to spy on you. He paid me extra to do it." The gap between us has closed and at least I'm no longer shouting. "That's why I have those pictures of you. Although, he didn't actually ask me to take those, but he *did* ask me to spy on you. I have other photos as well."

She stands there, silently taking this all in. Even if she thinks I'm crazy and killed her husband, some of this must ring true for her because their fights were ramping up; Nate was coming down on her.

"Listen, I really need your help. The cops think *I* had something to do with Nate's—" I can't form the word *murder.* "And you know I would never. You know how much I care for you guys—"

"Ha!" She tosses her head back, shakes it as if in disbelief. "I know how much you cared for *him*. The way you hung on his every word, followed him around like a little puppy. The way you were with him in the pool—"

"Okay, yes, I had a crush and I'm sorry about that," I blurt out. "But I really do need your help. Listen to me." I'm pleading now, my voice sounding like a creaky door. "I followed you that day to the Hilton."

She takes a step back, stares at me as if I'm psycho.

"And then, like, twenty minutes later, I swear to god I followed you home. But the cops are saying it wasn't you! But I saw someone who *looked* like you arguing with Nate in the living room." I stab the air in the direction of said room.

"I don't know what you're talking about. I *wasn't* here. But you were, Cassidy." She spits my name out as if it's an object of filth. "Now, get the fuck off my property."

"But what about Jessica? She looks just like you—" I hadn't intended to spill my theory for her, but it gushes out, a fire hydrant with its valve removed.

"You're fucking crazy. Get away from me!" She's shouting now. "I'm calling the police. I know you were in love with him, you back-stabbing freak show!"

I'm not technically *on* her property, I'm just on the sidewalk out front, but to Marisol, everything is her property.

She yanks the leashes; the boys give me one last look before following her inside the house.

66

I'M FLYING UP Highway 1, the Pacific at my side, wind whipping my face.

That was dumb, me going over there.

She's probably on the phone to the cops right now, telling them about my little surprise visit.

Great. I'll look even crazier and more suspicious than I already do.

I don't know what to think. She seemed genuinely dumbfounded when I told her that Nate was having me spy on her. I guess he stayed true to his word, never mentioned me. But I'm glad she now knows, even if she doesn't believe me.

Either she *is* in cahoots with Jessica or Jessica completely acted on her own. I regret spilling that particular tea, but I was desperate, wanted to reach her, to provoke her into saying something, to get some kind of reaction so I could know what in the hell is going on.

I know I saw her. Only, it wasn't her. So, it must have been Jessica.

I'm kicking myself for never getting her last name. At least I told

Detective Cruz about her; maybe she's looking into her at this very moment.

I veer onto the 10, speeding toward home, twisting through the hills until I reach my street.

My stomach lurches when I round the bend.

There, standing out front of my opened apartment door, is Mrs. Charlie, in her bathrobe. Her arms crossed, expression pinched.

The detectives' patrol car is parked out front.

When Mrs. Charlie sees me, she purses her lips.

"What's going on?" I ask, tumbling out of the driver's side.

"They had a search warrant; I had no choice but to let them in." She eyes me with suspicion. "Then they told me that Mr. Sterling was your boss. Guess I never asked who you worked for. And that he's now dead."

I don't have time to play games with Mrs. Charlie, so I scoot around her, step inside my apartment.

Detective Cruz is heading toward the door. "Cassidy," she says, sealing a plastic bag with what looks like a set of my journals, "you're going to need to come to the station with us. Answer some questions on record. Is this going to be a problem?"

And what if I say no? Is that when they'd slap the cuffs on me, push my head down as they wedge me into the back of their patrol car?

"No, not at all." Defiance surges inside me. "I haven't done anything *wrong*."

Gone are her kind eyes. Now she eyes me with a look that says, *Bitch, please.*

In the corner, Detective Simmons rifles through my dresser. Opening drawers, lifting contents off the top, bagging them up.

"Why are y'all going through my stuff?" I feel violated, empty.

"Because you are our number one person of interest." Simmons peels his latex glove off. "Any more questions?"

"I think we have everything we need here," Cruz says to Simmons.

I watch as they file out with my things.

"Hey, when will I get my stuff back?"

"That should be the least of your worries right now," Simmons retorts.

67

THE RIDE TO the police station is surreal. I feel like I'm having an out-of-body experience, like I'm watching Cassidy Foster, an actress on TV playing the role of murderess who's now being brought in for questioning.

Bile edges up the back of my throat and I can feel my nails digging into my palms.

My journals.

I can't believe they took my journals and god knows what else.

But my journals. My innermost thoughts.

Shit. My innermost thoughts about Nate.

I remember the day when he told me to go home, take the week off, that they were going to try and work it out, how angry I was. How hot and blinding my fury was.

I wrote it all down. I was in such a rage I don't even know what I wrote, but it was something to the effect of, *He can't just cast me off. I'll show him.*

Cruz and Simmons already read those lines—I know it—and are ready to blast me.

This is so bad. So freaking bad I don't know what to do.

I should get a lawyer. But I can't afford one. I don't even have a job anymore.

If it comes down to it, I'll just have to ask Lexie. She'll *have* to help me.

We arrive at a pecan-colored building.

Detective Cruz leads me out of the car, inside, and down a hall, soft hand at my elbow. Simmons trails us, a grumpy bulldog trudging down the hall.

The room they usher me into smells of Clorox and coffee. A squat black digital recorder sits in the middle of a long conference table.

"Please have a seat." Detective Cruz motions to the lone chair opposite the ones they plop down on.

"We just want to ask you some questions, Cassidy, clear some things up. Mind if I turn this on?"

I shake my head.

"Great." She presses a button and a red light blinks, signaling doom to me.

After she asks me to state my name for the record and all the other standard questions, Simmons rakes his chair forward, grates my ears with his agitated voice.

"Why don't you start by telling us about the last time you saw Nate Sterling." His hand works overtime holding his pen, tapping it on top of the table. A tactic meant to unsettle people, I'm sure of it.

"I've already *told* you. Friday. At his house. Through the living room window."

They exchange a glance.

"Cassidy," Cruz says, her voice soft, her hands closing around her coffee mug, "you were the last person to see Mr. Sterling alive. So, we need you to"—there's an irritated edge to her voice—"tell us the truth. You didn't just see him through the window, did you?"

Blood whooshes in my ears. I don't know how to convince them that no, I'm not the one who killed Nate.

"I never got out of my car," I say, struggling to keep my voice calm. "The last time I saw him? You wanna know my last memory of Mr. Sterling? Marisol, or someone who looks an awful lot like Marisol, was lunging at him. That's the last time."

She lowers her head, gives it a slow, sad shake.

"We've pulled your cell phone records. And yes, the location puts you at the Sterlings' address at the time of the murder. But nobody else. Not Marisol, and not someone who looked like her."

"Did you look into Jessica? Her body double?" I whine.

"Yes, in fact, we did. She was at her mother's home in the Valley all day on Friday. And yes, her mother was there with her," Cruz explains.

"But her mother could be *lying*. You ever think of that? Like, why wouldn't she want to cover for her daughter—"

"We pulled her cell records, too. She was definitely at home."

"Or her *cell phone* was at home!"

Cruz sucks in an exasperated breath of air. "Cassidy, I'm trying to help you. But I'm gonna be real honest. You're not making it easy for me. Ever since the beginning of this, you've been lying to us."

"I wanna ask about that day," Simmons says, "that Mr. Sterling discharged you from duty."

"He didn't discharge me! He just gave me the week off. So he could try to save his crumbling marriage!"

"That was on Monday, June nineteenth. Correct?"

"Yep," I gulp.

Simmons leans down, pulls a plastic baggie out of a duffel bag. Slits it open with his stubby index finger. Pulls out my journal. The one in which I raged about Nate.

"This is your journal, is it not?"

"It is, but—"

"I'm asking the questions here. I'm going to read something from this. You tell me if you remember writing it." He licks his fingers, turns the pages. "'He can't just cast me off. He can't just get rid of me. I'll make sure of that. I'll show him how wrong he is.'"

My stomach twists. Why do I have to be such a writer all the time? This looks terrible. It *is* terrible.

"Those your words?" he asks, rhetorically.

"Yes, but—"

"Hold on, it gets better." He grins. "'Take the week off. With pay. Fuck you.'"

"I—"

"Those your words, too?"

"Yes, but—"

He slams the journal shut, slides it to the side. "Sounds to us like you were pretty mad at the old boss man, eh? And sounds like you had more going on with him than just a cozy working relationship. This sounds like 'hell hath no fury like a woman scorned' stuff."

"I was worried about losing my job! Peeved that they could just send me home like that—"

"'Peeved' is putting it nicely." He's still grinning. "So, we're gonna ask you *again*, Ms. Foster, what was the nature of your relationship with Mr. Sterling?"

I feel Nate's lips on mine. Hear his voice telling me that he can be himself with me. That I'm full of surprises.

I may not be able to afford a lawyer—at least until I talk to Lexie—but I've watched enough police procedurals to know that they are fishing here.

They might be able to place me at the scene of the crime because of my cell phone, but there's no real evidence. No physical evidence linking me to Nate. So, they're fishing. For a motive, an angle. Cassidy, the scorned lover, goes batshit and kills her boss.

They have no way to prove the truth about my and Nate's relationship, and I'm not going to be the one to tell them.

"I told you this already. He was a kind boss. He was starting to let me read his scripts for him and yes, he confided to me about being concerned Marisol was cheating on him—"

"So, you started stalking her, spying on her, taking lewd pictures. What we think is this: you fell in love with Mr. Sterling and wanted to rip apart his marriage—"

"No, I told you *he* asked *me* to spy on Marisol—"

"It's just too convenient that that can't be confirmed." Simmons leans back, tucks his thumbs under his armpits.

"You were obsessed with him, Cassidy. Just admit it. That's what Ms. Torres told us. Those are her exact words. *Obsessed.*"

His words are like tiny knives in my chest.

"Said she saw you two together in the pool and it looked intimate. I'm not saying he didn't lead you on; we're all too aware of the Me Too movement, especially out here. But she said you were like a puppy dog with him, putty in his hands. She even caught you all dressed up ready to go out with him while she was supposed to be out of town. What do you have to say about that?"

"He was going to take me out, but only because I'm new here and he wanted to reward me—"

"For spying on his wife?" Simmons's face lifts into another smirk.

"We've also talked to their housekeeper," he went on. "She said one day you showed up dressed real nice, wearing Marisol's clothes? Do most people, Ms. Foster, dress like their boss's wife?"

"She gave me a bunch of clothes, I already told you—"

"She also said Mr. Sterling let her go early one day. So that you two could be alone."

I need to get to my phone. I need to call Lexie. I need a lawyer.

"I'm not answering any more of your questions without a lawyer."

A quick, sympathetic nod from Cruz. A glare from Simmons.

"But I was thinking . . . maybe Jessica and Marisol are working together. Jessica left her cell at home, then spied on me, then pretended to be Marisol leaving the Hilton. She then got into it with Nate, murdered him."

Even I can hear how dumb my words sound.

"You know what *I* think?" Simmons says. "I think that you're a writer and you like to make up stories, hmm?"

He thinks I'm crazy. Totally insane.

Even *I* don't know what to think anymore. But I'm still not ready to let my Jessica theory go just yet.

"I'm telling you, there's something off about Jessica, and I'm also telling you what I saw. She, or Marisol, struggling with Nate. If you don't have a reason to arrest me, I'd like to go home now."

They exchange another look.

They don't have shit.

I scoot my chair back with such vehemence it barks out a squeak.

I stand, snatch my bag off the table.

"Before you go," Detective Simmons says, "I have something else to show you."

Great.

I plop back down.

From a file, he slides out two sheets of typing paper, shoves one toward me.

It's the one that Nate showed me the night he asked me to start spying:

YOU NEED TO KEEP BETTER TABS ON YOUR WIFE

"Yes!" I practically shriek. "Nate showed this to me one night. So maybe the person who wrote this is the person you should be looking into."

"There were no fingerprints on the envelope, other than Mr. Sterling's," he replies coolly.

"But this one"—he taps the other sheet as dread expands in my gut—"has prints. Two sets. Yours and Mr. Sterling's." He slides it toward me.

YOU KNOW YOUR WIFE LIKES FUCKING ME BETTER THAN SHE LIKES FUCKING YOU

If I could shrink beneath the table, I would. I can't believe I stupidly typed those words out, left it for Nate to find. But I was desperate. And angry. My text with the photos of Marisol riding Andreas hadn't gotten me anywhere, so I tried this. Little did I know Nate would be murdered and it would come back to haunt me in such a profound way.

"Mind telling us what this is all about?" Simmons grins. He's basking in this.

"Not until I speak with my lawyer." I stand again. "And I don't need a ride. I'm taking an Uber," I say in the tone of a petulant teen telling off their parents. I turn to leave.

"And just because there's no prints on the first note," Simmons barks out after me, "doesn't mean that we won't trace it to you eventually."

Great. Now I'm on the hook for both of them.

68

AS SOON AS I'm back home, I call Lexie.

"Hey," she answers. Her tone is blank.

"Lexie, I need to come over. Right now." My words shake with the tears that are newly forming. Just hearing her familiar voice invites me to cry. It's like getting hurt on the playground and running over to your mom, dry-eyed, but the minute she comforts you the dam bursts and you're bawling.

I'm greeted with a low sigh. "Sure," she says, coldly.

"I'm sorry, is that a problem?" I ask, my range pitching higher. She'd better *not* be about to tell me that she and Harry need more alone time together.

"No, of course not. Just gimme a sec. I just got out of the shower. It's five. Let's say six?"

I PARK AT the bottom of their drive. This time, she doesn't come out to greet me.

I feel ashamed as I walk up their sidewalk, awkward about seeing Harry.

But that's silly, I tell myself. I've done nothing wrong here. And I need their help. Desperately.

I ring the doorbell. She answers, dressed in a simple black hoodie and joggers, her thick hair still damp at the tips.

"Come in, chica."

I glance around for Harry. As if sensing this, she says, "He's in his studio working. I told him to get lost for a second."

His studio is in their carriage house, a separate structure at the top of the drive that overlooks the massive deck.

I'm grateful he's made himself scarce.

"Want something to drink? I'm having tea but was about to go stiffer."

"Actually, tea sounds good."

Early evening light trickles into the kitchen as I sit on an uncomfortable barstool. Lexie heats fresh water, mixes herself a martini.

She's barely made eye contact with me; I'm starting to feel like a giant pariah.

"Do you really have to leave tomorrow?" I ask.

"Yep. Gotta get back. But don't forget, I'm home in eighty-two short days!"

"I'll probably be locked up by then."

This elicits a chuckle, but not a bright one; more sardonic, which sets me on edge even more.

"Lexie, the cops were at my place again today. With a search warrant. They took some of my stuff. And then brought me in for questioning. I'm freaking the hell out! They still think I did it! They said I'm their number one suspect."

She dunks the tea bags in and out of the pot, shakes her head.

I want to shake her.

"Well, say something, anything!"

Fresh tears well in my eyes.

Finally, she sets aside the tea bags and walks over to me. Gives me a one-sided hug. "Sorry, I'm just stressed."

"You think *you* are? About what?"

"About leaving. I'm stressed about leaving you. Like this. In this state. You're the reason I flew all the way back here, remember? I knew you were getting in too deep—"

"I don't need a lecture right now! I need help! I need my best friend."

"I know. Sorry, it's just . . . This isn't only affecting you, okay?"

"What are you talking about?"

"Cassidy, the police were *here* earlier today."

"What?" Dread clamps my chest.

"Yeah." She breaks away from me, pulls a mug from the cabinet. "Let's go outside. Talk there. I feel like I can't breathe in here."

"Me, either," I say, bitterly.

THIS IS THE second time in days I've been out on their gorgeous deck; I wish that it were under different circumstances so I could actually enjoy its magnificence.

"They were here about me?"

"Obviously."

"Well, hell, what did they want?"

"To know all about you. They knew, because I guess you told them, that I got you the job, that we are best friends, and so they asked me a bunch of questions."

"And?"

She sighs over the top of her martini glass. "Of course I raved about you. But I also told them about Carter—"

"You *did*? How *could* you?" I could throttle her right now.

"Excuse me? How could I *not*? Just because *you* lied to the police doesn't mean I'm going to. Are you nuts?"

"Well, what did you tell them exactly?" My mind is galloping, a pony that hasn't been broken in yet.

"The truth. Cassidy, I *had* to. Sorry, but they straight-up asked me about your past with men. They were going to find out from him eventually, and then he might have told them that I knew, and then—" She tosses her hands up.

She's right. Even though it hurts, I know how flustered anyone can be when being questioned by the police.

"And honestly—" She shakes her head. "I don't know *what* to think anymore. This whole thing is just crazy."

That creeping feeling slithers around my neck again, my fear that Lexie herself might think I'm behind Nate's murder.

"It *is* crazy, but *I'm* not crazy," I practically yell, sounding very much like I am, in fact, crazy.

"Okay, okay, calm down. Let's sit."

I follow her to the bench that rims the wooden rail. But I'm not calm. I'm livid.

"Listen, hear me out. I *saw* Marisol murder Nate! Except, it wasn't Marisol. It couldn't have been. She was still at the Hilton. I know that now. But I haven't told you about Jessica yet—"

"Who?" she asks, annoyance creeping into her voice, as if she's a parent whose patience is being tested.

"So, Jessica is Marisol's body double. Her stand-in. And the thing is, she was always hanging around the house, acting all flirty flirty with Nate, and then dissing Marisol behind her back. To me. And she called Nate a 'total snack.' I think she's been stalking them, that she knew I was watching them, then pretended to be Marisol murdering Nate because she knew I'd been following Marisol. She either thought she could frame her, or place me at the scene of the crime. I don't know, maybe she was obsessed with Nate but he didn't want her?"

Lexie peers over her cocktail at me. Her sculpted cheekbones are still sun-flushed from the beach. Her eyes pool with worry. "Well, what do the cops say about that?"

Great. Here goes. "They said she was at home all day in the Valley with her mom. Cell phone records show that, too. But, here's the thing, mothers lie all the time for their children and cell phones don't mean jack. She could've just left it at home and—"

Lexie rolls her shoulders.

"Well? What do you think? I mean—"

She shrugs, looks at me as if I'm off the wall.

"And also, I forgot to tell you this, but one night when we were together, Nate showed me this letter he got. A few months before I was hired. It was typed up like a ransom note. And it said, 'You need to keep better tabs on your wife.'"

Lexie stares blankly at me. So I don't tell her the rest, that I added my own, dumb note on top of the other one.

Her silence is maddening.

"Lexie! Please say something. Anything!"

"What do you want me to say?"

"I don't know, but I'm in deep shit and I need your help! This looks really bad for me. I need a lawyer, but I can't afford one, so I was gonna ask—"

"Are you kidding? Do you know how much that costs? I know you think we have this big lifestyle, but it's expensive to maintain and it's not like Harry is made of gold."

It would've hurt less if she had gone into the kitchen, retrieved a butcher knife, and stabbed me with it.

Fresh tears brew in my eyes. "But I have nobody else out here to help me! And not just out here. You know I have literally no one!"

"You should've thought about that before. I don't even know who you are anymore. I told you you were getting in too deep. I tried to warn you. Now I don't know what to think."

All I can hear is the gong of my heartbeat banging in my temples. I've never been so hurt, so furious. "But you're my *best friend*." I grab her shoulders, shake her. "Lexie, you don't honestly think that I—" I squawk between sobbing breaths, "that I murdered Nate, do you?"

My eyes rove all over her face, pleading, searching. As if looking for any sign, anything that registers my innocence. But her face is frozen, blank.

"I don't know *what* to think. Okay?" She leaps to her feet. "I love you, you are my best friend, you're my sister, but this shit is mad, okay? And don't get me started on what Harry thinks. When Marisol came up alibied, and you were the only one at their house when—well, I had to beg him to let you come over here tonight—"

I'm absolutely mortified; I want to shrink up and die.

"You're basically asking me to believe the impossible here," she continues. "I mean, as long as I've known you, you've had this obsessive personality. Maybe you *did* take things too far. Maybe things got out of hand—"

I open my mouth to defend myself, but only a tiny, pathetic noise squeaks out. I'm on the verge of breaking down, don't even know what to say. I can't believe I have to defend myself to my own best friend.

"I need to go inside, pee, get some space. But I'll be right back and we can talk about this further."

Without waiting for me to reply, she bounds across the deck to the sliding glass door.

All around me, night is sparking to life. The trees are shrouded in darkness, the canyon below a black pit. Bottomless.

Lexie is all but saying she thinks it's possible I killed Nate! What in the actual hell?

Tears come gushing, unbidden, but I let them roll out of me, a geyser that needs to erupt. I'm devastated, but on top of that, angry. How *dare* she suspect me. But even through my indignation, a small voice inside of me reasons that she has every right to. I've been withholding so much from her—Carter, Nate, *everything*—trickling it out piecemeal as it serves me. In all fairness she probably doesn't know *what* the hell to think. But still. It's *me*.

The glass doors whoosh open and when Lexie clocks my tears, her face falls. She comes over, sits right next to me, takes my hands in hers. "Oh, chica, I'm so sorry. I know all that was a bit harsh."

A *bit*.

I nod. Sniff.

"So, let's talk this through. If what you're saying is true—"

"It fucking *is* true!" I practically yell.

"Okay, calm down. I'm trying to help here. Let's figure this out. If it's true, and you think you saw Marisol kill Nate, but it wasn't actually her, you think it was this Jessica chick? Even though she has an alibi?"

"She has a *sort of* alibi. Just her mom's word and her cell records showing her phone was at home at the time of the murder. I'm kicking myself for never getting her last name."

"Pshaw. She's Marisol Torres's stand-in. Hold up, lemme check my IMDbPro." Her fingers fly across the screen. She almost has a tiny grin, as if she's proud of her detective skills. I eye her martini; it's nearly empty. She's tipsy.

"Here 'tis!" She taps the screen, spins it around so I can see it. "Bingo. Her name is Jessica Valdez."

Lexie leans back, rocks her body in satisfaction. Spins her cell around and begins pecking at it again. "You say she lives in the Valley?"

"Yeah."

I have no idea what she's doing, but I'm just happy she seems to be on my side again.

"There are three addresses popping up with that name. Hang on, lemme cross-check with social." The tiny grin curls her lips again. "This her?"

It's Jessica's Instagram and it's definitely her.

"Yes."

"Well, let's fucking go. She lives in Van Nuys. Ten minutes from here."

"You mean, go to her *house*?"

"Yeah! You know I have a bullshit detector like no other. Let's go suss this hussy out!"

69

LEXIE TAKES A nip off her roadie martini as we inch down Jessica's street.

The house is small, old, the windows lined with bars. No grass, just a concrete yard with a few potted plants out front.

"This it for sure?" I ask Lexie. I feel nauseated, queasy.

"Yesss," she slurs. "Park the dang car and let's roll!"

"But I don't even know what we're going to say—"

"Exactly. You're gonna let me do the talkin'." Her Texas accent is on full display, usually coming out when we're together and especially if she's boozing.

My hand is slick on the door handle; my nerves are beyond shot, but I clasp it, open it. I have no choice but to follow Lexie's lead—I don't know what else to do—even as panic squeezes my chest.

From the backyard, a dog barks. High-pitched squeaks that tell me he's tiny—all bark, no bite—but still, it makes me jump. I want to head back to Lexie's. This feels so wrong.

Lexie marches to the front door, not even waiting for me. She starts knocking. Then banging when no one answers. I wince at her drunken bravado. A room is lit from within, but the curtains are pulled so we can't see inside.

With shaky legs, I force myself to walk toward the door, looking over my shoulder as I do. What the hell are we doing?

Finally, the front door creaks open. A petite woman with white, wispy hair and wearing a muumuu stands before us. The lenses of her glasses are thick, her hands papery thin. She looks confused. "May I help you?" She seems like she could be Jessica's grandmother, rather than her mother.

"Hi!" Lexie says, oozing with charm, "we're here to see Jessica!"

The woman's mouth opens, her lips quivering. "I'm sorry, who are you?"

"We're her friends! From the movies!" Lexie deftly answers, without offering our names. Damn, she's good.

The quivering turns into a smile. "Okay, sure, of course. But Jessica's not here."

"Do you know when she'll be back?"

"Oh, dear, not for a few weeks, I'm afraid. You just missed her. She's on her way to the airport. Flying out to meet up with her boyfriend for a trip." Her eyes shift between the two of us.

Lexie looks at me, lifts her eyebrows. I swallow the bile that's moved up my throat.

Holy shit. Jessica's flown the coop.

I want to blurt something out, ask her about the day of Nate's murder, ask her *something*, but Lexie starts up again.

"Gotcha! Thank you!"

I grab her elbow, try to steer her away. Now that we have our intel, I want to get the hell out of here.

As we're halfway down the sidewalk, she spins around and slightly slurs: “Oh, and one last thing. I lost my cell and all my contacts—it’s why we’re stopping by instead of calling her. Can you give me Jessica’s number?”

The woman looks wary, but no one can stand up to Lexie’s aura.

“Uh, okay, I guess. It’s 818-555-0192.”

“Let’s go. Now,” I hiss into Lexie’s ear.

70

AS WE DRIVE away, my hands are even more slick, the wheel tossing underneath my palms like butter.

"Holy SHIT!" Lexie squeals, her glazed eyes dancing. "She's skipping town! Chica, I am *so* fucking sorry I ever thought anything else. But holy shit!" she repeats. "Check our shit out!"

My mind spins. But this time it's a more hopeful kind of spinning; we're getting closer to the truth. I think. I pray. I *still* wonder if Jessica is in cahoots with Marisol.

Instead of driving back over the hills, I head to the 405.

"Where are you going?" Lexie asks. "We need to get home and figure this shit out! Get you a lawyer, call the police, all of it!"

"I know, I know. I just . . . well . . . part of me still thinks Marisol could be working with her—"

"Tell me you're not driving us over to *their* house?"

"No," I say. But that's exactly what I'm doing.

We fly down the freeway and after we pass the Getty, I veer into Brentwood.

"Cass, this isn't your best idea. The police already think you're involved. What are you gonna do? Confront her?"

"I don't *know*!" I say, exasperated. "Just let me drive by. Please!"

"Fine." Lexie slugs back more of her martini. "But make it snappy. I gotta pee."

As we thread our way through the mostly darkened residential streets, my chest begins to tighten again. What *am* I going to do when I get to the Sterlings'? Last time I was there, Marisol threatened to call the cops on me. But now, the truth is on my side, or at least a sliver of it. Jessica has her hands in all this; I just know it.

"So, chica," Lexie asks, angling her body in the seat so she's facing me. "I know I'm a little liquored up, but it occurred to me that I never asked: How was it with Nate? The making out, I mean. Was it, like, super hot?"

I pound her biceps with my fist. "Really? You're asking that *now*? At this moment? Man, the way your mind is seriously twisted." But I'm actually grinning, for a moment. Lexie always has the strangest way of making the most serious situations lighter.

And her question, though it threatens to plunge me into grief—grief that I've been holding back because I need to prove my innocence—brings Nate's lips again to mine.

"*Super hot* doesn't even scratch the surface. More like *smoldering*. Like there are no words other than *I was lit on fire*."

"Hmph," she mutters.

I'm confused by the reaction; it's as if she doesn't believe me. I don't know how to read it.

"What?" I ask.

"Nothing. Sorry. I'm just over here thinking about your shitty luck. Well, it's not *your* luck and it's not your fault, but damn, woman, I haven't really thought about what you've lost until now. I'm sorry. It's so cruel of the universe."

"Tell me about it." I grip the wheel tighter as their neighborhood approaches.

"But Felix, from our party the other night. He actually asked Harry about you."

Actually? I think, but don't say it out loud.

"That came out wrong. I mean, in the midst of the news breaking about Nate and the chaos, he *still* asked about you, was checking you out. So, as soon as we bust you outta jail—"

I punch her arm again.

"Ow! Just kidding, god*damn*. But I'm setting y'all up."

I can't even think about Felix right now, but I know better than to argue with Lexie. "Well, yeah, sure. Oof, we're just about here."

As we round the bend, my stomach starts to quake. Fuck.

I pull into my customary spot, right by the Dead End sign, kill the engine.

As usual, their windows are bare.

Most of the lights inside the house are on. Even from this distance, I see Marisol sitting at the kitchen table, sipping from a wineglass.

Instead of fury, though, I feel a ping of sadness for her. For how lonely she looks sitting there, all alone. I'm probably crazy for ever thinking she was involved in Nate's death.

I shudder. I've seen enough. I want to get out of here. I'm ready to pull away when Lexie pipes up.

"Gimme those binoculars you've been using."

"Really?"

"Well, yesss!"

I sigh. "Okay. Glove box."

She pops it open, then orders me to recline my seat so she can have a look. "Dayum, even as a grieving widow, Marisol Torres is still smokin'."

Lexie continues peering at her, for longer than I'm comfortable with. I lean my seat back up, reach for the binoculars. She twists her arm away from me. "Just gimme a sec—" she says, breathily, the fog of gin rolling out of her mouth.

I inhale, then exhale an annoyed sigh. I'm getting nervous continuing to sit outside this house. I shouldn't be here, had no business coming in the first place. Why do I make such terrible decisions? What the hell was I thinking?

"Holy shit!" Lexie squeezes the binoculars, twists the lenses.

"What?!" I ask, my breath catching.

"Chica, bingo. Look."

I grab them from her, lift them to my face.

And gasp.

Jessica is standing over Marisol, refilling her wineglass.

"Bloody hell!" My hands shake as I hold the binoculars, causing Marisol and Jessica to look jumpy. "Those fucking hos! On her way to the airport, my ass."

"I mean, she *still* could be, we don't know, but dayum. Here, gimme—"

"No." I elbow her back and keep staring. After refilling her glass, Jessica takes a seat next to Marisol, tosses back her own glass. I see red.

"Maybe she's here to take Marisol with her?" I speculate. "But Marisol wouldn't be so stupid as to skip town right now."

Click, click, click. The sound of Lexie snapping pics on her cell causes me to lower the binoculars. "What are you doing?"

"Evidence, baby! If Jessica's mom lied to *us*, she's certainly capable of lying to the police." *Click, click, click.*

"Okay, stop it, I don't want your flash to alert them!"

"Fine!" Lexie sighs. "Chica, I gotta pee—"

"We're leaving—"

"No, I mean, right now."

"But—"

"It's fine," Lexie says, opening the car door, "I'll just go to the end of the trail."

She leaps out. It's pitch-black here; how the hell does she even see the trail? But I watch her find it as if she's been on it a million times. Maybe she noticed it the other day.

Blood thrumming, I put the binoculars back in the glove box. Fucking Jessica. If Marisol *is* oblivious to Jessica's murder of Nate—and she probably is—it gives me chills to watch her move through Marisol's house, fill her glass like she's her friend.

A ping, an alert on Lexie's cell, snaps me to attention. It's also on vibrate, so it zigzags across the seat.

I grab it, read the text.

Thank you for renting from Avis! When you have a free moment . . . the notification banner reads.

I want to look at the photos she's just taken, so I swipe at the notification to clear it. Instead, it opens, displaying the full message.

Thank you for renting from Avis! When you have a free moment, we'd love your feedback on your recent rental of the 2022 Black Convertible Mercedes.

71

THE CELL LIES limp in my hand. It's such a giant coincidence that Harry rented the same car as Marisol's—down to the exact year; I remember that tidbit from taking Marisol's Mercedes into the car wash.

Maybe it's not such a coincidence. This town is crawling with convertible Benzes. But still.

Also, why is the text going to *her* cell when Harry's the one who rented it? She *did* tell me he rented it, didn't she?

Before I can form another thought, the passenger door whooshes open.

I swipe out of her text messages.

Lexie hops into the seat and clocks her phone in my hand.

"What's up, chica?" she asks.

"Nothing. Just looking at the pics you snapped."

"Ah." She opens her palm for her phone, which I hand over.

"Let's get outta here."

As we cruise down Sunset, she yammers away. "First thing we're doing is calling the detectives. No, first thing, *I'm* getting you a lawyer. *Then* we'll call the police. I mean, if Jessica's mom—or whoever she was—was lying to us, then she's certainly capable of lying to the cops. Or else Jessica is duping her, too. Whatever, but damn, damn, I can't believe we busted her at Marisol's!" There's a schoolgirl squeak to Lexie's voice that I would've found charming, comforting even, a half hour ago, but now it sets my teeth on edge.

"Chica, why are you being so quiet?"

Because my brain is working double time.

"I'm not," I say, defensively.

Streetlights pulse past us as I drive.

A heavy silence fills the cabin, damp and weighty, like a wet towel.

"Hey," I venture. "What kind of convertible did you say Harry rented for you guys?"

A scoff erupts from Lexie. "*That's* a random question while we're trying to figure out who murdered Nate."

"I know, I know, I'm just trying to change the subject. My nerves are on overdrive. I guess what I'm asking is, when can I go with you guys to the beach?" I smile. A fake smile.

"Anytime. As soon as I'm back, okay? And it was a little Mazda Miata. Red. Can't believe I didn't snap some selfies."

Hmm . . . A red Miata, huh? Not a black Mercedes?

I'm about to mention the text from Avis, but something stops me; I swallow the question back down.

She's shifting in her seat. I glance over at her. Where she was giddy just moments before, she now seems pensive.

Why would she lie about this? Unease expands in the back of my throat like a balloon. I really don't like this.

I turn on my signal, pull into the parking lot of Chipotle. "Now *I* have to pee. Be right back."

Inside the stall, I type out a text to Harry. Even though he's wary of me right now.

Cassidy: Hey! Things are crazy rn, I know, and I can't imagine what you must be thinking, but just wanted to say thanks for loaning me Lex. She confided she's a bit stressed over wedding planning. After she leaves, I'm happy to help in any way! Currently out of a job. Lol. But LOVE that you rented the red Miata. She was raving abt that.

After a tense moment, Harry begins typing back.

Harry: Oh, Cassidy, no apologies! So sorry you're going through this insane mess.

Whew. Thank god he doesn't hate me. So . . . why did Lexie tell me he doesn't know what to think of me? Is he just being nice, or is she lying?

Another text bleeds into the screen.

Harry: And red miata? Not sure what you mean.

I feel dizzy.

Another text, from Lexie.

Lexie: You fall in? Let's fucking go!

I ignore hers, reply to Harry.

Cassidy: Um . . . yeah, for Laguna on Friday?

Harry: Ahh!

I'm swimming in relief. He's about to explain all.

Harry: I had to work all day Friday, recording at the house (more ambient sound bites) but yes, Lexie went to Laguna.

Well, thank god. I guess. Maybe I am really losing it?

But then Harry types a final text: She went in her own car tho.

My thoughts are spiraling; the closer I think I'm getting to an answer, the more slippery the truth feels.

72

WE RIDE THE rest of the way to Lexie's house in silence.

Once we step inside, she pads toward Harry's studio. "Gonna fill him in on the latest. Meet me on the deck, so we can war room, 'kay?"

"Sure!"

As soon as she's gone, I grab her phone off the kitchen counter. Tap my way back to the text, so I can view it again; I want to make sure I didn't hallucinate, that I'm not actually losing my mind.

But there it is, in front of me: Thank you for renting from Avis! When you have a free moment, we'd love your feedback on your recent rental of the 2022 Black Convertible Mercedes.

I force myself to keep staring at it, like gazing into the eyes of a monster.

I can't even begin to grapple with the reality of what this might mean. It would be an odd coincidence if she just happened to rent the same car as Marisol's, but it's altogether problematic that she felt compelled to lie about it. Downright creepy and disturbing.

Another thought edges into my obsessing mind. How *did* Lexie know about the hiking trail at the Sterlings'? I mean, it's plausible that she's been to their actual neighborhood before yesterday, hiked on that very trail with no connection to them, but still.

Also, she just hit town in time for Nate to be offed?

I claw my way into her email, and scroll through as quickly as possible, keeping an ear cocked for her footfalls.

Nothing. No email from Avis at all. Probably because she deleted it?

I go back to the notification, open it again. This time, I click on it. The survey springs onto the screen, and with it, the reservation.

Lexie rented the car on Friday morning. Returned it at five p.m.

Which *is* the window of time she was allegedly at the beach. But still. Why rush back and return it the same day? Most rentals are for twenty-four hours.

Hearing her steps from down the hall, I drop her phone on the counter as if it's a hot potato.

She's not even making eye contact as she saunters over, so it's doubtful she saw what I was doing.

The cell is still illuminated, though, which makes my eye twitch.

Finally, blissfully, it darkens, just as she approaches it.

"Sorry that took so long."

I can't help it; I'm staring at her.

"What?"

That's what I want to ask you, I think. If she rented a matching Mercedes to Marisol's, then . . .

I keep my eyes on her. This would never have occurred to me in a million years, but she's the exact same height, or damn near, as Marisol. Has the same model's body. Same sculpted cheekbones. All she'd need is a wig. And a matching pair of Marisol's oversized sunglasses.

But *why the fuck*?

Why would Lexie do this?

I'm not even sure what I think she did. None of this makes sense. But then the coincidences and her big, fat lie are too much to dismiss.

I see shadows all around me. The moon is high and streaking through the window. Fear rises up the back of my throat and I wonder, for the second time, if I'm slowly going insane.

"What's wrong, chica?" Lexie steps a little closer to me. "I mean, aside from the obvious. Looks like you've seen a ghost."

I shake my head, swallow.

I hold my hands in front of my face, count my fingers. Ten of them. I squeeze my eyes shut, recall my mother's face, her name: Angie Foster. She was unstable, but that, I believe, was mainly from the booze. She always had her wits about her. I silently recount to myself my driver's license number, the name of the current president, who, thank god, is *not* insane.

I'm not crazy. I know what I saw that day and I know it was real. As real as Nate being dead. As real as me sitting here.

"Cassidy, are you *okay*?" She plants her hand on my shoulder; I want to shake it off, but I don't.

"Yeah. I guess . . . I'm just feeling bad. Bad for what I've caused. For what I've put you through—"

"Oh, honey, I didn't mean to make you feel guilty." Her fingers sweep back my hair; I recoil inside. "You're going through *a lot*. You've been through *a lot*. And I know you had feelings for him, but what Nate did to you, it's kind of in Me Too territory, dontcha think? Like, I think it's messed with you. More than you know."

Tears leak down my cheeks. I sniff. Nod. Playing the role of pathetic little Cassidy. "You're right. You're so right. And I'm sorry I hit you up for money for a lawyer. I'm just—"

"Panicking. Look, I get it. And I talked to Harry, told him we are getting you a lawyer, especially with this Jessica stuff that just came up."

How very charitable of you.

"Let's go get some fresh air, hang out on the deck."

Wordlessly, I trail her outside.

When we sit, she starts tapping on her phone. "I'm Googling lawyers now, then we'll call the detectives." She gnaws on her bottom lip.

"You know what?" I say. "I think I *do* need something stiffer after all this. Would you mind making me one of your famous martinis? Maybe extra strong?"

"Sure." She springs to her feet.

Thankfully, she leaves her cell on the bench.

As soon as she's inside, I snatch it. Start racing through her texts, mind whirring.

Why in the world would she kill Nate?

Followed by: *No way in the world she killed Nate.*

Did she not like how he was behaving with me? Was she in some sick way trying to protect me from my past mistakes with men? I mean, I know she's my ride or die, but damn.

Her texts are all work, work, work, so I hop back into her inbox. It's more of the same, an endless sprawl of emails about the film.

I close out, open her phone and voicemail log.

Nothing.

I go back to the text from Avis, aim my own cell at it, snap a pic. Just in case.

Then, I open her photos.

A trove of Prague pics line the screen. Winding streets, cobblestoned alleys, ancient cathedrals spire the horizon. Tons of Lexie on set. Her aviator glasses on, full lips glossed. Selfie after selfie after selfie.

I keep scrolling back, as rapidly as possible, skimming the photos until I know I'm in pre-Prague territory.

Seemingly millions of shots of Lexie and Harry. Their cats. At

Catalina Island, their favorite getaway. On the coast. Pandemic photos of the two of them inside their house, some of which I recognize from Insta.

My hand sweats, but I keep swiping. What I see next makes my eyes about bulge from my head.

There it is.

My answer.

Or at least, a partial answer.

Lexie, her hair shiny as newly polished marble, a summer dress hugging her perfect figure. Her arm slung around Nate. Their too-pretty faces beaming at the camera, their heads touching, as couples do in selfies.

The pic is dated April 14, 2019.

Which would've been right before he met Marisol.

Holy shit. Lexie is the crazy ex Marisol told me about.

And the reason he became so private, so security conscious.

And now I remember her strong, odd reaction when I texted her Marisol's comment about Nate having a crazy ex.

So it *is* her.

But, if Lexie is indeed that crazy ex, the stalker, how and why did she land me my job?

Out of the corner of my eye, something moves. I glance up to see her staring suspiciously at me from the other side of the sliding glass door.

Watching me holding her phone.

Damn.

I look up at her, grin. Close out of the photos.

She toes open the sliding glass, steps out with our martinis, the glasses frosted.

I quickly type Nate's name into her web browser.

"Did someone call me?" she asks uneasily.

"No, I was just—" I falter. "I was looking up the latest on Nate. And, I kinda thought it'd be better if I didn't use my own search engine for that?"

"Ah. Good thinking. Here." She hands me my drink.

I take a chilly, biting sip, but just a small one. I need to stay sober, keep focused.

Lexie drinks, too, but hers is more of a gulp. "Mm-mm, just what I needed."

She sets down her martini, picks up her phone. Closes out the browser.

Whew.

But then her brow furrows.

Her fingers dance over the screen. She must be reading the text from Avis.

"I knew you weren't just Googling Nate. I watched you going through my phone."

"Lexie. Can you tell me what's going on?" My voice sounds disembodied, faraway. "Why is there a selfie of you and Nate? And why did you rent a black Mercedes on Friday? There was no red Miata, was there?"

A long pause hangs between us.

"Ah, chica. Trust me, you don't want to go there."

73

"I DON'T UNDERSTAND." My voice comes out cracked.

I honestly don't. None of this makes a damn bit of sense. It's 2023. The photo was taken in 2019. Lexie has been with Harry for the past five years, so . . . "You cheated on Harry?"

I ask her this as if it's the worst of it all.

"Shhh, keep your voice down."

Chills crawl over me. My best friend killed my boss. And framed me.

A wry smile trickles across her face. She fixes me with her icy blue eyes. "Yep. Nate was mine first. Long before he was yours."

What in the actual hell.

"We met at an after-party for a premiere. Not one of his films; it was some indie. I don't even remember the movie. That's funny," she says, almost wistfully. "I only remember *him*. His eyes were on me all night. So, I broke away from Harry, went to the bar while he was there. We were in bed, all over each other, the next night."

The thought of them sleeping together makes my stomach sick.

"And yes, I was still with Harry, so we kept it hush-hush, for obvious reasons. But we were together—sometimes for just an hour—every day for nearly four months. And Nate, well, you know, he was private, too, like obsessive-compulsively so, so it was easy to keep us under wraps."

My mouth feels like it's been filled with cement. I take another nip of my drink, just to water it.

"And," Lexie continues, as if she's not even talking to me but to the air. This is probably the first time she's ever told anybody she was with Nate. "Well, I was ready to leave Harry for him, the whole nine yards. I was in love, like never before. Like you said about him, he lit my whole body on fire."

I shudder, remembering his touch doing the same thing to me.

"But then, one day, out of the blue, he pulled away. Ghosted me. I was flipping out. He wouldn't return my calls, wouldn't text me back. I even showed up at his office under the guise of work and he was furious!" Her voice sounds nearly hysterical. "Told me never to do that again, that he was sorry but he'd met someone else."

I nod, but stay silent, hoping she'll keep talking.

"It was Marisol." A bitter laugh escapes her. "Like, who could compete with *that*? Anyway, I read about it in the tabloids, *Page Six*. Made my blood curdle. Then the pandemic happened. Everything shut down. Everything, that is, except for Marisol and her philandering."

"But how did you know—"

"Because. I wasn't working, so I started watching them. Watching her. I'm the first one who saw her with Andreas," she says, stabbing her chest with her forefinger, as if she's proud. "And I'm the one who sent Nate that letter about keeping better tabs on her."

I almost wish I had gone totally insane versus this being the actual reality.

"I wanted him to know what a big goddamn mistake he'd made."

She's almost shouting. "In leaving me for her. A cheater. But he stayed with her. Kept ignoring my calls. Married her, for Chrissakes."

"So, you're the crazy ex that Marisol told me about?"

Fury ripples across her eyes. It was a cheap shot but one I had to take.

"I can't fucking believe you did this to me, Lexie. But why, why on earth would you kill him? And why the hell would you get me involved?"

She laughs, sounding deranged. A guitar string out of tune. "Well, that was just the universe. I was getting ready to go to Prague and was devastated that I wouldn't be able to watch them anymore. To watch *her*. And then, out of the blue, Ramona sends a message out on this insider LISTSERV I'm on, wanting to know if anybody knew of anyone looking for personal assistant work. For Nate Sterling."

She lifts her martini, swills it around, takes a long sip like we're girlfriends meeting up for happy hour, gossiping. "And I thought of you immediately. Figured *you* could keep an eye on her, on them. Get the real inside dope."

Jesus Christ, I was a pawn for Nate with the spying and also, unwittingly, for Lexie. They all used me, played me.

I think back to Lexie's texts and realize that some of them were priming me. Fishing. Especially the one in which she said she was always up for good gossip, for me to spill it. I think about her reaction to Marisol calling her crazy, think about her acting "overly concerned" for me when I let her know about me and Nate.

"And so, when you texted me that they were having problems, I was thrilled! I thought, let them crumble, let them fall apart. Let him come begging back to me. I've never had to beg for a man; this was a first for me and it was brutal." She rolls her neck again. "But never in my *wildest* dreams did I imagine he would fall for *you*."

I bristle, let out a sharp burst of air.

"I mean, no offense. I love you, Cassidy. And you're . . . cute? You really are. But . . . c'mon. You're not exactly in his league."

Rage explodes inside of me. "Fuck you forever, Lexie."

"I don't mean anything harsh, but when you told me he was having you read his scripts, inviting you to dinner, well, I had to come on home and investigate what the hell was going on."

Of course; she underestimated me. Always has.

"So, Chris Evans doesn't have Covid?" I ask.

"No. I made up some shit. Got a week off."

"How could you *kill* him, Lexie?"

"Like I said, I couldn't believe y'all were having this—thing. Whatever it was. And then when I got back and you told me about how y'all almost had sex, your connection, I was enraged. But pacified by the fact that he flicked you out of their lives, like a dried booger."

What a goddamn evil bitch.

"And, I was elated that Marisol had only proceeded to double down with Andreas. Those pictures you took: priceless. When we got drunk the other night at your place? I copied them all, stashed them in a secret file. And then I took your copy of their key—well, I took all your keys—and went and had a copy made while you were blacked out."

A breeze gusts through the canyon, causing all the heat-parched tree limbs to shiver.

"I went and watched their house the next day. As soon as I saw her leave, I slipped in the back door. Found her planner open on the kitchen counter, made a note of her meeting at the Hilton the next day. I wanted to surprise Nate—I hadn't reached out to him in months and was hoping that he'd actually come around—but when he came down the stairs, he jumped back in horror. Started yelling for me to leave. Like I'm some crazy person."

Her eyes water. I might have been infatuated with him, but she was psycho obsessed. Like, beyond.

"I told him I loved him, that I knew he loved me, that Marisol was still cheating. I pulled out my phone, went through your pics, showed him. I pleaded. Begged him to come back to me. Even got down on my knees, tried to, you know," she says, making a gesture, like a blow job, "but he told me that we were over. Had been over. That he was sorry for the way things ended. But that if I didn't leave immediately, he'd call the police. I was so angry I could've strangled him then, but I'm smarter than that."

"Smart enough to frame *me* for it."

"Yes. Exactly. I mean, sorry." She seems like she's possessed. I don't even know who this person is. But I am aware that I'm talking to a sociopath. A murderous one.

"And I knew, even though I told you to stop, that you'd still be watching them. Stalking her. So, yeah, I dressed up like her, rented the car, did the whole shebang." Her voice is an icicle. "If I can't have him, no one can."

"Lexie—" I venture, keeping my voice stable, "I just need you to tell the police this—so I can—"

"Are you out of your goddamn mind? It's not my fault you went trolling through my phone. No."

"But—"

"No one will believe you anyway, if you tell them. With Carter, with your history with men, with you stalking Marisol, with everything. Honestly, if I were doing a movie, I couldn't have produced this any better."

"But the text, the photo—"

Lexie stands up, and to my shock, flings her phone into the abyss of the canyon. "There's your evidence, chica. And now, because you're the only one who knows the truth—"

Before I know what's happening, Lexie pulls out a paring knife, still in its sheath, from her back pocket.

I gasp, but before I can properly react, protect myself, she slides it out of its casing, clasps her hand around my neck. With one hand she's gripping me, yanking me up, pulling my body off the bench. In her other hand she grips the knife, the tip of it stabbing the surface of my skin.

Fucking psycho bitch!

I kick her hard in the groin, causing her to pause, my fingers using the brief moment to peel the knife from her hand, my nails digging into her skin as I do.

"Dammit!" Lexie seethes.

The knife clatters to the ground. I give it a good kick and it slithers across the deck, far out of reach.

This enrages Lexie so she grips my neck tighter. I tug at her arms, but they're longer, stronger than mine.

Now she's using her other hand to lift my hips. I can't believe it, but I'm teetering on the edge of the guardrail, her arctic-blue eyes searing into mine. My hands clamber for the rail, trying to get a grip. My feet flail in front of me, aiming for her, but the movement just puts me even more off-balance.

"He was mine. And you went and messed all that up—"

"Lexie," I gasp, "wait! He told me something. About you. But I didn't know it was about you."

She narrows her eyes.

"When we almost had sex that night. He didn't stop because Marisol walked in on us. I lied about that. She came home later. He stopped because he said he was in love with someone else still. His ex. The one he had before Marisol—" The lie rolls out, smooth as cream cheese.

Her grip relaxes, and her eyes spark with confusion.

Which buys me just enough time.

I grab the ends of her long hair, and pull.

Yanking harder than I've ever yanked anything in my entire life, I knee her in the forehead, pivot her around, still pulling her by her hair. I yank it higher, higher, and higher still, until she's the one on the edge of the guardrail.

But even though she's a murderer, I'm not. I pause.

But the second I loosen my grip, she's clawing at my wrists, tugging at me, eyes wild with scorn. "You're no match for me, Cassidy. Never have been," she spits out.

This bitch is gonna kill me if I let her. She's tearing at my arms, about to regain control.

So I suck in a deep breath, steel myself, and with all my force and fury, push.

Her fingernails claw my skin, but my shove is too hard, too fast for her to clasp on.

I stare into the canyon and watch as my best friend writhes through the air to the bottom.

Epilogue

TWO YEARS LATER

"CUT!" THE DIRECTOR'S voice, a female's, rings through the air, competing with the clapping sound of the ocean.

Even though I've been hearing that word constantly these past two months, I still get a little thrill from it.

I'm on an actual movie set.

One that I'm working on.

We're filming in the South of France, near the town of Èze, in a storybook estate just steps from the turquoise waters of the Mediterranean. It's late spring, and the air around the estate is flush with the scent of lavender.

The trailer door slaps open and Marisol pours out.

She's resplendent as ever, gold skin shimmering in the dazzling sun.

She's a brilliant Esme. Nate was right about that.

The next scene is an important one.

Esme is about to confront her controlling husband, Theo, for the first time.

The hair and makeup crew do last-minute touch-ups on Marisol, brushing more blush against her cheeks, scrunching up her hair to make it look even wavier.

She's dressed in a bronze-colored bikini; all eyes are on her as she gets primped, glances down at her index cards, which hold her lines for this scene.

After it all came out about Lexie murdering Nate and my name was cleared, Marisol reached out to me. Apologized. For everything. She even had me over to the house.

While I was there, we sat outside by the pool, the grounds splattered with crushed loquats. Everything in the house had pretty much gone to seed after Nate's death.

Elana was still coming over, but Marisol—at least for the first few months in the wake of his murder—had all but gone to seed herself, too. Letting her hair grow wild. Not leaving the house much. No longer getting facials. Keeping to herself mostly.

It came out that Jessica had been telling the truth all along. She was indeed at home during the time of Nate's murder, had stopped by Marisol's house on her way to the airport the night Lexie and I saw her there. She flew to Costa Rica to meet up with her boyfriend and, according to her Instagram, stayed put, working as an influencer at a green wellness retreat. Nate's murder and LA must've proved too much for her.

On that first day I visited Marisol, I told her about Nate's secret work, *A Kept Woman*.

Her umber eyes brimmed with tears. She was touched, beyond words, that he had written such an edgy, perfect script for her with the perfect femme fatale lead.

After all her hard work to land it, she had given up her role in Guillermo's film in the days after the murder, but Nate's vision gave her new life.

Sparked something in her.

She went on a mission to get it made. With the help of his production company—not to mention the notoriety and infamy surrounding the couple and the late director—everything fell into place rather quickly.

"Cassidy must get a writing credit, for all she's been through," Marisol insisted to Marta, Nate's right-hand woman.

I'm still a nobody out here, though, so I didn't get that credit, but they did bring me on as an assistant to the script consultant. Most of my days are spent fetching coffee, making appointments, and running unrelated errands, but I do have the opportunity to be on set, learn the ropes, see how a movie is actually put together.

"Rolling!" the director shouts.

I watch as Marisol steps to the edge of the water, turns around to have her face-off with Theo. She delivers her lines exquisitely.

"Cut!"

She's not only a brilliant Esme, she's also a brilliant mother.

The surf pounds the shore as a toddler waddles along the packed sand, away from the arms of Marta, her silver braids swinging as she walks after him.

"Nathaniel!" Marisol cries out with joy, running toward her son, scooping him up.

To be certain, she took a DNA test to make sure he was Nate's. But even without a test it's obvious. He's got his father's hazel-green eyes; he's got his mother's sparkling spirit.

My cell chimes. It's Harry. He's coming over from LA to visit me soon. We've been talking, texting more and more. First as friends and now it's feeling like something else.

When he heard me and Lexie hysterically arguing that night on the deck, he cracked open the window to his studio.

Listened.

As I suspected, Lexie didn't have to beg him to let me come over; that was just more of her lies. He never thought I killed Nate.

He heard most everything. Was shocked. When Lexie started admitting to it all, he nosed one of his mics out the window, pressed the record button, capturing everything she said. About Nate. About their relationship, about his murder.

We didn't need her cell, after all, to prove her guilt, but, of course, her texts were retrieved by the police and that photo of her and Nate lived on a cloud that Harry was able to pull up on her iPad.

He was devastated. Still is. But he's coming out of it. I'm hoping to help him come out of it fully.

AT NIGHT, THE city of Èze is a glittering snow globe, lights blinking against the dark sky, the hiss of the ocean breeze murmuring in our ears.

Marta is staying behind in the hotel with little Nathaniel so Marisol and I can go out.

Her stilettos click against the burnished cobblestone alleyway as she leads me to an underground bar in the basement of an ancient former cathedral.

Techno music thumps, but not so loud that we can't carry on a conversation.

She orders us the most expensive bottle of rosé.

"To us!" she toasts.

"To us!" The rosé hits the back of my tongue like spun sugar.

Glass votives hold flickering candles on our table, casting shadows across her face.

"It's ironic, don't you think? The title of the film?"

"Mm, what do you mean?"

My skin is flushed, ocean kissed, and I'm feeling more relaxed than I have in months. Each day bristles with new possibilities. I know I'm still on the bottom rung, but Marta sometimes slips me scripts to read like Nate used to. And then there's Harry. And what may come of that. After being played—by Carter, by Lexie, and even a little by Nate—I finally feel like I've come into my own.

"*A Kept Woman*," Marisol explains. "The title. It's ironic to me that Nate chose it. When I'm the one who came out on top."

She leans back, crosses her svelte legs, brings the rim of her wine flute to her lips.

Her words confound me. "What are you getting at?" I ask, genuinely confused.

"He only thought I was a kept woman. But I won, didn't I, after all that?"

Her eyes glimmer in the dancing candlelight. She takes down her whole glass, refills it.

"Cassidy, c'mon. You know by now, don't you? You're smart."

I have no idea what she's talking about.

"What?" I ask, playfully.

"I knew you were watching me."

A tiny ping of dread registers in my stomach.

"I played him. Played you. It was the role of my life."

I stare at her, unblinking.

A wicked laugh spills from her lips. "Ah, don't look at me like that."

I keep looking at her like that.

"This was my plan all along."

"To be in his movie?"

"Don't be daft. No. To be an unkept woman. I liked Nate, sure. But—and I can't believe you haven't figured this out by now—I married him for his money, his connections. Sure, I had money of my own, but not *his* kind of money. Old money. The kind that never runs out. And I needed my foot in the door in Hollywood."

Trepidation swims through my veins. "Yeah, it's funny how life works out sometimes," I say, wanting to wrap this line of talking up in a bow, put it on a high shelf.

"This didn't just 'work out.'" She claws the air with her long, manicured fingernails. "I *made* this happen. This was my plan all along. Well, almost all of it."

I feel my jaw drop open.

"When I got with him, he swept me off my feet, brought me to LA, to his goddamn mansion in Malibu. I was living the dream. But before we got married, his mother insisted on a prenup. I lost that battle and signed it. So the only way—"

A knife twists in my gut. "You could get his money is if—"

She nods. Puts her fingers to her temple as if pulling the trigger of a gun.

I want to vomit.

"Don't act so shocked. Look, I never intended to kill him, not at first, anyway. But during the pandemic, when he got super clingy and wouldn't let me breathe, I started fucking Andreas. Just to blow off steam, more than anything else. But Nate got more and more controlling. Possessive. Angry. There were times—and what's truly ironic is that this was before you came along and started spying on me—that I felt like I was being watched. Now I know I was. It was your sick little friend Lexie. The crazy ex. The loon that sent him that first letter—"

I gulp my wine, let the bubbles torch the inside of my mouth. What in the actual hell?

"I wanted out of our marriage then. But no way was I leaving him and all his money behind, so I thought, fuck it. If he thinks he owns me, mind, body, and soul, I'll show *him*. I'll drive him to the brink of insanity and then kill him in self-defense."

Marisol sways to the thumping techno, snaps her fingers to the beat.

I want to run from the table, race back to the hotel, and snatch Nathaniel away from her. But I remain seated, tongue dumb in my mouth.

"Then. It stopped. His anger. The feeling of being watched. So I was a good little girl. For a while. But then I couldn't help myself. I started seeing Andreas again. And then, voilà, you came along. Cassidy, I knew you were watching me the whole time. And reporting everything back to Nate, because he'd erupt at me after each encounter. I made sure Andreas's curtains were open that last time you saw us. I gave you the best performance of my career."

"But I thought you were in love with Andreas—"

"Hardly. He's just a stupid, horny man. I used him, and you, to drive Nate bonkers. Out of his skull. I was laying the groundwork for him to snap. To lose it. And then for me to take him out. But your crazy-ass friend beat me to it." She pats her hands together like she's dusting off flour. "I never even had to lift a finger."

"Why are you telling me all this now?"

Marisol smirks, tilts her head, winks at me. A chill shudders over me. I've seen this wink—and smirk—before. *It's how you handle them, how you stay in control.* Her words float back into my head.

The candlelight continues to shimmy between us. Expectantly, I look up at her luminous, glowing face, throbbing shadows dancing along her perfect cheekbones.

She leans back, fixes me with a devious grin.

Acknowledgments

Writing a book is hard, but I would argue that publishing a book is even harder. So I'm enormously grateful to everyone on my team who makes it look easy.

First and foremost, thanks to my incredible agent, Victoria Sanders, the best of the best. I'm so lucky to have you in my corner. Thanks for your friendship and unwavering faith in me. Huge thanks as well to Benee Knauer, book goddess and wonderful friend, for being in the trenches with me on this one, pushing me with love to make it the story we wanted it to be. Massive thanks as well to the rest of the amazing team at VSA—to Bernadette Baker-Baughman, Christine Kelder, and Diane Dickensheid—I'm so grateful for your incredible work behind the scenes on my behalf! Thanks as well to my amazing film agent, Hilary Zaitz Michael, for continuing to work miracles. And to Rebecca Cutter and Erwin Stoff, enormous gratitude for bringing my story onto the screen.

A huge thanks as well to my wonderful publishing team at Berkley, including my editor, Jen Monroe; Ivan Held; Craig Burke; Jeanne-Marie Hudson; Claire Zion; and Christine Ball. Also thank you to

Hannah Engler, Chelsea Pascoe, Dache' Rogers, and Bridget O'Toole. A very special thanks as well to both Candice Coote, for the extraordinary help and guidance, and my longtime publicist, Loren Jaggers, who's also become a treasured friend.

Thank you to my incredible friend Josh Sabarra for working PR magic and being so very unbelievably supportive. I love you.

This book is dedicated to my best friend, Amy Thompson, who I was lucky enough to meet when we were three (!) and I haven't let go of her since. Saying thanks isn't adequate, so I will say I love you!

My writing career wouldn't exist without the enormous support of my family, and a special thanks is owed to my wondrous parents, Liz and Charles, who cheer me on endlessly. Massive thanks as well to my sisters, Beth and Susie, for EVERYTHING, including taking my odd-hour phone calls for plot tips.

Huge thanks as well to my brother-in-law Paul (especially for the recent boat tour) and my amazing nephews, Xavier and Logan. Also big thanks to Joni, Courtney, Buddy, Marc, Kip, and Mac. And thanks to my extended family—Keegan, Slade, Dorthaan Kirk—and my East Coast family, T-Pa and Feeney, and David Ward.

This story is very loosely inspired by my work as a personal assistant, so big thanks are due to Ron and Lolita, who are nothing like Nate and Marisol, and who were the most wonderful souls to work for!

A special shout-out to my crime fiction writer pals, especially Samantha Bailey, Laurie Elizabeth Flynn, and Jesse Q. Sutanto (Unlikeable Female Author Coven Forever); Katie Gutierrez, Eliza Jane Brazier, Riley Sager, Rachel Harrison, Vanessa Lillie, Gabino Iglesias, Dan Mallory, Ashley Winstead, Hannah Morrissey, Robyn Harding, Jeneva Rose, Hank Phillippi Ryan, Amina Akhtar, Rachel Koller Croft, Mary Kubica, Don Bentley, Liv Constantine, and so many others I'm forgetting to name, because we truly are the warmest literary community even though we write murderous things!

Huge thanks as well to the wonderful Austin literary community, especially Marit Weisenberg, Amy Gentry, Owen Egerton, Suzy Spencer, Becka Oliver, Stacey Swann, Amanda Eyre Ward, and John Pipkin.

And enormous thanks to all the wonderful booksellers, reviewers, bloggers, bookstagrammers, and librarians who truly keep books alive, with a special shout-out to John and McKenna at Murder by the Book, Barbara Peters at The Poisoned Pen, Charley Rejsek at BookPeople, Amanda at Barnes & Noble at the Grove, Jane Estes at Lark & Owl, as well as Pamela Klinger-Horn, Maxwell Gregory, and Mary O'Malley.

Bookstagrammers are such a vital part of social media and word of mouth, and I can't thank the bookstagram fam enough for all your support! Special thanks to Abby Endler of @crimebythebook, Dennis of @scaredstraightreads, Gare of @gareindeedreads, Jordy of @jordys.book.club, and so many others! I'm so very grateful!

I could not, nor would I want to, do this without my fabulous husband, Chuck, who helped me figure out the plot twist in this one, and who will endlessly talk plot and publishing with me all day, all night. You deserve all the whiskey! I love you and J so very much!